Eladria

Eladria

Rory B. Mackay

Winchester, UK
Washington, USA

First published by Cosmic Egg Books, 2013
Cosmic Egg Books is an imprint of John Hunt Publishing Ltd., Laurel House, Station Approach,
Alresford, Hants, SO24 9JH, UK
office1@jhpbooks.net
www.johnhuntpublishing.com

For distributor details and how to order please visit the 'Ordering' section on our website.

ISBN: 978 1 78099 790 2

A CIP catalogue record for this book is available from the British Library.

Design: Stuart Davies

Printed and bound by CPI Group (UK) Ltd, Croydon, CR0 4YY

We operate a distinctive and ethical publishing philosophy in all
areas of our business, from our global network of authors to
production and worldwide distribution.

Dedication
For Mum and AJ, Holly and the Bees:
I couldn't have done this without your endless love and
support. Thank you!
And in memory of my beloved dog Jamie, who was never far
from my side and who supervised the writing of this book.

Chapter 1

The Fifth Day

There was no easy way to tell someone their entire world was about to be destroyed. Maybe that was why the old woman dispensed the prophecy in such a bizarrely offhand manner. Two short sentences. Two short sentences that would forever change the young princess's life.

"On the Fifth Day of Rusaak, darkness will fall. Your entire world will be lost."

The moment Eladria heard those words, her mind and senses froze and she stared at the woman in a blank stupor. She was certain the entire marketplace had simultaneously ground to a halt, for all went quiet. Of course, it was more likely that, in her sudden state of shock, her mind had simply tuned out all background noise. A sudden tightness in her chest forced a sharp intake of air.

Eladria insisted that the seer explain her words, but the old woman was unable to elaborate. "I'm sorry, my Princess," she mumbled, shaking her head slowly, the color draining from her wizened face. "I can say no more."

"What do you mean you can say no more?" Eladria demanded.

"It was a momentary flash," the woman responded, her voice broken and rasping. "It was gone almost the moment it came. The vision was taken from me."

"Taken from you?"

"It was as though someone, or something, blocked my sight. I don't understand it. This has never happened before. I'm sorry, Princess, but I can't continue the reading. Here, I will refund your payment."

"I don't want a refund. I want you to explain what you said."

"I can't. Please...forget I said anything."

1

But Eladria knew she would never be able to forget those words. The moment they left the old woman's lips they had been indelibly seared into her mind forevermore.

Three days had now passed since Eladria had made that fateful trip to the oracle. She had barely slept since then.

It was early morning and, as daybreak approached, the princess paced her palace balcony in a state of restless agitation. The stars shone down like celestial sentinels overlooking the royal city as it slept. Outwardly everything was peaceful, but Eladria's mind was a firestorm of unrest.

She had tried to dismiss the warning and chastised herself for paying heed to the ramblings of a deranged old fortune-teller. She didn't ordinarily believe in such nonsense and wasn't sure what had prompted her visit to the old woman in the first place. Perhaps it had been out of boredom, or simple curiosity?

She had done some investigation, looking over security logs and intelligence reports, and, aside from a series of unusual storms sweeping across the planet, there was nothing out of the ordinary. But try though she might, she couldn't shift the feeling that things were about to fall apart somehow; that some unspeakable tragedy lay just around the corner.

The princess came to a stop and wrapped her arms around her chest, shivering in the cool morning air. She gazed across the dormant metropolis that sprawled beneath the palace. Above the central plaza with its fountain and winding marble walkways, the city buildings—of varying size and structure—were illuminated as if by a million static fireflies glowing in shades of blue, white and green. The city was built in the hollow of a large moon crater and encased by a vast, translucent bio-dome. Beyond the arching glass barrier, the chalky moon surface gave way to an all-encompassing void of blackness, punctuated by the twinkling of distant stars and the ever-visible planet around which the moon circled. Dawn was creeping in and the first rays of sunlight were now visible, peeking from beyond the far side of the planet.

Eladria knew she wouldn't have to worry about the seer's words for much longer, because this was the day she had been warned about: the Fifth Day of Rusaak.

A hand on her shoulder startled her. She jumped, letting out an involuntary gasp but quickly realized there was no cause for alarm. It was only Narat.

"What are you doing out here?" he asked with a yawn, as he came to a stop behind her.

"I couldn't sleep," she said. "I've been awake most the night."

"Again? That's the third night in a row. I thought you'd sleep soundly knowing I'm beside you."

"Normally I would. I've just got some things on my mind," Eladria said distantly as she continued gazing across the horizon.

"Then maybe I can help take them off your mind?" Narat whispered in her ear, the warmth of his breath a marked contrast to the crisp morning air.

"You know you shouldn't be out here," Eladria said, turning and pushing him off the balcony and back into her chamber. "We have to be more careful, there are security cameras everywhere. What if someone saw you?"

"You don't have to worry about security," Narat responded with a laugh, his dark eyes glistening. "I *am* security!"

"Even so, we can't take chances," Eladria frowned as she slid the glass door shut behind her. "Father's due back this morning. If he was to find out about us, he'd..."

"He'd what?"

"He'd go insane."

"Maybe he'll surprise you. Besides, he's got to find out sooner or later."

"No, he does not. You can't begin to imagine the uproar. It'd be a scandal! I'd never hear the end of it; and as for you, I don't know what he'd do. At the very least he'd probably reassign you to the Narabulan mines."

"He might be shocked at first. But once he sees how much we

3

love each other, he'll surely—"

"Go against generations of tradition and let the Princess of Tahnadra marry a man from the lowlands of Rakata? Trust me, it'll never happen, Narat. My father's obsessed with tradition and protocol. This would push him over the edge. He'd probably lock me in my chamber for the next ten years, until he's found me the perfect husband."

"Is that so," Narat remarked with a smirk, running a hand through his short dark hair.

"It'd be different if my mother was still here," Eladria said softly as she sat down on the edge of her bed. "She'd have been happy for us. She'd maybe even have been able to talk Father around. But she's not here, is she? And there's no way my father would ever allow us to be together."

Narat sat down beside her and put his arm around her. "Times are changing," he said. "Perhaps the old ways don't work any longer, in which case we need to be open to new ways. Your father's a smart man. When he comes to see that, perhaps he'll be willing to make an exception and put your happiness—*our* happiness—above tradition and protocol."

Narat pulled Eladria toward him and looked deeply into her eyes. Although they'd been together for several months now, Eladria still felt a part of her melt each time she looked at him and was drawn into his smoldering dark eyes as if by a force of gravity.

"You know I'm right, don't you?" Narat continued. "I may not be of noble blood, but I can make you happy. I know I can."

Before Eladria could respond, she happened to catch sight of the timepiece on her bedside table. "Narat, you have to get out of here," she exclaimed. "It's later than I thought. Zinn will be here any moment."

Narat rolled his eyes, clearly unconcerned at the prospect of being discovered by Eladria's maid.

"Go." She pushed him off the bed with a scowl. "Now!"

4

"I'll try not to take that personally," he remarked as he picked his uniform up from the floor and dusted it off.

Eladria watched anxiously as he dressed, praying that he'd be gone by the time Zinn got here. The last thing she wanted was for anyone to find out about their secret liaisons. She loved Narat, and she wanted to be with him, but she knew that their destinies were divergent. She'd known that from the moment she'd invited the young head of security into her chamber and seduced him. He was charming, intense and vital—and he made her feel alive and excited—but she found it almost impossible to envisage a happy ending for them.

Now dressed, Narat put on his boots and walked over to the princess. Taking her hand, he pulled her up from the edge of the bed and wrapped his arms around her. "Things are going to work out, I promise you," he told her, his voice filled with conviction.

He leaned forward and kissed her with a passion that recalled their very first kiss. But Eladria was highly conscious of the time and she broke free of his embrace and pointed to the timepiece. "Quick! It's time you were out of here. Zinn will be on her way."

Narat took a step back and bowed before his princess. She acknowledged the gesture with a quick nod, before ushering him out the side door of her chamber.

The moment he was gone, she let out a sigh of relief. That particular disaster had been averted, for the time being at least. Although the risk of being found out added an element of excitement to their relationship, there were times when it was simply a burden that wore her down.

As it happened, Zinn was running uncharacteristically late this morning. By the time she arrived, Eladria had bathed and dressed. All the while, her mind was far elsewhere as she pondered Narat's curious assertion that things were about to change and again ruminated upon the prophecy of the seer. It was the Fifth Day and she could sense something strange in the air, as though an imminent storm was brewing.

A buzz at the door signaled Zinn's arrival. Eladria called her in and the maid entered, carrying her usual bundle of fresh linen. Zinn had been Eladria's personal maid since she was a baby, a cherished caretaker and companion and, in many ways, a surrogate mother. Zinn had changed surprisingly little over the years. Eladria supposed she was middle-aged, but could never discern exactly how old she was and had never seen fit to ask. She had a kindly demeanor and a warm face, her skin smooth and pale and her tousled mop of grey hair tied back and cascading down around her neck and shoulders. Despite her nervousness and propensity to fuss, Zinn was a curiously agile woman with considerable dexterity of both body and mind.

"Morning, my dear," she said as she deposited the linen on the bed and smoothed down her white tunic. "How did you sleep last night?"

"Not very well." Eladria frowned as she stood by her dressing table and absent-mindedly sifted through her jewelry box, picking out her favorite necklace, the one that had belonged to her mother.

"Oh. Why was that?" Zinn asked as she began sorting through the linen.

"Just things on my mind," Eladria answered vaguely.

"I'm always telling you to relax more. You need your sleep." There was an awkward pause before she continued. "I hope it has nothing to do with that young man..."

Eladria stopped what she was doing and felt a sudden tightness in her stomach. "What young man?" she asked.

"You know who I'm talking about," Zinn responded. "Young Narat. I'm not blind, my dear. I know what's going on."

Eladria was stunned. She thought she'd managed to conceal her liaisons with Narat, but evidently not well enough to fool Zinn. She didn't know what to do. Should she admit the truth and plead with Zinn not to tell her father? The rational part of her knew that it would be preferable to discuss the matter honestly and openly, but having been caught unprepared, she found herself opting to feign innocence.

"I don't know what you're talking about," she said haughtily. "Narat's just a friend, nothing more. He's one of the few people in the palace close to my age. Really, Zinn, sometimes the conclusions you jump to are ridiculous."

"Just so long as you don't get hurt, my dear," Zinn said. "I care about you too much to see that happen. Narat has both looks and charm, which is all very well. But when you add ambition to the mix, you've got a potentially dangerous combination. And from what I can see, he's got no shortage of that."

"What do you mean?"

"Think about it." Zinn looked over at the princess. "A young man of only twenty-four doesn't become chief of palace security without towering ambition, and you can be sure that it won't stop there."

"I didn't realize you were such a character analyst, Zinn," Eladria said, folding her arms, trying not to be too overt in the sudden defensiveness she felt about her lover. "Maybe you should stick to your job and leave others to theirs."

"That's fine with me, Princess," Zinn said as she laid away the last of the linen. "Speaking of which, you've a busy day ahead of you. Your father is due back in ten minutes and you're expected to greet him in the landing terminal. After that, you've just enough time for first-meal, then your appointments are fully booked for the morning. At midday, you're scheduled to dine with the Count of Sarabar before he leaves the palace. Oh, and in the afternoon your presence is required in the diplomatic lounge for another round of talks between the Ha'shon and True Way."

"Well that'll be a waste of time," Eladria muttered as she walked over to the balcony, pulled open the sliding glass door and stepped outside. "It's not as if they'll ever reach any kind of compromise. Neither side will be happy until they've completely obliterated the other. It's just a joke."

"Well, joke or not, you're obligated to attend," Zinn called after her as she tidied the princess's chamber.

"They've been holding these talks for over twelve years now," Eladria said. "And what difference has it made? Father's deluding himself if he thinks there's any hope of resolution, at least in this lifetime. I don't know why I have to sit there and watch the Ha'shon and True Way diplomats ranting at each other all afternoon. It's not as if I'm allowed to say or do anything. My presence at the negotiating table is just a pointless protocol."

Indeed, she often felt that her entire life here was just a succession of pointless protocols, one after the other, in rigid, dreary monotony. Her duties as Princess of the House of Chaldeen were excruciatingly dull. Such a life might suit someone like her father, but for a seventeen-year-old girl the thought of being stuck on this moon forevermore was almost more than she could bear. She often wished the royal family had never retreated to this lifeless hunk of rock. It may be safer up here, but the older she got, the more oppressive she found the isolation.

She gazed across the royal city and beyond the great bio-dome. Tahnadra itself was ever-visible, a spectacular orb in the heavens, its vast blue oceans punctuated by ragged continents of green and brown, dusted with wisps of cloud. Certainly, Tahnadra had its problems, least of all the infernal war between the two religious factions that had ravaged entire continents for centuries. *But there's life down there,* she thought wistfully. Life, adventure and excitement; the very things she craved most.

"Are you ready, dear?" called Zinn. "It's time we were going. Your father's transport will be here soon."

"Yes, I'm coming," Eladria sighed.

Upon leaving her chamber, Eladria perceived a subdued atmosphere in the palace. She wasn't sure why, but it was strangely quiet. Some of the palace personnel even seemed nervous and apprehensive. Sensing that something was wrong, Eladria reached into the folds of her blue dress and pulled out her handheld communication device. With the click of a button, she activated the spherical, palm-sized device and lifted it to her mouth. "Central Control, this is Eladria."

"Central Control," came the prompt response. "This is Administrator Jusaad. How may I help you, your Highness?"

"Has my father's transport signaled its approach yet?" she asked.

"Not as of yet, your Highness."

"Then it's overdue?" Eladria stopped in puzzlement and turned to Zinn.

"Correct, your Highness. They're almost thirty minutes overdue for check-in."

"That's unlike my father," Eladria said, her brow creasing. "He's never been late for anything in his life. Jusaad, I'm on my way to Central Control."

Something was wrong. It was unheard of for a royal transport to run this late. The words of the seer were still uppermost in Eladria's mind. If the prophecy was to be believed, then this was the day her entire world would be lost. She prayed that this prediction had nothing to do with her father. Certainly, they had their differences and she often resented his emotional remoteness following the loss of her mother, but she adored him nonetheless. The thought of losing him, the last of her immediate family, filled her with terror.

She strode along the white marbled corridor, Zinn rushing behind her, struggling to match her pace. Without a word, they took the elevator to Central Control, Eladria pacing back and forth like a caged animal.

Her father's entire trip was surrounded by an air of mystery. Although he was officially there for a routine visit to the Kalastrian province, unofficially he had gone to investigate reports from across the planet of strange electrical storms and a tear or crack of some kind appearing in the sky. The science ministry was at a loss to explain the disturbances.

This had, of course, caused widespread panic across the planet. The religious leaders had used it to their advantage, declaring the storms as heralding the 'end times'. As the True Way initiated a new wave of ritualistic sacrifice in an attempt to appease their deity, the Ha'shon had stepped up their crusade against all perceived nonbelievers. These were troubled times indeed. Perhaps it was little wonder that Eladria was put on edge by her father's unusual tardiness.

The moment the elevator came to a stop and the doors opened, Eladria and Zinn stepped into the vast, circular control room. Two interlinked tiers were lined with computer consoles and a large holographic display screen stretched across the room in a semi-circle. Central Control was a hub of activity as usual, but today the room was filled with an undercurrent of tension as the officers and technicians went about their duties, which involved coordinating the running of the moon and overseeing planetary activity.

Administrator Jusaad was the chief officer on duty: a stocky, middle-aged man with olive skin, deep-set brown eyes and short, neatly styled silver hair. Eladria had known him for many years and considered him an excellent officer and honorable man. Upon noticing her arrival, Jusaad stepped forward and bowed before the princess. "Welcome to Central Control, your Highness."

"Is there still no word from my father's transport?" Eladria asked.

"No," Jusaad shook his head. "There's been a complete communications blackout."

"Have you scanned for them?"

"We can't. Long-range scanners are offline for scheduled maintenance."

"Then get them back online now," Eladria ordered.

"I've already instructed the maintenance crew to reboot the scanners, but it'll be another ninety minutes before they're functional," Jusaad explained.

"What else have you done?" Eladria asked, looking around the room anxiously.

"We've sent two escort craft to intercept the king's transport. As of yet, there's been no word from either. We've been trying to contact them, but there's been no response."

"Have you contacted the planet surface? You could get one of the military bases to use their scanners and—"

"I've already—"

"Administrator!" interjected one of Jusaad's technicians. "The king's transport has just entered the peripheral zone of short-range scanners."

Eladria's heart leapt.

Jusaad joined the technician and leaned over the console to check the readings. "That's the royal transport all right, but it's not on the standard trajectory. It's off course by eighty-six tessits."

"Which means what?" Eladria asked.

"I don't know." Jusaad stood up and rubbed his forehead wearily. He turned to the communications officer. "Officer Nolahn, open communication channels."

The raven-haired communications officer complied. But after a moment she shook her head, a puzzled look upon her face. "We're getting a response, but it's text-only."

"Well, what does it say?"

"According to the message, they've been having problems with their engines, navigational and communications systems. They suspect sabotage. They managed to patch up their engines, but navigation remains affected and the visual communication system is inoperative. They request we initiate arrival procedures."

"That would explain a few things," Eladria said, relieved.

"Perhaps," Jusaad answered with a measure of uncertainty. "But they make no mention of the escort craft I sent to meet them. And I'm not entirely sure I believe this notion of sabotage. If a saboteur had really gained access to that transport, you can guarantee it'd be in a million pieces by now."

"So what are you saying?"

"I can't say anything for sure. It's just a feeling, your Highness...a feeling that something isn't right."

"Are you suggesting that someone's commandeered my father's transport?" Eladria asked, looking round at Zinn worriedly.

Jusaad nodded. "It's a possibility. Since we've had no visual communication, we've no way of verifying who sent that message. But we'll out find soon enough. When the transport reaches the bio-dome, they'll have to input the security code to disable the weapons platform and gain entry. If they are who they say they are, there won't be a problem. But if they fail to provide the right code, we'll know that whoever's on that transport, they're not officers of the royal court."

There was nothing they could do but wait.

By now, the royal transport was visible on the holographic screen. It limped toward the moon, its flight motion irregular and jerky. The technicians were all busy at their consoles, and Jusaad walked up and down the length of the room, peering at the monitors, seemingly braced for the worst.

"They've reached the checkpoint," one of the technicians reported, looking up from his station. "I can confirm they've received the request to input the security code."

Jusaad stood and folded his arms, his face creasing with grim resolve. Aside for the humming and bleeping of the electronic consoles, there was silence as they awaited the transport's next move.

"They've input the correct code," the technician informed them in a relieved voice.

Eladria exhaled loudly, unaware that she'd been holding her breath.

"Very well," Jusaad responded, clearly still concerned, for the strain lingered on his face. He turned to Eladria. "Your Highness, protocol dictates that you be at the landing terminal to greet the king. However, as far as I'm concerned there are still some unanswered questions. Until the king himself steps off that transport and explains what happened, I'm treating this as a suspicious situation."

"But they input the right code..."

"Maybe so, but I still insist that we proceed with caution. I think in this instance it would be safer for you to remain here while I have a security contingent meet me at the landing terminal."

"No," Eladria objected. "Have the security guards on hand if you wish, but I'm going to meet my father."

"Your Highness, under these circumstances, I recommend that—"

"My decision is made," Eladria interjected, her tone as authoritative as she could muster. She was tired of having decisions made for her. She was the princess and Jusaad was obliged to obey her commands. Her father would be expecting her to be there when he stepped off the transport and she wouldn't disappoint him. "Let's not waste any more time," she added. "Let's get down to the landing terminal."

"Very well," Jusaad said as he lowered his head in respectful deference.

As Eladria and Zinn made for the elevator, Jusaad instructed the communications officer to have Narat dispatch a full security team to the main landing terminal. Eladria felt a measure of comfort knowing that Narat would be there.

They took the elevator from the command center all the way down to the hangar level. When they arrived, Jusaad led the princess and her maid to the assigned landing terminal. With a swipe of his security card, the doors to the terminal slid open and they were greeted by Narat and a team of his security guards. There were around ten guards in total, uniformed in grey and black jumpsuits, each armed with an electro-pulse pistol.

Narat acknowledged Jusaad with a nod as they entered, before his eyes met Eladria's and, with a slight smile, he bowed his head. He seemed slightly nervous, which was unusual as Eladria had never seen him apprehensive about anything. The lingering glance between the princess and the head of security didn't go unnoticed by Zinn, who frowned disapprovingly.

They stood patiently in the reception area of the terminal, watching through the glass partition as the royal transport came into sight. Eladria shifted nervously as she watched the transport landing. The hangar staff readied the transport for disembarkation, signaling that it was now safe to enter the hangar.

Narat and his security team led the way. Jusaad was next, followed by Eladria and Zinn. The security team stopped before the transport, pistols in hand, Narat standing at the forefront. Jusaad motioned for Eladria and Zinn to remain at a discreet distance. They watched patiently as the hatch on the side of the transport began to open.

Come on, Father, Eladria silently implored him, biting her lower lip nervously. *I know you're in there. Come on out...*

There was silence as a figure stepped out of the transport.

It was the king. He took a few steps out of the craft and stopped. Although he was some distance away, Eladria could immediately tell that something was wrong. His skin was a deathly shade of white and his body was rigid and tense.

Jusaad stepped forward and greeted the king cordially.

But before he could reply, someone else stepped out of the transport—a male Ha'shon—and raised a gun to the king's head. Eladria let out a cry of alarm.

The man, who wore the uniform of a Ha'shon general, grabbed her father's arm and forced him down the steps onto the hangar floor. Five other Ha'shon emerged from the transport, each wearing the distinctive maroon and black uniforms of the Ha'shon military division, armed with electro-pulse guns and machetes. Like most Ha'shon males, they were tall and muscular with reddish-tinged skin and long black, braided hair and beards. The tattoos down their faces and necks identified them as Ha'shon militants.

Jusaad endeavored to take control of the situation and stepped forward, his voice strong and defiant as he challenged the intruders. "Please release the king now," he called.

"And who might you be?" the Ha'shon general snarled as he tightened his grip on the king.

"I am Jusaad, chief administrator of this facility. I don't know who you are, or what you want, but if you release the king now, we will be lenient. We'll set up a dialogue and listen to what you have to say. Just, please, drop your weapons now and let the king go free. No one has to get hurt."

"I think you fail to realize something, Chief Administrator," the Ha'shon sneered. "I'm the one who determines who does or does not get hurt."

Eladria watched in horror as the Ha'shon general released the king and aimed his pistol at Jusaad's chest. With a look of twisted satisfaction, he squeezed the trigger and fired, discharging a blast of crackling white energy that shot through the air and impacted the administrator squarely in the chest, electrifying his entire body. Jusaad fell to the ground in a heap, smoke rising from his wound as the sound of the blast echoed through the metal-plated hangar. The Ha'shon stepped forward and fired another shot at the fallen body. He then grabbed the king by the arm and dragged him forward as he approached Narat and the guards.

Narat will do something, Eladria reasoned. *He'll stop them…*

But what happened next was so perplexing that Eladria could scarcely believe her eyes. The general walked up to Narat and his face lit up in a broad smile. Narat nodded in greeting, then turned to his men and ordered them to lower their weapons. They immediately complied.

"I congratulate you, young warrior," the general addressed Narat. "Our plan worked perfectly. We could never have done it without you, not without those security codes. You have just assured yourself a place in the Great Light for all eternity."

Eladria stared at Narat in shock and disbelief.

Narat, for his part, couldn't bring himself to look at her. He motioned for his men to surround Eladria and Zinn and they complied without a flicker of hesitation.

Releasing the king to one of his subordinates, the general strode up to Eladria. "This must be Princess Eladria," he said, an insincere smile creeping across his lined, reddish face.

Eladria said nothing.

"Allow me to introduce myself," the Ha'shon said imperiously. "I am Kalon Estaran, First General of the Ha'shon Liberation Army. This is the start of an historic new era. After eighteen generations, the Royal House of Chaldeen has fallen. The Ha'shon now claim absolute rulership of Tahnadra. Any resistance will be met with swift and deadly retribution. As for you, Princess, your father's fate has already been sealed, but yours has not. You now have a simple choice. You can either surrender or die..."

Chapter 2

The New Order Rises

"I have nothing to say to you," Eladria stated defiantly. "The House of Chaldeen does not negotiate with terrorists."

"Is that what you think I am? A terrorist!" Estaran smirked.

Eladria remained silent.

"I'll tell you what I am," Estaran said, grabbing her arm and pulling her toward him. "I am now your *ruler* and what I say, you *will* do."

After eyeing her up and down lasciviously, Estaran let go of her and she pulled back, glaring at him with contempt.

The Ha'shon general rejoined Narat, who looked visibly uncomfortable. Narat had clearly been in league with the Ha'shon and had made some kind of pact with them. But it seemed events hadn't transpired quite as he had imagined. Nevertheless, he still appeared willing to co-operate with the Ha'shon invaders and he listened intently as Estaran briefed him. Eladria was unable to hear what was being said.

As she stood rooted to the spot, her eyes were drawn to her father. Although regal with his golden crown and long navy robes, he looked pale and defeated; a shadow of the man she knew. Was it just the shock of what had transpired, or had they somehow broken him? And what had Estaran meant when he said that her father's fate was sealed?

At Narat's orders, the security officers directed Eladria and Zinn to the elevator, guns pointing straight at them. It was hard enough to believe that Narat of all people would do this, but it was astonishing that all of his men were in compliance. She'd never have imagined that any of them would be capable of pointing a gun at a member of the royal family. What had Narat done to convince them to commit such treason? Was it just this set of security officers, or would the rest of the palace guard be prepared to stop them?

Eladria and Zinn were herded into the elevator, along with the king, Estaran and his men. They were joined by Narat and four of his guards, who kept their weapons trained on the captives. At Estaran's command, Narat set the elevator to take them directly to Central Control.

Not a word was spoken as the elevator ascended, the gentle hum punctuating the strained silence. Eladria stared at Narat disbelievingly. She wanted Narat to look at her, to assure her that this wasn't as bad as it looked, that he wouldn't let anything happen to her or her father. But he avoided eye contact, keeping his eyes fixed upon the ground, his olive-skinned face set in an expression of grim determination.

As the elevator made its way up the heart of the palace, Eladria felt like a bird imprisoned in a cage, simpering with desperation and determined to do whatever it took to escape. Surely there must be some way she could outwit her captors? But as she surveyed the palace guards and the Ha'shon terrorists, all of whom were armed and had Eladria, Zinn and her father locked in their sights, she realized the situation was hopeless.

The elevator finally reached its destination and, just as the doors were about to open, the Ha'shon and palace guards readied themselves for possible resistance. Eladria wondered if the control room staff were aware of what had transpired in the landing terminal. There were security cameras in all areas of the palace, but it was possible that Narat and his co-conspirators had taken steps to disconnect them. She realized that it may not have been coincidence that the long-range scanners were inoperative on this very morning. It would seem this whole operation had been meticulously planned in advance.

The moment the elevator doors opened, the Ha'shon and palace guards stormed the control room, weapons blazing. The control room personnel hadn't been anticipating the assault, for they were wholly unprepared and had no opportunity to react to the sudden barrage of fire.

Eladria had to avert her eyes as the control room officers and technicians were mercilessly gunned down.

She looked up at Narat whose face was taut and emotionless. How could he let this happen? These people were his friends and colleagues.

It took only moments for the Ha'shon to secure the control room. The battle for control of the palace was over before it had even begun and it had been nothing less than a massacre. The Ha'shon had deliberately spared two of the control room technicians, who were rounded up and given orders. Clearly these terrified-looking technicians were needed to operate the computer systems. Faces drained of color and their bodies trembling, the technicians nervously set about their orders, all too aware that there were a half dozen guns trained on them.

Estaran stood at the center of the control room and with a sadistic grin, surveyed the bodies strewn across the room. "This was even easier than I thought," he exclaimed.

He turned to Narat, who stood by his side, and put a hand on his shoulder. "We could never have done it without you, young warrior. May the Divine Father bless you. You've helped initiate a new era of greatness, an era that will put an end to the war and degeneration that has torn this world apart for centuries."

"Just so long as there's no more killing," Narat said flatly. "It wasn't necessary to kill all these people."

"I determine what is and is not necessary," Estaran said in a low voice, his face darkening. "And you'd do well to remember that, or you might quickly find you've outlived your usefulness here."

"My men would never follow you if anything were to happen to me," Narat responded sharply.

"I've no doubt," Estaran said, clearly unfazed by Narat's threat. "But if today has taught us anything, it's that loyalty is far from immutable. It can be bought, and allegiances can shift in the blink of an eye."

Narat was silent for a moment, before he answered in a hushed, indignant voice. "Just so long as you remember our deal, General."

"Oh, I remember," Estaran responded. "A Ha'shon never falls back on his word. By the virtue of the great Shon, I honor my deals."

Eladria couldn't help but wonder what kind of deal Narat had made with Estaran that would possibly justify his betrayal. Not that she really cared. Any remaining love she felt for him had instantly turned to hatred the moment Narat had allowed his men to slaughter the innocent men and women whose bodies littered the room. She could never forgive him for this.

Estaran had the remaining technicians activate the holographic display screens and they watched as a string of Ha'shon raiders approached the moon and streamed into the bio-dome. Estaran then opened communications and ordered the fighters to implement "order six".

The black, quadruple-pronged attack craft took formation over the royal city and began circling above the streets, houses and domes like ravenous birds of prey. Eladria watched in horror as they then opened fire. Weapons fire rained down upon the city. Buildings exploded and crumbled to pieces, sending flames and smoke billowing up from the smoldering metropolis.

Eladria cried out as she was forced to witness the carnage, pleading for them to stop. Even her father, who to his point had been silent, stepped forward and begged the Ha'shon to show mercy. "Please," he beseeched Estaran, his hoarse voice filled with desperation. "Those are innocent people! Spare their lives!"

Estaran turned to his captive, his face contorting into a sadistic smile, revealing a row of gnarled, rotting teeth, several of which were missing. "So, the king makes a final plea, does he?" scoffed the Ha'shon, clearly enjoying every moment of the horror. "It's sad that it must fall on deaf ears. The Ha'shon have planned this operation for many years, your Highness. The royal city is to be laid to ruin and any remaining resistance will be quelled. This moon will be ours and from here we will control the entire planet."

"It won't be as easy as you think," the king countered. "If you believe the planet will accept a Ha'shon dictatorship, then you're even more deluded than I imagined."

"Oh, I know we won't simply be accepted," Estaran laughed. "Our True Way adversaries will fight us to the bitter end, and I expect retaliation from those military bases we haven't already infiltrated. Yes, there will be much bloodshed. But we have the advantage and, in the end, we shall emerge victorious. It has been written; it is our destiny! With the Divine Father Shon shining his light upon us, we are unstoppable and we shall be triumphant."

"Even if you are triumphant," Eladria glared at the zealot. "By the time you've gone through with this, there may not be a planet left to rule."

"Whatever be the will of the Divine Father," Estaran responded, his eyes blazing with fire. "He shall not forsake us."

There was little point arguing with a Ha'shon. It was impossible to reason with someone who believed their every action to be sanctioned by a seal of Divine approval.

Eladria's attention returned to the assault upon the city. Her heart shattered as she watched the glorious city being pounded to rubble. She noticed several of the raiders targeting the headquarters of the Tahnadran Royal Military, a silver pyramid-shaped installation distinguishable as the second-largest building in the city, dwarfed only by the palace. It was home to the command hierarchy of the TRM, as well housing most of its weaponry, air force and soldiers.

Unprepared for the assault, the Royal Military was slow to retaliate. They tried to repel the attackers with anti-aircraft fire and launched a squadron of fighter craft, but the Ha'shon, having had the element of surprise, maintained their tactical advantage.

A furious battle was being waged, with several craft on both sides already destroyed or disabled.

Eladria knew their only hope was that the Royal Military could overpower the Ha'shon invaders, secure the moon and retake the palace. But this was not to be.

Estaran, incensed at the loss of several of his raiders, ordered his fighters to implement "order nine". His fighters pulled back, disengaging the military craft and hovering in formation above the TRM headquarters. Following the lead Ha'shon raider, the attackers simultaneously fired missiles straight at the heart of the installation.

Upon impact, the missiles exploded, shaking the entire moon. Eladria lurched as the ground moved beneath her feet. She watched in horror as what remained of the TRM installation was consumed by the aftermath of the explosion. The shockwave rippled across the city, tearing buildings to the ground as though they were made of sand. Most of the TRM fighters were caught in the explosion, while the remainder were targeted by the Ha'shon attackers.

Eladria reached out and took hold of her father's hand, desperate for some kind of comfort, for she knew that many of her friends and loved ones were dead or dying out there. Unable to stand the scenes of carnage any longer, she averted her eyes and looked down at the ground, her vision blurred by tears.

When the attack was complete, Estaran ordered all Ha'shon fighters to the palace. His men were to then fully secure the building and eliminate any resistance. No prisoners were to be taken.

Estaran directed one of the technicians to commence a planetary broadcast on all communications frequencies. The technician began operating the communications console, her whole body trembling as she prepared to initiate the planet-wide broadcast, something that was only ever done on the rarest of occasions.

With Estaran's attention elsewhere, Eladria looked up at her father. "Father," she whispered. "What shall we do?"

"There's nothing we can do," he said softly, a tear trickling down his face. "We must co-operate and hope to minimize any further loss of life."

"There must be something," Eladria implored.

"It's over," the king said with a shake of his head. "I'm sorry. I should have been able to prevent this. I've let you down. I've let everyone down..."

Eladria squeezed his hand tightly. She didn't like the way he was talking. Why was he resigned to defeat? There had be some way they could stop these terrorists.

The technician informed Estaran that the communications channels were open and the planetary broadcast had begun. Estaran stood upon the central dais of the control center, his chest puffed out and head held aloft and, in a loud voice filled with authority and self-importance, he began his address.

"People of Tahnadra, this is Kalon Estaran, First General of the Ha'shon Liberation Army. I speak to you from the Royal City on the third moon of Tahnadra. On this momentous day, the Royal House of Chaldeen has fallen. In its place a new regime rises. Tahnadra is now under direct control of the Ha'shon. By the grace of the Divine Father, Shon, the Ha'shon shall now lead Tahnadra to a new era of glory.

"The prophecies have been fulfilled. We now take charge and commence the restructuring of our world. We declare war upon all True Way degenerates and call for the complete eradication of their twisted and blasphemous religion. Those that surrender willingly and agree to convert to Ha'shon doctrine shall be spared and, indeed, shall be welcomed as our prodigal brothers. Those that refuse to repent must be destroyed, for their own sakes and for the sake of our world and its continued survival. The call goes out to the whole of Tahnadra: join with us, and be a part of this great new beginning. And let all who oppose us die!"

The general turned to his prisoners and ordered one of his men to bring the king to him.

"Behold, King Dulaan!" Estaran announced, gesturing to his prisoner, who was dragged alongside him on the central dais. "Last of a weak, ineffectual monarchy that have sat above us for centuries, doing nothing but simply watching as our planet descended ever deeper into chaos. They tried to compromise and placate, too weak to align themselves with either side and all they've done is prolong the agony, and intensify our suffering. They're responsible for the state of our world. For generations they have stood in the way of the Ha'shon rising to take their rightful place. But no longer!"

Eladria was unprepared for what happened next. It happened so quickly that her brain struggled to process the images her eyes relayed to it.

Estaran reached down to his belt, lifted his machete and plunged it into her father's chest. The king gasped and staggered back, while Estaran pulled out the blade and again thrust it into his torso.

Eladria screamed and tried to race toward him, but one of the Ha'shon restrained her.

With a cruel grin, Estaran twisted the blade and then retracted it. The king fell to the floor, clearly dead by the time his body hit the ground. A pool of blood poured from his wounds, running down the dais like a red river.

Estaran turned to the front of the control room, where his image was being instantly relayed to the planet below. He held the blade above him and roared triumphantly. "The king is dead and the old regime dies with him! The Ha'shon rule triumphant!"

Eladria's legs collapsed under her weight, but she didn't fall to the ground, for she was still being tightly held by her Ha'shon captor. She hung there, her chest and stomach knotted and convulsing in waves of sharp, spasmodic pain. As she stared at the lifeless body of her dear father, slumped in a pool of his own blood, she felt as though she herself had been stabbed in the heart.

Estaran's victory speech continued. His voice was filled with fire and venom, all the time becoming louder until he was shouting at the top of his lungs, in a voice filled with rapture and rage. "Let the nonbelievers try to stop us as we march to total victory!" he cried, waving his blood-soaked blade like a trophy above his head. "Let them come! Let them taste blood as we wipe them from existence. The Ha'shon have prepared for this day and have amassed an unstoppable military arsenal. Nothing can stand between us and world domination. Tahnadra is now ours! All praise to the Divine Father Shon!"

With that, he called an end to the transmission.

Eladria was barely aware of what was going on around her anymore. Eyes fixed upon the body of her father, she slipped into a strange state of delirium, only vaguely aware of disconnected snippets of what happened next.

She heard Estaran warning of possible counterstrikes by both the True Way and the remaining Royal Military forces. Their immediate priority was to secure the palace and seal off the moon. Upon the display screens she saw a stream of Ha'shon aircraft continuing to enter the bio-dome like a swarm of insects ready to devour a ripened crop. She was vaguely aware of Estaran ordering his men to take her to a cell.

Having lost all strength and feeling in her body, she could barely walk and was dragged along by Estaran's men. The last sight her eyes beheld, as she and Zinn were removed from the control center and bundled into the elevator, was her father's body lying upon the ground like a discarded garment casually tossed aside.

The lurching of the elevator made her nauseous. Still unable to stand of her own volition, she hung from the guard's arms like a limp doll, aware of little else but the shock of her sudden, devastating loss.

As they exited the elevator, Narat's men led the Ha'shon and their captives toward the palace security station. Along the way, they encountered some resistance from a number of palace officers and security guards who, unlike Narat's carefully selected group of turncoats, were still loyal to the house of Chaldeen and who fought valiantly to repel the invaders and their dissident allies.

A fight ensued and Eladria was certain that she and Zinn would be caught in the crossfire as the two forces fiercely battled. Unfortunately, the Ha'shon managed to kill most of their opponents while the rest fled in retreat.

Hopeless. It was all so hopeless.

They reached the security station and Eladria thought of Narat, for she would often visit him here while he was on duty.

Narat, why...why did this happen?

She and Zinn were led to the holding cells, which were dimly lit, furnished with a single bench and enclosed by metal bars.

By the time Eladria was deposited in her cell, she had just about drifted into unconsciousness, which was at least a reprieve from the grief that tore through her like a thousand sharpened blades.

Eladria slept, her mind drifting into a fluidic realm of images, memories and imaginings.

She found herself wandering the empty corridors of the palace, desperately searching for her father. But he was nowhere to be found. In a rising panic, she began running through the labyrinthine corridors, crying out for him. For some reason she felt drawn to the control room, but when she arrived there it wasn't her father that she found. It was her mother. She was encased in a beam of light so bright that Eladria had to shield her eyes.

"Mother!" she cried, overcome at finally having found her mother after all these years. "What are you doing here?"

"I need you," came the pained response. Her voice sounded weak and

distant, as though an entire universe separated them. "Please, Eladria, please...you must help me."

"What can I do?" Eladria pleaded.

But before she could answer, the scene shifted. Eladria was now on the planet surface, in the midst of a deserted city street, the sky overhead dark and stormy. She looked around, trying to ascertain where she was. As she wandered the eerily vacant street, the ground beneath her began to shake. Buildings started collapsing all around her, crumbling to the ground, sending up waves of dust and debris.

She stumbled and fell. Just as she was about to be crushed by a falling temple, the scene again shifted.

This time Eladria became aware of a whole other world: a world existing across an infinite void, closer than a heartbeat, yet an eternity away. It was a strange place, utterly unfamiliar to her, but it was somehow calling to her.

She saw the face of a young man she'd seen so many times before in her dreams, a handsome man with dark hair and dark eyes, a crystal amulet hanging around his neck. She didn't know who he was or why his face haunted her dreams, but he was calling to her...

Eladria felt as though she was been pulled in different directions. "Where do I go?" she cried. "What do I do?"

But there was no answer.

She found herself spinning into an infinite, all-consuming abyss of darkness, ensnared by its unrelenting gravity and unable to break free. All she could hear were the words of the seer, which echoed relentlessly through her mind as she was devoured by the void of blackness:

"Darkness will fall. Your entire world will be lost."

Eladria was awoken by a brusque shake. She opened her eyes and tried to throw off the lingering disorientation of sleep. She found herself lying on a bench in one of the security cells. The barred door was open and there were two men in the cell and another two standing outside, weapons in hand.

The Ha'shon...it all came back to her in an agonizing wave.

One of the Ha'shon knelt down and was shaking her awake and the other stood over her, arms folded, an expression of glee upon his lined and twisted face. It was their leader, General Estaran.

"Wake up, Princess," Estaran said as he looked down at her.

Eladria sat up on the bed and pushed the Ha'shon away from her. He stepped back and stood by Estaran's side, hand resting upon the leather holster that housed his firearm.

"What do you want?" Eladria looked up at Estaran, a tone of repugnance saturating her voice.

"I came to see that you were all right," Estaran answered. "I realize this must be a traumatic time for you. Contrary to what you might think, I abhor violence. Unfortunately, in this world, it is often a necessity. It is the force that drives change, the agent that initiates revolution. But although I had no love of your father, I derived no joy from taking his life."

Eladria stared up at the Ha'shon and felt a wave of hatred rising up within her. "I don't believe a word you say," she said. "You enjoyed every moment of what you did, because you're nothing more than a sick, twisted murderer."

Estaran's face darkened. "In accordance with the Sacred Texts, I hold all life sacred," he retorted. "What I do, I do because it has been ordained by the Divine Father. The nonbelievers must be subjugated and brought to the loving arms of Shon, or else purged from this world. The end times draw near and in order to save this world we are called to take whatever action we can. We do so in the name of Shon. He forgives us and washes us of all sin, because we follow only the sacred word."

"That's meaningless nonsense," Eladria shook her head defiantly.

Estaran bristled. It probably wasn't wise to push him, but she was determined to hurt him in any way she could. If she could have leapt up and strangled him on the spot, she would have done so. But her body was weak and her senses dulled. She knew that if she came within an inch of him, his men would strike her down in an instant. But she was fuelled by an insurmountable rage and the very sight of this Ha'shon butcher sickened her. Why should her gentle father have lost his life to this brainwashed abomination?

"You now have a choice, Princess," Estaran began as took a step closer, standing over her threateningly. "You can either repent and embrace us, or you will die as your father did."

"I will never join you," Eladria answered with as much fire as she could muster. "And it doesn't matter what you do to me, because you won't get away with this. People will rise up and stop you. Even your precious 'Divine Father' won't be able to save you. You'll be made to account for your crimes and you'll suffer for every man, woman and child you've slaughtered here today."

With a cold smile that didn't touch his eyes, Estaran reached down and stroked Eladria's face. She grimaced, sickened by the touch of his hand.

"I admire your strength, your fire and courage," he purred softly. "You certainly didn't inherit them from your father. He was weak and indecisive, whereas you're strong, spirited and *alive*. I shall regret killing you. I'd much rather have had you by my side. But you were offered the choice and you chose death over life and eternal damnation over salvation. You poor, deluded child. First thing tomorrow, I will again address the whole of Tahnadra, and once more I shall demonstrate our supremacy. With the entire planet watching, I shall execute you as I did your father. The message shall be clear and unmistakable. The old sovereignty has perished. The new order has risen."

Eladria sat with her back hard against the cell wall and she looked up at Estaran defiantly. She had nothing to say. A small part of her was fearful and compelled her to apologize, to plead for her life. But the greater part of her was resolute: she would not disgrace her father's memory by capitulating to this man. She would stand firm until the end and, if she was destined to die at the hands of the Ha'shon with the entire planet watching, then she would accept her fate.

Estaran frowned and shook his head from side to side, clearly disappointed by her reaction. Without another word, he turned and left. His subordinate closed the cell door with a loud clank. He input a code on the control pad at the side of the cell and with a reverberating click, the cell door locked. With that, they departed.

Eladria sat huddled on the bench, feeling more alone than she'd ever felt her entire life. Her thoughts turned to her father. How she yearned for him to come and save her...

Only he was gone.

Overwhelmed by an immeasurable grief, she lay on her side and cried for what felt like hours. Eventually her tears subsided and she lay motionless in a state of numbed emptiness. The faint hum of the ceiling light pierced the silence and there was a timepiece on the wall opposite the cell. It would soon be morning. Her death got closer with each rhythmic tick of the mechanism.

But what did it matter? She didn't know how she could go on living now. Not without her father. Not after her city had been blown to pieces, along with all of her friends and family. Not knowing that the world she had inherited was now under occupation by a cruel and insane dictatorship. And not knowing that the man she had loved was the one responsible for all of this.

No, after all that had happened this nightmarish day, she didn't want to go on living. There was nothing left to live for.

Chapter 3

The Long Night

It was ironic that what was to be the last night of Eladria's life was also the longest.

She lay upon the cold metal bench and, although physically and emotionally exhausted, her frenzied mind kept her awake the entire night as the hours slowly ticked by.

Again and again her mind replayed the murder of her father, the massacre in the control room and the destruction of the royal city, which now lay in smoldering ruins.

This shouldn't have happened...

Her thoughts turned to the Ha'shon, the perpetrators of these atrocities, and she felt a searing hatred rising in the pit of her belly, filling every cell of her being with rage. That they considered themselves to be acting upon some kind of Divine decree made the Ha'shon all the more despicable to her.

By now her tears had dried and she felt numb and hollow.

This is it, she thought to herself as she gazed vacantly at the wall. *There won't be an official coronation, but I suppose I'm now Queen of Tahnadra.* As sole heir to the throne, Tahnadra was now her world and those upon it were her subjects. Such a thought seemed strangely amusing to her. *The shortest, saddest reign in Tahnadran history: a single night spent in a prison cell...*

And, as with her father before her, it would end in her murder at the hands of Ha'shon terrorists. Perhaps that was just the way it was meant to be.

Her main regret was that there was nothing she could do to help her people. They were about to be subjected to tyranny under the Ha'shon. The Ha'shon Liberation Army would no doubt ravage the planet and kill countless people in their crusade to supremacy.

She shed a tear for her people, for the millions of innocent men, women and children that would die at the hands of the Ha'shon. She wished there was something she could do for them, that she could somehow save her world. If only she could stop the Ha'shon and make her father's death at least count for something.

But it was hopeless. She knew that. With a sigh, she lay back and endeavored to accept her fate. Perhaps one day someone would rise up and defeat the Ha'shon and overcome the ignorance and hatred that had destroyed her world.

She vividly recalled her father recounting the ancient legends of Tahnadra. She would be tucked up in bed at night, perhaps only seven or eight years old. Her father would sit by her side and tell her all kinds of incredible stories.

"There was a time when Tahnadra was a paradise, a land fit for gods," he had once told her. "There was peace, unity and a shared sense of purpose among its people. All worked together for the common good. These were gifts bestowed upon our world by the Lasan, travelers from beyond the stars. They had come to Tahnadra in the beginning times and brought civilization, culture and a rich sense of community and spiritual unity."

"What happened to them?" she had asked.

"For a time the Lasan ruled with great benevolence from the land of Atukaare. They later left this land to their children as they returned to the stars."

But over the generations, without the guiding hand of the Lasan, the wisdom of the Old Way was corrupted and two new religions were born: the Ha'shon and the True Way, two opposing ideologies that sought complete dominance, paving the way for millennia of war.

Atukaare was destroyed and the royal family, who were descendants of the Lasan, fled to the third moon. There they could rule the planet in safety and provide neutral ground for the two religious factions to attempt to reach some kind of peace.

Even from a young age Eladria had been cynical about such an endeavor. It seemed to her a wasted effort. Neither side wanted peace; they only wanted to win, to crush their adversaries. And why? Just so they could be *right*. It was pathetic and childish, yet the suffering that had been wrought by these self-proclaimed holy men was beyond imagining.

Centuries of unrelenting war had all but destroyed Tahnadra. It was an empty husk of a world, stripped of its beauty, freshness and life. The people were jaded, bitter and filled with hatred for the opposing side. All they wanted was victory and vengeance for the losses they had incurred.

The more she thought about the state of her world, the more she realized that she didn't want to be its queen, because no matter what she tried to do, she knew there was nothing she could do to save it.

Perhaps the Ha'shon were right: maybe these were the 'end times'. Maybe there simply was no hope and the whole planet was spiraling to its annihilation. And maybe that was the fate it deserved. All that her father, grandparents and forebears had strived for had died along with them.

Eladria lay in a state of defeat, resigned to her fate. If she was to die, then there was nothing she could do about that. There was no way out of this cell. Not without help.

It was at that moment that something caught her eye.

A creature scurried across the hallway. It was a yunpa, a small furry rodent, scuttling along the corridor that bridged the holding cells. It stopped in front of Eladria's cell and peered in. It was staring directly at her, its whiskers twitching wildly.

Eladria had the sense that this was no ordinary yunpa—and she was right, for it promptly began to change shape! The little creature grew larger and larger, its fur-covered body expanding and dissolving into an amorphous, shimmering mist.

Eladria leapt up from the bench. She stared in astonishment as the mist coalesced into solid form, with two arms, two legs, an abdomen, chest and head rapidly taking shape before her eyes. As the mist-like substance dissolved and the human form became clear, Eladria cried in amazement as she realized that she recognized this person.

Zinn! That little yunpa had just transformed into Zinn!

Eladria ran to the bars and cried out in delight. "Zinn! I don't believe it. Is that really you?"

Zinn stepped forward and smiled enigmatically as she smoothed down her tunic. "Yes, it's me, my dear," she said.

"But...*how?*" Eladria gasped, so utterly amazed she had to struggle to force the words out of her mouth.

"You've just learned something that I've kept secret for many, many years," Zinn said. "I'm what your people call a *metamorph.*"

"A metamorph?" Eladria echoed, pressing her hands against the bars as she leaned forward. "But I thought they were extinct?"

"Nearly, but not quite."

"I can't believe it..."

"The only person who knew my true identity was your father."

"But why conceal it?" Eladria asked, eyes still wide in amazement.

"There are very few of my kind," Zinn explained. "Because of our ability to change shape, we've always faced distrust, suspicion and persecution. Six hundred years ago, during the Last Reclamation, a law was passed outlawing my kind. Countless numbers were hunted and slaughtered. We learned to survive by carefully concealing our true nature, by endeavoring to pass ourselves off as 'normal'."

"But my father knew?"

"That's a story for another time, my dear. For now, time is of the essence. I was imprisoned in an adjoining cell. Emotional distress hampers my ability to change form. It's taken me all this time to muster the power to change shape. But once I did, I easily slipped through the bars, and now I must get you out."

Eladria's mind was galloping like a crazed rhastopod as she sought to reconcile this unexpected revelation. Having spent her entire life in Zinn's care, Eladria had assumed that she'd known everything there was to know about the kindly old maid. Yet it appeared she knew nothing about her at all.

Zinn began studying the control pad that operated the lock mechanism. "We need the code," she sighed. "I don't suppose you happen to know what it is?"

"No," Eladria shook her head. "But I do know the general override code for all palace systems. Unless, of course, it's been changed."

"Well, at your convenience," Zinn said, her body rigid with urgency.

"I think it's...nine seven eight four three...six?"

Zinn input the code but nothing happened. The console simply bleeped in error. Zinn shook her head.

"Four three...seven?" Eladria suggested.

Zinn input the code, but again it was to no avail.

Eladria sighed in exasperation and leaned against the cell wall, bringing her hand to her chin as she struggled to recall the correct code. As princess and heir to the throne, it was her responsibility to know the security override code in case of emergency. Every few months she was required to undergo a security briefing, during which she was expected to memorize a new override sequence.

Oh...what was it? It wasn't six...or seven...

"Nine!" Eladria exclaimed. "Try nine! Nine seven eight four three *nine*."

Zinn input the code and the lock clicked open.

Eladria pushed the door open and stepped out of her cell, relishing the sweet taste of freedom.

"We have to get you out of the palace and off this moon, your Highness," Zinn said gravely. "The palace is under control of the enemy. I don't believe there's anything we can do from here. We have to get you to safety."

"Then we have to get to the hangars," Eladria nodded. "If we can get to a fighter, I can take us down to the planet." Eladria was a trained pilot. She had been obsessed with flying since she was a small child and her father had reluctantly consented to flying lessons upon her fourteenth birthday. It was hardly customary for a princess to be piloting fighter craft, but then Eladria was anything but customary.

Eladria strode to the weapons locker and surveyed the firearms. She appropriated two electro-pulse pistols and quickly checked to ensure they were operational. "We can assume there are guards standing watch outside," she said as she strapped a holster around her waist.

"It would stand to reason."

"Your ability to change shape can be used to our advantage."

Zinn nodded.

"I want you to do what you did before," Eladria continued. "Change shape into something small; I'll open the door, you go through it and distract the guards. That'll give me the chance to catch them from behind."

"Just be careful, my dear," Zinn warned.

Without hesitation, they put their plan into action. With a look of concentration upon her face, Zinn began her transformation. Her form dissolved into a diffuse mist-like substance, which sparkled and glistened like sunlight upon dewdrops. Eladria marveled that even Zinn's clothes dissolved into the mist, suggesting they were merely a facsimile that could likely be altered with a single thought.

The mist swirled and coalesced in mid-air, decreasing in mass and gradually taking the form of a glitter-bee, a brightly colored insect with tapering wings that sparkled red and gold as they flapped. The insect circled Eladria's head with a melodic hum.

Eladria approached the door and stood with her back hard against the wall. Reaching up to the door control, she gestured for Zinn to ready herself as she mouthed a countdown. *Three....two....one....*

Eladria activated the door control and kept still as the door slid open.

Although she couldn't see them from where she was standing, she was nevertheless aware of two guards standing outside.

"What was that?" whispered one of the guards.

"There's no one there," responded the other.

Eladria held her breath and stood rigidly still. She had a pistol in each hand and she clutched them tightly, her fingers wrapped around the cold metal triggers.

She was aware of the insect form of Zinn, buzzing through the open doorway and circling the two guards.

"It's just an insect," grunted the first guard.

"Insects can't open doors," said the second suspiciously.

Eladria could tell that the guard was about to enter the security station, but that was when Zinn intensified her diversionary tactics. The glitter-bee buzzed around the guards, diving at their heads. The guards tried to swipe the insect away but Zinn wasn't going to let it end there. She began to transform herself in mid-air, the insect form dissolving into the sparkling mist as she initiated her metamorphosis. She had succeeded in getting the guards' full attention.

"What is that?" cried one of the guards in confusion.

Eladria realized that now was the time to act.

Her hands tensed as she gripped the guns and sprung into action, spinning round to face the Ha'shon guards. They had their backs to her as they gaped at the bewildering sight.

She had them in a clear line of fire. Their weapons were aimed at Zinn's coalescing form, and they made a motion to fire. Eladria pre-empted them. She pulled both triggers and felt her body lurch as the pistols discharged blasts of energy that slammed into the backs of the Ha'shon guards. The two men fell into the ground.

Eladria felt a wave of nausea as she looked down at their smoldering bodies. On one hand, she was repulsed at herself for having taken two lives, even if they were Ha'shon. But another part of her was simply relieved. There would be time for recrimination later.

Zinn had now resumed her usual form and Eladria stepped over the bodies and handed her one of pistols. Zinn reluctantly took the weapon. She was a gentle woman with an innate distaste of violence, but she knew the desperation of their situation overrode all other concerns.

"We have to get out of the open," Eladria said as she marched down the corridor, her blue dress swishing behind her. "The palace must be swarming with Ha'shon. Our advantage is that we know its layout, and they don't. If we take the next corridor to the right, we can access the maintenance crawl-ways and follow them down to the hangar level."

Zinn nodded as Eladria led the way. They cautiously crept along the corridor and managed to reach the maintenance hatch without incident. Once inside, they clambered through the innards of the palace, crawling down air vents and edging their way past power distribution stations, careful not to touch any of the buzzing wires. It was hot, the air was thin and the conditions cramped, but they kept on going regardless. Arriving at an intersection bridged by vertical ladders, they stopped briefly to rest, before continuing downward.

It was a long and exhausting climb down eight entire levels, but they eventually reached the hangar level. Breathless but relieved, Eladria and Zinn took a left turn, edging along the claustrophobic maintenance shaft in the direction of the aircraft hangars. The hangars comprised a vast network encircling the lower region of the palace and housed a variety of aircraft, from diplomatic transports to the trans-atmospheric fighters used by the Tahnadran Royal Military.

They came to an air vent above one of the hangars. Peering through the metal grates, Eladria was relieved to see two D-12 fighters sitting stationary in the middle of the hangar. In another stroke of luck, the hangar itself was deserted.

"What do we do now?" whispered Zinn.

"We get down there, take one of the fighters and leave for the planet."

They climbed down a thick metal pipe to ground level. Eladria knew her way around these crawl-ways and ventilation shafts better than most, for it was here she had escaped to when she was a child and was fed up with having to 'act' like a princess, when all she had wanted was to do her own thing. Here she would sit for hours, watching the military craft as they came and went from the palace, dreaming that one day she too would pilot them. In more recent times, she had sometimes met Narat here. It wasn't the most romantic location imaginable, but it was a place they could be together, away from prying eyes.

Eladria ran her hand along the inside of the wall, fumbling for the hatch that would open the access point. It was dark and there was barely room to move, but she persisted and eventually found it. With a heave, she cranked it open and climbed out of the ventilation shaft.

She stepped onto the concrete hangar floor, as Zinn followed behind her, and surveyed their new surroundings. She'd never seen the place this empty before. Normally it would be filled with engineers and maintenance personnel. Something wasn't right.

Regardless, she proceeded with haste to the main control booth. Her hands flicked across the control panel as she initiated the mechanized launch program and input the instructions. She set a four dessick countdown: that should be more than enough time to get the fighter ready to depart. Ordinarily there was a list of checks that had to be done prior to take off, but there was no time for that. She marched over to the nearest fighter, which, to her great relief, was already prepared for take off.

Just as she was about to climb into it, the sudden sound of the hangar door opening stopped her in her tracks. Her heart skipped a beat as she turned to the door and reached for her gun.

It was Narat. He was alone and unarmed. He approached her

slowly, hands raised in a gesture of surrender.

The very sight of him elicited a potent reaction in the young princess. She felt a wave of hatred pulsing through her blood. He was the cause of all this; he was the reason her father was murdered. She raised her weapon and tightened the trigger. She had loved him so much, but her passion had turned to an inextinguishable rage. Her eyes narrowed and she felt her face tighten as he came to a stop before her, hands held aloft.

"Give me one reason I shouldn't kill you now," she said darkly.

"Please just listen to me, Eladria," Narat said evenly.

"What are you doing here? How did you know I'd be here?"

"Because you were under surveillance the entire time. We knew you'd escaped the moment it happened."

"You were tracking us?"

Narat nodded. "We were ahead of you every step of the way. When I realized you were on your way here, I had the place cleared. I convinced Estaran that I would deal with you."

"How kind of you," she growled, raising the weapon.

"Eladria, listen to me," Narat pleaded. "I came here to talk. I have to explain what I've done. I have to make you understand."

"I understand that you betrayed my father and everything he believed in," Eladria shouted at him, her body shaking in fury. "You betrayed the monarchy and government. You betrayed *me*. You're responsible for my father's death and all the other deaths."

"No," Narat shook his head. "That wasn't part of the deal. Estaran said nothing about killing the king or destroying the city. You have to believe me. I didn't know it would come to this."

"Then you're a fool. If you make a deal with the Ha'shon, you're guaranteed of bloodshed. They speak about their religion, their beliefs, their Divinely-inspired ideals, but they're nothing but insane killers—and you're one of them now. I can't believe it, Narat. Why? Why would you ally yourself with those fanatics?"

"I may not agree with everything they've done, but I agree with their philosophy. They promise a new and better era for our world. I mean no disrespect to you, Eladria, but the royal family have done nothing for Tahnadra. They've sat up here in their little bubble, isolated and protected from the chaos down there. You've never lived on Tahnadra, but I have. I grew up on the streets and I experienced the violence, brutality and poverty—and the war. You've never tasted war, Eladria, you've never had to endure it. But I was there. The things I saw, the things I had to experience, the people I saw slaughtered, the towns and cities I saw laid to waste..."

"It wasn't us that waged that war, Narat," Eladria countered. "We've done all we can to bring peace to our world, to get the leaders to sit down and reach some kind of resolution. That's what my father worked for his entire life: peace and an end to the violence."

"Yes, and his father before him and his father before that," Narat responded. "And where has it got us? There can be no peace between the Ha'shon and the True Way. The only way for the war to end is for the victor to emerge triumphant. That victor is the Ha'shon. It has to be! They promise to transform our world from one of suffering, violence and struggle to one of peace and prosperity."

"You mean to say you actually believe their lies and propaganda?"

"You never asked me about my past. Well, I'll tell you why I had to side with the Ha'shon and why I've spent most my life a secret follower of their teachings. As you know I'm from the neutral land of Tamaru between the Ha'shon and True Way territories. When I was a child, my family lived in the northern province of Rakata, where we experienced such poverty that it was a daily struggle just to put food on the table. There were constant raids by both Ha'shon and True Way soldiers, both determined to claim the province for themselves."

"That's why my father stationed a TRM garrison there," Eladria intervened. "To secure those disputed territories and prevent incursions by either side."

"The garrison was a joke, Eladria," Narat objected. "The military sent only a minimal detachment of troops, just enough to secure the borders. But they turned a blind eye to the suffering of our people and did little to stop the abductions."

"If you have a point to make, I suggest you make it," Eladria growled, taking a step back and keeping her fingers coiled around the pistol trigger.

"I didn't realize it at the time, but I later learned that the Ha'shon care about liberating people," Narat began. "One night, during a raid, they rounded up fifty of us and took us back to Ha'shon territory, where we were offered a choice: the choice to embrace the Divine Father, or to die. Most of us repented and accepted the Ha'shon path. Some resisted and in so doing, accepted death. I pitied them. Having spent my entire life suffering, I could see that the Ha'shon offered us redemption and lives of purpose. My family and I were initiated into the Ha'shon and pledged to serve the Divine Father in all endeavors. They offered me something no one else had ever given me: belonging, purpose and the opportunity to help create this glorious new dawn."

"Then you actually believe the poison they spout?" Eladria asked in disbelief.

"Our world is dying, Eladria," he said. "What I did, I had to do. I served in the Ha'shon Liberation Army from the moment I was old enough to pick up a weapon. I fought the True Way and the Royal Military knowing that this was a holy crusade, that they had to be defeated, for only then could we save our world. I passed through the ranks and became noticed by the Ha'shon military hierarchy. Because I was a skilled fighter and wasn't of Ha'shon ethnicity, I was chosen to infiltrate the royal moon and serve as an operative here. This day has been planned for many years and I willingly laid the groundwork and brought as many Ha'shon sympathizers as I could into the palace where they could fight by my side."

"So this was all part of some plan," Eladria said, shifting on the spot. "What about me—about us? Was that part of your plan? Was I just some kind of pawn, an instrument to help you betray my father?"

"No, of course not," Narat said. "I couldn't have planned that, Eladria, I couldn't have planned falling in love with you. In many ways I wish I hadn't, because it's made all of this so much harder."

"You never *loved* me," Eladria stated. "If you'd loved me you could never have done this."

Narat moved closer, and Eladria raised her pistol to his head.

"You won't kill me," Narat whispered.

"Don't be so sure."

Narat stopped.

"Why did you come down here, Narat? What do you want from me?" Eladria asked.

"You're not going to escape, Eladria," Narat said. "Estaran won't let you. He wants you to join us. If the last of the House of Chaldeen joins the Ha'shon, it will hasten our march to victory. Instead of opposing us, those loyal to the monarchy will join us. It'll save thousands of lives, Eladria; lives that would otherwise be lost. Whatever happens, the Ha'shon are now in control of Tahnadra. If you join us, you can save so many lives and prevent untold suffering."

"Then what?"

"Then we can be together, as we've always wanted. Nothing will stand in our way and no one will oppose us. Just think of it, Eladria. You won't have to worry about those royal duties you so dreaded. We can live simple lives, doing whatever we want. We can be together."

Narat stepped closer. Eladria remained motionless, still pointing the pistol at him. Undeterred, he reached out, placed his hand upon the weapon and pushed it down. He stood directly in front of her. "You have to get over your anger, Eladria. You have to move beyond your grief," he said, looking into her eyes. "You know that I love you...and I know that in spite of all that's happened, you still love me too."

Eladria said nothing. She was letting him make the next move. All the time she was aware of Zinn in her peripheral vision, looking on in concern. Oblivious to Zinn's presence, Narat moved closer to Eladria and put his hand on her shoulder, angling his head toward hers. He closed his eyes and kissed her gently on the lips. Eladria let him. After a moment, he pulled back and looked into her eyes, seeking some kind of response from her.

Eladria dropped her gun and it landed on the ground with a clatter. She took Narat's hand and, without a word, gently led him a few steps back, until they were both standing alongside the hangar wall. Her face softened as she put one hand on Narat's shoulder and the other on the back of his neck. She leaned over and returned his kiss.

As her lips locked with his, she could feel him let down his guard. With great suddenness, and mustering all the strength she had, she smashed his head hard against the metal-plated wall. His head collided with the wall with such force that he immediately lost consciousness. His body drooped in her arms. She withdrew her arms and he fell to the ground.

"I'm glad you came to your senses," Zinn remarked.

"Part of me wanted to kill him, Zinn," Eladria admitted, horrified by the admission as the words left her mouth, her eyes stinging with held-back tears.

"But you didn't. The fact you felt that way simply means you've been hurt; hurt more than anyone ever deserves to be."

Eladria looked down at the man she'd once loved, the man who had so cruelly betrayed her, who had helped destroy almost everything she'd ever cared about. Realizing that she had little time to lament her losses, she gathered herself together and made for the nearest fighter, motioning for Zinn to follow.

"It's likely they've been monitoring all of this from Central

Control," Eladria warned. "In which case, they'll have a security force here in moments. We have to leave now, Zinn."

They climbed up the landing steps and boarded the stationary craft with haste. Zinn took the passenger seat, while Eladria sat in the pilot's seat on the right side of the cockpit. As they strapped themselves in, adjusting the seat belts in preparation for launch, Eladria activated the vehicle using voice control.

She readied the craft to leave and manually initiated the departure sequence. She fired up the engines and activated the launch pad, feeling the cylinders clicking into position as the launch pad beneath them rotated and ascended to the ceiling.

The ceiling hatch slid open and once they were on level with the exit shaft, Eladria disengaged the safety lock and took to flight. The vehicle lifted off the launch pad and shot toward the exit. With a flick of her console, she opened the exit door and the fighter sped out of the palace. She set course for the perimeter of the bio-dome, beyond which was open space. From there, she would take the craft into the atmosphere and down to the planet surface.

But this wasn't going to be easy. The moment they exited the palace they were surrounded by Ha'shon raiders. Ignoring them, she navigated toward the bio-dome exit and initiated full throttle. The fighter screamed ahead at full speed, piercing through the veil of black smoke rising from the dead city.

The Ha'shon raiders gave immediate chase. Although trained as a pilot, she had never been in a combat situation. Any analysis of the situation would have concluded it hopeless, but Eladria wasn't going to give up. She knew there was only one possible outcome now: she would escape, or she would die trying.

Chapter 4

Planetfall

Eladria kept on course, with one eye on the navigational console, the other on the four Ha'shon raiders in pursuit.

Her one advantage was that her D-12 fighter was technologically superior to the Ha'shon raiders, which looked as though they'd been cobbled together with parts scrounged from a dozen scrapyards. But it was altogether less easy to dismiss their weaponry. The Ha'shon were equipped with powerful electro-charge cannons and torpedo launchers. She had already seen them in action as they pounded they royal city to rubble, so she knew what they were capable of.

As Eladria kept her eyes glued to the display, she was only peripherally aware of Zinn in the passenger seat, gripping the cockpit with both hands in terror as the craft sped toward the perimeter of the bio-dome.

Through the shifting veil of smoke, the exit came into view: the rectangular aperture through which vehicles entered and exited the bio-dome. It was still open following the Ha'shon arrival, so all Eladria needed to do was pass through it. Once she'd exited the bio-dome, she would be able to leave the moon and set course for the planet.

But the Ha'shon didn't want her to escape. The lead craft fired two shots across her left wing, one of which clipped the left nacelle, causing a red light to flash upon her console. Her sole option was to employ evasive tactics. If there had been another pilot she could have launched a counter-offensive, but Zinn was unable to operate the weaponry.

The Ha'shon fired again, this time targeting her engines. Fortunately the damage was minimal. It would seem they had been ordered to disable rather than destroy her craft. Perhaps Estaran wanted to avoid any possibility of her becoming a martyr.

Whatever his plan, she knew she had to get the Ha'shon off her tail. Desperation often bred the best ideas and one immediately flashed into her mind.

She altered course, pulling the fighter upward, setting a direct course for the glass rim of the bio-dome. She tugged the control stick and initiated the throttle, putting the fighter into full speed.

She knew this would confuse her pursuers. Whether they thought she was attempting to smash through the bio-dome or was simply suicidal, it didn't matter: they fell for her trap and adjusted their course to pursue at maximum speed.

"Eladria, what are you doing?" cried Zinn, her voice shaking.

"Trust me," Eladria said, unable to take her eyes off the display.

"But we're headed straight for the bio-dome," Zinn gasped. "You know we'd never survive the impact!"

"I know what I'm doing," Eladria responded, as she calculated just how close she needed to get before she could execute her plan.

The vast curved rim of the bio-dome was getting nearer by the second. Eladria checked the readouts and smiled as she saw that the Ha'shon attack fighters were still behind her and closing in. They'd fallen for her bait.

Closer...

Eladria knew she was playing a dangerous game. If her calculations were even the slightest bit off she would collide with the bio-dome and that was an impact no one could survive. She involuntarily held her breath as she kept her eyes fixed upon the readout. As soon as she got to twelve hundred metrins she could implement her plan. But she had to be precise.

It was coming...

Coming...

NOW!

With a sharp tug of the control stick, she pulled the craft upward at full speed, looping around in a semicircle until she was behind the enemy fighters.

The Ha'shon, disorientated by the sudden move, were unable to change course in time. Their fighters collided with the great glass barrier. They were instantly obliterated, combusting into balls of flame as their engines ignited. The impenetrable glass barrier was undented as the flaming remnants of the Ha'shon raiders spiraled to the ground.

Eladria re-adjusted her course. She maneuvered the craft downward and sped toward the exit.

Alas, the Ha'shon had obviously been monitoring the entire incident from Central Control and, seeing that she was about to escape, they sealed the exit. As the gates closed, Eladria cursed loudly.

She didn't know the codes that would reopen them, unless, of course, her emergency override code would work? She quickly tapped it into the console and relayed it to the gate mechanism, but nothing happened. They must have changed the code after she'd used it to escape from security.

She had one final hope, however. Recalling something she'd learnt in her practical training, she reached over to the weapons console. She targeted the electro-charge cannons upon the third relay of the exit gate. A direct hit upon the relay ought to disable the entire mechanism, enabling her to escape.

With a silent prayer, she opened fire. The energy blasts hit their intended target, disabling the mechanism, causing the exit gate to once again slide open.

Eladria took her chance and the fighter punched through the gate at full speed.

They exited the great bio-dome, finding themselves in the icy black vacuum of space. The planet was just ahead of them. She plotted a course toward it, but was caught off-guard by sudden weapons fire. The craft lurched and a dozen warning lights flashed upon the console.

"What's happening?" gasped Zinn.

"They've activated the weapons platform."

The fighter suffered another direct hit and this time the damage was more severe. The vertical stabilizer was obliterated and the left wing damaged. It was futile to try to fight back. Eladria concentrated on dodging the incoming blasts while maintaining her trajectory.

"Atmospheric entry in point eight dessicks," Eladria said as her eyes darted between displays. The planet's atmosphere would provide a buffer, protecting them from hostile fire. But would they make it in time?

Another direct hit!

This time, the entire craft was rocked by an explosion. Zinn cried out in terror. Eladria felt her stomach lurch as she scanned her console and surveyed the damage. That last hit had shredded the left wing and torn off the nacelle. They were disabled. The fighter was operating on only half thrust and would be almost impossible to maneuver.

Yet they were fortunate to be alive. Ordinarily it would take only one direct hit from those charge cannons to destroy a craft such as this. This suggested to Eladria that either the Ha'shon were operating the weapons platform and their inexperience was working to her advantage, or the palace technicians were manning the guns and were deliberately trying to avoid killing their princess. Whatever the reason, she was grateful for any small favor she could get.

She tried to reroute additional power to the thrusters. The craft was flying erratically and she struggled to hold her course, while simultaneously dodging the incoming barrage of fire that rained upon them.

For some reason it brought to mind a childhood game in which someone threw a succession of balls and she had to catch as many as she could. Only this time she had to dodge what was being thrown at her. For the most part, she was succeeding. But it was simply impossible to escape each and every blast of the cannons. Again and again the fighter was struck. Sometimes the damage was only minimal as a blast clipped the wings. Other times the impact was more severe and the craft lurched violently, often knocking them off-course altogether. In such instances she had to scramble to regain control of the vehicle and re-navigate toward the planet.

Another savage strike and another direct hit...

Damn!

"The fuel tank's ruptured! We're leaking fuel."

But Eladria wasn't about to give up. They'd come too far to concede defeat. They were now in range of the planet and were about to enter the atmosphere. She adjusted the controls for atmospheric entry and braced herself for entry into the stratosphere. The counter-force of atmospheric pressure buffeted the fighter and slowed their descent.

Fortunately it also slowed the weapons fire and effectively dissipated the electro-charge blasts that were hurtling toward them. The only way the Ha'shon could target them now would be to fire missiles. But at this range, with their target descending through the atmosphere, even the most skilled weapons officer would struggle to hit their target.

Eladria turned to Zinn, whose eyes were wide in shock. "Zinn, that last hit not only ruptured the fuel tank, but it disabled navigation. So I don't know where we're going to land—and I don't think I can land us manually."

Zinn looked round in horror. "What does that mean?"

"It means we're going to crash. I'll try to make it as smooth as I can. But basically we're going to land wherever and however gravity takes us."

As they plummeted through the troposphere, land became visible through patches in the cloud beneath them. It was solid ground they were over at least; a lush mountainous region carpeted by dense forestland.

Eladria checked her displays and saw that they were now at an altitude of eighteen thousand metrins and rapidly falling. As gravity took its hold, their speed increased and the crippled fighter began spiraling, despite Eladria's best efforts to steady it.

She felt helpless. There was nothing she could do to regain control of the fighter. All they could now do was brace themselves for the inevitable collision. They were going to land in a forest or jungle. The dense greenery was now all she could see from the cockpit as the craft spiraled ever closer to the ground.

Eladria braced herself, tensing every muscle in her body, both hands gripped around the control stick, desperately trying to pull it up and elevate the nose of the vehicle.

They impacted the forest canopy. The craft sliced through the trees like a knife through butter. From then on, Eladria was aware only of her kinesthetic senses: the turbulence that shook her body, the sharp tug of the seat belt as it cut into her shoulders, chest and waist, holding her in place when otherwise she would have been slammed through the glass.

One final, violent lurch signified they had come to a halt.

The craft hung sideways, suspended in the trees and undergrowth. It was dark inside, a murkiness pierced only by the flashing warning lights that illuminated the display console.

Eladria was shaken and disorientated. Physically she seemed unharmed, except for some strained muscles and probable bruising.

She sat for a time, unable to move, unable to think or process information. It took her some time to regain her faculties. The first thing she realized was that they had to move. The fuel tank had ruptured and the slightest spark could ignite it.

She looked up at Zinn, who, at the angle the fighter had landed, was above her. "Zinn, are you all right?" Eladria called as she struggled to unfasten her safety belt, which dug so tightly into her abdomen and shoulders that her skin felt raw.

"Yes...I think so," Zinn responded hoarsely.

"We have to get out of this thing. Can you get yourself loose?"

"I...I'll try."

As Zinn fumbled with her safety belt, Eladria tried to activate the navigational display. She had hoped to use it to determine their position, but it was inoperative and she had no idea how to fix it. The communications device was similarly inoperative.

She reached into the aft section and tried to open the storage compartment. She knew that each fighter was equipped with a survival pack, including torches, flares, a compass and emergency rations. She held down the button and tried to pull the compartment open, but it wouldn't budge. She tugged at it with all her might, causing the whole craft to shake. It still wouldn't open. She swore loudly and noticed a disapproving glance from Zinn. Even in this dire predicament Zinn was reluctant to grant concessions when it came to her language.

We'll just have to manage without a survival kit, she decided. *At least we've still got the electro-charge pistols.*

Eladria pushed at the cockpit hatch, but it was stiff. She had to force it with all her strength until it eventually creaked open ever so slightly. She peered out the hatch. The craft hung suspended from the trees, wrapped in vines and undergrowth.

Heaving with all her might, Eladria forced the hatch open as far as it would go. She stepped out, carefully finding footing upon a tree trunk. She maneuvered out of the vehicle and climbed down the tree, gingerly holding onto whatever branches or vines she could get hold of, the craft swaying precariously above her with every movement. Zinn followed from above, nervously exiting the rocking vehicle.

"Wouldn't it be easier if you changed shape and flew down from there?" Eladria asked breathlessly after she jumped to the ground.

"It takes considerable energy and concentration to change shape," Zinn responded, careful not to lose her balance as she grabbed hold of the tree. "After all we've just been through, I very much doubt I'd be able to muster much of either."

Eladria reached up and helped Zinn down the trunk and safely onto the ground.

Above them the battered military fighter hung suspended vertically from the trees, entangled in branches and vines, its nose buried in the undergrowth. The damage sustained from the attack was extensive. With its fuselage battered, its wings and stabilizers torn and in some places completely destroyed, it was now little more than a smoldering hunk of metal.

Eladria scanned their surroundings. They were deep in the jungle. Exotic trees arched high above them, permitting only sporadic glimpses of the crimson sky. The jungle was alive with the chattering of birds and the calls and cries of various arboreal creatures. The air was warm and humid and insects buzzed around her face as she tried to swipe them away.

She had to figure out where they were and where they ought to go. There was no telling how far this jungle stretched or where the nearest inhabited lands were. But one thing was certain: they couldn't stay here. They had to get moving. Aside from the obvious danger posed by the ruptured fuel tank, it was likely the Ha'shon had been monitoring her descent. If that was the case, then they probably knew exactly where she had landed.

"Where now?" Zinn asked, looking around anxiously.

"Anywhere but here," Eladria said. She picked a direction at random and motioned for Zinn to follow as she began pushing her way through the undergrowth, trying hard to maintain her footing as she tromped across the uneven jungle terrain. Her dress and shoes were hardly conducive to this kind of activity, but as a princess she'd never had to consider practicality when it came to garments and footwear. She winced as her dress was torn by stray branches and thorns.

"What do you think the Ha'shon will do now?" Zinn asked.

Eladria's face darkened as she stepped over a fallen tree trunk covered in thick red moss. "I don't know. They now control the royal moon and by destroying the headquarters of the TRM they've virtually crippled the military."

"But there are other military installations on the planet..."

"Yes, which are all controlled and coordinated from the moon. And, from what Estaran said, it sounds like the Ha'shon coordinated simultaneous strikes at bases across the planet. They may even have seized control of them, especially if they had inside help, as they did with Narat."

"But they surely can't have vanquished every single base?"

"I hope not. If they haven't, then it's possible the remaining TRM bases could mount a counter-strike and try to retake the moon."

"Then there's still a chance we can still defeat them?"

"I don't know, Zinn!" Eladria snapped, frustrated by her questions. She cautiously stepped past a large twin-tailed lizard as it ambled along the jungle floor, before continuing. "I suppose there's always a chance. I just wish I knew what was happening across the planet...although that's probably the least of our problems right now. I mean, look at us! We're lost in the middle of some jungle, without communications, food or shelter. There's absolutely no telling where we might be..."

"I think I can narrow it down," Zinn said. She pointed off to their right. "You see these tall, red trees over there?"

Eladria nodded.

"Well, those are nucasta trees. Nucasta trees are found only in the jungles of Yahnas."

"Yahnas?" Eladria echoed. "Then this is neutral territory..."

"And that's surely a good thing," Zinn said.

"Well, it's certainly better than if we'd landed in the middle of Ha'shon or True Way territory."

Yahnas was a roughly diamond-shaped continent to the South of Da'mu. Although inhabited by isolated factions of both Ha'shon and True Way, Yahnas was predominantly nonaligned territory. It was a wild, uncivilized land, the terrain uneven and inhospitable.

"Are there any TRM bases here in Yahnas?" Zinn asked.

"Not that I know of."

"What are our plans now, then?"

Eladria didn't have to think before responding. "We keep moving. We have to get as much distance between us and that crashed fighter as possible. And we'd better be on the lookout for Ha'shon reconnaissance craft."

"You think they'll come after us?"

"Oh, you can be sure of it. Estaran's a strategist. He won't just assume I died in the crash. He'll locate and search the wreckage and when he finds no trace of a body, he won't rest until he's either captured or killed me. As heir to throne, I'm too much of a threat to him, and he knows that. Whatever he's planning, we have to get as far away from here as possible. So let's keep moving, Zinn."

They continued plodding through the thick undergrowth, their path illuminated by rays of sunlight filtering through the canopy. Eladria knew the jungle was teeming with life and was aware there would be predators aplenty. It was fortunate they still had their electro-pulse pistols, although without the facilities to charge them they would only last for a couple of days at best.

It was all about survival now. They would have to find food and shelter and come up with some way of navigating the jungle and finding civilization. It was a fortuitous stroke of fate that they had found themselves in neutral territory. Perhaps they would find a means of contacting the nearest TRM installation and get them to dispatch a rescue party. Then Eladria could rally her forces to retake the palace.

That seemed like a far-fetched hope, but if her father had taught her anything, it was that if one's cause was just, then nothing was unattainable.

Whether or not that was true, she did know one thing for certain. They had a long and dangerous journey ahead them.

Chapter 5

Mirror Of Souls

Storm clouds gathered overhead and the air was thick and heavy. Eladria had the sense that something strange was coming, but she couldn't fathom what, so she tried to dismiss it. It grew steadily darker as she and Zinn continued their trek through the jungle. The princess was reluctant to admit it, but they were wandering aimlessly, unsure of where they were or where they were going.

All the while her mind was strangely blank, as though she was awake but in a dreamlike state. Nothing seemed quite real anymore. Perhaps this was her mind's way of keeping her from facing the trauma of the past day. Her old life was gone, but she couldn't think about that now. She could feel her grief lurking beneath the surface, and she knew that if she gave in to it now, it would devour her.

"Princess, I need to stop," Zinn called.

Eladria stopped in her tracks and turned. "What's wrong?"

"I need to rest for a moment. I'm not as young as I used to be..."

Eladria shrugged and gestured for Zinn to take a break. Zinn sat down upon a fallen log with a relieved sigh. Eladria felt too restless to join her. Instead she began pacing the vicinity, trying to fight off the uneasy feeling that lurched in the pit of her stomach. Taking a deep breath, she looked down at her old maid and decided she wanted to learn more about Zinn's hitherto secret identity. "How old are you anyway?" Eladria asked in as casual a manner as she could.

Zinn looked up in surprise. "That's a rather personal question."

"Well, I can see roughly what age you appear to be," Eladria said, feeling a pang of indignation. "But that's just an appearance. In some ways, I feel like I don't know you anymore."

"That's not true," Zinn shot back, caught off-guard by the

princess's attack. "I'm the same person you've always known. I've never tried to deceive you in any way."

"But I don't even know what you look like, the *real* you," Eladria said. "I mean, that's not your real form, is it? What do you really look like?"

The conversation clearly made Zinn uncomfortable, but she knew that Eladria deserved some answers. "My natural form is diffuse, intangible," she explained. "You might perceive it as being like a cloud of vapor or mist."

Eladria nodded thoughtfully. "So why do your people disguise themselves as other forms?"

"Because we can, I suppose. It's our nature to do so. We take other forms in order to experience physicality, to explore, to relate, to do things."

"You said my father knew about this?"

Zinn nodded sadly. Eladria had forgotten how close Zinn had been to her father. She had been in his service for many years before Eladria was born. It hadn't occurred to her that Zinn might be grieving as well. Yet, with some measure of solemnity, the maid began to relate her story. "Many years ago, when your father was a boy, he and your grandparents were on holiday in Dumak. One day, as they relaxed in the palace complex, your father snuck out to play in the surrounding woodland. Unfortunately, he strayed too far into the forest, where he encountered a wild sabre-cat.

"I happened to be in the vicinity, in the form of a bird. When I heard his cry, I flew to the scene of the commotion and found your father cornered by the sabre-cat. I knew I had to rescue him, so I took the form of a large rhastopod and scared off the cat. Your father was safe, but he was astonished by what he'd just seen: a bird changing into a rhastopod and then into a person, for I then took the form you now see before you."

Eladria folded her arms and leaned against a tree trunk as she listened, fascinated by this tale of her father's childhood. In the back of her mind, she was aware of the sky growing increasingly darker, the thick grey clouds churning ominously above them.

"I tried to calm him down," Zinn continued. "I told him I was a metamorph and that he hadn't to tell anyone that he'd seen me. I explained that my people were endangered and had to live in secrecy, for fear of being hunted and killed. He agreed to keep my secret."

Eladria smiled. "So that's how you met."

"Yes. And every day during the rest of his stay in Dumak, he would come and meet me in the forest and we would play and talk. I became very attached to him, and he to me. I'd lost my family some years before and I'd spent so much time living in the forests alone, with only the animals for company. When I met your father, for the first time in as long as I could remember I had a friend, someone I could talk to and care for."

"So how did you come to work in the palace?" Eladria asked, aware of a sudden gust of wind sweeping through the trees.

"When he and his family returned to the moon, I travelled with them," Zinn said. "I suppose didn't want to lose my new friend. It so happened his parents were looking for a new royal maid. I applied for the position, and with a little encouragement from your father, they gave me the job. I took care of him and helped raise him until he grew up and eventually became king. When you were born, I was assigned to care for you as I had him. Your father was the closest friend I ever had. In some ways he was almost like a son to me. We trusted each other implicitly and often confided in each other. And he always he kept my secret, telling no one, not even your mother."

"I didn't realize," Eladria whispered, touched by the depth of their friendship. She felt a tear trickling down her cheek. She brushed it away and took a deep breath, fighting to push aside the rising tide of grief that stirred within her. She was about to speak, when she was distracted by a sudden noise. It was the sound of distant thunder reverberating through the jungle.

The sky had blackened and increasingly strong gusts of wind blasted through the jungle, shaking the trees and foliage. With alarming suddenness, the heavens opened and a steady stream of rain began lashing down, thundering through the jungle canopy and flowing across the ground.

This was the first time Eladria had ever experienced rain. Her initial wonderment quickly turned to alarm as she and Zinn tried to shelter beneath a broad-leafed tree. Her attention was drawn up to the darkened sky. Something strange was happening.

She watched in astonishment as a crack of light appeared in the sky, slicing through the air like a blade of fire. At first she assumed it was lightning of some kind, but the ribbon of light remained static in the sky, as though the sky had been ripped open like a piece of fabric. Waves of electrical force pulsated from the center of the crack. Lightning danced across the sky, while the ground below was rocked by convulsing tremors.

"What's happening?" cried Zinn.

"I don't know," Eladria called back. "But we need to find shelter!"

They began to run. Eladria didn't know where they were going, but she knew it wasn't safe to remain here.

The storm was intensifying. The crack of light pulsated wildly in the sky, sending out lightning in every direction. Some of the blasts struck the trees and ground, setting the jungle alight. As the booming thunder echoed throughout the jungle, flurries of terrified birds took to the air, screeching in alarm.

Filled with growing terror, Eladria and Zinn ran deeper into the jungle. Eladria found herself tripping over stray vines and struggling to maintain her balance as the wind buffeted her and the tremors rocked the slippery, rain-soaked land.

She didn't know how long a time they were running, but her heart leapt when she came across some ruins concealed amid a grove of lhuana trees. Crumbling stone pillars, most of which had toppled and lay covered in moss and undergrowth, were scattered around the remnants of a great wall. A series of stone steps led underground.

Ordinarily Eladria would have stopped to deliberate before entering derelict ruins, particularly those leading underground. But they desperately needed shelter from the storm. While struggling to keep her balance as another tremor rocked the ground, she approached the ancient stairway and motioned for Zinn to follow.

They descended the steps, relieved to at last be out of the rain and safe from the storm. The eroded green steps led them underground into a darkened passageway, seemingly part of a network of corridors. Drenched from head to foot, Eladria tried wringing the water out of her hair and dress as she shuddered in the cool, stale underground air.

"Are you sure it's safe down here?" Zinn asked, her voice echoing down the stone corridor.

"I'm not sure of anything. But it has to be safer than up there," Eladria responded, still trying to wring the excess water out of her skirt. She stepped forward to examine the exquisitely carved, cobweb-strewn walls, which were inscribed with obscure pictures and symbols.

Although it was a relief to have found shelter from the rain, wind and lightning, the tremors continued and the ground beneath them shook in intermittent bursts. Eladria knew that unless the tremors stopped, there was a danger the whole place might collapse around them.

"In all my years I've never seen a storm like it," Zinn exclaimed.

"It doesn't seem normal, does it?" Eladria looked round, her heart still pounding in her chest. "It has to be one of those electrical storms we've been hearing about, the ones they've been reporting all across the planet. Everything fits: the wind, rain and tremors—and that strange crack in the sky."

"I wonder how long we can expect it to last?"

"If it's like the others, it'll probably pass soon enough. But until it does, we're probably safer staying down here. The question is, what is this place?"

"I think I recognize these markings," Zinn said as she brushed away some of the cobwebs and ran her hand along the wall carving. "I encountered a temple like this once before, with similar inscriptions. If I'm correct, it belonged to an ancient tribe called the Ara'buno."

"The Ara'buno? I remember hearing about them in history lessons. They're extinct now, aren't they?"

"Yes, long since disappeared into the mists of time. All that remains of them are these vast underground temples."

"Well, until the storm passes, we might as well see what's down here," Eladria said, starting to walk down the corridor, trailing her hand along the wall, her footsteps echoing down the passageway. There was a pale green luminescence coming from somewhere in the distance. Eladria felt compelled to follow it to its source, strangely allured by this ancient subterranean world.

"I don't know if it's such a good idea to be wandering around here," Zinn called after her. "We don't know what's down here. It could be dangerous. A lot of these places are booby-trapped."

"Then we'll be careful," Eladria answered.

Zinn shook her head. "I really think we should stay put."

"You worry too much, Zinn," Eladria said. "There might be something important down here, something that might be useful to us."

Zinn sighed and reluctantly followed the princess as she wandered down the corridor. It wasn't uncommon for her pleas of restraint to be dismissed. Eladria's headstrong nature was something that, even after all these years, Zinn had yet to learn to counter.

The two explorers were nervous and on edge. Although they were by now becoming used to the ongoing tremors and the rumbling of the storm above ground, they were startled on several occasions by the flapping of bats and the scurrying of small rodents.

Eventually they came to the source of the light. Eladria passed through an arched doorway and found herself in an expansive rectangular chamber. She looked around in wonder as Zinn nervously followed. Thick columns encircled the clearly-ancient chamber, holding the ceiling aloft. The green-tinged sandstone walls were inscribed with indecipherable hieroglyphs and obscure images. There was no visible source of light, but a pale green radiance permeated the room, providing a dim light enabling them to see. Intriguingly, the chamber was lined by a series of rectangular glass booths carved into the walls, spaced at even intervals. Eladria stepped over to the nearest booth and peered inside, but it was dark, grimy and impossible to see what, if anything, was inside.

"This place is an archaeologist's dream," Eladria whispered as she looked around.

The chamber was empty apart from a single item placed upon a circular stone platform at the center of the room. Eladria felt drawn to investigate. As she approached, she realized it was an octagonal-shaped mirror of ancient design, cast in an elaborate emerald frame and covered in dust and cobwebs. As another tremor rumbled underfoot, she carefully stepped onto the platform and reached up to the mirror, using part of her dress to wipe the glass clean.

"Do be careful," Zinn called.

"I will," Eladria said as she studied the mirror, her reflection ghostly in the green light. "I wonder what this place was for..."

"Communing with the dead, most likely," Zinn shuddered, keeping her distance from the curious artifact.

"It's possible. Wasn't their whole culture centered around the afterlife?"

"Apparently so. That was why they built these temples, to serve as contact points between this world and the next."

"Then maybe this mirror was part of their ceremonies."

"It probably was. I believe it was called the mirror of souls, but no one quite knows what it was used for."

Another tremor shook the temple and Eladria was thrown forward, colliding with the mirror. Reaching out to steady herself, she inadvertently pressed a lever on the left side of the emerald frame. There came a deep, low-pitched grinding sound and the platform beneath her began to vibrate.

"What's happening?" cried Zinn.

"I accidentally pressed something," Eladria said, overcome by rising alarm. She sensed that something dangerous had been set in motion, as if a long-dormant mechanism had been activated.

Before she could react, the chamber burst into life. The green light grew brighter and the glass booths lining the room were illuminated, revealing an upright skeleton in each. There came a noise from above. Looking up, Eladria saw a circular ceiling hatch creak open directly above her. As it opened, a shaft of white light blasted down and struck the platform. Eladria tried to leap out of the way, but was too late. She was held firm by the light; a tangible energy force that encased her, seeping through her skin, penetrating her muscles, organs and bones, and irradiating every cell of her body.

Realizing that her body was all-but paralyzed, she let out a cry of alarm. In her peripheral vision she was aware of Zinn frantically trying to grab hold of her, only to be thrown backwards by the force of the electrical charge.

As the platform continued to vibrate, the energy intensified, growing stronger, brighter and more potent. Unable to move a muscle, all Eladria could see was her reflection in the mirror as she stood suspended in the beam of light. The energy continued to flow through her body as she felt herself being split apart atom by atom.

A sudden surge of energy discharged from her body and was swallowed by the mirror.

What was happening to her?

She was now aware of a change in the reflection in the mirror. It was still her face that stared back at her, but it was different in some way, as though it was out of sync.

She let out a cry of pain as the energy coursed through her body with increasing intensity. Amazingly, the reflection failed to mirror her movements. Even though Eladria had opened her mouth and cried out, the reflection remained motionless.

Overcome by panic, Eladria tried to reach her belt and get hold of her electro-charge pistol. With a great deal of exertion, she managed to remove it from the holster and aimed it at the mirror. Squeezing the trigger tightly, she felt the weapon discharge.

The blast from the pistol struck the mirror, which instantly shattered. All Eladria was aware of next was a vast explosion from the vicinity of the mirror. The explosion rocked the chamber, dispersing the beam of light and sending Eladria flying across the room.

As she landed on the stone floor with a thump, she looked up and watched as a surge of energy spewed out from the mirror, then contracted inward and imploded. The mirror was gone and in its place was a swirling light, like a vortex of energy, illuminating the hall in a brilliant blue-green radiance.

"What happened?" cried Zinn as she helped Eladria to her feet.

"I don't know," Eladria shouted above the howling noise of the vortex. "But we have to get out of here now!"

The temple was rocked by another round of tremors. Several of the pillars surrounding the room began crumbling and the ceiling showed imminent signs of collapse. They exited the hall and ran through the corridors, desperate to escape. They soon arrived back at the stairway and raced up to ground level.

Back in the water-soaked jungle, they ran from the ruins, determined to get as far from the temple as they could. The storm continued raging; the sky seemingly tearing itself apart while rain, wind and tremors bombarded the land beneath. And it could have been her imagination, but as they ran through the darkened jungle, Eladria was certain she could see ghostly figures lurking in the shadows, visible only in her peripheral vision.

She and Zinn ran as far and as fast as they could, often slipping in the mud or stumbling in the dense jungle undergrowth. Once Eladria was satisfied they were at a sufficient distance from the underground temple, they stopped to shelter beneath a sturdy old lacast tree.

Eladria's heart was still racing as she struggled to catch her breath. She was soaking wet, her saturated dress heavy on her skin and her hair and face streaming with water. Her ears were buzzing from the noise of the storm and she felt nervous and on edge.

Fortunately, it wasn't long before the storm began to subside. The wind ceased, the tremors stopped and the booming thunder that had reverberated throughout the jungle was supplanted by eerie quietude. Eladria looked up and was relieved to see that the crack of light was now gone from the sky.

The black storm clouds gradually dispersed, soon replaced by the returning sunlight. The air was tingling with static, causing the hairs on the back of her arms and neck to stand on end. The pronounced stillness that swept over their environment was almost alarming in its intensity, broken only by the dripping of water droplets falling from the leaves and plants.

"It seems to be over," Eladria whispered. "For now, at least."

"Back in the temple," Zinn ventured. "What happened to you?"

"I wish I knew. I must have triggered something on the mirror. That beam of light suspended me. I couldn't move. I felt this current of energy surging through my body—it was as though I was somehow being divided and split apart."

"Split apart?"

"That's what it felt like. I can't explain it. I suppose I panicked. That's when I grabbed hold of my pistol and fired. It was the blast from the pistol that caused the mirror to explode and created that vortex, or whatever it was."

"It was inexplicable," Zinn said with a shudder. "But we got out of there! We escaped and the storm's over. Everything's all right now..."

"I hope so," Eladria looked around helplessly. "Because I have this feeling I can't shake, Zinn..."

"What kind of feeling?"

"The feeling that I shouldn't have fired at that mirror...that I've somehow caused something terrible to happen..."

"Like what?"

"I don't know. It's probably best not to think about it, because there's nothing we can do about it now. But we have to be careful, Zinn. Between the storm, the temple and the mirror, this place is clearly dangerous. We'd best get away from here before anything else happens..."

Chapter 6

The Crystal Waterfall

"This is hopeless!" Eladria cried.

Exasperated, she threw the sticks to the ground. Having stopped by the banks of a river for the night, she had spent the last hour trying to light a fire, during which time dusk had fallen, gradually devouring the jungle in an oppressive darkness. The only source of light came from the moons, two of which were visible amid the star-filled sky. Moonlight rippled upon the river and all that could be heard above the sound of rushing water was the clicking of insects and the distant calls of nocturnal jungle creatures.

"Just look at us, Zinn," Eladria exclaimed, shivering in the cool evening air. "We don't know where we are or where we're going. We've no food, no shelter and no way of contacting the outside world. And it's probably only a matter of time before the Ha'shon catch up with us. You can be guaranteed they'll be searching the jungle already..."

Zinn was sitting on a rock peeling some rajah berries she'd gathered. She looked up at the princess but said nothing, a look of concern upon her careworn face.

"This shouldn't have happened," Eladria continued, finally succumbing to the anguish that gripped her soul. "We should be back in the palace, Zinn...with my father. None of this should have happened..."

"But it did happen," Zinn said softly. "And as terrible and horrific as it was, we have to learn to accept that and, in time, move on from it."

Eladria shook her head. "No. I can never accept what they did and I can never move on from it."

"It's the only way forward, my dear," Zinn gently countered. "You have to focus on what you can do *now*, on what action you can take next..."

Eladria turned and gazed into the moonlit river. "We shouldn't have come here. We ran away like frightened children when we should have stayed and faced our adversary. We should have found a way to defeat Estaran and not stopped until we'd killed every last Ha'shon in the palace."

"But you're not a killer," Zinn said.

"I wasn't. But I am now," Eladria said. She collapsed against a tree and slid to the ground, burying her head in her hands. "I'd never taken a life until I shot those guards outside security."

"You did what you had to do. There was no other way."

"But the worst part is that as I pulled the trigger and watched them fall to the ground, a little part of me actually felt a sense of satisfaction. They were Ha'shon! They'd invaded my home and killed my father. Part of me was glad I'd killed them. What does that say about me? Surely that makes me little better than they are..."

Zinn came and sat beside her, placing her arm around Eladria's shoulder. "You were hurt and grieving," she whispered. "But you'll *never* be like them. You'll heal and forgive yourself. Maybe in time you'll even come to forgive them. Whatever happens, you'll find yourself again, I promise you that. They can do all that they've done and more, but there's one thing they can never take from you: and that's who and what you are. It may be temporarily obscured, but it can never be lost..."

"My father...I miss him," Eladria said, struggling to fight back her tears. "I can't believe I'll never see him again. I feel so alone now. I've got nothing now...and no one."

"That's not true," Zinn assured her. "You've got me. I'll always be by your side. As long as I'm here, you'll never be alone."

Eladria didn't answer. She was indeed grateful that she still had her beloved Zinn. Yet everything had become too much to bear: the murder of her father and the loss of her home, the betrayal of the man she loved, their dramatic escape from the moon and the violent storm in the jungle. She also remained in a lingering state of shock following her experience in the underground temple. Something disturbing had happened to her there. She felt as though she'd experienced some inexplicable violation, as though something had been forcibly taken from her, although she wasn't sure what.

In a state of physical and mental exhaustion, she was unable to fight off her grief and despair. She sobbed uncontrollably, her stomach and chest heaving in spasms of grief, knocking the breath from her lungs, forcing her to struggle for each inhalation. She couldn't fight or resist it. There was no escaping the pain.

She remained in this state for what seemed like hours, resting in Zinn's tender embrace, unable to move or speak. It was a relief when eventually she lost consciousness and surrendered to the merciful release of sleep.

Her dreams were fitful and violent. She saw the royal city consumed by flames, its fearful inhabitants running and screaming, burning to death and being smashed beneath collapsing buildings.

She saw the halls of the palace running with rivers of blood, and she knew it was her father's blood. The Ha'shon were everywhere, laughing and jeering, jubilant in their victory. She ran from them, slipping amid the pools of blood, desperately seeking escape. Estaran was closing in on her. She ran as fast as she could, but he caught up with her and grabbed her by the arm. With a twisted sneer, he plunged his knife into her belly, just as he had done to her father.

As everything blacked out, Eladria was aware of a voice whispering soothingly to her from across the darkness. It was a man's voice, strong but gentle. Although she couldn't make out the words, she was comforted by it and melted into its warm glow.

She knew it was him: the stranger from across the void. She had dreamt of him since childhood, when he too had been but a child. Together they had grown up, separated by entire universes yet connected by their dreams. He was with her now. He could feel her pain and was trying to comfort and console her. She could sense that he too had suffered immensely, that he understood her desolation and was reaching out to help.

Yet her dream again shifted, and she found herself back in the jungle; only she was soaring above it like a bird. From this aerial perspective, she marveled at the lush, densely seeded trees. A turquoise river wound its way through the land, sparkling as the sunlight reflected upon the dancing waters. She felt compelled to follow the river upstream, driven by the inexplicable conviction that it would lead her somewhere special. As she flew above the jungle, she caught sight of a majestic waterfall: its white, foamy waters cascading down a cliff of glistening quartz.

The sunlight shone down from the crimson sky and combined with the water's mist to create rainbows, while the cliff-face sparkled in ethereal splendor. It was a place of magic and wonder, and Eladria felt a deep pull toward it, as though it was calling to her, enticing her toward it.

There was something here: something important...

When she awoke, the image of the crystalline waterfall remained etched in her mind. She was lying in Zinn's arms, her head upon the maid's shoulder, both of them resting against the tree by the river.

Eladria moved and stretched, aware of a dull ache in her back and neck, no doubt caused by the awkward position she'd been sleeping in. She was accustomed to sleeping in the finest of beds and had never spent a single night outdoors.

The air was hot and sticky and aside for the lively birdsong that greeted the new day, the first sound she heard was the trickling of the river. As she gazed into the water, she was overcome by a sudden realization: *the crystal waterfall of her dream was real.* She didn't know how or why, but she was certain of it!

"Zinn, wake up," Eladria called, nudging her softly.

"What is it?" Zinn blinked her eyes. "What's wrong?"

"Nothing's wrong. But there's something nearby—something

wonderful—and we have to find it."

"What?"

"A crystal waterfall. I saw it in my dream."

"In your dream...? You do realize that dreams are just dreams? They aren't real."

"Ordinarily I'd agree with you," Eladria said. "But this was real, I'm certain of it. It's here somewhere and we have to find it."

Zinn looked up, clearly confused. "What makes you say that?"

"I don't know. I know this must sound ridiculous, Zinn, but I'm certain I was shown it for a reason. I just *know* we have to find it."

There was a momentary silence.

"Very well," Zinn said as she got up from the ground and brushed herself off. "You're the princess, and wherever you lead, I will follow."

"I knew I could rely on you, Zinn," Eladria said with a nod. "Perhaps all we need to do is to follow the river upstream, as I did in my dream?"

"All right." Zinn held up her hand. "But first of all, you need to eat."

Eladria shook her head. "I'm not hungry."

Zinn frowned, clearly unhappy at the thought of her Princess missing meals. But, as usual, she realized it was futile to argue, so she reluctantly capitulated.

At Eladria's behest, they set off immediately. As they followed the winding river, Eladria was unable to shift the image of the waterfall from her mind. She knew this sudden obsession with an image from her dreams was both irrational and nonsensical. Perhaps it was simply because she needed a focus, some way of distracting herself from the horror of all that had befallen her. And if she didn't find it? If it turned out to be nothing but a fiction of her fevered unconscious? That was a possibility as well, of course. But she was somehow certain that this place existed, and that it was calling to her.

They walked for hours, stopping only occasionally to rest. It was getting hotter and stickier all the time as the sun beat down upon them. The place was alive with the chatter of birds, the buzzing of insects and the calling and cooing of various jungle creatures. Eladria remained on edge, ready to grab her electro-pulse pistol at the first sign of danger. She knew that there were all manner of jungle predators that might view the two of them as a hearty meal. They had already encountered snakes, lizards and several varieties of jungle primate, but thankfully nothing that had posed an immediate threat.

By midday, Eladria felt increasingly weak and light-headed. She realized it had been almost two days since she'd last eaten. Although her stomach felt knotted and she had little appetite, it was nevertheless a necessity that she stop to eat. Zinn had been collecting edible berries along the way, so they sat down to eat them by the river.

The berries were large, round and red in color. They tasted mildly bitter, but were succulent and filling nonetheless. They ate in silence for a while, before Zinn spoke up. "Why do you think it's so important that we find this waterfall?" she asked cautiously.

"I don't know," Eladria shrugged as she chewed on another berry. "I just have a feeling that there's something important there, maybe something or someone that can help us in some way."

"I do hope you're right."

Eladria could tell by the look on Zinn's face that she was skeptical. "I know you don't believe me, Zinn,"she said.

"It's not that I don't believe you," Zinn replied. "It just all seems a little unusual..."

"You're right, it is unusual. But I'm getting used to unusual," Eladria remarked wryly. "For instance, just yesterday I found out that the woman who's nursed and looked after me from the day I was born is actually a metamorph, something I didn't even know still existed. Now, *that's* unusual."

Zinn looked to the ground, unsure what to say.

"I was wondering...about your shape-changing abilities," Eladria continued.

"What about them?" Zinn looked up.

"How long can you maintain the shape you're in? Can you stay in it indefinitely?"

"As long as needed," Zinn said hesitantly. "But after long periods locked in a single form, I feel the need to return to my natural form, if only for a short while. I suppose it must similar to the way you feel after you've worn the same shoes all day long. After a while, you look forward to slipping them off in order to feel more comfortable."

"When I saw you changing form, your clothes changed form with you..."

"Because they aren't real clothes. They're just an approximation. When I assume this form, I simply *intend* the clothes I wish to wear and they appear as you see them now."

"They feel exactly like fabric to the touch. I'd never have known the difference."

"Well, I've had many years to practice and refine my skills."

Eladria nodded. She was slowly coming to come to terms with Zinn's secret identity. It was still disconcerting, for everything she thought she'd always known about her had suddenly been turned upside down. And yet Eladria supposed that, in every way that mattered, this was still the same old Zinn.

"Zinn, I have an idea," Eladria said. "In my dream I was flying above the jungle like a bird. Could you turn yourself into a bird and fly above the trees to look around? It might help us figure out where we are and where we have to go."

"Certainly."

"Good. We might as well use your skills to our advantage."

As soon as they'd eaten the last of the berries, Zinn did as Eladria suggested and transformed herself into a large red and green jacaht bird. She flapped her elegant wings and was soon soaring above the treetops, quickly disappearing from sight.

Eladria waited anxiously, pacing back and forth, only narrowly managing to avoid a large red snake that had appeared from one of the trees behind her. She cautiously stepped away from the reptile, which slithered by, seemingly unperturbed by her presence. Not long after that Zinn returned and retook her usual form.

"Well?" the princess asked impatiently.

"You were right," Zinn said. "There is a crystalline waterfall, and it's not far from here."

"I knew it!" Eladria let out a sigh of satisfaction.

"I could hardly believe my eyes," Zinn added. "I've never seen anything quite like it. It's beautiful! And all we need to do is keep following the river. After a while it'll fork to the right and soon after that we'll come to the waterfall."

"How long do you think it'll take us to get there?"

"It's hard to say, but I imagine we can make it there by dusk if we keep a steady pace."

That was all Eladria needed to hear. Filled with renewed energy and determination, they continued along the riverbank. They made their trek largely in silence, their attention focused upon the journey at hand. After a time, they came to the bend in the river that Zinn had spoken of. It forked to the right and they followed it round, confident they were getting closer to their destination.

The journey was often arduous, for even the banks of the river were riddled with thick undergrowth. Occasionally they were forced to wade in the fast-flowing water, vigilant lest they lose their footing and be swept away by the current. They would grab hold of stray vines and use them as safety lines, before stepping back onto the riverbank and allowing the sunlight to dry them off as they resumed their trek on land.

For the most part, their journey passed without incident, except for the jungle creatures they sometimes encountered along the way, including a large wildcat and several reptiles. Eladria was confident they would be safe from predators, for their charge pistols were more than capable of scaring away potential attackers. But there was one encounter they were unprepared for.

As they climbed over some moss-covered rocks, Eladria heard a commotion from above. It was the sound of an aircraft. Her heart skipped a beat as she looked up and scanned the sky. She couldn't see anything, but the sound was getting louder. Wherever the craft was, it was getting closer.

She wished it was possible to tell by the sound of the engines what kind of aircraft it was. If she'd ascertained it was a TRM craft, she'd have done whatever she could to make herself visible in the hope of being rescued. But she knew it was more likely to be a Ha'shon reconnaissance craft. They'd surely know she'd crashed in the jungle and had undoubtedly dispatched a search and retrieval squad.

Realizing this was the most likely explanation, she and Zinn scrambled away from the riverside and made their way into the depths of the jungle. In a way it was quite fortuitous they had landed in the jungle, for although it was a difficult terrain in which to travel, the thick canopy would make it difficult for a pursuer to spot them from the air.

They hid beneath a spiraling yaal tree, its sturdy trunk and broad-leafed branches hopefully concealing them from sight. From here, the canopy was so thick that barely a patch of sky was visible from the ground.

The droning hum of aircraft engines continued overhead. Sometimes it grew louder, at other times receding into the distance. It was evidently flying in circles.

"I wish they'd go away," Zinn frowned as they sat side by side, resting against the tree.

"So do I," Eladria said. "They seem intent on finding something, don't they?"

"You think it's the Ha'shon?" Zinn asked, her face creasing with worry.

"It's more than likely," Eladria answered. "In an ideal world it would be the TRM. Someone would have alerted them to what had happened and they'd have sent someone to rescue us. But sadly, Zinn, if we can draw any conclusion from the past two days, it's that we don't live in an ideal world."

"Maybe not," Zinn said. "But this isn't the end. Events may yet surprise us."

"I think I've had enough surprises already," Eladria remarked bitterly.

They remained beneath the yaal tree until they were satisfied the craft had left the vicinity. They then returned to the riverbank and resumed their journey. This time they were more cautious than before, remaining alert for any sign of the craft's return.

Perhaps their close encounter had hastened their pace, for it didn't take them much longer to reach their destination.

They rounded a bend in the river and Eladria's eyes were greeted by a sight that made her gasp in amazement. Ahead of them, amidst the jungle foliage, was a steep crystalline cliff-face, glistening as a flow of water cascaded down it, gathering into the river basin beneath. The mist from the waterfall was ignited by the sunlight in alchemical brilliance, casting shimmering rainbows in the air.

"It's beautiful," Eladria gasped. "It's exactly as I saw it in my dream!"

"Now that we're here, what do you suppose happens next?" Zinn wondered aloud.

They didn't have to wait long for an answer. Having been so mesmerized by the wondrous sight, they'd failed to heed the sound of rustling in the jungle thicket. Caught off-guard, they'd walked straight into an ambush.

The first Eladria knew of this was when she felt a hand clamp down on her shoulder and the sharp, cold edge of a knife pressed against her neck.

"Do not move," a man's voice whispered in her ear.

Eladria was in no position to resist. She couldn't believe it: she'd been led all the way here, to this place of her dreams, only to be lured into a trap.

Chapter 7

Voice Of The Others

"What do you want?" Eladria demanded as her assailant snatched the charge pistol from her belt.

There was no response.

There were six ambushers in all, tall muscular men with brown skin, dark eyes and closely-cropped black hair. They wore trousers, boots and sleeveless shirts in shades of grey and brown, each adorned with a crystal talisman engraved with the symbol of an eye. These men were clearly hunter-warriors, their countenance fierce and formidable, each of them armed with knives and crystal-tipped staffs.

Eladria and Zinn were rounded up and pushed forward. Eladria briefly considered trying to make a fight of it, but knew it would be futile to resist, for she and Zinn were unarmed and outnumbered. There was nothing they could do but comply with their captors.

Without a word, they were led toward the waterfall and across the crystalline rocks around it. The crystal was smooth and slippery and Eladria would have fallen more than once had her captor not kept a firm hold of her arm. They were taken to the side of the waterfall where, behind the cascading water, a large fissure cut deep into the rock-face. They were pushed forward, past the flowing water and through the opening.

They found themselves in a crystalline tunnel illuminated by a series of lanterns on the wall, each radiating a pale blue light. As they were led down the winding tunnel, the lanterns seemed to grow brighter and the walls sparkled in ethereal splendor. The sound of the waterfall receded into the distance the further they went, until all that could be heard was the echoing sound of their footsteps.

Their captors brought them to a circular, multi-tiered cavern, evidently a hall or meeting place of some kind. As in the surrounding tunnels, the empty hall was lit by a series of lanterns that cast a bluish light, causing the smooth crystalline walls to glisten and sparkle in an almost dreamlike manner. At the center of the hall a series of steps led up to an opaque glass platform, upon which sat a single chair. Resembling an ornately sculpted crystal throne, there were dozens of web-like tendrils extending from the tip of the chair, connecting to various points on the ceiling.

They came to a stop at the foot of the curious artifact. The men released them, but encircled them to prevent escape. With a nod to his comrades, one of the men turned and exited the hall, disappearing through the arched doorway.

"What is this place?" Eladria demanded.

"That you will find out soon enough," one of the men responded gruffly.

"Oh, so you *can* talk! Why have you taken us prisoner?"

"You are not our prisoners. You are our guests."

"Then you've got a strange way of treating guests. I demand to know why we've been taken here..."

"You will learn everything in time. Until then, I suggest you keep quiet."

Eladria frowned but grudgingly complied. They remained standing at the center of the great hall, the warriors evidently waiting for something, or someone. Eladria looked around, taking in every last detail of her surroundings. She felt helpless and caged; a feeling she hated, but she tried to relax and bide her time. There was nothing she could do right now, but if an opportunity to escape presented itself she would be ready for it.

They were soon were joined by a new arrival: a middle-aged man bearing a notable countenance of authority. Like the other men he was tall and muscular with brown skin and short hair, but he was dressed in a flowing azure robe with leather sandals, a navy cloak fastened at his shoulder by a bronze pin. He too wore a pendant inscribed with a large eye and was adorned with additional jewelry, including beads around his neck and golden earrings. Exuding an air of presence, power and a certain unspoken charisma, his face conveyed a mixture of gruffness and kindness. Eladria perceived something contradictory about him, as if he had perhaps been a warrior or hunter who had relinquished the blade in order to don the robes of a priest.

"I bid you welcome," he said as he approached, his deep, resonant voice echoing through the cavern.

"Who are you?" Eladria asked.

"My name is Lakandrian," he said with a slight tilt of his head as he stopped before them. He turned to his men and motioned for them to lower their weapons. "I apologize for the manner in which you were brought here. In spite of appearances to the contrary, we are not an aggressive people. But we could not risk you passing us by, not after you had come so far."

"What do you know of us?" Eladria eyed him suspiciously.

"We have known of your impending arrival for longer than you could possibly imagine," Lakandrian answered, his gaze fixed upon her. "You are not here by chance. Circumstances have conspired to bring you here. It was necessary, for all of us."

A procession of men, women and children of all ages began streaming into the hall. They were quiet, solemn and graceful as they filed through the doorway and gathered around the central dais, while the balconies above also filled with people. Eladria turned to Lakandrian, who continued watching her in clear fascination. "Who are you people?" she asked.

"We are the tribe of Ramaal," Lakandrian replied, his voice low and even. "We have lived here for many generations under the benevolent direction of the Others. The Others brought us here centuries ago, just as they have now brought you here..."

"No one *brought* us here," Eladria objected.

"Did you not dream of this place?" Lakandrian asked pointedly, raising an eyebrow. "And did you not feel an overwhelming urge to find it regardless of all else?"

Eladria said nothing. She tried to mask her sudden feeling of vulnerability by maintaining an even gaze.

"The Others implanted the image in your mind, in your dreams," he continued. "It was an invitation that you could not resist. It was imperative that they bring you here."

"Why?"

"Because only here can they communicate with you."

"Communicate with us?"

"Yes. There is much you must learn."

"Who are these 'Others'?" asked Zinn.

"They have many names," Lakandrian said as he began pacing the foot of the platform, arms clasped behind his back. "They have become part of the mythology of countless cultures across innumerable worlds. We simply call them the Others. They are beings from an intermediate dimension existing between and beyond all others. From there they observe and oversee the events of the mortal realm."

"For what reason?" Eladria asked, unsure if she liked the implications of such a notion.

"All components of existence—all worlds, dimensions and realms—are part of a grand universal symphony, one that binds the cosmos together in perfect balance," Lakandrian explained. "The universal balance must be maintained at all times. If it is lost, existence as we know it would lose cohesion. Entire dimensions would collapse and fragment. It is the task of the Others to oversee and maintain this delicate universal balance."

"How do you know all this?"

"From our communion with the Others. They tell us that the balance is now under threat; that dark forces are at work on this world and beyond. Events have been set into motion that threaten to disrupt the universal balance, with grave implications for us all."

"What does that have to do with us?" Eladria looked round at

Zinn nervously, before turning back to Lakandrian. "You specifically said they wanted to communicate with *us*. Why?"

"We have seen but small fragments of the overall tapestry," he said, stopping and facing the princess. "We were alerted to your coming. We know that you came from the sky and that you are of royal lineage. We know that you have recently suffered a great loss and are being hunted by a dangerous adversary. All this, we have been told by the Others. They made it clear to us that your arrival here was necessary and preordained. The rest they shall surely now reveal to you themselves."

Eladria was stunned. She had been ready to dismiss these people as some kind of deranged cult. But Lakandrian knew who she was, where she was from and what had happened to her. She didn't know how that was possible. In this remote and isolated jungle it was unlikely these people had access to any form of media. Feeling disarmed and vulnerable, she no longer knew what to believe. Perhaps there was an element of truth to his claim of being in contact with some form of otherworldly intelligence?

By now, the hall and overhead balconies were filled with people, who looked on in hushed awe. There was a sudden commotion amongst the crowd. Eladria watched as a young woman led a small figure in a hooded white robe into the hall and through the gathering. The crowd parted to make way for the arrivals, bowing reverently as they stepped aside. There was a respectful silence as they approached the central platform.

Lakandrian bowed his head before the frail figure. "Behold," he said to Eladria and Zinn. "It is my great privilege to introduce you to the sacred vessel, Javaan, the chosen Voice of the Others."

"Voice of the Others?" Eladria enquired as she looked at the figure in the hooded robe.

"Javaan is the last in a long line of chosen Voices," Lakandrian explained, a certain pride evident in his voice. "Such oracles are selected at birth. Their rare ability to bridge realms is recognized at a young age and developed through extensive training and preparation. Javaan has served our community his entire life, offering himself as a bridge and vessel, allowing the Others to communicate through him. It is a great gift, but a gift that comes at a terrible price."

Lakandrian turned his attention to the striking young woman who stood alongside Javaan, supporting him with an arm cradling his back. "How is your father, Muktaah?"

"His condition worsens," the girl answered, her voice choked with emotion. "Please, Lakandrian, I beg of you. Do not let him do this. He will not survive another communion..."

Lakandrian shook his head sadly. "It is not my choice, Muktaah. The Others have made clear their wish to commune. We cannot deny them their Voice, especially at this, of all times. Your father knows his duty, and he knows the price that must be paid."

"What price is that?" Eladria couldn't help but ask.

Muktaah's eyes met Eladria's and they were filled with sadness and anger. "This is the price," she said as she removed her father's hood, revealing his face.

Eladria was shocked at the sight that greeted her eyes. As she had surmised, Javaan was a frail old man of indiscernible age, but his skin had somehow crystallized. What was once flesh and blood was now an opaque, crystal-like substance. It had clearly been an agonizing transformation, for the suffering was etched in his translucent eyes.

"What happened to him?" Eladria gasped, unable to conceal her horror.

"The process of communion has done this," Muktaah answered.

"But how is this possible? His skin, his body—it's like crystal."

"We don't entirely understand the process," Lakandrian said. "But it has always been this way. Since the time our people were first led to these caverns, there has been a Voice and that Voice has had to pay the price of their gift."

"With each communion, the transfiguration worsens," Muktaah added. "I am certain he won't survive another. I say this has gone far enough."

"I understand your anguish, Muktaah," Lakandrian said, his gruff voice tinged with compassion. "But this final communion marks the fulfillment of our purpose here. Its importance cannot be overstated. It must proceed."

Muktaah looked at him pleadingly. "At the cost of my father's life?"

"It is not your choice to make, Muktaah. Your father alone must decide."

Lakandrian turned to the old man, who responded by nodding slowly. Every movement seemed to cause him great pain, but he was nonetheless resolute. Slowly and with great difficulty, he reached up and placed his hand on his daughter's cheek. A look of tenderness supplanted the pain in his eyes. He had given his answer.

Muktaah smiled sadly as a teardrop trickled down her face. Javaan gestured for her help and together they climbed the steps onto the platform, making their way to the ornate crystal chair.

"What is that?" Eladria asked Lakandrian.

"It is the means by which the Voice connects with the Others," he explained. "We believe these caverns were created by the Others in the beginning times. This chamber was here when our ancestors first arrived, exactly as you see it now. The first Voice was guided to sit in the chair, and from there, the Others were able to speak through him, facilitating our first communion."

"So it's a kind of transceiver?" Zinn asked.

Lakandrian nodded. "In a sense. There is a series of energy lines running across and within the planet. They form an invisible grid, and where these lines intersect are points of immense power. This is one such place. The power of the grid is amplified and focused by the crystal out of which these caverns are made. It is directed into the chair, enabling the Voice to serve as bridge between this world and the realm of the Others."

Eladria watched as the old man sat in the crystal chair, looking ahead expectantly. Muktaah reluctantly stepped off the platform and stood by Lakandrian's side, her eyes again filling with tears as she looked up at her father. Lakandrian put his hand on Muktaah's shoulder. "It is time," he said.

Almost as soon as he had uttered those words, the lanterns encircling the hall spontaneously dimmed. As the chamber darkened, the air became static and charged, causing Eladria's skin to tingle. She looked around nervously. There was silence as Lakandrian's people stood with their heads lowered, waiting with a sense of hushed expectancy. A low rumble seemed to emanate from all around, gently rocking the crystalline hall as it grew in intensity, as though some invisible force was building up to an explosion...

When it came, Eladria felt herself jump. With a flash of light, the walls and ceiling lit up, casting an iridescent blue luminescence. Sparks of silvery-blue light streamed down the synapse-like tendrils that connected the ceiling to the chair. Javaan's body was infused with the light, radiating through his translucent form like rays of moonlight.

Eladria looked at Zinn, who was staring in wide-eyed astonishment. Lakandrian's people were strangely serene as they watched Javaan. Some of them knelt on their knees in supplication, while others had their heads lowered in silent reverie. Lakandrian stood with his hands raised to his chest as he watched expectantly. Muktaah remained tearfully by his side, her body trembling as she watched her dying father undertake his final communion.

As he sat immersed in the pulsating shower of light, Javaan opened his mouth and a strange, otherworldly sound issued forth. It was a harmonious blending of hundreds of different voices, soft yet resonant and possibly the most beautiful sound Eladria had ever heard. At first it was distant and barely audible, but soon the interfusion of voices grew louder and clearer. A wordless song, an indiscernible melody, one that was enchanting in its hypnotic beauty. It filled Eladria like a warm ray of light, melting away a portion of the anger and grief she carried within her. So deeply relieved by this sudden and inexplicable release, she felt her eyes moisten with tears.

Then the sound began to change. The interfusion of unearthly voices began to form spoken words: uttered from Javaan's lips but clearly emanating from across an unfathomable distance.

"The connection is resumed. The final communion begins," the words echoed. *"May the daughter of the House of Chaldeen step forward."*

Eladria shifted nervously. Lakandrian gestured for her to step onto the platform. With some reluctance, Eladria took Zinn's hand and together they climbed the steps and took a few steps forward, until they were standing before the shimmering form of Javaan.

"Welcome, Princess Eladria," the voice greeted her.

Eladria felt an involuntary shudder at the mention of her name.

"As difficult as this may be for you to comprehend, you have been brought here for a reason. There is much you must learn. The scepter of responsibility has passed to your hands. Tahnadra is now your world and you must be made aware of the grave happenings that threaten to destroy it."

"You mean the Ha'shon?" Eladria asked weakly. "You're referring to the Ha'shon coup?"

"No. The Ha'shon are inconsequential."

Eladria's mouth fell open. The Ha'shon were anything but inconsequential! They had destroyed her home and seized control of her world...

"You face a far more dangerous adversary and there is a far greater threat than you could ever have imagined," the voice continued.

There was a pause. "What do you mean?" Eladria asked hesitantly.

"The mortal realm in disarray. A series of breaches has occurred...breaches between dimensions; tears in the very fabric of your universe."

"Tears?" Eladria asked.

"Yes. You have already experienced the effects," the voice said.

"I have...?" Eladria paused, suddenly recalling what had happened upon her arrival on the planet. "You mean the storms? The crack in the sky...?"

"Yes. We, as guardians of universal balance, cannot allow such breaches to occur; they are a threat to the continuation of life in all realms. We have endeavored to seal each breach as it occurred, but the situation worsens. Soon we will be unable to repair the damage from our realm."

"What's causing these breaches?" Eladria asked.

"They are not natural. They are being deliberately created, purpose-fully orchestrated: the result of a dark and dangerous experiment being conducted upon your world, in the land of Drantak."

"Drantak?" Eladria echoed. Drantak, the so-called 'forbidden land', was an island in the black sea, supposedly a barren wasteland with no known habitation. Eladria rubbed her head, struggling to grasp the enormity of what she was being told. "So you're telling me there's someone in Drantak deliberately creating these storms, these breaches? Why would they do that? Why would anyone deliberately endanger the planet?"

"There is a dark force from beyond the void desperate to claw its way into your realm. These entities are known as the Shadow Lords. Although sealed off in their own dimension, they have an operative on your world, one who is carrying out their directives. They have already tapped into the core of the planet, harnessing vast and powerful forces, with which they are violating the very laws of the universe."

"But why?"

"They intend to tear down the barriers between your two realms, creating a portal between dimensions, enabling them safe passage through the void. Once freed from their astral prison, the Shadow Lords

will invade your world: killing, destroying, feeding off whatever life they encounter. They are feared throughout the cosmos as destroyers of entire universes."

A feeling of terror swept over Eladria. She took a deep breath to steady herself as she gazed at the form of Javaan. The old man continued to sit in the light-infused chair, the otherworldly interfusion of voices streaming from his mouth. *"The experiment at Drantak must be stopped. If the Shadow Lords succeed in creating a stable portal, they will enter your realm, ready to obliterate an infinite number of worlds."*

"Assuming all this is true," Eladria began. "Why are you telling *me* this?"

"Because you, Princess Eladria, daughter of the House of Chaldeen...you must travel to Drantak and put an end to the experiment."

"Me?" Eladria shook her head, her voice wavering. "How am I meant to do that? I'm not a warrior, or a crusader or anything else!"

"Only you can save your world."

"But why? Why me?"

"You are now ruler of Tahnadra."

"Then let me send someone else," Eladria pleaded. "If I can make contact with the TRM, I can send an entire squadron to Drantak. They can stop whatever's happening there. Me, I can't do anything...not alone..."

"You must. Only you can go to Drantak. Only you can stop what is happening there. You are intimately connected with what is happening there, in ways you cannot yet begin to imagine..."

"What do you expect me to do?" Eladria cried in desperation. "Look at me! I'm nothing. I've lived all my life on the royal moon. I don't know anything about travelling, navigating or fighting. I can't do what you ask of me. And what of the Ha'shon? They now control this world and they're intent on hunting me down. What do you propose I do?"

"You will do what you must. There will be obstacles and dangers, but you are stronger and more powerful than you yet realize. In time, you will discover and come to master the innate power you possess. You will receive help and guidance where you least expect it. But you must also be vigilant and beware deception, for you may also be manipulated and deceived."

There was silence for a moment, before the voice continued. *"Your world has little time left. You must set off as soon as possible. Go to Drantak. Stop what is happening there. Save your world."*

Eladria wanted to protest further, but the words drowned in her throat. She felt a tear of desperation rolling down her face as she looked on helplessly.

"So ends our final communication," the voice stated, now addressing the entire gathering. *"You have served us well, children of Ramaal. Our gratitude and love will remain with you. You must now follow our previous instruction and prepare for the time of reckoning. The covenant is complete; the time of communion is over."*

With that, the voice fell silent. The pulsating energy that had electrified Javaan ceased and the cavern was plunged into darkness.

Chapter 8

Points Of Departure

There was a moment of silence as Lakandrian and his people lowered their heads in respect.

As the lanterns again illuminated the great hall, Muktaak raced onto the platform and rushed to her father's side. The crystallized figure sat motionless upon the chair, staring blankly ahead. As she had feared, this final communion had claimed his life. All that could be heard above the hushed whispers of the crowd were Muktaah's sobs as she knelt by her father and stroked his lifeless face. Eladria felt great empathy for her, as her own grief was still very much an open wound.

Lakandrian knelt in respect before Javaan and then got up and turned to address the gathering. "It is my sad duty to inform you that Javaan, sacred Voice of the Others, has now passed from this world. His life-force now travels across the void and into the great beyond."

There was a tangible outpouring of grief from the crowd. Clearly they were upset and frightened. After a moment's pause, Lakandrian continued. "Tonight we bid farewell to the last in a long line of Voices. And tomorrow we shall likewise bid farewell to this, the place that has been our home for so many generations. There is little time to waste, my people. You know your duties. We must go now and prepare for our departure."

With a nod of his head, Lakandrian dismissed the gathering. They began filing out of the circular cavern, the mood somber as they departed.

Lakandrian placed a reassuring hand on Muktaah's shoulder and told her to spend as long with her father as she wanted. He then turned to Eladria and Zinn. "You must both be tired and hungry," he said. "Please, allow me to offer you food and shelter for the night."

"That would be appreciated," Eladria said with a nod.

They made for the exit, following the last of the crowd out of the hall.

"We have much preparation to make," Lakandrian said as he led them down the labyrinthine crystalline corridors. "This night will be spent making final preparations for our departure."

"Why are you leaving?" Zinn asked.

"Because the Others have decreed it."

"Where will you go?"

"We have been told to travel eastward, across the Dranarian river, where we will meet the tribe of Ustai. There are ancient links between our ancestors and theirs. We have been in contact with them and have been assured safety and shelter."

"And you just do whatever the Others tell you?" Eladria asked.

"That is correct."

"Wouldn't you rather make decisions for yourself?"

"That is a question I used to ask a lot when I was your age and my answer, initially, was yes. But as I grew older and particularly once I was elected by the Others to lead my people, I came to realize just how limited our perspective is when compared with that of the Others. It is for this reason that we have dedicated our lives to them, surrendering our personal will to that of the greater good."

"What will you do now they've severed contact with you?" Eladria asked. "If you've relied on their direction all these years, how will you get by without it?"

"It will not be easy," Lakandrian admitted. "Many of my people are confused and fearful, for the future is indeed uncertain. All we can do is trust that it will unfold for the best. We must keep our faith, now more than ever..."

They arrived at their designated accommodation, one among dozens of hollowed-out compartments carved into the crystalline walls. It struck Eladria that this place was like a gigantic beehive, composed of an endless network of interlinked tunnels and chambers. Their compartment was small and functional, separated from the adjacent tunnel by a large curtain. Inside were two beds and a small wooden table, with a single oil lantern hung upon the wall.

"I trust you will be comfortable," Lakandrian said.

"Thank you, I'm sure we will be," Eladria replied as she looked around the small chamber.

"I will have some food brought to you. I myself must go now and oversee the preparations. We will be leaving before dawn, so it is unlikely we will see each other again."

"If I were you, I'd have a hard time leaving this place, regardless of what the Others say," Eladria remarked.

"It is not easy for us, but we know we have fulfilled our purpose here."

"Which was *what* exactly?"

"I would have thought that would be clear to you by now. *You were.*"

Eladria stared at him blankly.

"Do you still not see?" Lakandrian continued. "The Others exist in a dimension outside of space and time, in which past, present and future are one. They knew you would come here, they have known since the beginning of time. This place was constructed by the Others for a single purpose, for a single moment in time: your arrival. We have known of your coming for generations."

"That's overwhelming," Eladria exclaimed. "I honestly don't know what to believe, much less what to do..."

"That you alone must decide," Lakandrian advised. "I pray the Others will grant you the courage and faith to embark upon the path that stands before you."

"I don't share your faith in the Others," Eladria confessed, starting to pace the room nervously. "I've no reason to trust them; I don't know anything about them! Even if I do accept that they are supernatural beings with an elevated perspective on this world, how do I know they aren't just manipulating me, using me to serve some agenda of their own?"

"The Others have but one agenda and that is to safeguard this world and all others. Everything hinges upon your actions now. You have no choice but to trust them."

Eladria came to a stop and was silent for a moment. "I'm flattered by the confidence that's been placed in me," she began softly. "I just wish I shared it."

"I know this is difficult for you," Lakandrian said, looking deeply into her eyes, a look of empathy upon his face. "I had not expected one so young and inexperienced. But, as we must all eventually do, you must rise above your limitations and find the strength within yourself—the untapped power the Others spoke of—and you must use it."

"Why did they choose *me* for this? Your people have followed them for generations. Why didn't they send you?"

"Our task is complete, whereas yours is just beginning. You have been chosen for a reason."

"Because I'm heir to the throne?"

"No, there are far deeper reasons. As the Others said, you are connected with what is happening at Drantak in ways you cannot yet begin to imagine. You alone can embark upon this mission. You alone can save this world."

"But why?"

"I have told you all that I know," Lakandrian said. "The rest, I am certain, will be revealed in time. I understand your doubts, in your place I would most likely share them, but you must have faith in the Others. I urge you to look into your heart, for only then will know what you must do."

Eladria said nothing.

Lakandrian stepped forward. "I must now take my leave of you, Princess Eladria. I will arrange for you to be given food and supplies. It has been my great honor to have facilitated your communion with the Others. I pray that they be with you, to protect and guide you along your journey."

Eladria tried to muster a smile. "Thank you. I hope you and your people reach your destination safely."

Lakandrian bowed his head, bade them farewell and excused himself, leaving the two women alone in their room. The moment he left, Eladria began pacing again in a restless frenzy. Zinn tried to engage her in conversation, but Eladria wasn't ready to talk. She was trying to process all she'd been told, desperate to reconcile what seemed nothing short of insanity to her.

A short while later, one of Lakandrian's people brought them a meal of bread and honeyed fruit, which they hungrily ate in silence. Once she had finished, Eladria sat upon the edge of her bed and stared blankly at the wall, which sparkled as the lantern light illuminated the smooth, opaque crystal. Out of her peripheral vision she could see Zinn watching her worriedly, evidently unsure what to say. Eventually, after what seemed like an eternity of silence, Zinn spoke up. "If you want to talk about this, I'm here for you, my dear," she ventured cautiously.

"What's there to say?" Eladria responded wearily, not taking her eyes from the glistening wall.

"Quite a lot, I would think," Zinn answered.

Eladria looked round at her. "Do you believe them, Zinn?"

"I'm not sure what to believe," the maid admitted.

"Neither am I. I mean, according to these Others, I'm somehow the predestined savior of Tahnadra! That's inconceivable...isn't it?"

"Yet they seemed most earnest. They knew so much about us; about *you*. And what they told us about this experiment in Drantak, these 'breaches' between dimensions...well, it might explain the storms..."

"Perhaps." Eladria sighed. She was silent for a minute, her mind drifting, before she continued. "I wish my father was here, Zinn. He'd know what to do. He always knew what to do. But he's gone..."

"That may be, but I'm here and you don't have to face this alone," Zinn assured her.

"I don't know what I'd do without you, Zinn," Eladria tried to muster a smile. "This whole thing is like some kind of cosmic joke, isn't it? They want me to travel to Drantak, of all places, and prevent these *Shadow Lords* from invading our world. I haven't a clue how they expect me to accomplish such a feat."

"Then what are we going to do?"

There was a moment's pause as Eladria made her decision. "I don't see any reason to deviate from our original plan," she declared. "We'll get out of this jungle and find the nearest point of civilization. Then we'll do whatever we can to make contact with the TRM. In spite of anything else, we're at war, Zinn, and I have to be there to help my people overthrow the Ha'shon and retake the moon."

"But what if the Others are right? War or no war, they were quite clear that the Ha'shon are the least of our problems. What if the only way to save Tahnadra *is* to go to Drantak and stop this so-called experiment?"

"They've given me no evidence to substantiate their claims. I'm just supposed to take their word for it, and I'm not willing to do that. All I know for sure is that the Ha'shon have seized control of my world and they have to be stopped, whatever the cost. That's my priority."

"But it's hard just to dismiss what the Others said..."

"I won't forget what they told us," Eladria said. "It'd be impossible to forget, even if I wanted to. I just need some evidence, Zinn. Once I've made contract with the TRM, I can confer with them and then decide what to do."

"You said yourself before that we were brought here for a reason..."

"That may be. But I'm not going to let these Others make my decisions for me. Right now, my priority is to get to civilization and make contact with the military."

"It's your decision, of course," Zinn nodded. "Whatever choice you make, I'll be with you."

"Thank you, Zinn, I knew I could rely on you," Eladria said, unsuccessfully stifling a large yawn. It had been a long day and although her mind was still buzzing, her body was overcome by a wave of exhaustion.

"You'd best get some rest, my dear. Have a good sleep and things may well look differently in the morning," Zinn said.

"Best plan I've heard yet."

Eladria was relieved to remove her shoes, for they had been damaged during her jungle trek, causing persistent discomfort. As Zinn settled down on the adjacent bed, Eladria lay upon the mattress and pulled the thin cotton blanket over herself. The bed was surprisingly comfortable, and appreciated all the more as it was the first she'd slept in since fleeing the palace. In spite of her restless, troubled mind, the princess's exhaustion was such that it took little time for her to drift into a deep, dreamless sleep.

When she awoke, she felt as though she'd been asleep for days. Through misty, sleep-filled eyes, she looked around and recalled where she was.

"I was starting to think you'd never wake up," came Zinn's voice.

"How long was I asleep?" Eladria asked croakily as she propped herself up on the bed.

"I don't know for sure," Zinn answered, sitting on the edge of her own bed. "There's not a trace of daylight in these caverns, so it's easy to lose track of time."

"Are Lakandrian and his people still here?" Eladria yawned.

"No, they appear to be gone. I had a good look around the caverns and there's no sign of anyone."

"They must be on their way to their new home."

"They did leave some things for us," Zinn said, holding up a large leather bundle. "I found this outside our chamber."

"What's in it?"

Zinn unfolded the bundle and lifted out a folded parchment. "There's a map of the surrounding area...there's also a carrying bag, a compass, a knife, some clean clothes and several days' worth of food wrapped in these bundles here. Oh, and they've returned our electro-pulse pistols."

"That was good of them," Eladria said, pushing herself off the bed and placing her still-aching feet upon the smooth, glasslike floor.

"Can I get you anything, my dear?" Zinn asked, getting up from her bed and slipping back into the role of royal maid with consummate ease.

"Is there any water?"

"Yes, here," Zinn handed Eladria the flask of water that had been sitting on the table.

Eladria gulped down the cool water and let out a satisfied sigh. She then had a look at the clothes that had been left for them. Zinn had little need for garments, but Eladria would be glad to get out of the tattered blue dress she'd been wearing since that fateful morning the Ha'shon invaded the palace.

Her new clothes were similar to the garb worn by Muktaah and the other women she'd seen here. There was a sleeveless bluish-grey tunic along with a belt, dark leather trousers and brown boots. Eladria tried on the clothes, which fit remarkably well. She picked up the knife and ran her finger along the blunt edge, deep in thought. She then handed the blade to a startled Zinn. "I want you to cut my hair," she said.

"Cut your hair...? Why?" Zinn looked at her, curiously.

"Because when we meet other people I don't want to be recognized. I may not have your ability to change form, but I can at least make some minor alterations."

She bunched her hair together and lifted it behind her neck, motioning for Zinn to chop it off with the knife. Zinn reluctantly complied and Eladria's long dark locks fell to the ground. Eladria squinted to see her reflection in the crystal walls. Her hair now stopped just below her shoulders. She ran her hands through it, pushing it back from her face and tucking it behind her ears. She'd always been proud of her long, luxuriously wavy hair, but the time for vanity was long gone.

She examined the rest of the supplies left by Lakandrian's people. The food parcels were wrapped in cloth and comprised simple portions of bread, fruit and cooked meat. She lifted a piece of bread and took a bite as she unfolded the map. It was difficult to decipher, for she was unfamiliar with the symbols and text. But she managed to pinpoint their current position and located what appeared to be the nearest point of civilization.

"There's a village or town to the north of here," she said as she chewed on a mouthful of bread. "If I'm reading this correctly it's called *Niyastan*."

"How far away is it?" asked Zinn.

"I don't know, it's hard to tell from looking at this. But at least we now have an idea where we're going. Hopefully we can make it there within the next couple of days."

"Then what?"

"Then, with a bit of luck, we can try to make contact with the nearest military base."

"And if we can't? What will we do then?"

"Let's just concentrate on one thing at a time, Zinn."

The two readied themselves to leave, packing their supplies into the bag, which Eladria slung across her shoulder. They left their sleeping chamber and wandered down the deserted crystalline corridors. It was eerily quiet. The wall lanterns continued to illuminate the cavernous network of corridors and chambers, causing the quartz walls to sparkle in rainbow colors. Eladria didn't know what powered the lamps or how they activated upon their approach and dimmed again after they had passed. She wondered how these corridors had been so perfectly formed, as she had never seen workmanship of the like. Perhaps this wondrous place had indeed been created by the Others as Lakandrian claimed.

They made their way through the corridors, straining to hear the distant sound of the waterfall. Eventually they found it and followed it to its source. The tunnel opened at the mouth of the waterfall and they cautiously stepped out. Having spent so long in the dimly lit network of tunnels, Eladria initially found the harsh glare of daylight uncomfortable. She shielded her eyes as she and Zinn stepped past the vertical downpour of water.

As they climbed down the crystalline rocks, something caught Zinn's attention. "Look," she exclaimed, pointing back in the direction they had come.

Eladria looked round and watched as the fissure behind the waterfall began to shimmer and disappear. She could hardly believe her eyes. The mouth of the cavern, through which they had stepped only moments ago, was now gone, replaced by a solid wall of quartz.

"They sealed it," Eladria whispered in amazement. "They sealed the waterfall."

"Who...?"

"It must have been the Others. I suppose now that Lakandrian and his people are gone, the caverns are no longer needed. They must have wanted to prevent anyone else from accessing them."

"Remarkable..."

"It is." Eladria nodded, realizing with some consternation that it was now even harder to dismiss what the Others had told her. Clearly they *were* supernatural beings in possession of remarkable powers.

Eladria turned and made her way down the slippery rocks, onto the embankment, Zinn following close behind her. She took one last look at the waterfall as it cascaded over the quartz embankment. "It certainly is a place of beauty," the princess remarked. "But even so, I'll be glad to get away from here."

She put down her bag, took out the map and together they

began plotting the quickest route to the town of Niyastan.

Chapter 9

Bounty Hunter

It had been raining for several hours. Although drenched from head to foot, Eladria and Zinn kept moving, all the while hoping the deluge would soon subside. It didn't. As the water continued pouring down from the heavens, the jungle became like a swamp, the ground thick, muddy and slippery.

Eventually conceding defeat, Eladria decided to stop and shelter beneath a giant lakast plant. As they sat beneath the plant's broad, rubbery red leaves, they watched as the rain continued its relentless downpour.

"I remember these tropical storms well," Zinn remarked as she sat next to Eladria, both leaning against the thick stem of the towering jungle plant.

"You used to live in these jungles?" Eladria asked.

"Yes, for a time," Zinn said. "I lived in many different places all across the planet. My people live a migratory existence, never staying too long in any one place. We try to avoid inhabited areas as much as possible, so jungles like as this are ideal for us."

"How many of you are there?"

"I don't actually know. I suspect there are very few of us left now. We've long been a species on the verge of extinction."

"Why is that?"

"As I said before, single-formed beings such as yourself have generally feared and distrusted my kind, and fear and distrust can so easily turn to hatred and violence. We quickly learned that it wasn't safe to reveal ourselves to non-changers. If any of us were seen to change form, we were likely to be hunted and killed, particularly after the Last Reclamation. That's what happened to my family..."

"I'm so sorry, Zinn," Eladria exclaimed.

"It was a long time ago," Zinn said softly, pausing before

continuing. "We may be different to non-changers in so many ways, but we *feel* as you do. We love...and when we lose our loved ones, we grieve so very deeply."

Zinn stopped and took a deep breath before continuing. "Yet I was one of the few lucky ones. I found a new family and have lived all these years in safety and protection. The wounds of the past are still there, for I don't think they ever fully heal, but I've lived a long and happy life with you and your family. The love I have for you and the joy I've experienced at being able to raise both you and your father...well, it was more than I could ever have dreamt of following my loss."

"I wish there was something I could do to make it better, Zinn," Eladria said. "When this is all over, maybe there's something I could do to protect your people?"

"That's a nice thought, dear one, but I fear it may be too late. My people dispersed far and wide and went so deeply into hiding that it would take many years to find the last of my people."

"But there must be something we can do. You taught me never to give up."

"I taught you wisely then, and I was right. But there are times when you simply have to surrender to life and accept things the way they are. Sometimes that's the only way you can ever be at peace. Sometimes the more you struggle and hold on to things, the more suffering you create for yourself and others."

"So how do you know when it's best to keep on fighting and when it's time to simply give up?"

"You just know," Zinn said. "There are some things you know you can change and there are others you just have to accept. Like this rain, for instance. We can't fight it or make it stop and it's futile to even try. We just have to accept it and deal with it as best we can."

"What about things that have happened in the past?"

"The past we most certainly have to accept, because no matter how much we might wish it were different, nothing can change what has already occurred."

"I can't accept what's happened to me," Eladria said bitterly. "And I won't. Because it shouldn't have happened."

"Perhaps not. But it did, and until you accept that, you're bound by it, trapped in a prison of your own suffering. I know, because that's what happened to me when I lost my family."

Eladria looked away. She was painfully aware of the tangled storm of emotion that raged inside her and she made a conscious effort to push it aside. She was determined that she wouldn't give in to it.

The pair remained silent for a time, and all that could be heard was the relentless drumming of raindrops on the jungle canopy. Having been lost in her reverie, Eladria turned to Zinn and decided to share her thoughts. "I've decided something," she began. "Try though I might, I can't dismiss what the Others told us. As incredible as it all seems, if there's even the slightest possibility that what they said is true, then I'd be foolish to ignore it."

Zinn nodded. "I'm inclined to agree."

"As soon as we've made contact with the TRM, I'll dispatch a team to Drantak. They can investigate and tell us if there truly is anything going on there. I'll do what the Others suggest, Zinn, but I'll do it on my own terms."

"I think that's wise."

Before Eladria could respond, she spotted something out of the corner of her eye. In the undergrowth nearby was a large jungle cat with a mane of shaggy grey fur and piercing blue eyes. The cat was watching them intently as they sheltered beneath the lakast plant, its fur dripping wet as the rain continued to fall. Eladria suspected it was sizing them up as a potential meal. She reached for her pistol, just in case it decided to make a sudden move at them. But the cat suddenly leapt in the opposite direction and disappeared into the undergrowth. Something had startled it—but what?

Eladria didn't have to wait long for an answer. A man

appeared through the foliage not far from where the cat had stood. With sudden dread, she realized it was a Ha'shon bounty hunter. Wearing black body armor, his head was shaven and his coarse-skinned face was twisted and unpleasant. He was armed with a large pulse rifle, with an assortment of blades hooked upon his belt.

Eladria jumped to her feet and the bounty hunter immediately caught sight of her. If it hadn't been for the relentless deluge of rain and the distant rumbling of thunder she might have heard his approach and been better prepared, but it was too late now.

"Surrender!" cried the Ha'shon, his voice deep and booming.

Eladria had no option but to comply. There was nowhere to run and nothing she could do to fight him. He had his rifle trained on them and she knew that any resistance would be met with swift retribution. She raised her hands and Zinn did likewise.

The bounty hunter sneered as he walked over and brusquely disarmed them, casting their weapons to the ground, keeping his rifle trained on them. "Did you really think you could escape the Ha'shon?" the man said with a smug grin. "You've no idea the size of the reward they put out for you. Sixty thousand crasadas, dead or alive. That kind of money will set me up nicely for retirement."

"I'm so happy for you," Eladria muttered, glaring at him defiantly.

"I warn you now," the hunter grunted, narrowing his eyes. "I'm willing to take you in alive, but I'd be just as happy presenting your lifeless corpses to Estaran."

Eladria said nothing.

"Put your hands on your heads, both of you!" the man barked.

They did as he said and he stepped behind them. Pushing his rifle into the small of their backs, he motioned for them to move.

Eladria's mind was racing as they were marched through the rain-soaked jungle. She was desperately trying to come up with a means of escape. She couldn't bear the thought of ending up Estaran's prisoner once again. There was no way she'd assist him or legitimize his coup in any way. The moment he realized that, she would unquestionably be made to suffer the same fate as her father. The royal lineage of Chaldeen would end with her death and the final link in the chain would be broken. She had too much to live for now. Tahnadra was her world and she vowed she would do what she could for it. She owed it to her people, for that's what they were now: *her people.* Realizing this, she was now determined that she would live.

The storm was intensifying. The deluge worsened and the sky grew ever darker, lit up by bursts of lightning followed by the angry rumbling of thunder. Blasts of gale-force wind swept through the jungle.

Eladria's eyes were drawn to the sky, for something strange was happening above. As she'd seen during the first storm, a crack of light appeared in the heavens, like an incision slicing the sky open.

Eladria looked round at the bounty hunter, who was rooted to the spot, staring up at the sky in surprise. She knew that with his attention momentarily elsewhere, this was her chance to act. She reached out and tried to snatch the rifle from him. Although caught unaware, his reflex response was to lash out and he elbowed her in the ribs causing her to stagger back and yelp in pain. Turning his full attention to her, he took a step closer and raised the weapon, pointing it straight at her head. His eyes narrowed and his lip curled in anger as his finger tightened around the trigger.

Eladria was about to close her eyes and brace herself, when something caught her eye behind the Ha'shon. With his full attention on Eladria, he'd apparently forgotten about Zinn, or else deemed her not to be a threat. In an uncharacteristically bold move and with great struggle, the maid had picked up a fallen log and crept up behind the bounty hunter. Had it not been for the screaming noise of the storm he'd probably have sensed her approach, but he was taken completely unaware as, with an almighty heave, the maid smashed the log against his head. The Ha'shon slumped to the ground, his legs buckling and the rifle falling from his hands.

Eladria was unsure whether he'd lost consciousness or was simply stunned, but she seized the opportunity and reacted swiftly. She stooped down to the appropriate the weapon. It was even heavier than it looked, but she wasn't going to leave it in the hands of the Ha'shon, for he was already stirring, rolling over as he lifted a hand to his head. Eladria stood over him and, acting on a sudden impulse born of desperation, she lifted the rifle and struck him over the head. She marveled at her own strength as the burly Ha'shon slumped over.

She turned to Zinn and shouted at the top of her lungs: "Run!"

The two raced into the depths of the jungle, leaping over logs, vines, rocks and shrubs, while attempting to keep their footing in the mud underfoot.

The electrical storm continued to light up the heavens. To her horror, Eladria noticed something emerging through the tear in the sky: creatures of some kind, streaming out of the breach and darting across the sky at dizzying speed. The bat-like creatures circled the land beneath and some of them began swooping down into the jungle, leaving a trail of red fire in their wake.

Eladria glanced behind her and saw that the bounty hunter was in close pursuit. Larger, stronger and faster than they were, it wouldn't take him long to catch up. But, for now at least, Eladria had the upper hand, for she had the rifle. As she continued running, almost slipping in the mud on numerous occasions, she tightly clutched the weapon as if it was some kind of coveted prize. The rifle was so heavy it was almost certainly slowing her down, but she was determined to hold onto it, for it was her one advantage.

The ground beneath them began to shake as the jungle was rocked by a wave of tremors. Eladria lost her balance and was sent flying to the ground. She tried to get up, but the ground continued shaking, making her dizzy and nauseous. She looked round at Zinn, who was nearby, similarly floored and disorientated. The tremors, like the wind, were intermittent. She took advantage of the lull to get back onto her feet and, after picking up the fallen rifle, she went over to Zinn and helped her to her feet.

That was when she felt a hand clamping down on her shoulder. She turned to see the Ha'shon bounty hunter glaring down at her. While keeping hold of her with one hand, he reached out and snatched the rifle from her. She struggled, desperate to escape him, but his steely grasp was unrelenting. Zinn tried to come to Eladria's aid, grabbing the hunter from behind, but with a thrust of his elbow, he knocked the maid to the ground.

"You're going to pay for that, little lady," the man said with a rasping sneer.

Before Eladria could respond, a tremor rumbled underfoot, sending them flying to the ground. This time, a crack formed along the jungle floor. As the land parted, trees and shrubs were uprooted and devoured by the crumbling abyss.

Eladria got to her feet and tried to run, but the bounty hunter grabbed hold of her ankle, preventing her from moving. She managed to break free of his grip and raced to Zinn's side, again helping her up from the ground.

Another tremor struck, causing the crack that etched across the land to widen exponentially. The jungle was being torn to pieces: fire, wind and rain consumed it from above, while the ground was crumbling from below.

The Ha'shon bounty hunter began closing in on Eladria and Zinn, his rifle poised to fire. "Don't move," he snarled. "Like I said, I'd just as happily take you in dead as alive..."

He reached down to his belt and produced two metal cuffs. With his gun pointed at her head, he ordered Eladria to put out her hands. She saw no option but to comply. She held out her hands, glaring at him with simpering hatred. As he was about to fasten the cuffs around her wrists, Zinn took advantage of his distraction and changed form. Eladria watched as Zinn's familiar shape dissolved into a swirling mist and re-formed as a large blue eagle.

The Ha'shon was astonished by the sight, but reacted swiftly by taking aim and firing. Fortunately Zinn was too fast for him and she deftly dodged the rifle fire. She circled overhead, causing the Ha'shon much consternation as he again took aim and fired. Again he missed.

Eladria seized her chance and with all her might she rammed herself into the Ha'shon, attempting to push him into the chasm that was just a few feet behind him. But she wasn't strong enough to budge him. Enraged, the Ha'shon lifted his rifle and locked her in his sights.

But before he could fire, Zinn swooped down and, with claws outstretched, dived at his face. The Ha'shon dropped his weapon and reached up to shield his face. Zinn dive-bombed him again, causing him to stagger backward and fall headlong into the chasm. His cries were largely drowned out by the noise of the storm as he disappeared from sight. Eladria peered over the edge of the fissure and could see no sign of him.

Zinn returned to land and resumed her human form. Eladria ran over to her and embraced her tightly. "Zinn, you did it," she exclaimed.

"That's one problem sorted at least," Zinn said. "But we have others."

Eladria looked up at the sky, which was still consumed by the breach as the circling bat-like creatures filled the heavens. Many of them were diving into the jungle, leaving trails of flames as they swooped through the treetops. The ground rumbled fitfully and wind blasted through the jungle in intermittent spurts.

She knew they had to find shelter. But before either of them could move, one of the shadow creatures dived toward them. Eladria leapt back in alarm. The creature flew back upwards, before again swooping down at them, setting the trees alight with red flames.

Eladria and Zinn raced through the undergrowth. Thankfully they managed to evade the creature and, as they scrambled over fallen tree trunks and uprooted foliage, they became aware of a lull in the storm. The wind had ceased, the tremors dissipated and, as Eladria stopped to look up at the sky, she was relieved to see no sign of the crack in the heavens. And whereas moments ago there had been hundreds of the bat-like creatures circling above and swooping through the trees, now there was nothing to be seen. The storm had ended and they were gone along with it.

Flames still leapt up from the trees and the ground was uneven and contorted by a series of cracks and chasms. But there was a sudden stillness and Eladria let out a cry of relief.

The rain continued lashing down, but Eladria welcomed it. She stood and held out her arms, allowing the rain to roll down her face and saturate her already water-soaked clothes and hair. The rain was also dousing the red flames, which would otherwise have consumed the jungle.

She let out a jubilant laugh and felt tears of gratitude rolling down her face, mingling with the raindrops. They had escaped the bounty hunter and survived this latest breach. Amid laughter and tears, she sunk to her knees, dislodging a wave of mud as she descended.

The tears continued to flow, only this time they were not just tears of gratitude, but of shock and trauma. She had been through so much and had endured so much. She had been pushed to the brink and beyond, experiencing more terror and despair than she'd ever thought possible. And it wasn't over. She somehow knew that in spite of this temporary reprieve, the worst was almost certainly yet to come.

Chapter 10

Janak

Silence followed the storm. Aside from birdsong and the sound of their feet squelching in and out of the mud, all that could be heard was the gentle tapping of water dripping from the trees and vines.

Signs of damage were plentiful in the wake of the storm. Uprooted trees and plants littered the jungle floor, some of them burnt and charred. The ground was uneven and in places had divided, forming chasms they had to jump across or maneuver around.

The destruction caused by the dimensional breach made Eladria all the more inclined to believe the Others and their warning that a dangerous experiment was threatening to destroy the planet. If this was a taste of what lay in store for them, then she realized she would be foolish indeed not to heed their words.

They made frequent reference to the map and compass as they made their way through the jungle, endeavoring to take the quickest route to Niyastan. There had been no further sign of Ha'shon pursuit and in spite of frequent encounters with jungle creatures, including wild cats, karrick-bears, several snakes and an oversized scorpion, their journey passed without incident.

It was on their third day of travelling that they came to the town of Niyastan. Situated in a jungle clearing, the metropolis was encircled by a defensive wall, heavily fortified and lined with lookout towers, cannons and guns. The town itself looked barren and run-down, with dents in the ramparts and buildings and rooftops exhibiting varying degrees of damage. It looked as though the town was in the midst of a war zone. Eladria realized she had been foolish to assume that, being the nearest point of civilization, Niyastan would automatically provide some kind of safe haven.

"I don't like the look of this place," she confessed to Zinn as they stood at the edge of the jungle, surveying the town.

"Neither do I," Zinn agreed, her brow furrowed.

"I'm not happy strolling into this town without first knowing something about it."

"Then allow me to do some reconnaissance," Zinn suggested. "In the form of a bird, I could enter the city undetected. Once I find out who lives there and have an idea of how safe it is, I'll come back and we can decide whether it's worth proceeding."

"That's a good idea," Eladria agreed.

She watched as Zinn transformed into a small grey bird, unobtrusive and unlikely to draw attention to itself. The bird flapped its wings and circled Eladria affectionately before fluttering toward the dismal grey town. Eladria remained at the edge of the jungle, partially hidden among the trees and foliage. She watched as Zinn disappeared from sight.

It was some time before she returned.

Eladria sat down against a tree trunk in silent contemplation. So much had happened in such a short time. Her life had transformed beyond all recognition. She'd gone from being a princess living a life of pampered excess to being a fugitive in a hostile and dangerously unpredictable land. She again wondered what to make of the Others and their assertion that whatever was happening at Drantak would spell disaster for the entire planet and beyond. She still wasn't sure whether the Others were to be trusted. She knew nothing about them and was utterly overwhelmed at the immensity of the task they had handed her.

What she did know was that everything had gone wrong and it was up to her to make it right again. But she would do so on her own terms. There was no way she could go to Drantak alone. She was unprepared and ill-equipped for such a task. That was why her best chance was to make contact with the TRM and have them send an expedition to Drantak.

She glanced ahead at the shabby town, its turrets and domes glinting in the sunlight and she mused that, as this was now her planet, this was essentially her town. And yet, there was no fanfare, no red carpet and no loyal subjects lining up to do her bidding. On the contrary, many of the inhabitants would be less likely to bow to her than they would to hand her over to the nearest Ha'shon authority. Or perhaps that was doing them a disservice. It was extremists that had seized control and inflicted so much harm, and they were still the minority. Most of the planet's inhabitants were just decent people struggling to survive amid turbulent times.

It wasn't long before the little grey bird fluttered back into the jungle. It stopped in mid-air and transformed back into the familiar form of Zinn. "What did you find out?" Eladria asked as she got up from the ground.

"Quite a bit as it happens," Zinn answered. "The town is under jurisdiction of the True Way and the streets are patrolled by True Way Patriarchs. The only entrance or exit appears to be a check-point at the periphery of the town. It seems the town is at war with a nearby Ha'shon outpost. From what I gather, there have been battles both in air and on land, as well as regular incursions into enemy territory by both sides. It's not a nice place, Princess. It's poor, overcrowded and from what I've seen the streets are filled with thieves and narcotic dealers."

"Definitely not ideal." Eladria sighed. "But I suppose we can at least be grateful it's not a Ha'shon town."

"Even so, I don't know how safe it is," Zinn cautioned. "What if the True Way are looking for you as well?"

"There's no way they'd be in league with the Ha'shon," Eladria said. "The Ha'shon are in control of the moon, so they probably control most of the news networks as well. I can only imagine the kind of propaganda they've been sending across the airwaves, but it's unlikely they've made our escape public knowledge. That's not their style. They like to be in control, or at the very least *appear* to be in control."

"So, should we should risk it or not?"

"I don't think we've got much choice. We need food and supplies. And I have to find out what's been happening since the coup, and see if there's any way I can contact the Royal Military."

"Do you think anyone will recognize you?"

Eladria shrugged. "Well, I have a new haircut and I'm not exactly dressed like a princess anymore. And I don't suppose they'll be expecting to see a royal figure strolling about their town. But it's still risky. We'll have to try and make ourselves as inconspicuous as possible."

Eladria removed her gold necklace and carefully placed it in her pocket. The necklace originally belonged to her mother and she wore it almost every day. She ruffled her hair and pulled it forward, using it to conceal as much of her face as she could.

"I'd scarcely recognize you myself," Zinn remarked.

"You'd better do something to change your appearance as well," Eladria said. "Just in case the Ha'shon have posted descriptions or pictures."

"That I can do quite easily," Zinn smiled.

Eladria watched as Zinn's entire face began to change. Her features melted and re-formed into those of a much younger woman. Her wavy grey hair became long, dark and sleek, cascading behind her ears. Eladria was taken aback. Zinn looked like a completely different person, one that was at least thirty years younger. Whereas before Eladria couldn't fathom why people would be so fearful and distrustful of metamorphs, she now had an inkling. It was disconcerting to see a person's face change so radically before one's eyes and it was hard to accept that the young woman standing before her was in fact Zinn.

"What do you think?" Zinn asked expectantly.

"I can hardly believe it's you," Eladria said, almost at a loss for words.

"Well hopefully that's the reaction any potential pursuers will have as well," Zinn answered, her voice still exactly the same as it was before, in spite of her metamorphosis.

"I wish I shared your abilities," Eladria remarked, turning her gaze to the town ahead. "You said there's a checkpoint at the entrance to the town?'

Zinn nodded. "It's manned by True Way Patriarchs. They ask each person who they are and what their business is in town."

"What should we say?" Eladria wondered.

"We could say that we're sisters? In town to visit relatives..."

"What if they want proof, or ask who our relatives are?"

"From what I saw most people are let through without any further questions. I imagine they only stop people they think look suspicious."

"In that case we'll have to try our best not to look suspicious," Eladria said, not entirely confident they would succeed in such an endeavor.

She and Zinn left the relative sanctuary of the jungle and made their way to the grim-looking town. Zinn led Eladria to the checkpoint, where a small number of people were coming and going from the town. Trying to act as casually as they could, they joined the line of people waiting to enter the town. Eladria's heart was thumping and her stomach knotted. Although she had disguised herself as best she could given the circumstances, she was still concerned that, as something of a public figure, she would be recognizable.

They came to the checkpoint booth, which was manned by a Patriarch, one of the True Way's warrior-priest caste. As with most Patriarchs, he wore a hooded grey habit beneath black body armor, with prayer beads around his neck and a band of metal chains winding around his chest and waist. The man, muscular with pale bluish-tinged skin, looked them up and down, his cold dark eyes drinking in every last detail. In a low, guttural voice he asked what their business was in Niyastan.

Zinn did the talking, explaining that she and her sister were in town to visit a sick relative. He asked their names and Zinn, a far better liar than Eladria would ever have imagined, told him they were called Jelandra and Shazay. Eladria was worried the Patriarch was going to ask for papers or proof of identification, in which case they would be in deep trouble. But he simply waved them through and turned his attention to the next in line.

With a heartfelt sense of relief, Eladria followed Zinn through the town gates, which were bookended by two Patriarchs brandishing rifles and large black ceremonial staffs. While the Ha'shon were outwardly more militant and aggressive, there was something even more sinister about the True Way, especially its Patriarchs. They were invariably pale-skinned with a haunted, deadened look about them. Whereas the Ha'shon radiated fiery aggression, the True Way exuded a joyless and calculating coldness that never failed to unnerve Eladria. True Way doctrine was rooted in pain, suffering and sacrifice. Historically, that sacrifice had been exacted through austerity and renunciation of worldly pleasures. But in recent years, as the socio-political situation on Tahnadra had worsened, the True Way had taken to the ritualistic killing of young men and women and captured enemies. It was thus little wonder that for all she now loathed and despised the Ha'shon, there was something equally if not more repellent about the True Way.

Eladria kept her eyes to ground as she walked past the Patriarchs, who stood like stone sentinels either side of the town gates. She was desperate not to make eye contact or engage them in any way. Again, she was overcome by the terror that they might recognize her. But like the man at the checkpoint booth, there didn't seem to be any flicker of recognition and they duly allowed her and Zinn to pass without incident.

She could barely repress a smile of relief as she and Zinn stepped into the town. They found themselves on the edge of a bustling, ramshackle promenade, filled with shops and market stalls, selling everything from food and clothing to medicines, jewelry and livestock. They cautiously walked down the street, senses bombarded by an array of sights, sounds and smells, careful to avoid drawing attention to themselves. It was a loud and raucous town, filled with activity as the townspeople went about their business. It was populated by an assortment of people, some of them fair-skinned like the Patriarchs and others with a darker skin befitting the region. While the men and women busily went about their duties, children played freely, their laughter and shouting mingling with the sound of barking dogs and clucking fowl above the general noise of the marketplace.

Eladria noticed the sick and elderly sitting or lying on street corners looking dejected and unwashed. She had never seen such squalor and deprivation. It broke her heart to see the old and infirm cast aside and left to rot on street corners while the general population engaged in their covetous marketplace transactions. Every so often she'd see a True Way Patriarch patrolling the street and she felt an immediate repulsion at the mere sight of them.

They approached a small tavern and the smell of cooking wafted out, making Eladria's mouth water as she realized just how ravenous she was. They'd finished the last of their rations the night before and she was overcome by hunger. The problem was they didn't have currency.

"Food and accommodation are our priorities," Eladria whispered to Zinn. "We also need to find access to the communications net."

Eladria was suddenly knocked forward as someone bumped into her. She turned round to see a young man, perhaps in his early to mid-twenties, short in stature with tousled black hair, several days' worth of stubble and a dark complexion. He wore a tattered white shirt, black trousers and boots. The man bowed his head and raised his hands in a gesture of apology. "I sorry, good lady," he said. "I not mean to disturb you. Please, please forgive clumsy Janak."

Eladria curtly nodded, not wishing to engage him further. With another small bow, the man crept off and Eladria turned back to Zinn, putting her hands in her pockets. The moment she did so she realized that her mother's necklace was no longer there. That man must have stolen it. He must have picked her pocket when he bumped into her!

Filled with sudden rage, Eladria ran after the thief. He was immediately aware of her pursuit and quickened his pace as he darted through the crowd. Eladria was determined not to let the thief escape and she soon caught up with him, catching hold of his arm and using her defense training to apprehend him in one fail swoop. She reeled him in, twisting his arm and, administering a sharp kick to the back of his knee, she brought him to the ground.

Conceding to her fighting skills, the man began sobbing and begged her not to injure him. "Please, lady, please, not hurt me," he cried.

Eladria hushed him, looking around cautiously, hoping that he hadn't elicited undue attention. "My necklace," she said angrily. "Where is it?"

"Necklace?" the man echoed. "Wh-what necklace?"

"You stole it from me," Eladria snapped. "I know you did! Empty your pockets."

The man shook his head slowly. Eladria tightened her grip on his arm, twisting it back until he yelped in pain. With his free hand he reluctantly complied, reaching into his pockets and emptying them onto the ground. The people in the marketplace seemed uninterested and undeterred by the commotion. It was likely that such scuffles were commonplace.

Eladria was astonished at just how much was contained in the thief's pockets. There were two bags of gold coins, various pieces of jewelry, keys, rings, brooches, pendants and, of course, Eladria's necklace. She reached down and took hold of it. She also decided to take advantage of the opportunity and confiscate the bags of coins, for they were no doubt stolen in the first place.

"Please no," the thief protested. "Not take those. I need them."

"I need them even more," she retorted.

It was at that moment that she became aware of one of the robed, ashen-faced Patriarchs approaching through the crowd. The Patriarch walked slowly but purposefully, staff in hand and rifle slung over his shoulder on a leather strap. Eladria felt the blood drain from her face. It seemed the commotion had drawn the attention of one of these sinister officials and she inwardly cursed while trying to steady her nerves and remain calm.

"What is happening here?" the Patriarch demanded as he stood over Janak.

"We just had a slight disagreement," Eladria said, trying to imitate the local accent. "But it's all right now. We've settled it."

"Did this man steal from you?" the Patriarch asked, looking down at Janak, who shifted nervously on the ground.

Eladria also looked down at the rather pitiful man and she shook her head. "No, this is my cousin," she said, trying to sound as convincing as she could. "We were just having a friendly disagreement. We're always teasing each other and bickering, but we love each other really. Isn't that right, cousin?"

Janak looked up at her, bewildered, before forcing himself to respond. "Uh—yes, yes, is true!"

Eladria mustered an affectionate smile, hoping that the Patriarch wouldn't mention all the money and jewelry lying at Janak's side.

The Patriarch nodded slowly. "As long as there is no trouble. As you know, thievery is punishable by execution."

"Just as well there are no thieves here then," Eladria said with a shrug of her shoulders.

The Patriarch looked down at Janak, then back up at Eladria, his eyes cold and penetrating. Then, thankfully, he turned and left, disappearing into the marketplace.

"You save my life," Janak looked up at Eladria in clear bewilderment. "Why you do that after I steal from you?"

Eladria helped the man to his feet and together they gathered his scattered loot. "I've done you a favor, now I expect a favor in return," she said.

"Anything! I do anything for you!"

Janak reached out to take the bags of coins from her, but she pulled back and shook her head. "That's the first part of the favor," she said sternly. "My friend and I need currency, so we're taking these."

"But what I do without money?" he asked worriedly.

"I assume you didn't exactly have to work hard for *this* money," Eladria said.

"Not so!" Janak objected. "My work is extremely hard—and dangerous!"

"Then tell you what, I'll keep one bag and you can have the other," Eladria conceded. "But before I give it back to you, you'll have to earn it. My friend and I need accommodation for the night, and we need access to the communications net."

"I see," Janak began. "Janak stay at Araban apartments, two blocks from here. Landlord gives Janak free accommodation in exchange for supply of certain...items. You stay with Janak tonight. As for access to communications net, I arrange that."

By now, Zinn had caught up with them and she came to a stop by Eladria's side. "He's clearly not to be trusted," she warned Eladria. "He just robbed you and I'm certain that given the chance he'd do it again in a flash."

"Maybe so, but I have his money and I assume he'll be eager to do whatever it takes to get it back."

Janak smiled, his chestnut eyes twinkling mischievously as he nodded his head. "I know where I get hold of portable comm device. It enable you access to communications net. Now, you go to apartments and ask for room twelve B. Say you friends of Janak, staying for night. There be no questions asked. Is not unusual for Janak to be entertaining lovely ladies."

"All right," Eladria said, resisting the urge to roll her eyes. "But I warn you, there had better be no deception. Otherwise you'll never see your money again and I'll report you to the authorities."

"Not to worry, not to worry," Janak said with a small bow before rushing off into the marketplace.

"Do you really trust him?" Zinn asked.

Eladria looked round and was momentarily surprised when, in spite of Zinn's familiar voice, it was an unfamiliar face that looked back at her. It would take her some time to get used to her new appearance. "No, I don't trust him in the slightest. But I do trust that he'll be back for his money. In spite of our close call with a Patriarch, it seems our meeting this thief was a stroke of luck. We now have currency and accommodation."

"Do you think the Patriarch recognized you?" Zinn asked.

"No, I don't think so. At least he didn't give any outward sign that he did. But I can't tell you how grateful I'll be when we leave this town. Next time I'm eager to rush to the nearest town, just remind me of this place."

"Shall we go to apartment and wait for him, then?"

"Let's go back to that tavern first. I don't know about you, but I'm in need of a good meal, and thankfully we can now afford one."

By the time they left the tavern it was late. The sun had set and darkness had crept in, the stars twinkling high above them as they made their way down the streets, in search of their accommodation.

For a while they seemed to be walking in circles and Eladria didn't feel safe, for gangs of thugs patrolled the streets and brawls broke out with regularity. Again, she noticed the poor and elderly huddling for warmth as they sat in doorways and on street corners and her heart went out to them. She'd never before seen such deprivation and it pained her. In spite of all that and transpired, these were her people and she hoped that someday she would be able to help them.

They eventually found the Araban apartments. It was a dingy

building with doors hanging off hinges and walls that were uneven and cracked. It was hard to imagine that anyone would pay to stay in such a run-down, unclean, disorderly environment.

A middle-aged man with unkempt grey hair and a beard sat behind a wooden desk in the main hallway. They told him that they were staying with a man named Janak in room twelve B. The man smiled lasciviously and licked his teeth in a manner that Eladria found quite repulsive. She did her best to hide her disgust and politely thanked him after he showed them through the darkened, shabby halls to room twelve.

Eladria repressed a grimace as she entered the room, which comprised nothing more than a single wooden bed with a thin, tattered sheet crumpled on top of it and a rickety old table with a paraffin lamp. She could imagine more luxurious prison cells. Eladria sat down on the bed with a sigh, the mattress creaking loudly as she sank into it. She looked around the room in resignation, the flickering lamplight casting shadows upon the cracked, stained walls.

"Oh well, it may not be up to palace standards, but it's better than sleeping outside again," Zinn said, trying her best to sound optimistic. "And we won't have to worry about predators tonight at least."

Eladria grunted. "That remains to be seen. I think the landlord probably qualifies as a predator."

Feeling dispirited, Eladria lay down upon the lumpy, uneven bed and decided to rest until Janak returned. As it happened, it wasn't long before the thief joined them. He entered the room and looked at Zinn quizzically. "Who your friend?" he asked.

"This is Zinn," Eladria answered, before remembering that they were supposed to be using cover names. "You met her earlier in the marketplace, don't you remember?"

Janak shook his head. "No. In marketplace you with beautiful young lady, much like yourself. This an old woman, like your grandmother or something."

Eladria suddenly realized that Zinn had changed her appearance back again. Of course Janak wouldn't recognize her. "That's right, my mistake," she countered. "That was someone else. You haven't met Zinn. She's my dearest friend and travelling companion."

Janak bowed his head and smiled roguishly, while Zinn shot him a disparaging glance, perhaps unhappy at being likened to Eladria's grandmother.

"Well, is nice for Janak to come back and find such beautiful lady sharing his bed," Janak grinned at Eladria.

"I'm not sharing *anything* with you," Eladria responded tersely. "Zinn and I will sleep on the bed. You'll sleep on the floor."

"That hardly any way to thank Janak," the man replied, closing the door behind him. "After all, I bring you comm device you want—and for you, is free of charge! My debt to you is repaid. So perhaps now you return my money?"

"You'll get it back when I decide it's time for you to have it back," she answered. "Now, bring me the comm unit."

Janak handed Eladria the handheld communications device. She took it eagerly. It was an outdated and very basic design, with a large, cracked rectangular screen, a scuffed black plastic frame and silver finishing. As it was a battery-powered unit, she hoped it had enough power to function. Janak watched as she activated the device and started tuning the receiver.

"Why you need comm device anyway?" Janak asked, taking a bag of nuts from his pocket and placing one in his mouth.

"That's my business," Eladria said.

"Is it working?" Zinn asked.

"Yes...I think so," Eladria said as she scanned the available channels. "What we first need to do is connect to the newsnet. We need to find out what's happening. And then, with a bit of luck we can open a communications frequency to the Royal Military."

"For ladies you do the strangest things," Janak commented as he rustled the paper bag, reaching for another nut. "Most ladies I know have no interest in news or communications, except their own gossip."

Eladria shot him a withering glance then returned her attention to the device. It was now displaying a list of broadcasting channels. She selected the interplanetary news channel and held her breath as she waited for it to connect. A faint, crackly picture appeared on the screen and the sound of newscasters could be heard. The signal was weak, but it would hopefully suffice. Zinn peered over Eladria's shoulder as she held the device in her hands and watched anxiously.

The newscasters were initially discussing the recent storms and disturbances that were sweeping across the planet with increasing severity. "Experts are still at a loss to explain the phenomena," a female newscaster said, as images of lightning storms, fires and strange weather patterns flashed across the screen.

"There are hundreds of reports of a 'crack' appearing in the sky, and a variety of inexplicable occurrences. Though each event is relatively short-lived, the destruction that has been caused is widespread across the planet. Entire towns have been destroyed by earthquakes. Many have experienced strange visions, reporting ghostly figures, creatures and 'monsters' emerging from the cracks, causing destruction and terror. Religious leaders have declared these almost-supernatural happenings as being signs of the end times, as predicted in the sacred texts. According to Ha'shon authorities, these occurrences are the very omens that precipitated their dramatic rise to power."

Eladria listened intently as the newscasters went on the discuss the recent 'Ha'shon ascendancy'. It didn't take her long to realize that the Ha'shon had indeed commandeered the media, for the tone of the broadcast was celebratory. Several commentators praised the Ha'shon's "brave and audacious" rise to power and noted that the benevolent Ha'shon rulership offered hope for the future. According to the newscasters, many of Tahnadra's populace, terrified by the freak storms, were now looking to the Ha'shon for deliverance.

The broadcast went on to summarize recent events, displaying footage of Ha'shon armies marching into towns and cities and images of Ha'shon raiders engaged in aerial combat with both the True Way and TRM.

"The Ha'shon rise to power has sent shockwaves across the planet," a male newscaster announced. "This is in spite of the fact that many believed this transition to be inevitable, especially given longstanding disillusionment with the old lineage of Chaldeen. Despite sporadic opposition from the Royal Military and True Way, the Ha'shon march to victory proceeds apace and they continue to quell all remaining pockets of resistance. They have sent out a planet-wide call for the opposition to lay down its arms, assuring them amnesty, pardon and peaceful coexistence under benevolent Ha'shon rule."

Eladria was unable to contain her disgust. It sickened her to hear such blatant propaganda. She wasn't sure if this broadcast could be trusted when it spoke of only sporadic opposition. She hoped that the Ha'shon's "march to victory" hadn't been as easy as they were making out.

"I can't believe it," Zinn whispered softly, shaking her head as they continued to watch the broadcast.

"I *don't* believe it. Not a word of it," Eladria frowned. "Neutrality of the media is clearly not permissible on a planet under Ha'shon occupation. They might have control of the palace and the media, but there's clearly still opposition from the Royal Military. The TRM have the superior craft and weaponry, if they can just coordinate themselves and create a cohesive strategy—"

"Why you interested in such affairs?" Janak cut in, sitting against the wall, watching them curiously. "What happens out there is no concern to likes of us."

Before Eladria could respond, her attention was brought back to the news broadcast. They were talking about the death of her father. "Although the Ha'shon have gone out of their way to ensure the population that their takeover was non-violent and bloodless, many have questioned General Estaran's killing of former monarch King Dulaan in a live broadcast to the planet."

Eladria was unprepared for the images that followed. They displayed clips of her father being stabbed by Estaran in the command room of the palace and slumping to ground as Estaran jubilantly declared victory. She turned her head away from the screen and closed her eyes tightly, trying to remove the image from her mind. It was enough that she'd been forced to witness it with her own eyes, but to see it replayed was more than she could handle. Zinn put her arm around Eladria, holding her tightly.

Although it was long moment before she could bear to look at the screen again, she listened as the newscaster continued his monologue. "The Ha'shon ruling council have expressed regret at the haste with which Estaran acted. But they are nonetheless resolute that it was a prudent move to ensure a swift end to any conflict between the Ha'shon and royalist forces. They claim victory was swiftly attained, with as little bloodshed as possible. The House of Chaldeen has fallen and it was announced earlier today that the king's only child, Princess Eladria, was also sadly killed as she attempted to leave the palace."

Eladria looked round at Zinn, her eyes wide with surprise. The newscaster continued: "The exact circumstances of the princess's death are as yet unclear, but the Ha'shon have denied responsibility and claim that, as she fled the palace in a stolen aircraft, she experienced engine problems. It is believed her craft exploded as it entered the atmosphere. The possibility of the princess having survived such an accident has been ruled out by Ha'shon officials. They claim this was a tragic and unnecessary accident and that they had hoped to work with the her to avert any potential conflict between the Ha'shon and royalist forces."

"They're saying I'm *dead*," Eladria gasped. "Why would they do that?"

Eladria had completely forgotten that Janak was present and had been listening to every word. The young thief got up from the floor and stared at them in disbelief, his jaw wide open. "But...they talking about the *princess*," he spluttered. "You—you *are* the princess?"

"That's a discussion for another time," Eladria responded.

"Then is true!" Janak laughed in glee. "You the princess— Princess Eladria! But why you here, in Niyastan? They saying you dead!"

"Yes, all right, it's true," Eladria admitted. "But you mustn't tell anyone, do you hear me?"

"Why would Janak tell anyone?" he asked, cocking his head to one side in a manner that reminded her of her old pet grudik.

"I don't know, perhaps because you figure you'll get money for handing me to the authorities?" she fixed him in a steely gaze.

Janak shook his head vigorously. "No, of course not. You Janak's friend. I never do such a thing to a friend!"

Eladria got up from where she sat and approached the diminutive thief, trying to look as intimidating as she could. "Just as well," she said, lowering her voice. "Because they'd be just as likely to kill you as they would reward you. Life means nothing to the Ha'shon, least of all the life of a lowly thief. They wouldn't hesitate in running you through the belly with a blade, just as they did my father. That's if I didn't manage to kill you first."

She reached down to her belt and drew the knife she'd been given by Lakandrian's people, lifting it to Janak's neck. Janak stepped back until he was hard against the wall and he trembled as Eladria pressed the blade against his skin. She fixed him a penetrating stare that she hoped would scare him into compliance.

"I promise," Janak cried in alarm. "Not harm me! I never betray you. You my friends!"

Eladria lowered the knife but kept her eyes locked with his. "You're not to tell anyone who we are," she cautioned.

"I not tell anyone," he answered, slinking away from her. "You have Janak's word of honor."

Zinn frowned. "The honor of a thief carries little weight."

"Maybe not," Eladria said, still staring intently at the young thief. "But it will have to do. Janak knows not to betray us, because doing so would result in his almost certain death."

"You ladies mean business," Janak exclaimed with a raised eyebrow and let out a sharp exhale of air.

Eladria was satisfied that she had intimidated him into compliance and turned her attention back to the communications device. They were still discussing the recent coup. They listed a number of towns, cities and provinces that had fallen to the Ha'shon, who had evidently launched a full-scale offensive across the planet the moment they had secured the palace.

It was a grim picture and Eladria felt her heart sink further as the newscasters relayed details of numerous Ha'shon victories against TRM forces. They claimed to have commandeered several TRM installations with the help of inside forces: or, in other words, traitors like Narat. Eventually she could stand no more, so she switched off the news broadcast and shook her head in resignation.

"I don't know what to believe," she said to Zinn. "Is it really as bad as they're making out or is that all just Ha'shon propaganda?"

"Who can say? At least with the news spreading that you've been killed, no one will be looking for you. So unless anyone recognizes you—"

"But the Ha'shon know I'm not dead," Eladria interjected. 'They know my craft didn't explode in the atmosphere. They're just saying that because they don't want the TRM or the True Way knowing that I'm out here. They know I'm still a threat to them. They want people to think that any hope of returning to the old regime is gone. They want the royalists to simply give up the fight."

"More than likely," Zinn said sadly.

"Well, I can't stop what's happened, but I can make it as hard for them as possible," Eladria said. "I can maybe use this device to contact the TRM. There must be an installation within communications reach."

Eladria turned her attention back to the device. She began trying to trace the nearest TRM frequency in the hopes that she could open a transmission. Janak and Zinn watched in silence as she tapped away at the box, trying to master the archaic user interface. She eventually located a TRM frequency. It was weak and intermittent, but it was the only one she could see. She dialed it up and hoped they would be able to respond—and that it wouldn't be one of the installations commandeered by the Ha'shon.

The moment she tried to initiate a frequency, she was blocked by a security wall encoded with the Ha'shon insignia. Evidently the Ha'shon had found a way to block all frequencies. She tried to bypass the security wall, to no avail. In a fit of frustration, she threw the device to the floor, where it smashed into pieces.

"It's no use!" she cried. "There's no way to contact them. The Ha'shon are everywhere. There's no getting past them."

There was a long silence as she considered her options. "I don't know what to do now. Do we try to find the nearest military base on foot? Or do we just give up and head off to Drantak alone like the Others suggested?"

"That I don't know," Zinn said. "But I do think it's time you got some sleep, my dear. You're exhausted and you need rest."

Eladria knew she was right. Although frustrated and in pain, having had her grief reignited by the images of her father's death, she tried to settle down and get some rest. She shared the lumpy, uneven bed with Zinn, while Janak settled himself on the floor and soon began snoring loudly.

Eladria found it difficult to sleep, for a terrifying thought arose in her mind. What if the Ha'shon had been monitoring all communications and had been able to trace her attempt to dial the TRM? It was likely that anyone trying to contact the TRM would be an immediate target for Ha'shon attack. What if she'd inadvertently led them straight to her?

She tried to dismiss this disturbing notion and after what felt like hours of lying awake, uneasy and restless, she eventually drifted into a light sleep.

A sleep that was soon to be disturbed...

Chapter 11

The Siege Of Niyastan

Eladria awoke to the sound of thunder.

She jumped up in bed and looked around in disorientation. It didn't take her long to realize that it wasn't the sound of thunder at all. It was gunfire. Flashes of light streaked through the windowpane, accompanied by the roar of blazing artillery.

"What's happening?" Zinn cried.

Eladria looked down at Janak, who sat upon the ground shaking his head. "Must be Ha'shon again," he muttered. "Third time they attack this week..."

"Why are they so intent on attacking this town?" Eladria asked, her heart skipping a beat every time there was another blast of weapons fire.

Janak shrugged. "Is just what they do."

The noise outside was worsening. Eladria went over to the window and pulled back the curtain just enough to peer outside. The town appeared to be under aerial bombardment by the Ha'shon. Aircraft cannons were ablaze, apparently inflicting significant damage upon the beleaguered town. Even from this limited vantage point, Eladria could see buildings ablaze and thick reams of smoke rising up from the town. The True Way was retaliating, launching anti-aircraft missiles in a sustained exchange of fire.

"What are we going to do?" Zinn fretted as she sat upon the edge of the bed.

"I'm not sure," Eladria answered. She turned to Janak. "What usually happens during the raids? Will we be safe here?"

"Previous nights they not manage to enter town," Janak said. "So we probably be safe here. Is best not to worry."

Nevertheless, Eladria couldn't help but worry. They were in grave danger here. Was this simply part of the Ha'shon's ongoing war with the True Way, or did they suspect that she was here, having intercepted her attempt to contact the TRM? She took a deep breath and tried to throw off the tension that constricted her chest and gut. There was no reason to be paranoid, at least not yet.

She remained at the window watching as the town was relentlessly pounded in the assault. After a time, the sound of gunfire and explosions began to diminish. She prayed that the Ha'shon had been driven away. But she quickly realized that this was not the case, for she caught sight of something that made her freeze in terror. Storming down the street were Ha'shon warriors brandishing rifles and machetes.

Those on the street fled in terror, while a handful of True Way security forces, headed by the Patriarchs, engaged the Ha'shon insurgents in combat. Alas, the Ha'shon were too great in number and the True Way were quickly vanquished.

Eladria watched in horror as the Ha'shon began raiding houses at the far end of the street. They forced their way into the buildings and dragged the inhabitants onto the street where they were lined up and surveyed by the Ha'shon generals. The prisoners were then marched down the road until they were out of sight. The remaining Ha'shon continued moving down the street, systematically raiding each house.

"They're coming this way," Eladria said. "We have to get out of here."

"And go where?" Zinn asked.

"Anywhere! We can't stay here. They're rounding people up and marching them off to who knows where. We should never have come here, Zinn. We've walked straight into the hands of the Ha'shon."

"Janak come with you?" Janak asked.

"Please yourself," Eladria said as she made for the door.

"I rather take my chances with you than with Ha'shon," Janak muttered. He reached beneath the bed where Eladria had stashed his money and slyly pocketed the bags of coins.

They left the room and made their way down the darkened corridor. They reached the entrance lobby where the landlord was trying to calm a crowd of frenzied tenants, who were shouting and gesticulating, a number of children crying and screaming.

Eladria, Zinn and Janak slipped past them and exited the building. Eladria cautiously peered down the street in the direction of the Ha'shon. They were continuing to ransack the street, systematically raiding each of the towering, dilapidated buildings and dragging the terrified occupants onto the street.

Eladria turned to Zinn. "Zinn, we need to find a way out of this place without running into the Ha'shon."

Zinn nodded, understanding Eladria's request. She began changing shape, her human form morphing into a swirling mist and then re-forming as a small bird. Janak, unaware of Zinn's shape-changing abilities, cried in alarm. "Wha-what happen to your friend? Why, she—"

"Quiet," Eladria hushed him, sharply tugging his arm. "I'll explain later. For now, we have to keep quiet and remain as inconspicuous as possible."

Zinn flapped her wings and rose into the air, where she began circling above the rooftops. Eladria watched, hoping she'd be able to find the best way for them to escape the town undetected.

Her attention was drawn down a side lane adjacent to the main street. She saw some of the town's inhabitants running in terror as a scuffle broke out between a Patriarch and three Ha'shon. The Patriarch was about to open fire on the approaching insurgents, but was ambushed from behind. The attacking Ha'shon disarmed him and took great delight in beating and slaying the disarmed Patriarch. Eladria turned away in disgust.

Thankfully, it appeared that Zinn had found a way for them to proceed. Her bird-form swooped down toward them and as she flew down one of the side streets, she turned, looking back at them.

Eladria and Janak followed her, only too happy to leave the main street. They raced down the uneven stone paving, where a number of frightened townspeople had congregated and were discussing how to escape the encroaching Ha'shon. Eladria and Janak continued to follow Zinn, maneuvering past the anxious gathering, unerring in their direction. They soon found themselves at the marketplace on the edge of town.

There were Ha'shon soldiers everywhere, streaming in through what had been the checkpoint but which was now just a smoldering mound of rubble. Outside the town, through a screen of smoke, Eladria saw at least two stationary Ha'shon aircraft.

The True Way had yet to concede defeat and the Patriarchs and security guards continued to battle the Ha'shon. The two forces exchanged volleys of electro-pulse fire, causing a steady stream of casualties. There were bodies strewn across the marketplace, while the buildings danced with flames, thick black smoke spiraling upward, casting a murky pall upon the decimated town.

Eladria and Janak hid behind an outbuilding, observing the fighting from a distance. Zinn rejoined them, resuming her human form.

"Why did you lead us here?" Eladria demanded. "This is a battlefield, Zinn! It's swarming with Ha'shon."

"It's also the only way out of the town," Zinn said.

"The moment we step out there we'll be in the line of fire," Eladria sighed, slamming her fist against the wall. "We don't stand a chance."

But as she began to rethink her strategy, something happened that immediately changed the rules of the game.

At first Eladria thought a bomb had detonated. The entire town shook and a flash of light was accompanied by a sharp gust of wind. The ground began shaking in intermittent bursts. Stripped of solid foundations, buildings began to buckle under the stress; walls crumbling, rooftops caving in and windows smashing. There was a howling noise, like the sound of a raging tornado scouring the land.

Looking upward, Eladria saw that once again the sky had been sliced open as if by a giant blade, leaving an open wound pulsating with lightning, dispelling the darkness and creating an eerie luminosity. It was another storm, or what the Others called a dimensional breach.

Eladria turned her attention to the battlefield and saw that the fighting had temporarily ceased. Both sides now had a different and far more unpredictable adversary. The Patriarchs broke their lines and fled deeper into the town, while the Ha'shon regrouped to confer with their general.

"What happening?" Janak cried, his face drained of color and his eyes wide in terror.

"Either things have just got a whole lot worse or we've been given an opportunity," Eladria answered, having to shout to be heard above the storm. "This might be the distraction we need to slip past the Ha'shon and get out of here. But we have to wait until the time is right."

"You crazy," Janak shouted back. "We should go hide! Is dangerous here!"

"You're welcome to do whatever you want. If you want to go hide, then do so. But we're getting out of here."

Janak looked round at Zinn, then back at Eladria. "Well, is hard to believe, I know, but I...I not have many friends. So when I do find them, I stick with them. We go together!"

The tremors continued shaking the land, intensifying with each round. The buildings were crumbling, some gradually, others with alarming suddenness. The Ha'shon raiders were nearly caught beneath a collapsing tenement. They leapt away from the falling building and looked around in escalating alarm, unsure what to do: were they to continue their assault or concede defeat and retreat?

Eladria knew they had to get out of here now, but their timing had to be right. Although the exit was in sight, the moment they made a run for it, the Ha'shon would see them and open fire.

The howling wind increased as the storm grew more intense by the moment. The noise of the storm was almost deafening and Eladria was certain she could hear voices intermixed with the tempest: millions of voices howling in unison.

Another tremor rocked the town, this time causing the ground to split. As a crack travelled along the marketplace, crumbling buildings fell into the fissure. The Ha'shon were disbanded by the chaos, some killed by collapsing buildings, others falling into the widening chasm. The remaining insurgents appeared to lose their resolve and began to retreat, running in any direction they could to escape the chaos.

The crack in the ground was spreading in every direction, causing the concrete paving to split and uprooting even the sturdiest of buildings. Eladria knew that in order the reach the exit they would have to cross the chasm.

The sky was ablaze with lightning, which spewed out of the tear and forked across the sky. Each blast of lightning seemed to intensify and it began to strike the ground, causing buildings to burst into flames. The screaming voices continued to carry on the wind and Eladria knew that they weren't coming from the townspeople, but from some place beyond the breach.

It was time to make their move. She turned to Zinn and Janak and waved her arm, motioning for them to follow. Zinn nodded and changed form, once again becoming a bird. This time she became a great lastar, a gigantic bird of prey that swooped into the air, struggling against the blustering winds. Eladria couldn't help but envy her. How much easier would it be if she too could change shape and fly away from this disaster zone?

Although every fiber of her being compelled her to flee in the opposite direction, she steadied her resolve and began running into the open marketplace. She and Janak came to a stop where the chasm split the land in two. They had to find a way to cross it, for just beyond it was the town exit.

By now, she'd attracted the attention of some remaining Ha'shon. She thought they'd all retreated, too busy trying to save themselves to bother about two escapees, but she was wrong. Two of the burly, reddish-skinned Ha'shon warriors had remained in the vicinity and were now closing in on her and Janak, rifles drawn, their long braided hair blowing into their faces.

Fortunately, as she clambered over the remains of a collapsed building, she found a place she could cross the chasm. With a jump, she managed to reach the other side, just as another tremor rattled underfoot, causing the chasm to widen further. Janak was still on the other side and the chasm was now too deep to safely jump. He looked at Eladria helplessly as the two Ha'shon soldiers closed in on him from behind.

Another quake was accompanied by a blast of wind and a prong of lightning that knocked Janak and the two Ha'shon to the ground. Before the Ha'shon could get to their feet, they were caught beneath a collapsing building behind them. Janak managed to dart out of the way, narrowly avoiding being crushed by a falling pillar. However, as the ground began shaking again, he lost his footing and fell headlong into the chasm, screaming as he tumbled down.

Eladria watched in horror, helpless to assist. At that moment she was certain that Janak's fate had been sealed. Another tremor struck, forcing Eladria to step back as the ground in front of her gave way.

But just as all seemed lost, Zinn—still in the form of the giant lastar bird—swooped down and shot into the chasm. Eladria watched in amazement as the bird reemerged from the abyss, clutching Janak in its great talons. The bird deposited Janak on the ground beside Eladria and flew back up to the sky. Janak was dazed but unhurt. Eladria helped him to his feet and urged him to get moving.

They made their way along the cracked paving and reached the exit point. All that remained of the checkpoint was a pile of rubble and the town gates had been blown to pieces. It was with a profound feeling of elation that Eladria climbed across the debris and exited the town.

Just outside the town were the two stationary Ha'shon raiders. The ground had also cracked and separated here, causing one of the craft to dangle precariously over the edge of a chasm. The other sat motionless, with no apparent sign of life. It appeared they had been left unmanned while the Ha'shon stormed the town.

For a brief moment Eladria considered commandeering the craft, but realized that such a notion was foolhardy. It would take her some time to figure out how to pilot it and time was one thing they didn't have.

They had to head back into the jungle. That was their best chance of finding cover.

She began running. Janak followed behind her, and above them she was aware of the bird-form of Zinn, still struggling against the wind.

They kept moving until they were deep in the jungle, surrounded by the trees and undergrowth. The jungle had also been hit hard by the storm and the tremors continued to rattle the land. They made their way with haste and care, on more than one occasion almost being caught beneath falling trees.

Fortunately, the breach soon began to subside. The crack in the sky, which had been visible even from the jungle floor, gradually vanished. As it dissolved into darkness, the lightning, winds and tremors also ceased. Eladria's ears had grown so accustomed to the noise that the sudden silence was quite shocking. The sky was dark again, no longer lit by the unnatural luminescence of the breach.

Satisfied that their ordeal was over, Eladria and Janak came to a stop. Zinn circled above them and then landed on the ground, changing back into her ordinary form. Although not a word was spoken, their shared relief was profound and palpable.

Eladria sat down upon an uprooted tree. It took some time for her to catch her breath and to steady her pounding heart as her body and senses remained in a heightened state of shock.

She didn't know what they would do now, but following the horrors of the storm, the stillness around them was an almost heavenly respite. She felt a tear trickling down her face. It was a tear of gratitude. In spite of all the odds, they'd made it. For now at least, they were safe.

Chapter 12

Skyfire

The wildcat was intent on catching its prey.

Eladria watched as the animal raced through the undergrowth, darting over logs and leaping across boulders. Its prey was a single dwarf borra, running for its life. The furry creature was hopelessly outmatched by the jungle cat, but it put up a good chase. Eventually, however, the cat caught up with the borra, snatching it from the ground in its mighty jaws.

The cat turned and made its way toward Eladria and Janak as they watched from the vicinity of their campfire. The cat skulked along, its belly swinging from side to side and its head down low as the unmoving borra dangled from its mouth. Far from triumphant, the cat looked dejected as it neared them. In that moment, Eladria knew she had done a bad thing.

The cat approached the campfire, deposited the dead borra and turned to leave.

"Zinn, I'm sorry," Eladria called after it. "I know you didn't want to do that."

The feline stopped and began to shimmer and dissolve, transforming back into Zinn's familiar form. "It had to be done," Zinn said sadly. "You have to eat, after all."

"But there should be another way," Eladria went over to her and put her hand on the maid's shoulder. "I promise I won't ask you to do that again."

Zinn nodded kindly and withdrew, moving just beyond the campfire, clearly in need of some space to herself. Eladria knew that Zinn deplored violence of any kind. Zinn herself rarely ate meat, preferring to stick to a simple plant-based diet. Eladria greatly appreciated what she had done, for both she and Janak were extremely hungry and there was little edible vegetation in this part of the jungle. But seeing how much it pained her friend, she vowed that she would never again make such a request of her.

Eladria turned her attention to the borra. She had never had to prepare a meal for herself before. She didn't have a clue how to prepare a dead animal for cooking and the mere thought of doing so made her squeamish despite her hunger. Fortunately, using her knife, Janak was able to skin and fillet the borra, before roasting it over the crackling campfire.

"You've obviously done that before," she commented as she watched him cook the meat.

"Yes," Janak nodded. "I live on my own since I was child. I learn to do whatever it take to stay alive."

"Don't you have any family?" she asked as she sat down and watched him.

"No, not now," he shook his head sadly. "I come from Dabastak province. My family live there for generations. When I ten years old, my family killed in Ha'shon raid. Ha'shon stormed city, killing hundreds of people. My mother tried to get us safety, to hide us away. But Ha'shon found us and killed her and rest of my family. Only I manage to escape."

Eladria felt a deep sorrow for the man and horror at this terrible story. She'd known about these raids for many years but had never met any of the victims firsthand. "I'm sorry," she said. "I had no idea. What did you do? How did you survive?"

"I survive by doing what I had to do," Janak said, staring down at the campfire over which he held the roasting borra, skewered on Eladria's knife. "I learn to steal whatever I need. I know what you think about thieves, but Janak had no education, no prospects, no home, no family, no food! I learn to adapt, to survive. Is not a life I proud of, but it is at least a life."

Eladria didn't know what to say. She'd been judgmental and disparaging toward him from the moment she'd met him and she suddenly felt ashamed of her condescending attitude. She vowed to be more tolerant and understanding toward him.

"So," Janak said, looking up at the princess, changing the

subject. "You are Princess Eladria? You live on royal moon?"

"That's right," she nodded. "I did live on the moon, but not anymore. I had to leave. The Ha'shon invaded my home too and they killed my father."

"Ha'shon are disgusting pigs," Janak said, his voice low and trembling. "Janak hate them. They have no remorse. All they do is kill and kill."

"There's been too much killing," she agreed. "I wish there was some way I could stop it. But, unfortunately, I'm a fugitive in my own world now."

"So what are you going to do now?" Zinn asked, sitting at a discreet distance from the campfire.

"I suppose I've no option but to do what the Others said," Eladria answered. "These storms—or breaches, or whatever they are—are getting worse all the time. It seems the Others were right. They do appear to be our most immediate danger and I have to do whatever I can to stop them."

"Then we're going to Drantak, on our own?"

Eladria nodded. "I tried making contact with the military and you saw what happened. I hate to say this, but I think we're in this alone, Zinn. I haven't a clue how we're going to get there or what we're liable to find once we do, but yes, we're going to Drantak. We have to. The Others were adamant that only from there can we stop whatever's happening to the planet."

"Others?" Janak asked, his face creasing in a perplexed expression.

"I don't entirely know who or what they are," Eladria said. "We encountered them prior to our arrival in Niyastan. They claim to be beings from another dimension. They warned us that something terrible is happening in Drantak, that an experiment is being conducted by creatures desperate to invade our world. It's this experiment that's responsible for the storms—and it clearly has to be stopped."

"And if is not?"

"Then this world will be invaded and destroyed, or so they claim."

"You believe this?"

"I have no choice but to believe it. I tried to dismiss it, but if there's any chance at all that what the Others told me is true, then I have to act on it. I have to go to Drantak."

"How will we get there, Princess?" asked Zinn. "And once we do, what are we supposed to do?"

"I wish I knew. All we can do is take what the Others told us and use that as our starting point. The map Lakandrian gave us is helpful. Using that we can plot a route out of the jungle and toward the northeast coast of Yahnas. Then we'll have to find a way of travelling across the Raskabari sea to Drantak."

"You think we can make it all that way?"

"It won't be easy, but we have to try. And who knows, perhaps along the way we'll find a way of contacting the TRM. Although we can't count on that. I fear this is a journey we'll have to undertake ourselves."

"Wherever you go, I go with you," Janak said with a resolute nod.

"You can come with us if you want but I should warn you, it's going to be dangerous."

"Janak's life's been one danger after the next. I quite used to it by now."

"Very well then," Eladria said, approving his decision. She still wasn't entirely certain he was to be trusted, but she would keep a close eye on the diminutive pickpocket.

Janak declared their meal ready to eat. He divided the roasted borra into two portions, Zinn having again declined the invitation. The two ate ravenously, relieved to finally satisfy their hunger.

By the time they had finished eating it was dark and the trio settled down for the evening. Eladria and Janak tried to make themselves comfortable as they lay by the campfire. Zinn, who seemed not only to need less food than they did, but also less sleep, offered to keep watch as they slept. In the form of a plume-tailed green owl, she perched upon the branches of a tree overlooking the campfire, quietly watching the vicinity.

In spite of Eladria's exhaustion, she found it difficult to sleep. The sounds of the jungle kept her awake: the cries of nocturnal creatures in the distance, the rushing of a nearby stream and the humming and clicking of various insects. She rolled over on the thin mattress of leaves she'd arranged on the ground and tried to block out the background noise. She knew that Zinn would alert them to any danger.

Following their escape from Niyastan they had kept on the move, barely stopping at all. Eladria still feared that the Ha'shon knew, or at least suspected, that she was in that town. She was worried that, having failed to find her, they would redouble their efforts and head into the jungle in search of her. Perhaps her fears were unfounded, but it was prudent that they kept moving. If she knew anything about the Ha'shon it was that they possessed a relentless resolve.

Her attention was suddenly drawn up to the sky. As she looked up, she saw the sky coming alive with light and color. A shifting screen of reds, pinks, blue and violet suffused the black void of the heavens. It moved in waves, like the ocean rippling against the shore and was accompanied by a sound like distant thunder mixed with the tinkling of bells.

At first Eladria was worried that this might be symptomatic of another impending breach. But it seemed different somehow. Absent was the fear and ominous dread she felt prior to the storms. This was a benign sight, intoxicatingly beautiful and strangely serene. She was aware that Janak had also noticed the celestial display.

"What is that?" she asked, not taking her eyes from the heavenly marvel.

"Skyfire," Janak answered excitedly, getting up from where he lay. He gazed up at the sky with a look of childlike wonder upon his face. "It only happen occasionally and only visible in darkest night."

"Skyfire," Eladria echoed. "I remember one of my school teachers telling me about it. It's caused by the interplay of solar and magnetic forces, isn't it?"

Janak shrugged. "I not know what causes it," he admitted. "But is beautiful!"

"I've seen pictures of it, but never imagined I'd see it with my own eyes. I suppose having lived on the moon my whole life there are so many things I've missed. After my mother disappeared, my father was reluctant to let me visit the planet unless it was absolutely necessary. Until a few days ago, I'd never slept beneath the stars..."

"There are so many wonders for you to see," came Zinn's voice from behind them. Eladria looked round and saw that Zinn had flown down from the tree and was back in human form. She stood gazing up at the sky, a look of detached awe upon her face.

"You've seen this before?" Eladria asked.

"Oh yes, many times," she answered. "Back when I lived on the planet, wandering from place to place, I loved nothing more than to sit at night and watch the sky. I saw the skyfire quite frequently. It's a remarkable sight, isn't it? And usually when the skyfire appears, the Riders are close by, drawn to it like luna-flies to a flame."

Eladria turned to the maid in surprise. "The Riders? I thought they were just a myth?"

"Certainly not," Zinn said with a shake of her head. "I've seen the Riders with my own eyes, many times."

"What are they?"

"No one quite knows. They're mysterious, semi-corporeal creatures, only visible at certain times. It's said that they ride the planet's energy currents, following the magnetic grids like stones skimming across the surface of a pond. On nights like this, when the heavens are alight with skyfire, they can sometimes be seen, if one looks closely enough."

Eladria looked back up at the ever-shifting screen of translucent light visible above the treetops. After a time she became aware of streaks of light shooting across the sky, dancing and spiraling, riding in waves. They were like giant fireflies high up in the sky, chasing the kaleidoscopic light stream as it shifted and undulated. There must have been over a dozen streaks of light, like shooting stars, and they all moved in the same direction, as though drawn by some invisible magnetism. It had to be the Riders!

She was unable to take her eyes from the wondrous sight, but soon her neck began to ache as she craned her head upward, so she lay back down upon the ground. As she gazed up at the sky, she felt like a little child, enthralled by the light display. Her troubles and traumas melted away and she felt renewed and refreshed. It was amazing how the world could change in an instant from being a place of darkness and terror to a land of magic and wonder.

As she and Janak lay by the dimly glowing fire, they continued watching the morphing lights and the playful dance of the Riders as they moved back and forth.

Janak began recounting the various times he'd seen the skyfire and the Riders. Eladria found his stories somewhat meandering and pointless, but she let him talk. Since learning of his difficult life and the tragic loss of his family, she had a newfound empathy for him. He was a wounded soul and although she would never trust him around money or possessions, she could at least let her guard down around him.

She realized now how hardened and closed-off she'd been. Was it possible that growing up surrounded by opulence and luxury and cut off from the suffering of the planet's populace had made her unsympathetic and self-centered? It was a sobering realization that she perhaps lacked the qualities that made her father great; his kindness, selflessness and wisdom. The very least she could do to honor his memory would be to cultivate those qualities in herself. Maybe then she would actually be worthy of leading this planet and its people.

The skyfire eventually began to fade. As the shifting kaleidoscope of color receded into the darkness of the night sky, the Riders disappeared from sight. The sky was now empty, a vast blackness punctuated only by the twinkling stars.

Janak's ramblings also subsided and, as he drifted off to sleep, he began snoring softly. Zinn was again in the form of the green owl, keeping watch from a branch overhead.

Eladria rolled onto her side and tried to get off to sleep, but her mind was active and she soon became aware of what sounded like whispering voices. At first it was faint and she dismissed it as her imagination, but the whispering seemed to get louder and more frequent; indiscernible words carried upon the subtlest hint of a breeze.

Disturbed, she sat up and looked around, but there was nothing to be seen. Zinn was still perched upon the branch, seemingly unperturbed. If there was any danger lurking nearby, Zinn would had spotted it.

Was it all in her imagination? Perhaps the traumas of the past few days had taken their toll and were affecting her mind?

She lay back down upon the ground, the leaves rustling as she tried to make herself comfortable. The whispering continued in intervals and she was certain she could see shadows and silhouettes lurking amid the trees and foliage.

She tried to dismiss the voices and shadows. This was easily done in the case of the shadows, for all she had to do was close her eyes and keep them closed. But it was less easy to block out the eerie whispering, which continued to unnerve her.

Now that the beauty of the skyfire had subsided, she was again reminded of what a dangerous and unsettled world this was. It was almost as though the veils that separated realms were collapsing, making every moment unpredictable and potentially deadly. It was hard to relax, never knowing when another breach might occur.

By now she'd given up hope of enlisting the help of the Royal Military. Even if she could find a way to bypass the Ha'shon security block and contact them, there was probably little they could do to help her. They had a war on their hands and their top priority was obviously to prevent the Ha'shon from achieving complete world domination, assuming that hadn't already happened.

Her only chance was to get to Drantak. She didn't know how she was going to get there or what she was meant to do once she arrived, but she knew that this was where she had to go.

Tahnadra was her world, and she would do whatever she had to in order to save it. She was just troubled by the possibility that if the storms continued as they had, by the time she got to Drantak there might not be much of it left to save...

Chapter 13

Snare

There was nothing but swampland as far as the eye could see. The ground was wet, muddy and sticky and a rancid odor permeated the air. The travelers' discomfort was worsened by a grimy mist that obscured visibility and clung to their skin. The trees were wiry and gnarled, their bare branches outstretched like rickety old limbs. It was a place of inhospitable deadness.

Eladria stopped again to study the map. Since leaving Niyastan, their sole concern had been to get a safe distance between them and the Ha'shon, so they had been desperate to steer clear of any potential Ha'shon settlements. Eladria had selected a general northeasterly heading, for that would take them in the direction of the Yahnas coastline. Unfortunately, it had also led them here.

The three travelers continued through the swamp, struggling to maintain their footing as they waded through the thick, slippery mud. Their spirits were low and there was little conversation along the way. Food was scarce and they had to rely on berries and other fruit they'd gathered earlier in their journey. Eladria was unsure how long the supplies would last, but they would suffice for now.

As they later sat upon a large log and ate their meager rations, Eladria had the sense of being watched. It was a strange and inexplicable feeling. She looked around anxiously, but couldn't see anything through the murky mist that pervaded the swamp.

"What's wrong?" asked Zinn, sensing her unease.

"I don't know." Eladria shrugged. "It's probably nothing. But we should get going. The sooner we're out of this place, the happier I'll be."

"And happier I be also," Janak said ruefully. "Janak never been in such a place."

They ate the rest of their frugal meal and readied themselves to move on. But, as they resumed their journey, Eladria could sense that something wasn't quite right. She had a feeling of unease in her pit of her stomach; a sensation that usually preceded imminent trouble. But there didn't appear to be any immediate sign of danger and she was uncertain what option they had but to keep on moving.

This part of the swamp was darker than the rest. The clouds were heavier and the mist thicker, and between the two they swallowed up just about all trace of daylight. Eladria looked around nervously. Again she had the disquieting sense that someone or something was watching them. She tried to dismiss it and they continued traipsing through the marshy ground, their feet squelching in and out of the mud.

Alas, it wasn't long before her suspicions of danger were confirmed. Taking a step forward, she collided with something, as though she'd walked into an invisible wall obstructing her path. Her body was held rigid. Whenever she tried to move, a sharp electrical shock surged through her body and she could momentarily see a web of interpenetrating cords fizzling with electricity. She yelped in pain, her alarm increasing as she realized that she was completely helpless.

"Zinn, Janak! I'm trapped in something. Are you all right?" she called, hoping they hadn't also become entangled in the invisible web. Unable to move, she couldn't look round and had no idea what had happened to them. All she could see was straight ahead and even then she was unable to see far for the encroaching mist.

"No, I'm caught as well," came Zinn's panicked response. "I don't know what happened. I was walking along and suddenly I became *stuck*. I can't move and I can't change shape. Whenever I try, I experience pain."

"I-I caught as well!" cried Janak, his voice choked with clear distress. "I not move! What should we do?"

"Try not to panic," Eladria said, knowing that they had to remain calm and levelheaded. But that was easier said than done.

She felt a rising sense of alarm as she saw a figure appearing through the mist ahead of them. It was a man, trudging through the mud, holding a flaming torch in one hand and a large knife in the other. He had seen them and was moving straight toward them. Was it he that was responsible for trapping them?

Eladria watched helplessly as the man approached. She felt a pang of dread as she saw that his large build, reddish-brown skin and rough, hard-set features were unmistakably those of a Ha'shon. He was an older man, perhaps in his early to mid-sixties. His posture was impeccable and he walked with a graceful, purposeful gait. His face was framed by a short beard and long, greying hair that fell down over his shoulders. Although he had the tattoos of the Ha'shon military down his face, he wasn't dressed in military attire, instead wearing a long charcoal overcoat, a brown tunic and dark trousers and boots.

The man remained silent as he neared them. His face was calm and expressionless, so Eladria found it impossible to discern his intent. He stepped toward Eladria and raised his knife. In that moment Eladria was certain the man was going to kill her. He'd ensnared them and was now moving in for the kill...

But a noise disturbed the Ha'shon and he turned his head, listening intently. Without a word he then swiftly retreated, darting back through the marshland and disappearing into the mist. Eladria was initially relieved, until she realized that something had obviously frightened him off. The question was what?

She didn't have to wait long for an answer. Something was stirring amid the swamp. Much to Eladria's horror, a massive eight-legged creature emerged through the mist and bounded toward them. The creature's elongated body trailed through the mud as it scuttled through the marsh. Its head was studded with three large red eyes and dominated by a set of razor-sharp jaws.

The beast's segmented grey body was heavily armored with a prickly exoskeleton and as it moved it emitted sparks of electrical charge.

Eladria recognized the creature as an arachoid. She'd seen pictures of them and that alone had been enough to terrify her. She'd never dreamt she'd ever have the misfortune of encountering one of these electrical predators in the flesh. As she recalled, arachoids were solitary creatures that lived in the depths of the jungles and marshlands. They spun invisible electrical webs and lay in wait as their unwitting prey were ensnared.

Eladria struggled to escape the web, but each movement was painful and soon she could no longer feel her body. The arachoid was quickly upon them. Eladria was nearest, so its attention was upon her. It stretched out its long, multi-jointed front legs and took hold of her, dislodging her from the web and reeling her toward itself.

She cried in terror as she tried to break free of its grip, but the creature was too strong. It bound her tightly and administered an electrical shock that coursed through her body. The shock was enough to cause unconsciousness. Everything blacked out...

Eladria drifted in and out of consciousness over a span of time that was impossible to discern. In the brief moments in which lucidity returned, she was aware of being carried by the creature as it scurried through the marshland. Her mind and senses were obscured by heaviness and beset by a dull, throbbing ache, making it difficult to focus her attention. As the creature moved, sparks of electricity surged from its body, again rendering her unconscious.

When Eladria gradually awoke, she felt drowsy and disorientated, as though she'd been hibernating for months.

She found herself encased in some kind of cocoon, suspended from the ceiling of a darkened cave. She tried to break free, but was unable to move a muscle. The cocoon was woven around her chest and abdomen and her arms were tightly bound by her sides. Only her head and lower legs were free of the casing.

The cave was strewn with webbing and numerous other cocoons hung from the ceiling and walls, but most were empty. She looked around in search of her companions. There was no sign of them. She called their names but there was no response.

Again she tried to move her arms, but she was tightly constricted and could barely feel her body. Feeling helpless and defeated, she felt a tear trickling down her face. It couldn't end like this, could it? She was hung up like a piece of meat in a larder, soon to be devoured by an arachoid and there was nothing she could do.

In spite of all the terrible things that had happened to her, until now there had always been a seed of hope. At times that hope had been but a distant flicker, like the farthest star in the infinite blackness of the night sky. But it had been there nonetheless, and she'd been able to hold her attention there and trust that this one spark of light would in time enable her to overcome the oppressive darkness. Only this time there was no hope. There were no stars in the sky; it was empty, dark and dead, and she knew that very soon she too would be dead.

Eladria didn't know what, if anything, lay beyond death. She was unsure if she believed in an afterlife. The insanity of both the Ha'shon and the True Way had left a bitter taste in her mouth when it came to religious doctrine.

Yet during her childhood she had, for a time, received tuition from a man claiming to be a master of the Old Way. The Old Way comprised the spiritual teachings as taught long ago, before the Ha'shon and True Way factions had emerged, each claiming the monopoly on truth. It was said that the Old Way was brought to Tahnadra in a time of darkness by the space-faring Lasan. For several generations they ruled the planet in benevolence from the mystical land of Atukaare, before again returning to the stars.

The essence of their teaching was rooted in harmony, balance and regard for the whole. The Old Way taught a mystical understanding of life that transcended mere physical observation. According to its precepts, the body, far from being the entirety of one's being, was merely the instrument of a non-localized source. It was but a temporary container for an essence that remained formless and untouched by the ravages of time.

The old man that had instructed Eladria in the basics of Old Way mysticism had been kind and patient, although Eladria had found his teachings difficult to fathom. But the lessons had nonetheless planted a seed in her consciousness. It was funny that now, in her most desperate hour, her thoughts returned to those lessons. Perhaps it was because they offered her the glimmer of hope that she needed, the possibility that her consciousness would survive the death of her body and that maybe she would be reunited with her father again in some other dimension. Her instructor had been adamant that the world of the senses was but one among countless dimensions of reality. He had told her that one's true essence, when freed from the mortal shell, was free to traverse these dimensions as easily as one could leaf through the pages of a book.

Eladria had now conceded that her death was inevitable. She hoped that it would be painless, though she somehow doubted it. Her main regret was that she was unable to help her friends. She assumed they were somewhere nearby and were also going to end up on the arachoid's menu.

She also wished that she'd been able to help her world. She wondered what would happen now. Without anyone to prevent it, would it indeed be torn apart by the breaches or invaded by the Shadow Lords as the Others warned? Perhaps it was just as well she wouldn't be here to find out.

It was at her moment of deepest despair she realized that she had perhaps been wrong to give up. In spite of the bleakness of her predicament, there was a single star of hope shining amid the dark.

At first she wondered if it was her imagination, but there literally was a light shining in the darkness. It came from the passageway that led into this grim larder. It was distant at first, but it soon grew brighter. Eladria's heart skipped a beat as she saw a figure stepping out of the corridor and entering the cave.

It was a man brandishing a fire torch. Eladria immediately recognized him. It was the Ha'shon that had approached her in the swamp when she was ensnared in the web.

The man looked around the chamber and soon spotted Eladria, the only incarcerated specimen still alive. "Are you unharmed?" he asked, looking up to where she hung suspended from the ceiling.

"I think so," Eladria answered, finding it difficult to speak due to the constriction on her chest. "But I can't move. And I don't know where my friends are."

"There are dozens of these chambers," the Ha'shon answered, his voice deep and calm. "Come, I will get you down from there. I don't know where the creature is right now, but these arachoids are renowned for their sharp hearing, so we must keep as quiet as possible."

Although Eladria wanted to gracefully accept his help, her distrust of the Ha'shon was so pronounced that she couldn't help but question his motivation. Was this just another bounty hunter, intent on capturing and handing her over to the Ha'shon authorities? "Why are you risking your life to help me?" she asked.

"Because I am," the man said evenly. "I was watching from a distance when you stumbled into the creature's trap. I could not let harm come to you, so I intervened."

"Who are you?" Eladria asked suspiciously.

"There will be time to discuss that later. For now, you must keep quiet and I will get you down from there."

The man placed his fire torch upon the ground and drew his blade, a hefty ceremonial dagger studded with gemstones. He gathered some rocks and a pile of the white webbing and used it as a step to reach Eladria. Once within reach, he carefully plunged his knife into the cocoon encasing her. Eladria was concerned that he might stab her, but he was skilled in his use of the blade and in very little time had managed to cut the webbing away from her body.

The moment he freed her from the cocoon, they both tumbled to the ground. The man, who was surprisingly limber for his age, quickly got to his feet and reached down to help her up.

"Thank you," she said as she got to her feet and looked into his intense dark eyes.

"We must get out of here now," the man said.

Eladria shook her head. "I have to find my friends. I won't leave without them," she declared.

"Very well. I came across a number of passageways and chambers as I made my way through the creature's nest. I know where we might find them."

The Ha'shon picked up his torch and led Eladria out of the web-filled cave, into a labyrinth of winding, rounded tunnels. As they wandered along the tunnel, the Ha'shon kept his dagger drawn and Eladria likewise reached for her own blade. She didn't know where the arachoid was, but it was bound to be here somewhere. Even the slightest noise made her jump.

Moving through its lair, they came across different compartments strewn with webbing, with cocoons suspended from the walls and ceilings, containing various creatures that had stumbled into the arachoid's snare. Most of the creatures were long-dead and some were in a clear state of decay.

It was a nauseating task as they searched each compartment for Eladria's missing friends. She eventually found them in a single compartment, both encased in cocoons and suspended from the ceiling as she had been. They were alive, conscious and understandably relieved to see her.

"I so happy you here," Janak cried in delight, his eyes welling with tears. "I thought I was spider food!"

"Keep quiet," Eladria said as the Ha'shon set to work freeing them.

"Who's he?" Zinn asked suspiciously, as he climbed up and set to work freeing her from the cocoon.

"He Ha'shon," Janak spat angrily, his jubilation of only seconds ago supplanted by a hateful distrust. "Ha'shon *not* to be trusted!"

"He's our only chance of getting out of here," Eladria hushed him. She was also eager to know more about this man. He wasn't at all like the other Ha'shon she'd encountered, but her curiosity would have to wait.

Eladria caught Zinn as she fell from the ceiling, successfully freed from the dangling cocoon. Eladria's body was still weak from the electrical discharge of the arachoid, and she was unable to bear Zinn's weight. Both collapsed on the ground and landed amid a tangled heap of webbing. As they got up, their Ha'shon rescuer successfully freed Janak, who momentarily seemed to forget his innate hatred of Ha'shon as he beamed in relief.

Now they were all free, it was time to leave this place, as quickly as possible. They hurried down the web-filled corridors. The Ha'shon led the way, his torch in one hand and dagger in the other. Eladria was filled with dread at the prospect of again encountering the arachoid.

Her heart leapt with delight as she saw what looked like the exit just a little way ahead of them. The tunnel narrowed, growing steeper as a shaft of daylight shone through the opening. They'd nearly made it; they were just a few steps away from freedom.

But before they could reach the exit, they were forced to stop in their tracks. The arachoid appeared silhouetted in the exit. It had left its nest unattended, only to return to find its prey on the verge of escaping. The creature came bounding toward them. Bursts of electrical charge lit up the tunnel as it launched its attack. Eladria froze in terror. She didn't know what to do. The only place to run was behind them, back into the creature's cavernous nest—and that was the last place she wanted to be. They had to somehow get past the creature and escape to the surface.

Fortunately, the Ha'shon knew how to respond. Instead of running from the arachoid as it charged at them, he moved toward it and waved his fire torch at it. The arachoid stopped, startled by the fire, stunned into a motionless stupor.

Both Eladria and the Ha'shon had their knives drawn, but it would be impossible to defeat a creature of its size with two small blades.

Zinn, however, had a plan of her own. She'd evidently recovered enough energy to change form, for she assumed the guise of a large rhastopod, a towering elephantine mammal with rough, brown skin and three horns. Eladria backed off, while the Ha'shon looked round in surprise. Both he and Janak stepped aside, allowing the rhastopod to charge past them and lunge at the startled arachoid.

The two creatures collided and the arachoid was thrown to the ground, howling loudly, its legs flailing as it tried to get up. The rhastopod kept it pinned to the ground with its horns.

Seizing their opportunity to escape, Eladria, Janak and their Ha'shon rescuer ran toward the exit, slipping past the two creatures locked in desperate struggle. As a rhastopod, Zinn clearly had the greater strength, but the arachoid was a formidable opponent and was unleashing bursts of electric charge, causing Zinn to buckle. Eladria was concerned for her friend and prayed that she would escape unharmed.

They exited the underground lair and stepped into the surrounding swampland. Now all that remained was for Zinn to join them. Eladria called to her, and held her breath in anticipation.

Nothing happened. They could still hear the sound of the struggle: the arachoid's hideous shrieking and the blasts of electricity. Eladria looked at Janak helplessly, wishing there was something they could do to help her.

Come on, Zinn, she pleaded inwardly.

The sound of the scuffle soon abated and Eladria waited anxiously, staring at the entrance to the nest. More than anything in the world, she wanted to see the mighty rhastopod emerge from the ground victorious. But it wasn't the rhastopod that appeared: it was a small bird, shooting out of the nest and into the sky above them. Eladria knew it was Zinn.

She was closely followed by the arachoid, which scrambled out of its lair and assumed an attack posture, apparently undeterred by the struggle.

Realizing that her knife was probably useless, Eladria grabbed the nearest object, a small log lying upon the ground, and she lifted it up with a heave, ready to use it to repel the attacking creature.

The Ha'shon advanced toward the arachoid, brandishing his fire torch. The arachoid clearly hated fire, for it backed off with each advance the Ha'shon made. Eladria used this opportunity to take the offensive. She lunged forward and threw the log at the creature. Even though she had taken aim with all her might, the branch simply bounced off the beast with impunity.

"Your torch," Eladria called to the Ha'shon. "Throw your torch at it!"

"No," the man shook his head. "We just need to repel it. There's no need to inflict harm."

"You must be the only one of your kind that wouldn't jump at the chance to inflict harm," Eladria snapped back, baffled by his inexplicable pacifism.

She knew what needed to be done. There was no way they could escape the creature. The moment they turned to run, it would follow them. Surging with adrenaline and infused with the indefatigable will to live, she grabbed to torch from the Ha'shon and flung it at the creature. The creature roared and hissed as flaming torch struck its head and, with a yell of terror, it retreated into the underground lair.

Eladria turned to the Ha'shon defiantly. He seemed aggrieved by her intervention, but she didn't care. She'd done what she needed to do. Now they had the opportunity to escape.

Zinn had now rejoined them in human form. Eladria motioned for her and Janak to run. It didn't matter where; they just needed to flee the vicinity. But the Ha'shon abruptly stopped her, grabbing hold of her arm and glowering at her. "You must follow me, or you'll end up trapped in another of its snares," he warned. "I know this place. I know the safest routes. Follow my steps carefully and do not stray from them."

Eladria agreed and they immediately set upon their way. As they retreated from the arachoid lair, wary of a potential counter-attack, they followed the Ha'shon without deviation.

Eladria just hoped they hadn't been rescued from one trap only to be led into another…

Chapter 14

Van'garat

"Stop!" Eladria called.

They had been striding through the swamp, eager to get as far from the arachoid nest as they could. Their Ha'shon rescuer had led the way, his sense of direction beyond anything Eladria had ever seen. He was almost like a wild creature, relying upon instinct and intuition to guide him. But although he had saved their lives, she still harbored a deep and unshakable distrust of his people.

As they came to a halt beneath a spiky-limbed borast tree, all eyes turned to the Ha'shon, who looked at the princess, his eyebrow raised quizzically.

"Before we go a step further, I want to know exactly who you are," she declared, eying him warily. She was reasonably certain that they were now at a safe distance from the arachoid and she was determined to unravel the mystery of their Ha'shon benefactor.

"Very well," the man spoke calmly, his voice deep and placid. "My name is Van'garat."

"Tell me about yourself, Van'garat," Eladria said, her tone of voice a little more challenging than she'd intended.

Before he could respond, Janak stepped forward and interjected. "Janak warn you, not listen to anything he say. Ha'shon not to be trusted, even this one! Do not be fooled because he rescue us. He have hidden motives, of that you can be sure."

The Ha'shon looked round. "Your suspicion is certainly understandable, my little friend."

"Who you call little?" Janak exploded, bounding toward Van'garat, fists clenched.

Eladria pulled him back and tried to defuse the situation. "If we're to go anywhere with you, you first need to allay our suspicions," she said to the Ha'shon. "What are you doing here? Where did you come from and why did you risk your life to rescue us from that creature?"

Van'garat sat down upon a mound of stone, his face creasing with a light smile. Although she was reasonably certain he was unlikely to turn violent, Eladria found it difficult to read his intent. He was utterly unlike any Ha'shon she had ever encountered. He seemed calm and even-minded, yet she detected an element of sadness and unease about him. It wasn't overt, but it was there nevertheless, hidden just beneath the surface of his stoic exterior.

"To answer your first question, I live around these parts," the Ha'shon began.

Eladria narrowed her eyes. "You live here? In the jungle—alone?"

"Well, the jungle is filled with life, so I never consider myself truly alone. But no, there are no others with me. I live and travel in solitude.'

"Why?" Eladria pressed.

"Ah, you wish to hear my story," Van'garat remarked, his tone mildly sardonic. "I have little use for stories, my young friend, and the past is something I find is generally best forgotten."

"Maybe so," Eladria said. "But I'm not going another step with you until I know exactly who you are and what you're doing out here alone."

There was a lingering silence. The princess and the Ha'shon locked eyes. Again Eladria found it impossible to discern what the man was thinking. He exuded an air of detachment and seemed unperturbed by her insistent questioning, as though he wasn't taking it quite seriously.

"Very well," Van'garat began with a hint of reluctance. "A personal history lesson, make of it what you will. I was born the third child of a noble family in Esta'bak, the capital of the Ha'shon empire."

There was a pause. Eladria and the others were silent as they waited for him to continue. "Although I was provided with every-thing a child could want, it was not a happy childhood. After many years of bickering and in-fighting, my family was torn apart over territory disputes and escalating socio-political conflict. My parents separated and I remained with my father and younger brother. Realizing from an early age that I had no aptitude for politics and little interest in his vast estate, my father had but one ambition for me. He arranged for me to join the military the moment I was of age. There I would climb the ranks and become an officer as his father had been. Seeing that I had little choice in the matter, I did as he desired."

"You were in the military?" Zinn asked.

"For a time," Van'garat answered, indicating the tattoos down his face.

This was almost too much for Janak. "I tell you he not to be trusted," he declared angrily. "He just another killer, like all other Ha'shon! How I know was not him that invade my home and kill my family?"

Eladria turned to the irate thief. "Janak, calm down. Let him speak."

Van'garat nodded in appreciation. "As I was saying, I did join the military, but it didn't take me long to realize that it was not something to which I was suited. I found that, unlike my comrades, I had no taste for killing and no appetite for violence. For a time I tried to fit in, to be like the others and to do what was expected of me, but ultimately the price was too high and the taste too bitter. So I left the military and, in so doing, I brought dishonor to my father and the rest of my family. I never saw any of them again."

Eladria sat down on a nearby log as she listened.

"Prior to my experiences in the military, I'd spent my youth in a haze of luxury and excess," Van'garat admitted. "I wanted for nothing and yet through it all, a nagging discontent gnawed at my soul. No matter what I did or how much I had or attained, I could never find peace. Following my dishonorable discharge from service, I had nothing. My wealth was stripped from me and I had nowhere to go and nothing to do. I decided that, more than anything else, I had to be true to myself. Deploring violence and yearning for peace and solitude, I knew I wanted to know more about the nature of existence and what we were meant to do with that existence."

"So what did you do?" Eladria asked.

"I figured the only way to find the answers was to renounce the world and join the priesthood. Surely if I was to find answers anywhere, it would be there. But this was not the case. I found the same ignorance and corruption in the priesthood that was so pervasive in the military."

"In what way?"

"I saw that our religious institutions had distorted the ancient teachings simply to legitimize my people's militaristic thirst for conquest. It became clear to me that our religion was merely an instrument to justify our desire to conquer and subjugate, to make ourselves right and the rest of the world wrong."

"You condemn your own people?" Janak asked, his face still set in an expression of distrust and contempt.

"Yes, I condemn them, as I would condemn any that conduct themselves in such a manner," Van'garat said, looking up at him, then returning his gaze to the ground. "At the root of it is a warped need to bolster themselves by trampling the rest of civilization to the ground. I found the teachings empty and hollow, raped of their holiness and stripped of all meaning. All that was left were deadening conceptualizations that didn't even make sense to a rational mind. Yet my people continue to lap them up, for they provide self-validation and purpose. Hungry minds and empty hearts devouring deadened lies, like carrion birds stripping carcasses of every last morsel of flesh."

Eladria watched him, dumbfounded. She had never expected

a Ha'shon to deliver such a blistering indictment of his own people.

Van'garat smiled, a sad and faraway look upon his face as he continued. "It was strangely liberating to be able to see through the lies and delusions that have kept countless generations perpetuating the same cycles of violence. I could not be a part of it. I left the priesthood and retreated from the world, no longer wanting to among what is so laughably called the 'civilized'. I entered a self-imposed exile here, in this vast untamed wilderness. Here I have been for many years and here I began to fulfill my deep yearning to understand life. Here I began to awaken."

"What do you mean?" asked Zinn, watching him with rapt attention.

"I encountered an old hermit living in the forest," Van'garat explained. He got up and began pacing slowly back and forth, hands clasped behind his back as he continued. "His name was Ustabak and he was the most remarkable man I'd ever met. Quite how old he was I never knew, but he possessed an unfathomable power within him. He lived in total balance and alignment with life. He was, I learned, one of the last remaining adepts of Ko Tra Pah."

"Ko Tra *what?*" Janak asked, narrowing his eyes suspiciously.

"Ko Tra Pah," Van'garat answered. "It's an ancient system of martial arts and energy mastery as practiced by masters of the Old Way. I wanted to know everything about it, to learn all that he knew. He accepted me as his disciple and we lived together for many years, he as my master and I as his student."

"What did he teach you?" Eladria asked.

"A great many things," Van'garat stopped and looked at her, his eyes twinkling. "Master Ustabak began instructing me in mastery of the physical body, teaching me movements, poses and breathing techniques that enabled me to strengthen, attune and refine my physical form. I was trained in the art of meditation, which freed me from the bondage of mind and thoughts. He later taught me to consciously connect with the primordial essence. Unfettered by the prison of mind and unconstrained by the flesh, I developed and honed certain abilities."

"What kind of abilities?"

"Some of the many benefits of Ko Tra Pah include razor-sharp intuition, extrasensory perception, and the limited ability to direct energy and manipulate matter."

"So what happened to this Master of yours? You said you live alone now."

A sadness passed over the Ha'shon's face and he lowered his head. "My Master was killed by a group of True Way raiders," he answered softly. "That was over a decade ago. I remained in the forest and have lived alone since that time."

Eladria got the impression that there was more to this story, that there was something he wasn't willing to share with them. She wasn't at all sure what to make of this most unusual of Ha'shon. "Let's suppose I believe that you turned your back on your people and that you live alone in the jungle," she said. "Why did you risk your life to save us? It was one thing to find us in the arachoid's web and try to free us, but you risked your life to enter its lair and save us. Why did you do that when we're complete strangers to you?"

Janak stepped forward. "I know one thing," he said. "He may claim to be different, but all Ha'shon are same. All they care about is conquest, glory and power. Is in their blood! And in spite of what he say, I certain this is all some kind of Ha'shon trick!"

"I'm sorry you feel that way," Van'garat responded. "I understand your distrust of my people, because I share it. Beyond the blood that runs through my veins, I have nothing in common with my people and no allegiance to them. I have renounced them and, on that, you will simply have to take my word."

"Word of Ha'shon means nothing," Janak shook his head. His joy at being rescued had been short-lived indeed, but Eladria understood his suspicion and his hesitancy to trust the stranger.

"You must have had some motive for risking your life to save us," Eladria insisted.

"There are always motives, my young friend," Van'garat smiled. "Everything in this world has its motive and that motive is *life*. I do what I do because I am so directed by life. I had to save you because I knew it was my purpose to save you. You are more important than you could possibly imagine, young Princess."

"How do you know who I am?" Eladria gasped. She had been careful not to divulge her identity.

"I told you about my intuition and my ability to see things that others cannot," Van'garat said. "I foresaw your coming in a vision. I knew that a princess would fall from the sky, seeking escape and finding herself embroiled in a quest to save the world, wrestling with forces beyond her comprehension."

"What do you mean?" Eladria asked, feeling the color drain from her face.

"You have a higher purpose to fulfill. I saved you from certain death in order that you might fulfill your part in the great unfolding. I know of your quest and I ask that you allow me to accompany you on your journey, for I believe I can help you."

"Janak will not travel with Ha'shon," Janak exclaimed angrily.

"You must move beyond your prejudice, my friend," Van'garat responded. "Do not allow it to distort your view of the world and of others. Know me as I am, not as you think me to be." He turned to Eladria. "I ask that I be allowed to join your quest, because I believe that you need me."

"Why would I need you?" she asked.

Van'garat lifted his hand to his chest and took a slight bow. "Because I can guide and direct you. My powers may be of help to you and it is my hope that I can teach you to develop and hone your own such abilities." There was a moment of silence before he continued. "I'm offering to join you not out of personal desire, but because I've been directed by the tides of fate to join your expedition. And whenever I feel the promptings of fate, I invariably comply."

Eladria considered this for a moment. Although, like Janak, she harbored a deep distrust of all Ha'shon, she was nevertheless inclined to believe Van'garat. There was something inexplicably different about him. She didn't entirely understand him, but they needed all the help they could get, and if he knew as much as he claimed, his insight and guidance might prove invaluable.

She decided to speak with Zinn and Janak in private before she accepted Van'garat's offer. He was satisfied with this and allowed them some time to confer in private as he wandered off into the misty swamp.

Janak was of course vehemently opposed to allowing the Ha'shon to join them, whereas Zinn was uncertain but not averse to the possibility. Like Eladria, she readily admitted that they needed as much help as they could get and had a hunch that Van'garat might be of significant aid to them. Eladria overruled Janak and called Van'garat back.

"Although we still have some concerns, we've decided to accept your request to join us and would be grateful of any help you can offer," she told him. Zinn stood by her side, while Janak quietly fumed several paces away.

"I appreciate your trust in me," Van'garat said with a gracious nod.

"So what do you know of our quest?" Eladria asked.

"I know that you must travel to a dark land; a place of great evil, eclipsed by a veil of darkness."

"You know of Drantak?"

"Only from what I have seen in my visions. In my mind's eye, I perceived a dark force manipulating susceptible minds and holding innocent people against their will, forcing them to create distortions in the very laws of the universe. I saw a tear between realms—a rip in the fabric of the universe—and a force of evil desperately trying to pass through the void, into this world."

"That's more or less what I was told," Eladria said, astonished by just how much the mysterious hermit appeared to know. "The Others, the beings that communicated with me, told me that I have to go to Drantak, that only I can stop what's happening there."

"That's correct. You started it, and only you can end it."

"What do you mean, *I started it?*"

"I can't say for certain. It's just an impression I get, a feeling that somehow, in some unknown way, it is you that has caused this entire situation."

"That's impossible," Eladria exclaimed. "I've done nothing. I've spent my whole life in the royal palace, in seclusion from the rest of the world. How can you possibly say that I'm responsible for what's happened?"

"It's not yet clear to me," the Ha'shon said. "I've only been able to piece together fragments of my visions. The answers, I'm certain, will be revealed in due course. For now, may I suggest that we resume our journey out of here with haste. The sooner we leave this swamp, the less likely we'll be to encounter another arachoid."

Eladria concurred and they set on their way again, Van'garat briskly leading them through the swamp, displaying an impressive degree of agility for a man of his years. Eladria was relieved that she now had someone to guide her, even if he was an enigma—a renegade Ha'shon living as a hermit, seemingly in possession of a curious extrasensory vision. Of course, it was wholly possible that he was deceiving them and was leading them into some kind of trap, but she tried to push such a thought from her mind.

As they plodded through the swamp, Eladria walked alongside Zinn and a huffing Janak, who was still aggrieved that his concerns had been waived.

Her mind kept returning to Van'garat's inexplicable assertion that somehow *she* was responsible for all that was happening.

Such a notion seemed insane, yet she found it hard to dismiss his words.

What if he was right? What if she had inadvertently initiated this entire chain of events? What if this whole sorry nightmare was somehow her doing?

Chapter 15

Revelation

By the third day, the swamp was but a distant memory. The travelers found themselves in a region of hills and valleys thick with jungle brush and arduous to traverse. Exotic plants surrounded them in bursts of red, yellow and blue, while the breeze that rustled through the trees sent a stream of pink and white blossom spiraling down like snowflakes, carpeting the jungle floor.

The jungle was vibrant and filled with life. There were plentiful birds, snakes, lizards and occasionally monkeys, wildcats, rhastopods and markots; twin-tusked, long-haired mammals that were thankfully placid by nature. But the most prevalent creatures were the insects, for there was a multitude of bugs: flying, crawling, buzzing and all too often biting and stinging.

Since leaving the swamp their journey had been uneventful. Only once did they encounter an aircraft passing overhead. At Eladria's behest, they hid in the undergrowth until it was gone. She couldn't tell whether or not it was a Ha'shon craft, but was unwilling to take any risks.

A lingering quietude had settled over the jungle. The last storm had occurred back in Niyastan and although there had been nothing of that magnitude since, there were, as Van'garat described them, a number of small 'hiccups'. The sky would suddenly crackle with blue lightning and a ribbon of light would appear high above the jungle. But each incident was short-lived and after a few moments would settle, leaving behind nothing more than a static tingle in the air.

"These are but the symptoms of a great sickness," Van'garat had remarked after one such distortion. "The fabric of reality is being warped, distorted and stretched. The barriers between worlds are deliberately being smashed." But he didn't elaborate further. It was rare that he explained his cryptic words. Eladria repeatedly tried to coax more out of him, with little success. She was curious as to how he was privy to such knowledge. Was it possible that he was somehow in communication with the Others? She once asked him this, but his response was vague and noncommittal.

In spite of Van'garat's enigmatic nature and his unwillingness to divulge all that he appeared to know, tensions between the travelers diminished as they journeyed onwards. In spite of his reticence to be forthcoming and his tendency to keep to himself, Eladria found herself becoming somewhat fond of the renegade Ha'shon. Zinn also appeared to be more relaxed in his presence.

Janak was more hesitant to accept Van'garat and continued to hold him responsible for the crimes of his people. In his bitter hostility and blatant prejudice, Eladria saw some of her own darker qualities mirrored back at her, and it wasn't something that she liked. She realized that she too carried a raging anger toward the Ha'shon for murdering her father and enslaving her world. She was aware of a deep and lingering hatred within her, wrapped around her heart like a serpent coiled in a suffocating death-grip. Van'garat was so unlike his people in all but appearance that it was easy to deflect that hostility from him, but she was still aware of it burning within her. She didn't like the feeling, but no matter how hard she tried, she couldn't shift it.

That night they sat around the campfire. They had finished their evening meal, which had again been prepared by Janak. He was a surprisingly able chef and could make reasonably palatable dishes using only the simplest of ingredients appropriated along their jungle trek. Eladria sat staring into the flames, her mind on the future and the immensity of the task before her.

Van'garat approached her and asked to speak to her. "There is something I must tell you," he said enigmatically.

"What?" Eladria looked up at him in surprise.

"Perhaps you would prefer to hear what I have to say in private," he suggested.

She shook her head. "No. If you have something to say, you can say it in front of Zinn and Janak. There are no secrets between us."

"Very well then," he said, sitting down upon the log beside her. "It is about your mother."

"My mother?"

Van'garat nodded. "As I told you, some time prior to our meeting in the swamp, I experienced a series of visions. They were disjointed and fragmented, but I clearly saw the forbidden land of Drantak. I saw images and faces, labyrinthine corridors and a magnificent crystal buried in the heart of the land. And I saw a group of prisoners, people being held there against their will."

There was a pause before he continued. "Among them was your mother."

Eladria was stunned. It took her a moment to formulate a response. "My mother is dead," she exclaimed. "She disappeared years ago, when I was just a child."

"You maybe assumed that she was dead," Van'garat offered. "But did you ever find her body?"

Eladria shook her head slowly, remaining silent.

"That's because she is still alive," Van'garat said as he looked into her widened eyes. "From what I saw and from what I deduced, she was taken to Drantak, where she is being held against her will. And more than that, unless I am very much mistaken, she was instrumental in creating the very breaches that now threaten to destroy this world."

"That's impossible," Eladria growled. "My mother would never do anything to endanger this world."

Van'garat lowered his head. "I did not mean to suggest otherwise," he said. "But she has been used by the dark forces against her will, as an instrument of potential annihilation. You probably never knew this, but I believe your mother has certain powers and abilities that make her a crucial part of this experiment."

"If what you say is true, then why didn't the Others tell me this when they had the chance?"

"I'm sure they had their reasons. Perhaps they did not wish to overwhelm you. But I felt it necessary that you know. Perhaps now you can see how you are linked with what is happening at Drantak and why, above all else, you *must* go there and do whatever you can to end the experiment. Only then can you rescue your mother and save this world."

Eladria locked eyes with him, trying to ascertain the truth of his words. She could see no trace of deception in his dark eyes, simply an earnestness coupled with a jaded weariness. "But it doesn't make sense! What use would they have with my *mother*, of all people?" she asked. "How could she have had anything to do with this experiment, with these dimensional breaches?"

"I don't possess all the answers," he admitted. "All I can tell you is what I saw. Your mother is not alone. A number of others have been abducted and taken to Drantak over the years, all of them possessing unique abilities that have been exploited by the dark forces at work there."

Eladria got up from where she sat and began pacing. There was silence as Zinn and Janak looked on anxiously.

After a time, Eladria broke the uneasy silence. "Am I expected just to take your word for all this?" she asked.

"You can take my word for it, or you can wait and find out for yourself, as you inevitably will," the Ha'shon answered.

"I warn you before, Princess," Janak interjected. "You not believe a word he tells you. He trying to confuse and deceive you..."

"Janak, I think it's best that we stay out of this," Zinn advised in a hushed voice.

"Fine, but not say I not warn you," the thief retorted with a measure of petulance.

Eladria stopped and looked down at Van'garat, who remained seated by the campfire. "I believe that you're no ordinary Ha'shon," she began. "I'm even inclined to believe that you do have some kind of extrasensory vision or insight. But what you've just told me is hard for me to accept..."

"I can understand that," the Ha'shon nodded.

Eladria felt the need of some space to herself. She picked up one of the flaming torches they'd lit around the campfire and wandered into the forest, a very old wound having suddenly been reopened within her. Zinn followed, eager to be with her princess at this difficult time.

Eladria came to a stop by a small stream. The water glistened, reflecting sparkles of moonlight streaming through the trees above. Zinn came to a halt beside her, but said nothing, allowing the princess to speak first.

"I can't help but wonder," Eladria began. "What if it's true? What if she *is* alive...if she really was captured all those years ago and is being held at Drantak?"

"You think it's really possible?" Zinn asked.

Eladria stood staring vacantly into the stream as she held the fire torch aloft, the flame reflected in the water as an orangey-yellow glow. "I believe anything's possible," she answered. "We never did find out what happened to her when she disappeared on that trip to Nukarean province, did we? Father spent years searching the planet, but there had to have been places he overlooked. Drantak was likely one of them. After all, it's just a barren wasteland, so I doubt he'd have sent a search and rescue team there."

"Then you think she could still be alive?"

"Deep inside I always believed that she was still alive and that someday, somehow, she'd come back to us. I know Father eventually gave up hope and came to accept that she was dead, but I never did. Not truly. Maybe I just couldn't. Maybe I just wasn't ready to let her go."

"We still don't know much about Van'garat," Zinn cautioned. "It could be that he's just told you what you wanted to hear. Perhaps he knew about your mother's disappearance and is using it as a way to manipulate you."

"Manipulate me into doing what?" Eladria shrugged.

"Into going to Drantak?" Zinn suggested.

"But I'd already decided that was where I was going and he knew that," she said, pausing for a moment. "No, the more I think about it, the more I'm inclined to believe him. Maybe it's just wishful thinking on my part, but if there's any chance that he's correct, that my mother's alive and is being held against her will at Drantak, then I can't ignore that. Now more than ever, I have to find a way there, to stop what's happening and to find out the truth."

"I suppose that is the only way you'll ever know for certain," Zinn said.

"You're right." Eladria paused for a moment. "Zinn, you go back to the campsite. I need some time to myself, to work this out in my head."

Zinn nodded reluctantly and took her leave of the princess. Eladria sat down on a large rock by the stream and placed the torch in the ground beside her. She gazed into the water as it flowed over the stones and boulders in an unending rhythmic dance, but her mind was elsewhere.

She couldn't stop thinking about her mother. She had only been seven years old when Queen Anarah had disappeared. She could vaguely recall her mother leaving the palace to attend a conference on the planet. As the ruling monarchs of Tahnadra, the lives of her parents had been busy ones and she was accustomed to being parted from either or both of them for days or weeks at a time. At this tender age, Eladria hadn't been privy to the details, but she was aware that her mother had been gone far longer than usual and she was acutely aware of the distress her father was in. There had been an atmosphere of despair hanging over the palace, although Zinn had tried her best to keep the young princess sheltered from it.

Eladria had grown increasingly despondent and she cried herself to sleep every night for weeks. Her father explained that her mother had been 'detained' and promised that she would return soon. She'd believed him and, upon waking each morning, she prayed that this would be the day her mother would return, that she'd enter her chamber and run over to embrace the little girl with warmth, tears and a promise that she'd never leave her like that again.

But that never happened. One day, her father sat her down and explained that her mother had been lost, that they'd looked everywhere for her but couldn't find her—and that, in all likelihood, she wouldn't be coming back. Part of Eladria died that day. Her happy, carefree childhood became a dark and lonely one, scarred by a heartache that would linger for the rest of her childhood and adolescence.

In spite of her father's tireless attempts to scour the planet in search of her, he'd been unable to find any trace of Queen Anarah. It was strange that no one had ever claimed responsibility for her capture. There was apparently no motive and no reason for her disappearance. What kept Eladria going was the fact they never found a body. That was what fostered the thin sliver of hope that her mother was still alive and would someday return to her.

Eladria took a sharp inhale of breath and wiped away her tears. There was nothing she could do for her father now, but there was a chance that her mother was still alive and she vowed that she would do everything in her power to find her. If that meant travelling all the way to Drantak and fighting an as-yet unknown enemy, then she would gladly do so.

Before the torch burned out, Eladria made her way back to the camp, where everyone had already settled down for the night. Janak and Van'garat lay some distance from each other around the campfire, while Zinn was waiting for Eladria's return. Satisfied that she had safely found her way back, Zinn changed into a large furry matah-mouse and crawled up the limb of a lacast tree. There she sat upon an outstretched branch and kept watch over her comrades.

Eladria lay down upon a bed of leaves and endeavored to make herself as comfortable as she could. But she found it difficult to sleep, for the ground was cold, hard and uncomfortable. As she tossed and turned for what felt like hours, she was unable to slow down her frenzied mind. She found herself endlessly pondering her predicament, anticipating what might lie ahead and whether it was possible she would be reunited with her mother. The thought that she might not have lost her family altogether helped allay the terror of whatever dark forces were waiting for her in the so-called forbidden land.

She turned on her side and let out a weary sigh, frustrated by her inability to sleep. Judging by the snoring that came from his vicinity, Janak was fast asleep and had been for some time. She was unsure about Van'garat, who hadn't made a sound the entire night.

Her restlessness was exacerbated by an ominous feeling that something was about to happen. The air was heavy and tingled with a faint electrical charge. She'd experienced this before prior to the breaches, which made her suspect it was a precursor to another impending storm.

She was right. It wasn't long before she became aware of a bright flash of light from above. Looking up, she saw the sky tearing open as a bluish-white ribbon of light devoured the black void, crackling like electricity, sending fingers of lightning spiraling in every direction. A peal of thunder echoed around them, as the electrical storm illuminated the jungle in a pale bluish light.

Janak and Van'garat staggered to their feet, staring up in bleary-eyed bewilderment. Zinn scurried down from her perch and resumed human form, drawing close to Eladria's side.

It was one of the more intense storms. Sparks of light shot across the sky as an aperture formed at the heart of the electrical storm. The ground beneath their feet began to shake as a wave of tremors rocked the jungle. They struggled to retain their balance as a blasting wind swept through the jungle in intermittent bursts, strong enough to snap the branches off trees and sending waves of perched birds fluttering into the sky in alarm.

Eladria became aware of shadows all around them; silhouetted figures only visible out of the corner of her eye. It was as though two realities were being superimposed, the walls between them loosening and crumbling.

Something then began to emerge from the apex of the storm — the same bat-like creatures she'd seen before. The shadow creatures soon filled the sky, circling like birds of prey and dive-bombing the jungle, leaving trails of fire in their wake.

"We must find shelter!" Van'garat called above the noise.

Eladria nodded. One of the creatures was directly above them and it swooped toward them. As it descended through the jungle canopy, it ignited the trees in blazing red flames.

With Van'garat in the lead, they made a hasty retreat, successfully evading the bat-creature as they raced through the jungle, struggling to get through the thick undergrowth. The light from above enabled them to see their way for the most part, as it bathed the jungle in an eerie blue glow.

They continued to run, often stumbling over branches, vines and undergrowth, or knocked down by the rumbling tremors. Each time they scrambled to their feet and began running again. Van'garat was decisive as he led them onward, as though he knew where he was taking them.

After a time they came to a lagoon at the base of a steep cliff. At the bottom of the cliff was a network of caves. Eladria didn't know whether Van'garat had known about this place or if it was simply a stroke of luck, but they now had somewhere to shelter and wait out the storm. But just as Eladria was about to race toward the nearest cave, Van'garat put out his arm and restrained her.

"What's wrong?" she cried. "We'll be safe in there!"

"I'm not so certain," Van'garat responded. "I sense danger."

"It can't be any more dangerous than remaining out here," Eladria answered. She shook free of his grasp and began running toward the nearest cave. The others followed.

As they ran, they were pursued by several of the shadow creatures, diving down through the trees. Fortunately, as they made it into the cave, the bat-creatures broke off pursuit and soared back up to the sky. Eladria let out a sigh of relief. They were safe, for the moment at least.

She looked around the craggy cave, which cut deep into the cliff-side, dimly illuminated by a pale light filtering in through the mouth-like entrance. The walls and ceiling were dripping with water, stagnant pools of which collected on the ground, and there was clearly a nest of bats nearby, as evidenced by the occasional flapping and squeaking in the darkness.

Taking some time to catch their breath, they agreed to remain here until the storm passed. Everyone was exhausted and few words were exchanged as the travelers tried in vain to get comfortable. Eladria sat down on as dry a bit of ground as she could find, resting her back against the cavern wall. As the adrenaline pumping through her body began to subside, she surrendered to her exhaustion and after a time drifted into the sweet embrace of sleep.

Her dreams that night were intense, vivid and fragmented.

She saw images of distant islands, forests, deserts, cities and towns, all of them unfamiliar and alien-looking.

A face kept appearing before her: that same young man, little older than she was, his handsome face framed by locks of dark hair and his penetrating brown eyes gazing at her as if from across an infinite void — so far apart, and yet so intimately connected.

Although she had never met him before, she had seen his face so many times, perhaps in her dreams, or perhaps as part of a long-forgotten memory, a distant recollection obscured by the haze of time and space. She was drawn to him, compelled by a magnetism she found impossible to resist.

Yet when she tried to reach out to him, his face vanished like a reflection on water dissipated by a ripple.

She found herself alone again in a distant and inhospitable land, wondering why she'd been forsaken in this most alien of places. She searched for the enigmatic stranger who so allured her. Who was he, and where had he gone? Why did she feel that their fates were connected, even though they were separated by vast distances of space and time...?

"Princess, wake up! Wake up!" a voice startled her.

She opened her eyes to find Janak nudging her awake, a panicked expression upon his face.

"What is it?" she asked sleepily.

"We have company," came Van'garat's curt response.

It was now morning. She looked round and saw daylight streaming through the mouth of the cave. It was there, at the cave entrance, that she saw a figure standing silhouetted in the light, brandishing a large stick or staff of some kind.

Alarmed, Eladria reached down and grabbed her dagger. She got up and stood alongside Van'garat and Janak, while wondering where Zinn was. The figure at the entrance of the cave remained still, watching them intently.

"Who are you?" Eladria called.

The figure moved closer, stepping into the cavern. Van'garat remained calm and motionless, while Janak visibly tensed, shifting nervously on the spot. As the stranger approached, Eladria saw that it was a middle-aged man, wearing the hooded grey cowl and apparel of a True Way Patriarch, the band of chains around his chest and waist clanking as he moved. She immediately felt a lurching sensation in her stomach.

"Who I am is of no consequence," the Patriarch responded as he came to a stop before them. In common with most other Patriarchs Eladria had seen, his blue-tinged face was pale and expressionless and his eyes empty and deadened. "I am but an instrument, a servant of the mighty Antas, the True God of Tahnadra. I live only that I may glorify his name and carry out his divine will."

"What are you doing here?" Eladria asked.

"Just as you were led here, so too was I," the Patriarch replied.

"What-what you want with us?" Janak asked weakly.

"You will come with me back to the sacred town of Arnaast," the man answered.

"We're not going anywhere with you," Eladria said forcefully.

"But you are, Princess Eladria," the Patriarch responded darkly. He smiled at Eladria's visible alarm at knowing she had been recognized. "Yes, I know who you are. The mighty Antas said you would be here, on the run from the Ha'shon and desperately trying to stop the resurrection from happening. But you will never stop what is destined to be. Indeed, you will be an important part of it."

"I don't know what you are talking about," Eladria growled.

"No matter. You will soon learn of what I speak." The Patriarch closed his eyes, raised his staff and began to chant strange words that Eladria had never before heard.

"Beware, he's casting an incantation," Van'garat warned.

Eladria stepped forward and raised her dagger. "Stop!" she shouted.

The Patriarch continued, ignoring her. The words poured from his mouth like an obscure song from an ancient, long-forgotten world.

Eladria was prepared to stop him with physical force, but before she could act the Patriarch snapped open his eyes and raised his staff. From the tip of the staff, a burst of energy shot outward, encircling her, Janak and Van'garat in a ring of black fire. The crackling black flames closed in on them like a lasso, coiling around their bodies in a snake-like manner. The black fire was cold to the touch yet tingled with electrical charge.

Eladria and her comrades struggled to break free but, like the arachoid web, it had them completely incapacitated.

She looked helplessly at Van'garat and Janak who were pinned next to her. The three of them were like helpless animals caught in a hunter's trap. They couldn't fight and there was no way to escape.

Chapter 16

The Cult Of Arnaast

That morning, Zinn was awake long before the others. As a metamorph with an entirely different physiology to her comrades, she needed little in the way of sleep. Rather than staying in the cave, which she found dank and miserable, she went outside to take a look around.

Aside from the chirping and cooing of birds and the humming of insects, it was surprisingly quiet and serene. The morning sun shone down from a cloudless sky of pink and orange, making the droplets of morning dew upon the trees and flowers glisten like tiny stars.

As she approached the turquoise lagoon, she assumed the form of a golden swan and happily immersed herself in the cool, crisp water. As she swam across the lagoon, she surveyed the surrounding jungle and marveled at just how much had changed from last night. When they arrived here in desperation and terror, the conditions around them had been nightmarish. But just a few hours later this place was a paradise; tranquil, quiet and so very beautiful.

She stepped back onto land and shook her entire body, flapping her wings from side to side to dry off. She then changed into a blue raven and took to flight, cruising high above the treetops, exploring the area, trying to figure out where they were.

That was when she noticed a commotion not far from the lagoon. Through a clearing in the canopy, she saw that an aircraft had landed in the jungle and there were a number of people gathered around it. At first she assumed it to be the Ha'shon. But as she flew closer to the land and perched upon a tree to get a closer look, she realized that these were not Ha'shon warriors. In hooded grey robes with black armor and ceremonial staffs, she recognized them as True Way Patriarchs and alongside them were civilian guards brandishing rifles.

She hopped from branch to branch, trying to get close enough to see and hear what they were doing. One of the guards held out a large map and was conferring with two of the Patriarchs. They spoke in an obscure tongue, snippets of which were recognizable, but the syntax and dialect were unfamiliar to Zinn. From what she could gather, they were searching for something.

Realizing that whatever was happening would most certainly bode ill for Eladria and the others, she decided to get back to the cave and warn them. She spread her wings and was soon soaring above the jungle. Every so often she caught sight of movement below and would slow down to investigate. The True Way were combing the jungle, wasting little time as they hacked through the undergrowth.

Zinn hastened her speed and returned to the lagoon and surrounding caves. She was just in time to see one of the Patriarchs approaching the mouth of the cave where Eladria and the others were presumably still asleep.

She knew she had to do something. She began changing form in mid-air and by the time her feet touched the ground she had assumed the form of a large rhastopod. It was an odd feeling being in the body of such a large, bulky creature. Its body was powerful yet cumbersome and every movement took a certain degree of effort. But once it had gained momentum, it was an unstoppable predator. Indeed, herds of rhastopod had been known to trample entire villages to the ground.

Letting out a warning roar, Zinn charged toward the lone Patriarch, who stopped and turned in surprise. The Patriarch was momentarily stunned, but as the creature raced toward him, he lifted his staff and fired a burst of black energy. The discharge hit Zinn and surged through her body like a thousand knives tearing into her flesh. The Patriarch fired another energy bolt, which this time knocked the rhastopod to the ground with a thud.

The pain was excruciating. Zinn's body was screaming in

agony and her mind was disorientated, as though she'd been bludgeoned across the head and was unable to think or react.

The Patriarch took a step forward and used his staff to fire one last shot. As the energy electrified every cell of her body, Zinn found herself unable to maintain her shape. The form of the rhastopod melted and she found herself dissolving into a pool of viscous liquid that trickled across the ground. She was unable even to return to her natural form, for she didn't have the strength or focus. Her consciousness rapidly faded and all went dark.

Ensnared in the black ring of fire, the three prisoners were led from the cave and dragged through the jungle like cattle. With his staff held aloft, the Patriarch walked ahead of them as they were forced to trail behind.

Eladria didn't know where Zinn was. She only hoped that, perhaps having sensed the Patriarch's approach, she had retreated in order to avoid capture. If that was the case, then she might be their only hope of escape.

After some time they came to a True Way craft landed amid a clearing in the jungle. The aircraft, a mid-range vehicle with curved wings and a tapered cockpit that jutted out like a bird's beak, glistened as a ray of sunlight struck the aluminum fuselage. Either side of the craft was emblazoned with the insignia of the True Way: two blue circles joined by a red triangle. There were two other Patriarchs and half a dozen civilian personnel in navy fatigues gathered around the craft. They greeted their comrade in congratulatory fashion upon sight of his captives.

The Patriarch lowered his staff and released his prisoners. Eladria's immediate impulse was to try to escape, but the True Way guards immediately grabbed hold of them and they were taken aboard the vehicle and bundled into the aft compartment. One of the guards, a young pale-faced man with short dark hair, stood over them, rifle in hand.

The craft remained stationary for some time. It appeared the

True Way had been searching the jungle and it was a while before all of them returned.

The Patriarch that had captured them had claimed that Antas, their deity, had led them here to find and capture her. Eladria had always dismissed belief in the supernatural as symptomatic of a weak and gullible mind. But now that she'd witnessed so many wondrous and inexplicable occurrences, she was starting to re-evaluate that assumption. After all, she'd encountered the Others, who were non-corporeal beings guiding the mortal realm from beyond this dimension. It was therefore not unreasonable to assume that there were other beings out there, such as the deities worshipped by the True Way and Ha'shon. It was a disturbing thought. Perhaps there was some kind of cosmic battle being waged across space and time, in which the mortals of Tahnadra were but pawns?

Eventually the remaining True Way personnel returned and they prepared for departure. With all aboard, the engines were powered up and before Eladria knew it they were flying over the jungle, a vast expanse of green, dotted with hills and valleys and intercut by winding rivers sparkling in the morning light. The flight was uneven and jerky. Eladria was certain that she herself could have piloted the craft better.

Her thoughts again returned to Zinn. Where was she? She had evidently managed to escape and hide, but would she be able to find them again?

After a time they reached their destination, another part of the jungle filled with equally dense trees and vegetation. The True Way craft landed upon a runway in the center of a wide valley. They disembarked and Eladria and her friends were escorted down the steps and onto the concrete runway, the guards keeping their weapons trained upon them at all times.

Eladria's attention was immediately drawn to an ancient town just ahead of them, nestled in the heart of the valley. The sun shone down upon the predominantly white and grey masonry;

clusters of houses, towers, temples and archways, largely still standing, but eroded by the passing of the centuries. Around these crumbling monuments to a long-forgotten past stood a number of modern buildings. The True Way had apparently built a settlement in and around this ancient town. Dominating the heart of the town, atop a flight of ever-narrowing steps, was a large temple overlooking the valley.

The prisoners were ushered along the runway, which housed several warehouses and hangars, as well as four other stationary aircraft. They were led toward the town, at the perimeter of which several armed guards stood on patrol.

As they passed through the checkpoint and entered the town, Eladria looked around in curiosity. The town, an incongruent mixture of ancient and modern architecture, was a hub of activity, with Patriarchs and guards patrolling the well-worn streets, as well as monks and nuns dressed in hoodless grey robes. The majority of the town's inhabitants were True Way civilians, recognizable by their pale, slightly blue-tinged skin, dark hair and piercingly dark eyes. They watched the arrivals in curiosity, stopping their activities to observe as the prisoners were marched through the town, down the cobbled courtyards and under archways that looked liable to collapse at any moment.

Arriving at the heart of the town, they found themselves at the foot of the imposing temple perched upon the stone steps. This part of the town was deserted, possibly being reserved solely for ceremonial functions.

The prisoners were lined up. The glaring sunlight forced them to squint as they looked ahead. They were joined by a group of nine Patriarchs. These Patriarchs wore black and silver robes, gold belts, pointed black ceremonial hats and carried staffs carved of pure gold, identifying them as this sect's ruling council.

The Patriarch that had captured them bowed and introduced the prisoners to his superiors. The Chief Patriarch stepped forward and nodded, a satisfied sneer twisting his pale wrinkled face. He surveyed the prisoners one by one, looking each of them up and down. He was little interested in Janak, but he seemed simultaneously delighted and repulsed to have a Ha'shon in his midst. His attention settled on Eladria, his smile widening as he took in every last detail with his jet black eyes.

"Welcome to Arnaast," the Patriarch said. "We knew you could come, Princess Eladria. Guided by the mighty Antas, it was both your destiny and ours."

"What is this place?" Eladria asked defiantly, narrowing her eyes as she glared at the wizened old Patriarch.

"Arnaast is one of our foremost religious communities," the man answered, his voice low and rasping, yet filled with pride. "It is a most sacred place, a place of the ancients, built at a time when our world was young. Eighteen cycles ago, our Order was led to find this place and guided to set up a community here. Here, we have awaited the end times."

"What's so special about this place?"

"Arnaast is built upon one of the strongest energy conduits of Tahnadra. When this power is channeled in exactly the right way at exactly the right time, our centuries-long goal of resurrecting the great emissary, Kahnos, will be realized."

"So you're here to resurrect Kahnos?" Eladria frowned. She knew from her religious-historical lessons that Kahnos, supposedly the emissary to the True Way's deity Antas, had been slain by the Ha'shon emissary Shon. True Way doctrine purported that when Kahnos had been slain, the whole world had been damned. In order to appease the wrath of Antas, the True Way religion was built around austerity, sacrifice and penance, which in recent times had even escalated to include ritual sacrifice. In addition, Eladria had heard that some True Way sects were intent on somehow resurrecting Kahnos.

"Many do not believe it can be done," the Patriarch said. "They fear that Kahnos cannot be resurrected as was foretold. Such disbelievers will burn with the Ha'shon filth as our world is consumed in flames. We stand apart from the central True Way hierarchy. They are content to expend their energy on politics and war, whereas we know that the only way to save ourselves is to resurrect the great emissary. It was written so many centuries ago that only the return of Kahnos could lead us to our promised land. With his divinely bestowed power, he will slay our adversaries and lead us to the land of purity. You, Princess Eladria of Chaldeen, you and your companions have come at precisely the right moment. Do you not see?"

Eladria looked at him blankly.

"The storms, girl, the storms," the Patriarch exclaimed. "That is the link between worlds. With each storm, the great Kahnos comes knocking upon our door, seeking to get back into this realm, to save and deliver us! We have gathered here, where we can harness the unique energies of Arnaast. The sacred temple above us is the conduit that will allow us to combine and utilize our focused intent. We will use this to open the doorway that will allow Kahnos back into our realm. Only then can he save and deliver us—only then!"

"You actually believe that?" Eladria asked. "You really believe you can bring Kahnos back from the dead?"

"It was foretold. Our Order has spent thousands of years deciphering the ancient texts. We were led here by divine guidance, just as you were led here. Do you not see the important role that you play?"

"No, I don't," Eladria narrowed her eyes.

"We must offer Antas the sacrifice he seeks," the Patriarch explained, his eyes ablaze with fervor. "He demands it. But not just any sacrifice, no. He demands a special sacrifice—one of royal blood. Only then will the great Kahnos have the power he needs to return to us. And we will not have to wait long. Now that you are here, we can proceed as soon as the next storm commences. The next time Kahnos knocks, we will answer..."

Eladria said nothing.

"Do not fear, girl," the man added. "Your death is necessary, but we are not cruel. We will make you suffer no longer than is necessary. Your death will herald new life. Only that all could make such a glorious sacrifice!"

"What if we're more valuable to you alive than dead?' Eladria ventured. "The Ha'shon want us captured at all costs. They've seized control of Tahnadra, but I can stop them. If I can rally my forces and mobilize the neutral territories, I can—"

"No, no, no," the Patriarch interrupted with a shake of his head. "The Ha'shon will be of no consequence. Kahnos *will* deliver us. He will avenge his murder and slay all those Ha'shon animals. It has been foretold. You were led here for a reason, led here to your noble sacrifice. You must accept and rejoice. For it is the only way, and it is coming, so very soon."

"What do you mean?"

"The seer has predicted that the next window will arise tonight—this very evening! We shall be ready."

Eladria saw the futility of challenging the Patriarchs. They had made up their minds. She was to be put to death, and her friends along with her.

The Chief Patriarch stepped back to confer with his fellow council members, before summoning the guards. They spoke in a dialect Eladria was unfamiliar with, but she saw the old man pointing at her, Van'garat and Janak and then motioning toward something at the far end of the courtyard. It was a large rectangular enclosure, comprised of a metal frame set with thick panes of glass; evidently a cage of some kind.

As the Patriarchs departed, the guards led the prisoners to the glass cage. One of the men unlocked the door and three of them were ushered up a series of metal steps and forced into the enclosure. The guards closed and locked the door and, once satisfied that the prisoners were secure, slung their rifles over their shoulders and departed.

Eladria paced the glass prison in a fit of desperation. The sun blasted through the glass and the heat was almost unbearable, the air so thick it was difficult to breathe. She tried to force the door open, to no avail. The glass was scorching hot and so thick as to be unbreakable.

She slumped to the ground in defeat. Janak and Van'garat looked down at her. Janak's entire body was trembling and he looked like a desperate, terrified animal. Van'garat, however, had a look of detachment and resignation upon his face. It was almost as though he had somehow expected this to happen and was resigned to his fate.

"I don't suppose either of you have any idea how we're going to get out of here?" Eladria asked with a sigh.

Neither answered.

"I didn't think so..."

When Zinn eventually regained consciousness, it was a slow and gradual process. Awareness did not return all at once. First to come were impressions of tall trees and dense jungle foliage, a turquoise lagoon and a network of caves.

Then came the sense of 'I', the realization that there was a witness to these images. It took a comparatively longer time for her to fully regain her sense of self, to remember who she was and to recall what had happened. The droplets into which she had dissolved after the attack had now coalesced into intangible wisps of vapor that mingled with the air.

But something was terribly wrong.

She was badly injured. Whatever the Patriarch had done to her, it had affected her at a core level. It was difficult for her to formulate thoughts and the continued pain made it even harder to function. She didn't know what to do, for she'd never experienced such injury before. Normally a speedy return to her natural state remedied any injury accrued while in corporeal form, but not this time.

She couldn't let the pain stop her, though. She had to find out if Eladria was safe. She had no idea how much time had passed while she'd been unconscious. She tried to resume human form, but found it extremely difficult to do so. It took numerous attempts and a significant degree of pain before she finally managed to force herself into physical form. As her feet touched the ground and she looked down at her hands and body, she noticed that she still looked the same as before, but she was so weak that she could barely stand, much less walk.

Yet she forced herself to move. She hobbled over to the cave and cautiously entered. As she feared, it was empty. She called out, but there was no answer. She slowly and painfully searched the length and breadth of the cave but there was no sign of anyone. She knew they wouldn't have left without her, not unless they'd been forced to leave against their will. The Patriarch must have overpowered and captured them.

She slumped to the ground, her back resting upon the cave wall and she began to weep. How would she ever find them? She could barely move!

She didn't know what to do. It still hurt to think, so she had to struggle to gather her thoughts and consider her options. She realized that her own pain mattered little. She had to find Eladria and rescue her. That was all she cared about.

And so she dragged herself up from the ground and made her way out of the cave, holding onto the walls for support as she forced one leg in front of the other. Once outside, it took considerable effort to change shape once more into a bird and with great exertion she took to the air and rose above the treetops. Each movement, each effort to direct her will and control her form hurt immensely, but the force of her love for Eladria enabled her to endure the pain as she began searching for her dear child.

She flew erratically above the jungle, trying to keep her scattered mind fixed upon her goal. She scanned the lands below, finding no trace of the True Way or the craft they'd arrived in. They were gone, but she vowed to find them. With luck, they had a settlement somewhere in the region, although she knew it was a possibility that they had come from another country or even continent, in which case she might spend the rest of her life searching and still never find them.

Zinn didn't know if she believed in a deity or divine force. But having encountered the mysterious Others at the crystal waterfall, she now knew that there were forces beyond mortal understanding, and seemingly benevolent ones at that. She didn't know if it was possible for them to hear her thoughts, the thoughts of an injured metamorph flying above the jungle. But she nevertheless called out to them and asked them to help her, to guide her and to lead her to her beloved Eladria.

If they really needed Eladria to save this world and do whatever it was she was supposedly destined to do, then it was vital that Zinn find her. For wherever she was, she knew that Eladria was in extreme danger.

Chapter 17

Resurrection

"I not want to die here!" Janak exclaimed as he paced the cage, repeatedly throwing himself against the glass in a futile bid to break out.

"None of us do," Eladria said. She didn't know where Janak got his energy, for it was all she could do to open her mouth to speak. She was slumped alongside Van'garat on the floor of the cage, exhausted and drenched in sweat. The day had stretched on endlessly, all the while the sun streaming through the glass, heating their prison like a furnace.

"There must be some way," Janak cried. "I mean we escape from arachoid and storms and even Ha'shon! There must be way out of here! Perhaps we somehow reason with them?"

"No, they're beyond reason," Eladria sighed. "You must have seen the look in their leader's eyes. He was crazed, irrational…insane. Nothing we can say will possibly change their minds."

"I not want to die! I not ready to die," Janak cried angrily, again pushing against the glass with all his might.

Eladria turned to Van'garat. "Why do you suppose they're doing this?" she asked.

"They're frightened, desperate people," Van'garat answered. "They see the chaos in the world around them, they know they're threatened with annihilation and this is their reaction. Digging their claws into life, desperately grasping at survival."

"I can't help but wonder though," Eladria began, wiping a band of sweat from her forehead. "What if there's something more to it? What if they really are in communion with some kind of entity? *Something* must have led them to us in the cave. It wasn't coincidence they found us like that. If the Others exist and are guiding Lakandrian's people, isn't it conceivable that Antas also exists and is guiding the True Way?"

Van'garat was silent.

"Well?"

"There's very much more to life than we can perceive with our physical senses," Van'garat admitted. "There *are* beings out there, intangible and unseen, that seek to manipulate the people of this world."

"Why would they want to manipulate us?"

"Why do children play with toys? What's the fascination that makes us want to explore, acquire and control things? There are beings out there engaged in perpetual conflict, much as we mortals are. They're all ultimately of the same source, the same primordial essence, but until that realization is attained, the apparent duality remains and the battle continues without end."

"Then we're in the middle of some kind of cosmic battle?"

Van'garat nodded. "Yes, and we're seeing symptoms of it all around us. Everything that's happening here is a manifestation of this conflict. This world is a focal point and whatever's happening at Drantak is at the apex of it: an incursion into this realm that must be stopped at all costs."

Eladria sat up and stared at him. "So the True Way deities actually exist and are somehow involved in this?"

"It's possible there's something—an energy force, a dark entity—that has latched onto these people for millennia," Van'garat said. "The same may be true for the Ha'shon. Perhaps their deities are real in a sense, but they're certainly not divine. Two antagonistic forces from beyond this dimension, engaged in a state of perpetual conflict."

"If that's true, then the war between the Ha'shon and the True Way has its roots in some other dimension?"

The Ha'shon nodded thoughtfully, as if only having just come to the realization. "It would seem that each side has been manipulated by dark entities threatening to encroach upon this world."

"Like the Shadow Lords—the beings the Others said were

trying to invade this realm? Do you think they're one and the same?"

"That I cannot say, but it's entirely possible."

"I not listen to another word," Janak cut in, folding his arms and glaring at Van'garat with indignation. "You may be fooling her, but I not believe your Ha'shon lies and I never will."

Eladria looked up at him. "Janak, you're not helping."

"Actually I am! You need reminder he is *Ha'shon*," Janak declared angrily. "Ha'shon never to be trusted! You forget it was *him* that led us to cave where we captured. Was all a trap! He is clearly reason we here."

"You're mistaken," Van'garat responded, a hint of annoyance in his voice.

"No," Janak countered. "You filled with lies and deceit. You claim to have premonitions, so why not you warn us we be captured and brought here?"

"Actually, he did try to warn us," Eladria recalled. "But I ignored him."

"Well, I still not believe word he say and neither should you," Janak retorted.

"Listen, Janak, the last thing we need to do right now is turn on each other," Eladria said. "In case you hadn't noticed, Van'garat is in this cage with us."

She turned to Van'garat, who looked back at her blankly. There was still so much she didn't understand about the renegade Ha'shon. She knew there was certainly more to him than met the eye. He carried a secret of some kind, something deep and burdensome. But what was it he wasn't telling them?

"This 'inner vision' of yours, how does it work exactly?" she asked.

"It's a result of my training in Ko Tra Pah," he said. "My master taught me to sharpen and refine my senses and to hone my intuition. As a result, I have the ability to see beyond the surface level of objects and appearances. This deeper awareness comes to me in visions and dreams and occasionally in flashes of insight."

"Do you have the ability to see the future?"

"Yes and no. The future is not yet written, so I often intuit different probabilities simultaneously. Some come to pass, some do not."

"How you know where to find those caves?" Janak challenged him. "You seem to know exactly where they were, just as True Way did..."

"I sensed the caves ahead of us and knew they would provide shelter. I reached out with my mind and simply followed my intuition," Van'garat explained.

"Why did you warn me before we proceeded?" Eladria asked. "Did you know that the True Way were coming for us?"

"I felt there was possible danger, but I was uncertain what it was."

"It sounds like your intuition is rather vague," she noted.

Van'garat nodded and was silent for a moment. He continued, with a measure of some reluctance. "I didn't tell you this before, perhaps because I didn't even want to admit it to myself, but from the time these breaches began, my ability to see has been somewhat compromised..."

"In what way?"

"My inner vision has become patchy and unreliable, as though a blindfold has been placed over me. Some things I can still see, but others I cannot."

"I take it this hasn't happened to you before?"

"No," Van'garat replied, shaking his head, a look of puzzlement upon his face. "It takes immense power to block the vision of an adept of Ko Tra Pah. There's something out there, something powerful and dangerous, and it's aware of my presence and is attempting to restrict my inner vision. Perhaps I've been deemed a potential threat."

"I don't like the sound of that," Eladria said. "But right now, none of us is much of a threat to anyone. We're locked in a glass cage and if the heat doesn't kill us first, we'll be sacrificed in their resurrection ceremony." She looked up to the sky. "The sun is starting to set. Assuming they're correct and another breach is due to occur tonight, we don't have much longer."

"Is hopeless then," Janak exclaimed, sinking to the floor of the cage. "We really going to die here..."

As they grimly discussed their fate, they were unaware of a bird landing on the courtyard not far from their glass prison. The bird hopped toward the enclosure and began to change shape, dissolving into a vaporous mist and re-forming into the shape of a woman.

Janak was the first to catch sight of the arrival and he cried out as he pointed her out to Eladria and Van'garat. Their hearts leapt as they realized it was Zinn. But the first thing Eladria noticed was how different she looked. She seemed so much older and weaker. As she approached the cage she had a noticeable limp and her entire body was strained and tense. There was a look of pain upon her face.

"Zinn," Eladria called out. She got up and placed her hands on the glass, before quickly removing them again, having forgotten how hot it was.

"She find us," Janak cried in excitement. "We saved!"

"What happened, Zinn?" Eladria asked in concern.

"I was detained," Zinn responded weakly, looking up at the princess and mustering a small smile. "I was attacked by a Patriarch. It wasn't easy, but I made it here..."

"How did you find us?"

"I don't know whether it was by luck or some hidden intuition. But after hours of aimlessly circling above the jungle, I felt pulled in this direction, across hills and valleys...where I eventually came across this strange old town..."

"Well, however you did it, I've never been happier to see you," Eladria beamed.

"You don't look well," Van'garat observed.

"I don't feel well," Zinn admitted. "I don't know what the Patriarch did to me, but I...I am not myself."

"You get us out of here?" Janak asked eagerly.

Zinn surveyed the lock and shook her head. "No, I would need the key."

"Is there any way you could smash it open?" Eladria suggested.

"I don't think so," Zinn said. "Not right now. I don't have the strength."

"We can't stay here, Zinn. They're going to execute us— tonight!"

"Give me some time," Zinn said. "I must rest and regain some strength. I can barely hold my form. But I'll do what I can, when I can."

"Our lives are in your hands," Eladria said.

"I know," Zinn said. "Trust me, I won't let anything happen to you. I must rest and then, when the time is right, I will act. Be prepared."

"Prepared for what?" Janak asked.

"For anything."

Zinn stepped back and her form dissolved into a mist, dispersing into the air.

"She really doesn't look well," Van'garat said.

Eladria nodded, concerned. "I hope she's all right."

"She has to be," Janak said. "She our only hope. Without her we all dead."

"I know," Eladria said. "And like you, Janak, I'm not ready to die. Not yet."

The town center had been deserted all day, but once the sky began to darken, it became a hub of activity. Eladria watched as a group of Patriarchs began preparing for the impending ceremony. Flaming torches were positioned around the steps leading up to the old temple. Incense was lit and flags and banners were tied to buildings and pillars.

The town's inhabitants—all clad in hooded navy robes with sinister black masks concealing their faces—soon began streaming through the archways, gathering around the temple steps. For the moment, the prisoners in the glass cage were being ignored. It was almost as though they'd been forgotten, although Eladria knew this was merely wishful thinking on her part.

After a time, a group of Patriarchs and guards approached the cage and unlocked the door. The guards dragged them out of the cage and forced them to bow before the Patriarchs. With rifles pressed into their backs, there was nothing they could do to resist.

Eladria wondered where Zinn was. There had been no sign of her, but Eladria knew she wouldn't forsake them. If she was at all able, she would try to mount a rescue. But now was probably not the right moment. With guns trained on each of them, they would be killed at the slightest provocation.

The prisoners were forced to their feet and dragged along behind the Patriarchs as they made their way through the gathering and toward the temple. As they were marched up the temple steps, the crowd began chanting an obscure incantation as the pounding of drums reverberated through the town.

Eladria and her comrades were weak from their day spent in the glass cage, but they were granted little concession as they were forced up the ancient stone steps. As they neared the top, Eladria looked down and observed the townspeople encircling the base of the temple, a sea of masked figures wrapped in hooded robes, reciting their strange chant in unison. It was now dark, the only source of light coming from the fire torches and sporadic glints of moonlight filtering through the clouds.

They reached the temple and were brusquely escorted inside. Dozens of candles illuminated the temple in a warm flickering glow. Although clearly built many centuries ago, it was still largely intact. The walls and stone pillars were weathered but largely undamaged by the passage of time. Ancient statues of long-forgotten gods and demonic gargoyles lined the interior walls. The ceiling showed signs of decay, with a large gap overhead revealing the night sky above. At the heart of the temple was a circular well surrounded by wide stone slabs. The well seemed to run deep underground, far beneath the temple.

Eladria, Van'garat and Janak were lined up by the well. They were joined by what appeared to be the ruling council of Patriarchs, clad in red and silver robes, bedecked with talismans and beads. As with the rest of the townspeople, their faces were covered by black masks. In spite of his mask, Eladria immediately recognized the Chief Patriarch by the crazed expression in his bulging dark eyes.

"So it begins," the lead Patriarch said as he stepped forward, somewhat out of breath after having climbed the steps. "The great Kahnos awaits us, and we await him. Let us now pray in supplication, that we may succeed in our sacred endeavor."

The entire assemblage, including a dozen Patriarchs and six guards, formed a circle around the stone well and dropped to their knees. Eladria, Janak and Van'garat were also forced to kneel. The guards knelt beside them, guns poised, ready to react to the slightest sign of trouble.

As she knelt, Eladria looked around anxiously and noticed that the stone slabs surrounding the well were stained with blood. They were clearly sacrificial altars, which meant that this place, far from being a holy sanctum, was in fact a slaughter-house.

The sound of drumming and chanting continued outside and was soon accompanied by a distant peal of thunder. The Patriarchs opened their eyes and looked up in expectation. A moment later came another rumble of thunder, this time louder. The air tingled with static charge. Eladria knew what was happening, for she had experienced it many times now: another breach was imminent.

A series of flashes came from above. Looking up through the

hole in the ceiling, she saw the same twisting, blue-white ribbon of energy that had accompanied previous breaches filling the sky and sending ripples of lightning shooting outward.

Outside, the townspeople roared in excitement, their cries of joy just audible between bursts of thunder. The Patriarchs rose to their feet, picking up their staffs and staring down at Eladria and her comrades. The expression on their faces was a curious mixture of rapture and bloodlust. Eladria could tell it was time for the executions to begin.

"The princess," the chief Patriarch addressed the guards. "Prepare the princess."

Eladria struggled as the guards grabbed her arms and forced her forward.

"Fine, if you want to execute me, then do it!" she cried at the onlooking Patriarchs. "You said you needed to sacrifice someone of royal blood and you've got me for that. But you don't need my friends. They have nothing to do with this. Let them go."

"That is not possible," the Patriarch shook his head. "They are our enemies, and we are especially grateful to have Ha'shon blood to offer Kahnos. They will also be sacrificed to ensure that Kahnos is given all the life-force he needs to return to this realm."

Eladria was dragged before one of the bloodstained slabs and forced to lie upon it. Two guards pinned her down, one holding her legs and the other her arms as she kicked and struggled with all her might.

The Chief Patriarch stepped forward and closed his eyes, remaining silent for a moment. "It is not quite time," he said as he opened his eyes, raising his voice to be heard above the rumbling thunder and the gusts of wind sweeping in through the temple door, causing the candles to flicker. "We must harness the energy conduit. Form a circle, my brethren. We must use our combined power to activate the conduit."

The Patriarchs formed a circle around the well. Joining hands, they began chanting, looking ghostly and menacing in their red robes and expressionless black masks. Above them, the sky was consumed in an explosive blaze of fury. Eladria continued to struggle against the guards as they pinned her down on the stone slab.

It was then that Eladria noticed something strange. The well at the center of the temple began to glow. The air was tingling with electrostatic charge and Eladria could sense waves of energy radiating up from the well. As the air crackled with increasing charge, the glow intensified and a shaft of red light shot up from the well, passing through the temple and out of the ceiling.

"We have harnessed the power of Arnaast," called the lead Patriarch. "The window is open. Mighty Kahnos, we call to you now! We beseech you to return to us. We have brought you the sacrifice you need. Take her life-force, use it to manifest your new form."

The Patriarch reached into the folds of his robe and produced a ceremonial dagger. He moved toward Eladria. As the guards continued to restrain her arms and legs, the Patriarch stood over her and raised the dagger above her chest. Eladria continued to struggle wildly, but the guards were too strong.

This must be it. Realizing that struggle was futile, she suddenly let go, resigned to her fate.

She looked up and watched the shaft of red light streaming from the well out through the ceiling. High above, the sky was consumed in a chaotic dance of electrical chaos as the pulsating anomaly crackled, spewing out fingers of lightning, each accompanied by an explosion of light and sound.

She became aware of an aperture forming at the center of the breach, as though something was clawing at the very fabric of this universe, struggling to pierce the membrane between dimensions, desperate to pass from one realm into another.

Another aperture began forming in the temple, right above her, where the shaft of light from the well met the crack in the ceiling. At the center of the opening she saw what looked like distant figures, lurching and contorting, flickering like flames consuming a burning log. It was accompanied by the image of a face that filled her with terror; a nightmarish apparition, twisted and gnarled. Reddish in color, its eyes were swirling pools of all-consuming hatred. Whatever it was, the creature was trying to force its way into this world. She could sense its desperate need to satiate its appetite, its hunger for life. It wanted nothing more than to devour this world until nothing remained.

Eladria cursed that the last sight her eyes were to behold was this vision of evil. She closed her eyes and braced herself, for she knew that any second the Patriarch would plunge the dagger into her chest. Her life, which had been little more than a succession of cruel blows, was about to be snatched away in one final violent strike.

But she was granted an unexpected reprieve.

All of a sudden something flew into the temple. It was a large, winged reptilian. Chaos erupted. As the dragon-like creature thrashed its mighty wings from side to side, the macabre ceremony came to a halt and the Patriarchs and guards reacted in panic. The Chief Patriarch staggered back and cowered behind one of the statues.

The guards were about to open fire, but the creature lashed out, knocking them to the ground and sending their rifles flying across the temple.

Eladria knew then this was no ordinary creature. It was Zinn. As if in confirmation, the creature turned to her and lowered its head in greeting.

The flying reptilian continued to hold off the Patriarchs and guards, aggressively flapping its wings and reaching out to snap at any of them that made the slightest move. By now Eladria was on her feet and, along with Van'garat and Janak, she edged her way to the door.

"It's Zinn," she called to them above the noise of the storm. "She's come to rescue us!"

Zinn had planned the escape and taken the form most suited to a rescue mission. After taking one last swipe at the guards and sending several of them flying across the temple, the dragon creature turned and flew toward the exit. It stopped beside Eladria and the others and, with a twist of its head, indicated for them to climb onto its back.

With only the slightest hesitation, Eladria did so, grabbing hold of the creature's thick scaly neck, while Van'garat and Janak climbed on behind her. As soon as they were upon the creature's back, it took to flight, shooting out through the temple doorway and flying high above the townspeople as they watched in uncertainty.

Above them, the storm continued to rage. The sky blazed in fury as the crack of light danced and pulsated, illuminating the land below in sporadic flashes.

Eladria glanced behind and saw that the guards were standing at the temple door, firing at the creature as it escaped with their prisoners. She also saw that the shaft of light from the well had indeed interfused with the storm to create a rupture, a concentration of light and energy that throbbed in a relentless pulsing motion. Whatever it was she'd seen in the temple, that face of evil, she knew it was desperate to enter this realm. It was as though she could still sense it pounding at the thin gate bridging the two worlds. Even without its sacrifice, she knew it was close to breaking through.

Zinn suddenly lurched in the sky. She had been hit by a rifle blast. She managed to steady herself and prevent her passengers from falling to the ground, but she began descending.

"No," Eladria cried. "We can't stop! We have to keep going."

But Zinn was injured and could fly no further. Eladria and the others held on tightly as the wounded metamorph plummeted to the ground. They landed at the edge of the town. Eladria and the others dismounted and Zinn dissolved from the winged reptilian into her human form, which lay upon the ground, racked with pain and struggling to breathe.

"Zinn," Eladria cried.

"I'm sorry, my dear," she gasped. "I can't...can't go on,"

"Don't apologize," Eladria said, distraught as she cradled her beloved friend. "You saved us, you got us away from there. A moment later and I'd have been dead. Zinn, what can we do for you? How can we help you? There must be something."

"No," she shook her head. "I fear I have reached the end..."

"We can't stay here," Van'garat warned, hovering above them.

"He right, they coming!" Janak exclaimed. "They coming through town. Toward us!"

"We'll carry you," Eladria said, getting to her knees and trying to lift her. She noticed that Zinn's face was gradually melting, as though she was unable to maintain her solidity.

"No," Zinn said, pulling back from her. "You must run. I'll only slow you down. I have just enough strength to change shape one more time. I can hold them off. You must go."

"No, I'm not leaving without you." Eladria looked up at Van'garat desperately. "Van'garat, there must be something we can do," she implored him, praying that he'd know what to do.

"I'm afraid she's right," he said gently, his eyes filled with sadness. "I don't believe there's anything we can do for her now. We must leave."

Eladria looked down at Zinn, her eyes welling with tears. "Zinn," she said. "I'm sorry this had to happen. I wish I hadn't asked you to—"

"Don't apologize, dear one," Zinn said. She tried to muster a small smile, but her features were rapidly dissolving. "I'm just glad I could save you. You've always been so dear to me. I love you as I would my own child..."

"They here!" cried Janak.

Eladria looked round and saw that he was correct. The Patriarchs had directed the townspeople to pursue the escapees and they came storming out of the town, brandishing flaming torches, led by a dozen armed guards.

"You don't have to do this, Zinn," Eladria said, looking down at her.

"I do," Zinn said, a strangely serene look upon her now almost unrecognizable face. "Go now! Please!"

Before Eladria could say another word, Zinn began to change shape one last time. Her human form dissolved into a large, slightly misshapen rhastopod. The mighty beast looked round at them and then turned and began charging at the oncoming townspeople.

"I'm sorry, Zinn," Eladria called after her. "I'm sorry..."

Van'garat grabbed her arm and pulled her toward him. "If we're to leave, we must do so now!"

Eladria found it almost impossible to move as she watched the rhastopod, her dearest friend, charging to her own death. The True Way guards were on the defensive and they opened fire at the rhastopod. She didn't know whether or not Zinn had been hit, but she kept charging toward them.

Eladria's eyes were briefly drawn to the temple overlooking the town. The swirling rupture above it was growing larger and brighter. The storm had reached its zenith. She could somehow sense that something was about to happen.

Within seconds, the rupture exploded and a flash of light shot outward in ever-expanding waves. It was accompanied by the sound of an explosion and a blood-curdling shriek that chilled her to her core.

Whatever dark entity the True Way had summoned, whether it truly was Kahnos or something even worse—it had arrived. The True Way had succeeded in their goal, but they were wholly unprepared for the fury they had unleashed.

Janak had already begun running from the outskirts of the troubled town. Van'garat dragged Eladria along with him, forcing her to follow as he took Janak's lead and made for the surrounding jungle.

Eladria felt as though she'd left her heart behind her, with Zinn.

They raced through the undergrowth, jumping over fallen logs and trailing vines, Eladria barely able to see through her tear-filled eyes.

The heavens continued to burn in effervescent fury, a pulsating blue and white light illuminating the land in dizzying flashes. Tremors rocked the land, and shadowy ghost-like figures appeared around them, like lost souls adrift in an immense foreign wilderness.

Eladria's beloved friend had sacrificed her life to enable them to escape. But it had possibly been for nothing, for something terrible had been conjured from a dark netherworld, something that had pierced the membrane separating realms and was now here on Tahnadra. Eladria had no idea what this meant. As far as she could tell, the entire world was falling apart, and maybe that was the fate it deserved.

Chapter 18

Apparition

Van'garat led the way as they ran through the jungle and up the hill at the edge of the valley. Exhausted and breathless, they stopped and looked down at the town of Arnaast, which lay cradled in the heart of the valley. Lightning danced across the sky as the tear consumed the heavens, illuminating the darkness in flickering bursts of blue and white.

The focal point of the storm was now centered on Arnaast. A funnel of light descended from the crack in the sky and connected with the ground through the ancient temple. The light crackled and swayed as it bridged sky and land, sending waves of energy shooting across the valley.

The True Way had succeeded in creating a doorway allowing Kahnos, or whatever it was, to cross the void and step into this world. Eladria didn't know how exactly, but she could sense a dark force had penetrated this realm. After being locked away for possibly aeons, it had finally been released and it had a ravenous hunger.

An explosion rocked the valley and hillside and a wave of light shot out from the center of Arnaast. Eladria, Van'garat and Janak were thrown to the ground.

By the time they made it to their feet, they were relieved to see that the storm was subsiding. The crack in the heavens had sealed, the funnel of light had disappeared and the sky was darkening once more, except for the occasional flicker of light.

In the sudden darkness, it was difficult to see into the valley. But it was the silence that struck Eladria most forcibly. Her senses had been bombarded with relentless noise ever since the people of Arnaast had gathered around the temple and begun drumming and chanting. Now there wasn't a sound to be heard.

"It over?" Janak eventually broke the silence, his voice hoarse and filled with uncertainty.

"It would seem so," Van'garat answered. "For now, at least."

"What do you think happened?" Eladria whispered.

"I don't entirely know," Van'garat said. "But it appears the people of Arnaast knew exactly what they were doing."

"It got through," Eladria said, repressing a shudder. "Kahnos, or whatever it was. It got through. I could sense it."

"As could I," Van'garat confirmed.

"It still here?" Janak gasped, eyes wide in terror.

Van'garat closed his eyes and was silent for a moment before turning to Eladria. "It's gone," he said, an undercurrent of alarm spilling into his voice. "But something terrible happened down there. As it left, pulled back into the void, it took the townspeople with it..."

Eladria stared at him, dumbfounded. "What do you mean?"

"I closed my eyes and reached out with my inner vision," Van'garat said, shifting uncomfortably. "And I saw it! The creature was between two realms, one foot in this world, the other in its own, struggling to pass through the void and force its way into corporeal existence. It had just about done so when the breach was sealed and the doorway closed. It was forced back into its own dimension. But its energy had already expanded to encompass the entire town. As it was sucked back into its own realm, it pulled the souls of the townspeople with it. All of them...they're all dead. Their souls were forcibly ripped from their bodies, which were then incinerated in the explosion. All killed in the blink of an eye..."

"Zinn," Eladria gasped. "What happened to Zinn?"

Van'garat lowered his head. "I'm not sure. But I do know that she saved us. If she hadn't stayed back to distract the towns-people, they would have recaptured us and we'd have shared their fate."

"But what happened to her?" Eladria demanded, grabbing him by the arms in desperation. "You must have seen what happened to her?"

"I'm sorry, but I didn't," he responded with a solemn shake of his head.

"We should never have left her," Eladria growled as she let go of Van'garat and began running back down the hillside. She didn't know whether her friend was dead or alive, but she feared the worst. Her relief at witnessing the end of the storm had transformed into an inconsolable grief, tinged with bitter regret.

Forgetting her exhaustion and weakness, Eladria ran through the jungle, frequently tripping over vines and struggling with the undergrowth as stray branches and thorns tore into her clothes and skin. Her mind was curiously blank as she made her way back to the town. Time had somehow shattered, losing all fluidity and distinction.

She found herself back at the edge of the town, around the same place they had left Zinn. There was nothing to be seen now. There was no one here. The town itself was still standing, but was eerily quiet, without any sign of life.

Eladria cautiously entered the town, walking down its empty, winding streets and vacant buildings, desperately searching for a sign of her dear friend.

Surely Zinn hadn't been killed with the townspeople? She couldn't have been. Zinn didn't belong here and she had nothing to do with this. The people of Arnaast were responsible for this; they'd been meddling with forces they didn't understand and couldn't control. In a way, they deserved what had happened to them—but not Zinn, the kindest and gentlest person Eladria had ever known. If there was any fairness at all in life, Zinn would have been spared...

But there was nothing here. No life, nor even any signs of death. Just nothing.

The immensity of the power that had surged through the town, coupled with the tremors and that final explosion, had caused significant damage. A number of buildings, old and new alike, had been pulverized and now lay in ruins. It was a bitter irony that one of the structures that remained largely untarnished was the temple. Eladria stared up at it, her heart seething with hatred. It was the source of all that had happened, the catalyst for all this death and destruction.

Yet she felt inexplicably drawn toward it. She climbed the steps, aware that the last time she had done so it had been as a prisoner being marched to her death. Ironic that she was now one of the only survivors of a cataclysm that these people had brought on themselves.

Inside the temple, the signs of destruction were plentiful. One of the walls had caved in and two of the pillars had fallen, making the dilapidated ceiling even more precarious. The round stone well at the center of the temple was still intact, as were the surrounding slabs and most of the statues.

Feeling a swell of rage rising within her, she grabbed the nearest object—a piece of stone that had broken off one of the statues—and, using it as a club, she tried to smash the temple to pieces. It was futile, of course, for in her weakened state she was unable to so much as dent the hideous statues as she pounded them angrily. Throwing the club to the ground, she tried to push over the stone slabs, but they were fixed to the ground and wouldn't budge.

She found herself drawn to the stone well. She stopped and looked down into it. A warm updraft struck her face as she tried to see what was at the bottom. There was definitely something down there, for she could see a faint glow emanating far below. An energy conduit, the Patriarch had said, but she didn't entirely know what that meant.

Gripped by sudden resignation, she slumped to the ground, her back resting upon the stone well, her vision blurring as her eyes filled with tears. "Zinn, where are you?" she sobbed as she pulled her legs close to her chest and wrapped her arms around them, cradling herself, allowing the tears to roll down her face like raindrops upon a windowpane.

Was it at all possible that Zinn had survived?

If she had, then surely she'd have found her by now? But then Eladria remembered how injured she had been. She had struggled to move, or even to speak. It was as though Zinn had known she was going to die and had accepted it. That was why she'd so readily stayed behind to hold off the townspeople, for she knew that her death was inevitable.

If it was true that she was no longer here, then Eladria wanted to know how she'd died. She was horrified by Van'garat's assertion that the souls of the townspeople had been snatched from them and their bodies incinerated. What if Zinn had shared this fate? She tried to dismiss this thought. In all likelihood Zinn had been killed by the townspeople long before the entity had pulled them back into the void with it.

I shouldn't have left her, Eladria chastised herself. In spite of their predicament, there must have been something she could have done.

Zinn had been like a mother to her. She'd cared for her, nurtured her and been there for her, from the moment she was born. There wasn't a single time Eladria could remember when Zinn hadn't been close by. Certainly, a lot of the time she had taken her for granted, just as she'd taken *everything* for granted. But the bond between them had been enduring and unbreakable. Eladria couldn't begin to imagine life without Zinn, without her comfort, guidance and love. Zinn had been the last remaining link to her old life, to her childhood and adolescence, to all the old memories, the good times and the bad. And now she was gone. Without her steadying presence, everything had unraveled.

Eladria sat rooted to the spot, consumed by her grief. Her chest and abdomen wrenched in spasmodic waves, and she let out intermittent sobs as the tears continued to flow. Her mind was haunted by a single thought, which played itself over and over without end: *she's gone.*

Van'garat and Janak appeared at the temple, having followed her from the hillside. They tried to console her, but she told them she needed to be alone. They agreed but promised to remain nearby should she need them. They left and she was alone once more, huddled in the middle of the darkened temple.

She sat awake for hours, overcome by a deadened numbness. She'd lost everyone she'd ever cared about and nothing seemed to matter anymore—not the Others, not her mission to Drantak, not even the fate of her world.

Eventually she succumbed to her own exhaustion. As though a plug had been pulled, she found her consciousness ebbing away like a receding tide. She slept fitfully, frequently waking to find herself lying upon the temple floor, the black night sky and glistening stars visible through the open ceiling. Upon waking, her grief returned to her in waves. Each time she would remain awake for a while, craving to be reunited with Zinn and helplessly wishing there was some way she could turn back time and change what had happened, as if there was some way she could avert the whole tragedy.

When morning came, she remained in the temple. Quite why she didn't know, but she didn't want to leave it. Even though she hated it, she had nowhere else to go, and above all else, she wanted to be alone. She sat watching the sun as it climbed above the horizon and made its way across the sky. Her mind was curiously blank. Her grief was still raw and she found herself frequently in tears.

Around noon, Janak appeared at the temple, bringing food and water he'd found in the town. Eladria thanked him, asked him to set it down and leave.

"Is anything else Janak can do?" he asked, looking at the princess worriedly.

"No...thank you, Janak," she said softly.

"Zinn, you know, she not want you to be like this," Janak said.

Eladria shook her head. "I don't want to talk about it," she said. "I just want to be alone please."

Janak nodded and left, disappearing as he descended the steps leading down to the town.

Eladria hadn't eaten in over a day and, although she didn't feel hungry, she nevertheless forced herself to eat some of the food. Afterward she continued to sit, staring out the temple door, across the dead town and into the surrounding jungle and hills. She didn't know what she was still doing here. Perhaps, she reasoned, some part of her believed that Zinn was still alive and would come back to her, although the better part of her knew that she was gone and that she would never see her again.

She didn't know what she would do now. She was too hurt, too numb, too overwhelmed to begin to think about what she would do next. She just wanted to remain here for now, alone with her pain.

The hours passed slowly. She spent the day in battle; battling her own thoughts and emotions, wrestling with her grief and despair. The onslaughts came like the rise and fall of a tide, crashing over her and then subsiding for a time before the next wave. Physically and emotionally exhausted, she remained seated on the temple floor, staring blankly into space. She was worn out and tired of the struggle. After a time, she gave up fighting the emotions as they came. She just let them come and wash over her. What did it matter if she got lost in them, if they swept her into oblivion?

It was dusk. The sun had disappeared and the sky began to darken. Eladria was aware of a cold blast of air suddenly sweeping through the temple. It was accompanied by an eerie luminescence coming from behind her. She got to her feet and turned to the source of the light.

As had happened before, during the True Way ceremony, a shaft of red light rose from the center of the stone well up to the ceiling, illuminating the temple in a hazy glow. Eladria watched in nervous fascination, her pulse quickening and an uneasy feeling creeping into her stomach.

A figure began to appear in the pillar of light. Eladria stepped back, her entire body tensing. Her immediate impulse was to run, but something kept her rooted to the spot as the ghostlike figure took form before her eyes.

It was a semi-transparent figure, its face obscured by a dark hooded robe, a crystal pendant hanging around its neck. Eladria had the sense that it was a woman, which was confirmed when, much to her surprise, the apparition spoke to her.

"*Eladria,*" came a deep, resonant female voice.

"Who are you?" Eladria demanded, trying to muster a tone of authority, and again resisting the urge to flee the temple immediately.

"*My name is Zanel,*" the hooded figure responded.

Eladria couldn't believe that she was evidently having a conversation with a ghost. "What are you doing here?" she asked. "How is it I'm seeing you?"

"*I speak to you from across a great distance, from beyond the void itself,*" the woman answered. "*You have already had communication with my kind...*"

"I have?"

"*At the crystal waterfall.*"

"You mean the Others? You're one of the Others?"

The ghostly figure nodded, her face still hidden beneath the hooded robe. "*We knew you were here. We were able to utilize the conduit of Arnaast to break through the dimensional barrier, to again communicate directly with you.*"

"It's just as well," Eladria said. "I have so many questions for you."

"*The answers must wait. Time is limited. Sustaining this line of communication takes great effort.*"

"It can't wait. I need answers now," Eladria objected. "You told me to travel to Drantak to end this 'experiment' you spoke of. But I'm not going any further without knowing how I'm to get there and what I'm supposed to do once I'm there."

"I know we have asked much of you. You will find the answers you seek only when you reach your destination. But you won't be alone in this endeavor. I am to be your guide. The connection has now been established between us. I will help and direct you as much as I can. Listen to me now. Since our last communication, there has been a change. You must resume your journey to Drantak, for it is imperative that you get there. But first there is something you must find and take with you."

"Something I must find?" Eladria echoed. "What?"

"It is called the Dragon Star."

"The Dragon Star?" Eladria gasped. "I've heard of it. But it's just a myth, a legend."

"It is real," Zanel assured her. *"Millennia ago, as your legends state, an advanced race of space travelers came to your world and bestowed the gifts of civilization, technology and culture. As you know, they eventually left your world to travel onwards. But before they departed, they left one final gift, a means of unlocking the secrets of the universe and ensuring order and peace: the Dragon Star. This mystical artifact has remained hidden for thousands of years, safeguarded and ready to be used only when it was needed. And it is needed now, in this time of chaos...*

"The Dragon Star is now the only thing that can stop the Shadow Lords from invading your realm. You must find it and take it with you to Drantak. There you will be guided to use it, to undo the damage that has been caused, to safeguard the future and to seal the rupture."

Eladria shook her head, confused. "Why wasn't I told of this before?"

"Circumstances have changed," the ghostly figure responded. *"The situation has worsened and the damage is far greater than previously realized. Greater measures are called for. That is why you must find the Dragon Star and take it to Drantak."*

"Where will I find it?"

"It is located in the fabled 'Heart of the Dragon', a secret location in the volcanic island of Naaryu in the Raskabari ocean."

Eladria took a step back, feeling overwhelmed and helpless. "How do you expect me to get there?" she exclaimed. "I have no way of travelling. I have nothing..."

"You have already overcome seemingly impossible odds. Do not underestimate your own resourcefulness. You will find a way to do what you must. Of this we are certain."

"I may have come this far, but I've lost so much along the way," Eladria said bitterly.

"This we know. If there was a way we could make your path easier, we would..."

"Why should I risk any more? Why should I be the one to find this Dragon Star and travel to this place of great evil? I'm not an adventurer or a soldier and I'm certainly not a hero. Why should this fall to me?"

"Because it is your destined path and it always has been," Zanel responded, her voice echoing through the temple.

"I don't believe in destiny," Eladria said with a growl.

"You may believe what you will, but belief or lack of belief are immaterial; they do not change what is. You must do this..."

"I think I've done enough already. It's been all I could do to escape with my own life. Others, like Zinn, were not as fortunate."

"You stand to lose far more if you do not act. Your world will be destroyed; this we have foreseen. And many others beyond will be jeopardized. You are the only hope that remains. Only you can safeguard your world and the lives of your friends...and your mother."

"Then it's true," Eladria said slowly. "My mother *is* at Drantak?"

"That is correct."

"But why? What happened to her? Why would she be captured and taken there?" Eladria asked.

"She has been a prisoner for many years and has suffered greatly. She is being used and manipulated, forced to act against her will. She needs

you, Eladria. You must go to her, to Drantak. And you must go with the Dragon Star. The Dragon Star is the only hope."

"But I don't even know what it is!" Eladria cried in desperation. "I don't know how to get to Naaryu, or what I'm supposed to look for once I get there."

"You will be guided," Zanel said. *"Behold!"*

There was a flash of light in mid-air and something fell to the ground. Eladria looked down and saw that it was a red ring. She reached down and picked it up. It had appeared out of nowhere but was solid and tangible. She ran her finger along its edge, marveling at its unique beauty. She'd never seen a ring like it. It was entirely red, made of a metal she couldn't identify.

"Wear the ring," Zanel instructed. *"Whenever you need instruction, simply close your eyes and focus on the ring—and on me. It will bridge your consciousness with mine. I will impart the information you need. I will lead you every step of the way."*

Eladria slipped the ring on her finger and nodded. "Thank you," she said, relieved to know that she wouldn't be travelling blindly.

"You must go as soon as possible. Find transportation to Naaryu, where you will locate the Heart of the Dragon. I will lead you there. The Dragon Star is guarded by the Daykeepers, a race that has protected it for aeons. They will only give the Dragon Star to one of royal blood and noble virtue. That is why you alone can take possession of the Dragon Star and bring it to Drantak, where it will be used to save your world. You must set off on your journey as soon as possible. There is little time to waste."

Eladria nodded. Things were clearer to her now. She watched as the robed figure began to dissolve and disperse. The red light from the well dimmed and Eladria found herself alone in the darkness.

She sat down by the well, her mind reeling from all she had learned. Whereas before the words of the Others had been disconcertingly vague, Zanel had filled in a great many missing pieces of the puzzle.

It pained her deeply to hear that her mother was being held against her will and forced to serve the dark forces that threatened to destroy her world. Eladria buried her head between her knees. She had lost so much: her home and everything she'd ever known, her father and now Zinn. If the Others were to be believed, then all that now remained was her mother.

Zinn had sacrificed her life to enable Eladria to escape, so she could continue her quest and carry out her mission. Eladria silently vowed that Zinn's sacrifice would not be in vain. And she promised herself that, no matter what, she would save her mother and put an end to whatever was happening at Drantak.

She felt wholly unprepared for such an undertaking, in spite of the immense trust the Others had placed in her. She was just a spoilt girl who had never had to worry about anything other than what shoes she would wear that day.

Yet she owed it to her mother to do everything she could to free her and to save her world. What happened after that she couldn't begin to imagine. Even if they succeeded in ending whatever horrors were being perpetrated at Drantak and escaped with their lives, what would she and her mother do? Would they find a way to overthrow the Ha'shon and regain control of the planet?

The future, she realized, was out of her control. All she could do was take charge of the present moment; to do as she had been directed and to embrace her so-called 'destiny'.

"I have to try," she muttered, as she looked down at the red ring. "I have to try. I owe it to them..."

She sat lost in her thoughts for what seemed like hours. But after a time, exhaustion took hold again and she slipped into a deep, yet restless slumber.

In her dreams she was being pursued by an unseen force and chased deep underground into a cavernous maze. She saw many people around her: Zinn, her mother and father, Van'garat, Janak and the enigmatic hooded figure of Zanel. The mysterious boy with the dark hair and sparkling brown eyes was also present; someone with whom she felt an inexplicable affinity, but who always seemed just out of reach.

Even amid the ephemeral vista of her troubled dreamworld, Eladria was aware of one thing with certainty: the time was coming. The wheel of destiny was turning and all spokes converged upon a single moment in time, a moment that was fast approaching and of which Eladria was intrinsic. She was somehow the key. The fate of an entire world, of an entire realm, rested with her.

Chapter 19

Preparing To Leave

Eladria awoke to find herself bathed in sunlight. She stretched and felt a dull ache in her back, for she'd been lying upon the cold stone floor the entire night. Still, comfort was a luxury she had rapidly become accustomed to living without.

She looked up at the cloudless crimson sky as the morning sun illuminated the temple in a warm yellow hue. But even in daylight, it was a sinister and unwelcoming place. As she got up, her thoughts again returned to Zinn. This time, to her surprise, no tears came. The sharp intensity of her grief had been superseded by numbness. She knew there was nothing she could do for her now, however much she wished differently. But she vowed that her death would not be in vain.

Eladria looked around the temple and decided it was time to leave. She didn't know what had drawn her here in the first place, or why she'd felt reluctant to leave. Perhaps Zanel and the Others had somehow directed her here, as they had to the crystal waterfall, so they could make contact with her.

As she climbed down the temple steps, she recalled her conversation with Zanel. In spite of everything that had happened here, she felt a spark of determination igniting within. Now that she knew a little more, Eladria was resolute that she would find the Dragon Star and take it to Drantak. Some dark force was threatening to destroy her world, and she would fight to stop it. She had to make things right again: for her father, for Zinn—and for her mother. Eladria would do everything in her power to save her.

Her newfound resolve was like a healing balm that took some of the edge off her pain. She'd always been headstrong and determined, two qualities that often worked more to her detriment than her favor, but this time she needed them. They would keep her going. In spite of all that had occurred, in spite of losing everyone dear to her and being hunted like an animal, she realized that she still possessed that reservoir of inner strength.

It didn't take her long to find Van'garat and Janak. They had been awake for some time and were wandering the deserted town. Both were relieved to see her, although each expressed their feelings in different ways: Janak was exuberant like a child, while Van'garat was typically calm and measured. She was impressed that they had managed to remain in each other's company without killing each other. The trauma of what had happened had evidently forced them to bond and it seemed Janak had finally formed a grudging tolerance for the Ha'shon mystic.

Eladria didn't immediately tell them about her encounter with the ghostly apparition. She decided she would wait for the right time before sharing what Zanel had told her. Instead she joined them as they searched the town for food and water.

Wandering the ghost town was unsettling. The streets were pervaded by a deep silence not even broken by the sound of birdsong. Eladria felt a lingering aftereffect from the cataclysmic events of the other night. It was as though the sense of evil, the shock and fear, was somehow tangible and lingered in the air like an invisible mist. This, however, didn't deter Janak from looting and pilfering various trinkets and valuables from the buildings. Eladria voiced her disapproval, but it seemed the instinct of a thief was impossible to quell.

They came to a large hall. Like most of the buildings in Arnaast, it was of ancient design but had been renovated by the True Way cult. As they ventured inside the weathered grey-stone building, they realized it must have been a communal banquet hall, for it was filled with long wooden tables, many of which had been damaged in the storm and tremors. The walls were cracked, the windows smashed and a portion of the roof had caved in, shattering a wooden balcony on the second level. Carefully maneuvering around the damage, it didn't take them long to find the kitchen and larder, in which they found enough food to last them for several months. There was an assortment of vegetables, fruit, meats, bread and baked goods, as well as fruit juices and various other drinks. All three of them were hungry, so they generously piled their plates and then returned to the hall, sitting down at one of the undamaged banquet tables.

As they ate, no one dared speak of Zinn, although she was clearly foremost on everyone's mind. Eladria found it almost impossible to stop thinking of her. Her absence was painful and frequently she felt herself on the verge of tears, only no tears would come, as though she had already expended every last drop.

It wasn't until they finished their meal and began to talk that Eladria told them of her vision. As she relayed the details of her encounter—the way Zanel had appeared to her, and her directive to travel to Naaryu and find the Dragon Star—Van'garat and Janak listened intently.

"So that's what she told me," Eladria summarized. "We have to find the Dragon Star and take it with us to Drantak. That's the only way we can stop what's happening there."

"I no understand," Janak said. "What is a...Dragon Star?"

"I don't actually know," Eladria admitted. "According to mythology, it was a mysterious artifact, a gift from the gods, supposedly to heal the planet in a time of great crisis. No one knows more than that. I don't even know what it looks like."

"Then how we find it?" Janak asked, scratching his head.

"Zanel said she would lead me to it."

"And you trust her?" Van'garat asked, his brow creasing as he spoke.

"Well, if she's one of the Others, I've no reason not to trust her," Eladria answered. "If, as they say, they're beings from a dimension beyond this one, then they can see things that we can't. They can see the bigger picture and they seem to know exactly what we need to do to save our world. Without them, we wouldn't have a clue what was happening, we'd just be stumbling around in the dark."

"Because they have an expanded perspective doesn't necessarily mean they're working in our best interests," Van'garat warned.

Eladria was taken aback by his response. "Why the sudden skepticism?" she asked.

"I simply feel the need to urge caution."

"I don't understand, Van'garat. You claim to have some kind of mystical vision. So you tell me, is Zanel to be trusted or not?"

Van'garat leaned back on his seat and took a deep breath. "As I said before, my inner vision has been curtailed. I wish I could say with certainty who we can trust and who we cannot, but at this point I'm unable to."

Eladria was silent for a moment. "What do you know of the Others?" she asked him.

"I know that they're a race of beings existing outside of time and space," he said. "They have many names: the First Ones, the Overseers, the Guardians. It's believed they're responsible for overseeing the events of the mortal realm, for maintaining balance between the multiplicity of universes and dimensions that coexist and interpenetrate. Any significant imbalance in one realm threatens all the others. And certainly, whatever is happening at Drantak is a grave threat indeed."

"Then you think we can trust them?"

"Ordinarily perhaps. But you must realize they are not alone. There are many other beings out there, besides the Others..."

"Like one we encounter here?" Janak offered. "Kahnos, or whatever it was?"

Van'garat nodded. "The utmost vigilance is required when dealing with discarnate entities. Some genuinely work for our best interests, but many do not. When contact between realms is established, they can easily manipulate the beings of this world into doing their bidding."

"You believe that's what Zanel is doing?" Eladria asked.

"I don't know. When I close my eyes and try to gain insight, to tune into her as you did, I see nothing. I can't penetrate the barrier that's been placed around me. She may indeed be a representative of the Others, directing you to do what's necessary to save this realm. What I do know is that you, Princess Eladria, are the key to what is happening here. You have a pivotal role to play in determining the fate of this world. What that role is, and how you are to fulfill it, I cannot yet say..."

"It comes down to me then. It's my decision," Eladria realized. "In spite of your warning, Van'garat, I feel I can trust Zanel."

Van'garat nodded. She noticed him glancing at the ring Zanel had given her with a look of mild suspicion, but he remained silent.

"I'm going to do this," she continued, determination spilling into her voice. "I won't forget Zinn's sacrifice. She gave her life so that I could complete this mission and I won't let her down."

There was a moment of silence before she continued. "I intend to leave here today. If you either of you want to come with me, you can. But this is my journey, not yours and I'll understand if you'd prefer to stay here. After all, it's going to be dangerous. I don't know what might be waiting for me out there."

"I not like sound of that," Janak said. "But Janak has nothing else to do and nowhere else to go. I trust you, Princess. Where you go, I follow. Besides, when you back in charge of the planet, maybe you can find position for Janak?"

"What kind of position?" she asked.

"I not know," he smiled, eyes twinkling. "But if you ever looking for a king, I sure we be very happy together."

"I...don't think that arrangement would work somehow," Eladria said with a slight smile.

"Then perhaps I be in charge of trade and commerce?"

Eladria shook her head. "No offence, but I think a field such as that might prove too much temptation for someone with your...work-related history. But I am impressed by your cooking skills, so how would you like to become royal chef?"

"Yes, yes! I happily cook for you in palace," Janak beamed proudly.

"It's agreed then. Assuming all goes well, you'll be my royal chef." She turned to Van'garat. "What about you, Van'garat?"

"I harbor no such ambitions for the future," he replied. "But I will continue to travel with you, for I was led on this journey for a reason, as we all have been."

"Very well," Eladria said. "We'll leave here as soon as we can."

"But how we going to travel?" Janak asked.

"I have an idea," Eladria said as she got up from the banquet table. "Once we're out of here, I'll show you."

Before leaving the hall, they returned to the kitchen. There they found some cloth bags which they filled with as much food as they could carry. It seemed a prudent move, for they were unsure when they would next have access to such plentiful food.

The princess led them down the derelict courtyards and along the deserted streets to the periphery of the town. Here she was overcome by another wave of grief, for this was the last place she had seen Zinn. It was here she must have died. Taking a deep breath, she tried to set her grief aside. There would be time to deal with her feelings later. For now she had to focus on the task at hand.

Eladria led them to the runway on the outskirts of the town. Five True Way aircraft remained on the runway, three of which had been damaged by the storm and tremors.

"We take one of these?" Janak asked as they approached the stationary fighters.

Eladria nodded. "It's our only option. The only way we'll ever get to Naaryu and Drantak is by air."

"But wait," Janak exclaimed. "I not know how to fly and I not suppose Ha'shon knows either. You know how to fly one of these?"

"Not yet, but I think I can learn," Eladria said as she stepped toward one of the seemingly undamaged vehicles. "Much to my father's consternation, I was trained to pilot TRM craft and I was considered a fairly competent pilot, too. That's how Zinn and I managed to escape the palace when the Ha'shon invaded."

"But surely these are quite different to the ones you're familiar with," Van'garat noted.

"Obviously they're different, but they're based on similar principles."

Eladria surveyed the True Way fighter. It was larger than the TRM fighters she was accustomed to. Fortunately, she found the craft was unlocked and prepared for takeoff. Clearly security hadn't been a priority for the people of Arnaast, their isolation in the deepest regions of the jungle perhaps accounting for their complacency.

Eladria climbed aboard the fighter, stepped into the cockpit and looked over the controls. The layout was different but she was reasonably confident that, with a little time to familiarize herself with the operational system, she could pilot the craft.

"I think this initiates the engines," she said, pointing at a lever on the right-hand side of the console. "This controls altitude and flight path...and this must be the throttle."

"Do you think you can pilot it?" Van'garat asked.

"It's a basic interface, far cruder than TRM technology, but I think so. And we have one thing in our favor."

"What's that?"

"See this?" Eladria pointed to a silver box-like device that sat atop the cockpit. She flicked a switch and activated it. "This is a navigational device. Again, it's crude, but if I input our destination, it ought to show us where we're going."

It took her several failed attempts, for the user interface was unlike anything she'd seen before, but she finally managed to input Naaryu into the navigational control. The display screen revealed a map and began to plot their course, which took them northeast across the continent of Yahnas and over the Raskabari sea to the small volcanic island of Naaryu.

"This will keep us on course."

"And once we arrive on Naaryu?"

"I suppose I'll have to rely on Zanel to lead me to 'the Heart of the Dragon', as she called it. But we have to get there first."

Before takeoff, Eladria spent some time familiarizing herself with the controls and layout. She experimented firing up the engines, controlling the hydraulic system and maneuvering the craft across the cracked, tremor-damaged runway. It was a matter of trial and error and ideally she could have done with a day or two to fully master the controls, but she knew they had to leave now, whether she felt ready or not. She was reasonably confident she could pilot it once in the air, although she wasn't nearly as confident about landing.

"Get seated and strapped in," she called, as she fastened her own belt. Van'garat, who sat beside her in the cockpit, fastened his belt securely as he looked around in curiosity. Janak sat behind them and, only now admitting to a fear of flying, was extremely apprehensive. "Please make it smooth ride," he called nervously.

"I can't guarantee anything," Eladria said, concentrating hard as she readied the craft for takeoff.

She followed her flight training and went through all the necessary checks and procedures as best she could. As she initiated the thrusters and put the vehicle into motion, it sped across the runway in a jerky, uncontrolled motion, causing the passengers to lurch in their seats. Janak let out a cry of panic but Eladria ignored him, concentrating upon the archaic control panel as she maneuvered the fighter ahead and pulled the throttle.

The craft lifted off the runway and shot upward. It was a less than smooth takeoff, however. As she struggled to control its movement, the craft jerked uncontrollably and began spinning in circles. While Janak cried in alarm and Van'garat held on to his seat tightly, Eladria tried to regain control of the fighter as it cut through the trees, sending branches flying in every direction. The controls were stiff and she had to pull at the control stick with all her might, but she eventually steadied the vehicle and evened its trajectory.

Before long they were flying high above the jungle. Unlike the TRM fighters with which she was familiar, this machine was difficult to control and required constant manual adjustment. But for now, she felt confident it was under her control. She referred to the navigational system and adjusted her course to bring it in line with their intended flight path.

She felt a surge of satisfaction. They were airborne and on their way to Naaryu. After what seemed like weeks of wandering through the jungle, aimless and lost, they were finally making headway.

Chapter 20

The Daykeepers

Their journey was largely made in silence. They flew across jungles and mountains, canyons and deserts, and all the while Eladria kept a close eye on the remote sensor readings. There was a great deal of aerial activity across the planet and she wanted to avoid any entanglement with the Ha'shon or the True Way. As a lone fighter on an undesignated heading, they would be an easy target. Eladria had spent all her time learning to fly the craft and didn't have a clue how to operate the weapons systems. Upon catching sight of any other aircraft, she immediately altered course to avoid them.

Fortunately this part of the planet was largely uninhabited and, as far as she knew, the island of Naaryu was also unpopulated. As she adjusted her flight path to avoid three Ha'shon raiders on the periphery of sensor range, she again wondered what had been happening in the days since the coup. Had the Ha'shon completely overthrown the Royal Military and the True Way, or was there still a battle being waged for rulership of Tahnadra?

She felt helpless. Here she was, legitimate heir to the throne, and she had no involvement as the various groups vied for power. Still, she had a more important mission now. If she failed in her quest to stop what was happening at Drantak then none of it mattered anyway; for if the Others were correct there wouldn't be a planet left for anyone to fight over.

They left the continent of Yahnas and began their flight across the Raskabari sea, which bridged Yahnas and Da'mu, the latter being the largest landmass of Tahnadra. Da'mu was divided between the True Way territories in the north and the Ha'shon regions of the south. A thin belt separated the two warring regions: the neutral lands of Tamaru. Despite their neutrality, these territories were the source of frequent skirmishes between Ha'shon and True Way forces, as both fought to advance upon the other's territories. Eladria was glad that Zanel hadn't asked her to travel anywhere near these war-torn regions, for if she had, their chances of survival would have been marginal at best.

Eladria kept to the course outlined on the navigational chart, travelling across the ocean toward Naaryu, which lay alongside three other small islands. She didn't know what to expect when they arrived, but she could only trust that Zanel would be true to her word and would guide them once they landed. She looked down at the red ring on her left index finger, which glistened as rays of sunlight streamed in through the glass cockpit.

The hours passed and Naaryu eventually came into sight, a small landmass with steep volcanic peaks and dense green valleys and forestland. The surrounding ocean was rough and choppy with large white waves crashing upon the sandy coastline.

"This is it?" Janak asked, leaning forward and staring out the cockpit.

"This is it," Eladria confirmed.

"Where will we land?" Van'garat asked.

"I don't know," she answered. "I suppose now would be a good time to ask."

"Ask?"

"Zanel said that whenever I needed direction, I only have to close my eyes, focus on the ring and she would guide me."

"I see," Van'garat said.

Eladria took a brief moment to close her eyes and directed her attention to the ring. Almost immediately, she could sense Zanel's presence. Content that she'd established a connection, she inwardly asked her question: *where are we to land on Naaryu?* The answer came immediately: *the southwest coast of the island, by the Garatiano volcano.*

Eladria opened her eyes and immediately plotted the course.

"I take it you received an answer?" Van'garat asked.

Eladria nodded as she maneuvered into position and prepared to initiate landing procedures. It was difficult to find a suitably flat stretch of ground upon which to land, but she eventually located a clearing amid the trees not far from the southern shore.

With great care she brought the craft down. It sliced through the treetops, its wings like twin blades cutting through branches and leaves, sending waves of nearby birds fluttering into the sky. They landed with a bump, but Eladria was nonetheless pleased with her piloting skills. She hadn't been trained to fly this archaic old fighter, and she'd had to rely on her wits as much anything, but they'd made it.

As they prepared to disembark, Eladria went to the weapons locker in the aft compartment. Both she and Janak armed themselves with a True Way electro-pulse pistol, but Van'garat declined the offer. Eladria knew it would be futile to argue with him, but as far as she was concerned it was a necessary precaution. After all, they didn't know what might be lying in wait for them.

As they stepped out of the craft, the forest was rocked by a sudden tremor.

"What was that?" Janak gasped as he steadied himself against the aircraft's fuselage.

"I'm not sure," Eladria frowned. "Could it be the start of another breach? Because that would be the last thing we need right now."

"I don't think so," Van'garat said with a shake of his head. "Normally I can sense them before they happen. That felt to me like a normal seismic tremor."

"Normal or not, is still not good," Janak murmured.

"What do you think caused it?" Eladria wondered as she surveyed the surrounding forestland.

"My first assumption would be *that*," Van'garat pointed behind her. Eladria looked round and saw the Garatiano volcano towering above the treetops: an imposing rocky mountain with wisps of smoke rising up from its peak.

"I thought the volcano was extinct," Eladria said.

"It not look extinct to me," Janak exclaimed.

Another tremor rumbled underfoot and Eladria raised her arms to balance herself.

"You not think is going to erupt soon, do you?" Janak asked nervously.

"How would I know?" Eladria snapped.

"Whatever we're here to do, I suggest we do it as quickly as possible," Van'garat advised.

Eladria nodded.

"So where do we go, Princess?" Van'garat asked, looking at her expectantly.

"Give me a moment," she said. She closed her eyes and again focused upon the red ring. As before, it wasn't long before she felt the presence of Zanel. She mentally reached out and sought direction. She immediately received an answer and it was much to her consternation.

"The volcano," Eladria said, opening her eyes and turning to Van'garat. "She's directing us *into* the volcano..."

"Are you certain?"

"Yes. That's where we have to go. The volcano itself is the 'Heart of the Dragon' and the Dragon Star is somewhere within it."

"No!" Janak stepped back in alarm. "Janak not going anywhere near volcano,"

"Fine, you can stay here and watch over the craft while we're gone," Eladria said. She looked at Van'garat questioningly, and saw not a trace of fear in his eyes. As ever, he was imperturbable and seemed more than content to follow her.

"Is not that I scared, you know," Janak added, puffing out his chest in exaggerated bluster. "Is just I feel is best I *stay*...and guard craft, like you said."

"Good," Eladria looked round. "It's an important job too,

because we don't know what might be lurking in the forest."

"What you mean?" Janak's chest suddenly slumped and a look of fear crept into his wide eyes. "You mean there are *things* in forest...?"

"I don't know, but I'll feel happier knowing there's someone watching over the craft while we're away."

"Yes," Janak said, his face draining of color. "I do that. But I think I stay *inside* it, just in case."

Eladria repressed a smile. "Suit yourself. We'll be back as soon as we can."

Eladria and Van'garat made their way through the forest toward the volcano. They trudged over the dense foliage and under-growth, across rocks, vines and logs. The tremors continued intermittently, shaking the entire forest, and each time Eladria felt a sense of foreboding, as though they were portents of an impending danger. Part of her wanted to leave the island immedi-ately, for she knew it wasn't safe here, yet she was here for a reason and she wouldn't leave without the Dragon Star.

"What do you know of the Dragon Star?" she asked Van'garat as they crossed a small stream.

"The usual stories," Van'garat said. "It was apparently a gift left to the people of our world by the Lasan. This gift, the Dragon Star, was a mystical device capable of unlocking great power, designed to bring peace and balance to the world. But it was of such unfathomable power that it had to be protected from those that would misuse it, so it was taken to a hidden location and there it has remained for millennia. No one on Tahnadra knows its whereabouts, although countless have tried to find it over the centuries."

"That's much the same as I was taught," Eladria said, as she gingerly climbed across a large boulder obscuring her path. "Though I didn't pay much attention during my history and mythology lessons. I wasn't much of a scholar. I was always dreaming of being out there—out *here*—exploring the world instead of being stuck in a classroom on an isolated moon."

"It seems that you got your wish," Van'garat noted.

"I suppose I did," she said with a sigh. "But I was young and arrogant. If I could go back and change one thing it would be to appreciate what I had back then. I had everything I could ever have possibly wanted. I had my mother, for a time at least, my father and Zinn, and family and friends, and it still wasn't enough for me."

"We live to learn," Van'garat said as he helped her across another boulder. "And in time, the wiser among us at least, not only live to learn, but learn to live. The two go hand in hand."

As they continued through the forest, they found numerous signs of stress upon the land. Cracks had formed across the ground in several places, creating chasms of varying sizes and a number of trees had been uprooted. Eladria didn't know if these were caused by the volcanic tremors or the dimensional breaches, which she assumed had struck with equal ferocity here.

They reached the edge of the forest, beyond which an open rocky expanse led to the base of the smoldering volcano. The first thing Eladria noticed was a series of metal pylons encircling its perimeter. She wondered who had placed them there and for what reason. She was about the step forward, when Van'garat put out a hand to stop her.

"Be careful," he warned, squinting his eyes, as if straining to see or sense something.

"Why?"

"There's danger here. I sense a trap..."

"I don't see anything. Whatever those pylons are, they don't appear to be active. Besides, we can't turn back now."

She pulled away from him and took another step forward. At that moment the metal pillars activated with a loud, resonant hum. A wave of electricity discharged, jumping from pillar to pillar, connecting to form a web of light encircling the base of the volcano.

Eladria staggered back. It was clearly some kind of defensive grid designed to keep intruders out. She picked up a nearby rock and threw it at the web of energy. As it hit the violet web of light, the rock disintegrated and dispersed in a puff of smoke.

"Thanks for warning me," Eladria gasped as she turned to Van'garat. "What are we going to do now?"

"That, I don't know..."

"Perhaps it's time to ask Zanel," Eladria answered. She closed her eyes and took a deep breath, trying to settle her mind and focusing all her attention upon the ring. She inwardly called to Zanel, beseeching her guidance. Again, almost immediately the answer came to her.

She opened her eyes, slid the ring off her finger and handed it to Van'garat, who reluctantly reached out and took it from her. "Why are you giving this to me?" he asked.

"She told me to take off the ring and step through the barrier," Eladria explained.

"Step *through* it?" Van'garat's face darkened as he placed the ring in his pocket.

"She assured me I'll be able to step through it unharmed," Eladria responded with a nervous shrug. "She told me before that only one of royal blood and pure heart would be permitted entrance to the Heart of the Dragon."

"That's a large leap of faith to take. Do you really trust her enough to risk your life like that?"

"I have to. I'm not going back, not without what I came here for. I'm here for a reason and I can't believe that reason is to die. I can do this. I know I can. Wait here for me."

"Very well," Van'garat said, shifting uncomfortably.

Eladria took a deep breath and began walking toward the barrier, which continued crackling with electrical charge. She could feel the heat being emitted by the energy as it danced from pylon to pylon, encircling the volcano and rising at least twenty feet above her. There was clearly no way around it, or above it. There was only one way, and that was through it.

She felt a rising terror as she contemplated walking directly into the electrical barrier. This went against all sense and reason and her instincts for survival were screaming at her to turn and walk the other way. If Zanel was wrong, she would be killed instantly.

But Eladria was determined. If this was the only way to save her world and rescue her mother, then she had to take the chance. This wasn't the first time she'd been called upon to risk her life and, assuming she survived this, it probably wouldn't be the last.

She took a deep breath and tried to steady her quivering legs as she silently counted to three. Upon the count of three, she stepped into the barrier...

As she passed through the wall of electricity, she could feel the energy dancing upon her skin. It tingled sharply, but there was no pain. The current was being repelled from her as though her skin was some kind of energy-resistant armor. Not daring to stop, she kept moving until she reached the other side and was beyond the barrier.

In unspeakable elation, she cried out in triumph and fell to the ground laughing. "I did it!" she cried. "I actually did it!"

After taking a moment to savor the delicious relief of still being alive, she got to her feet and turned to the entrance of the volcano. Ahead of her, a series of stone steps led to an arched doorway cut into the side of the mountain.

"I'm at the entrance," she called to Van'garat. "I'm going in. I'll try to be as quick as I can."

She climbed the steps and passed through the stone doorway, which led into a rocky passageway. The hot, winding tunnel veered downward and was lit by a dim reddish glow coming from the distance.

She proceeded with both caution and haste as the passageway led her deeper into the volcano, occasionally branching off into side-paths. Eladria was never quite sure which way to proceed. If she still had the ring she would have sought Zanel's guidance, but that was no longer an option. She wasn't sure why she'd been advised to remove the ring before entering the volcano, for she needed it now more than ever. She decided it was best to follow the tunnel straight ahead and not take any of the side-paths.

The tremors continued with increasing frequency. She often had to stop and steady herself against the wall, careful to avoid debris falling from the rocky ceiling. The further she went, the hotter and thicker the air became, making it harder to breathe.

She eventually came to the end of the corridor, which led into a vast underground cavern. As she stepped forward, she looked around in wonder. Illuminated in a warm red glow, the cavern ceiling arched high above her, the ground interspersed with pools of steaming water and craters of fire. There were a number of man-made structures as well, made of glass and gold, with bridges and walkways leading to a number of entrances and exits dotted along the walls.

As she walked across one of the gold bridges leading over the pools of water, rock and fire, she caught sight of a small man, only half her height. He was scurrying past one of the glass buildings, wearing a plain brown robe and sandals, his arms filled with a pile of dusty old books. With a curiously mouse-like appearance, he was bald with large ears, had small round black eyes and a thin, wiry frame with large, stubby hands and feet. Upon catching sight of Eladria, the man stopped in his tracks and stared incredulously, remaining silent.

Eladria cautiously approached, stepping off the bridge and moving toward the rodent-like man. "Hello," she called. "My name is Eladria. I'm looking for the Daykeepers..."

"My word," the man twitched nervously as he continued staring at her, not once blinking. "You've finally come! Finally come, after all this time."

"Then you've been expecting me?"

"Yes, of course, yes," the man responded, putting down his armful of books and scurrying toward her. He took hold of her hand and looked up at her, his eyes penetrating and enquiring. "You are just in time. If you had come any later...any later...you would not have found us. Please...please, come! No time to waste. Hurry, hurry."

Still holding her hand, the man led her through the cavern, along the gold-paved walkways, through one of the exits and down a darkened corridor. The corridor terminated in an even larger cavern, at the heart of which sprawled a vast subterranean city, comprising an assortment of domed buildings, dwellings and temples, all constructed of glistening gold and glass. Eladria marveled at the beautiful fairy tale-like city hidden deep within the volcano. Again illuminated by a fiery red glow, the city was surrounded by pools of water and fire beneath a network of inter-linking gold bridges and pavements.

But it wasn't a peaceful place. Its mouse-like inhabitants were frantically scurrying to and fro, carrying armfuls of belongings, boxes, tools, implements and books. There was a great urgency about them that verged on panic.

The cavern was suddenly shaken by a tremor, dislodging rocks from the ceiling, pulverizing buildings and walkways as they crashed to the ground. The mouse-people reacted in heightened alarm, desperate in their efforts to get where they were going in spite of the obstacles around them. Most of them seemed to be scurrying toward one of the exits.

"What's happening here?" Eladria asked her guide as they crossed one of the bridges and entered the heart of the city.

"Wait...wait here," the man said, gesturing for her to remain where she was.

She nodded and did so compliantly, watching as the miniature people darted about like oversized ants. Some of them looked up at Eladria in curiosity as they passed, but quickly carried on their way. Eladria got the impression that she was the first visitor they'd had in a very long time, but there was obviously no time for fanfare.

The man that had brought Eladria here soon returned and was accompanied by an older man. He had the same mouse-like features, only he was wearing a long-sleeved burgundy robe and an ornate headdress studded with multicolored gemstones and topped with long golden feathers. Clearly struggling with the ravages of old age, he walked slowly and awkwardly, relying on a spiraling wooden cane to support him. But he nevertheless had an air of dignity and power that greatly exceeded his physical stature.

"Here she is, here she is," the first man muttered as he pointed to Eladria.

"Yes, yes, I can see that," the old man nodded with a trace of irascibility as he came to a stop before the princess. "You may leave us," he said, dismissing his subject, who bowed reverently, then scurried off to join the others.

Eladria stepped forward and introduced herself. "My name is Eladria," she said, with a polite tilt of her head.

"Yes, this I know," the old man nodded. "I am Ru'archa, ancestral First Priest of the Daykeepers. Here, deep in the Heart of the Dragon, my people have lived for millennia. It is my honor...great honor...to welcome you, Princess Eladria."

Eladria lowered her head in acknowledgement.

"You are the first mortal to have entered the Heart of the Dragon in the long history of my people," Ru'archa continued. "All others have been forbidden. The barrier around this mountain was installed long ago to keep intruders out. Only *you* could enter the inner sanctuary."

"Only me?"

"When we were first brought here all those millennia ago, the ancient ones told us that, at some point in the distant future, one would come to claim the Dragon Star and that, until that time, all others had to be kept out. Many have tried and failed to pass the threshold. But the ancient ones foresaw your coming. They knew the day would dawn when the Dragon Star would be needed to play its part, to enable the fulfillment. Trusting their words, we knew you would come. And you have made it just in time...just in time!"

Another tremor caused more of the cavern ceiling to collapse.

"In time for what?" Eladria asked.

"We are evacuating," the old man responded. "We must leave here immediately. Some of us wanted to leave sooner, but I kept us here long enough, just long enough. The volcano has been activated, triggered by the dimensional collapse. It is about to erupt and it will be a major eruption. Nothing will remain. Our underground sanctuary will be destroyed. So we are leaving...leaving now, and taking as much with us as we can."

"Where will you go?" Eladria asked, looking at the desperate and frightened little people as they continued to pack up and flee their homes.

"Deeper underground," Ru'archa replied. "A place of safety has been found. What lies next for us, we do not know. Whether this world will endure beyond the dimensional collapse, no one can say. The future has never been more uncertain. Now, come, Princess...come and you will be given the Dragon Star. Time grows short, so let us make haste!"

Chapter 21

The Dragon Star

Ru'archa led Eladria through the crumbling underground metropolis to an open courtyard at the heart of the city. The courtyard was dominated by a colossal gold statue of a man with outstretched, birdlike wings. Ru'archa approached the statue and Eladria followed. As she studied the monument, wondering what it signified and why it occupied such an important place at the heart of the city, Ru'archa bowed his head and uttered an obscure incantation.

The moment the words left his mouth, there came a loud grinding noise and the statue began to move and transform. Eladria stepped back in surprise as it opened up to reveal a cylindrical glass booth inside. Ru'archa moved toward it and beckoned for Eladria to join him. They entered the booth, which was apparently an elevator of some kind. The door closed behind them and Ru'archa pressed a button on the gold-plated control panel. With a loud hum, the elevator began to descend, taking them down through layers of rock and sediment.

"Where are we going?" Eladria asked.

"To the Dragon Star, of course...to the Dragon Star," Ru'archa muttered, looking straight ahead, his expression solemn.

Down the elevator went, deeper and deeper underground. It was lit by a rapidly intensifying red glow and the further they went, the hotter it became. Eladria marveled at the ingenuity of the Daykeepers, for they evidently possessed an astonishing level of engineering skill and technological ability.

The elevator soon came to a halt. The door opened and Ru'archa stepped out, motioning for Eladria to follow. They had arrived at the edge of an immense funnel-shaped crater in what appeared to be the heart of the volcano, a rocky basin stretching high above and far beneath them.

Ahead of them a circular stone platform was supported by four walkways branching out like the spokes of a wheel. Each walkway terminated in a doorway carved into the rock-face, one of which being the elevator in which they had arrived. Ru'archa carefully made his way along the walkway to the central platform.

As Eladria followed, she was struck by the immense heat, which she could almost feel blistering her exposed skin. The air was thick and laden with smoke and ash, making it difficult to breathe. Beneath was a sheer drop, at the bottom of which bubbled a bed of swirling molten lava. The princess crossed the walkway with the utmost care, extending her arms to steady herself as the volcano rumbled and shook.

With a sigh of relief, she made it onto the platform alongside Ru'acha. At the center of the platform stood an altar. Tall, narrow and carved of stone, it housed a triangular case made of black metal. The case emitted a halo-like golden glow, with sparks of light dancing around it like merry fireflies.

Ru'archa stepped toward the artifact and lowered his head before it. "Behold...behold, the Dragon Star," he said. He reached out and opened the casing. A light of almost blinding intensity blazed outward, forcing Eladria to shield her eyes and look away.

"That's the Dragon Star?" she asked, trying through squinted eyes to get a decent look at the mysterious object. "What exactly is it?"

"Starlight," Ru'archa answered. "A spark of starlight, gifted from the Lasan, the ancient ones. It is told that this starlight comes from the Lasan's own solar logos...that it is pure creative power, pure potentiality."

"What am I to do with it?" Eladria asked. "I can't even look at it! How am I to take this to Drantak?"

"You will not take it...it will take you."

"I don't understand."

"The Dragon Star is not a possession to own...no! Neither is it an object to be acquired. You must become *one* with it..."

"Become one with it? How?"

"Open yourself...be receptive to it. Allow it to take hold of you. Invite it into your heart..."

"But what will happen?" Eladria demanded.

"That I cannot say. For it has never been done before."

"If it's never been done before, then how do you know it's even possible to become 'one' with it? How do you know it's safe?"

"There is no guarantee...but then there is no guarantee of anything in life. It is time. You have been led here, and not by chance. Allow it to become one with you, to become a part of you."

"I'm afraid to," she admitted, immediately ashamed of the admission.

"Fear is a natural response," Ru'archa said with an understanding nod. "But you must go beyond it...beyond it...or all has been for nothing..."

She knew he was right. She'd been through too much to give in to her fears now. She didn't know what would happen if she followed Ru'archa's advice and merged with the Dragon Star. Would it kill her, or transform her? Would she somehow lose her sense of self, or identity? That would be tantamount to a death of sorts.

The tremors were increasing in both frequency and severity. As another shook the mountain, Eladria almost fell to the ground, and was suddenly very much aware of the long drop beneath them.

Their time was limited and Eladria knew she couldn't afford the luxury of a lingering deliberation. She set her fears aside and did as Ru'archa suggested. She took a deep breath and, through shielded eyes, looked ahead at the Dragon Star, which blazed radiantly with the power and intensity of a sun. In spite of all her fears, she mentally opened herself to it, reaching out to it with her mind, inviting it to enter her heart.

The invitation was immediately accepted.

She was surrounded and filled by a river of light. The breath was knocked from her lungs as the light surged over and through her skin, into her muscles, organs and bones, flowing through her mind and senses, penetrating every cell of her being.

She felt as though she was melting, dissolving into a vast sea of light, until nothing remained but the blinding luminescence that devoured her.

Yet, awareness still remained; a pure, undifferentiated awareness...

All pervasive and sublime...

Unlimited and non-grasping...

How long a time Eladria spent in this state of altered consciousness, she was uncertain. It felt like an eternity stretched into a mere second. Yet it passed. The light dimmed and she again became aware of her body as thoughts returned to her mind. She struggled to understand what had just occurred, but knew it had been something extraordinary and profound.

She opened her eyes. In front of her was the altar with the glass case, which was now empty. The light was gone. The Dragon Star was gone! The place was now illuminated only by the fiery glow of the swirling lava beneath them.

She turned to Ru'archa, who was watching her intently.

"The Dragon Star," she whispered. "Where is it? What happened?"

"It is within you. It is part of you now," Ru'archa responded, one of his eyebrows arched. "The Dragon Star is now you...you *are* the Dragon Star."

When Eladria had been told to come here and find the Dragon Star she'd expected it to be a trinket, or a jewel or ornament, an artifact she could simply have lifted and taken with her to Drantak. Now there was nothing to be seen and nothing to take possession of. The Dragon Star had somehow dissolved into her. She now *was* that which she had sought.

"But I don't really feel any different," she admitted.

"Its power will be revealed in time. Until then, you must get used to its presence. You must integrate...integrate."

"I've been told I must take it to Drantak. Do you know anything about Drantak, Ru'archa? And about what I'm supposed to do once I get there?"

"No," Ru'archa shook his head. "We keep only to our own business, to our own affairs and we leave others to theirs. Only that all would do this, the world above ground would be a far more harmonious place. But that is of little importance to us...little importance. We have fulfilled our mission. It is over and we must move on..."

"This place your people are evacuating to, will you have enough time to get there?" she asked, steadying herself as again the mountain shook.

"The future is uncertain, but we will do what we can. Now it is time, Princess of the Dragon Star. It is time that you leave here."

Ru'archa pointed to one of the walkways leading from the central platform to an exit in the rock-face. "Go there, Princess...follow the passage all the way, do not deviate. It will take you back to the surface. But you must hurry...hurry!"

Eladria looked down at the high priest and bowed her head politely. "Thank you," she said. "Thank you for everything. I wish your people well."

Ru'archa nodded and extended his hand, placing it in front of Eladria's heart. Unfamiliar with the gesture, Eladria simply smiled.

"Go now, Princess...go now," he said.

With a parting bow, she took her leave of Ru'archa and carefully crept along the narrow walkway. Behind her Ru'archa returned to the elevator and soon disappeared from sight.

Eladria found herself in a long tunnel leading upward in a series of steps. She ran up them as fast as she could, swayed by the increasingly severe tremors. She was relieved to be out of the blistering heat of the volcano crater, but was struggling to find her way in the relative darkness. Occasionally, small passageways forked to the left or right, but Eladria stayed on course, following the steps onward and upward.

They led to a long winding corridor, which she raced along as fast as she could. As she ran, another round of tremors shook the mountain, causing a large chunk of the ceiling to fall, blocking the path ahead.

She was fortunate not to have been caught beneath the falling rock, but her way was now obstructed.

She cursed in dismay and tried to pull away the rocks. She heaved with all her might, but they were simply too heavy to budge.

In desperation, she slumped to the ground, tears of despair rolling down her face.

She didn't know what to do, but she knew she'd come too far to give up now. Overcome by a surge of determination, she got to her feet and, following an instinctive impulse, focused all of her energy and intent upon removing the obstruction.

She felt her body begin to glow, as though every cell of her being had suddenly ignited. Something was building within her; a tingling, electrical charge, getting stronger and stronger by the second. She remained still, but continued to stare ahead: hoping, praying, *demanding* that the obstruction be cleared.

Incredibly, that was what happened! She watched in amazement as the boulders suddenly disintegrated and disappeared. In mere seconds, the fallen rocks had crumbled into dust and dispersed into nothingness. The way was now clear. She was astonished, but there was no time to question it.

She began racing down the rocky passageway once again. It was some time before she reached the exit, a small opening leading outside, into daylight.

The tremors had exacerbated immeasurably. She could feel the volcano being torn apart from the inside out. Once clear of the mountain, she passed through the electrical barrier with impunity, just as the pylons began to collapse, uprooted by another round of quakes.

"Van'garat!" she called as she caught sight of her friend. He had already spotted her and was running toward her.

They caught up with each other just as a violent tremor carved a fissure in the ground not far behind them. As the ground cracked open, a stream of lava spewed outward, running down the surrounding land like a scalding, viscous river of golden-red.

"Back to the craft!" Eladria cried.

They ran as fast as they could. The ground continued to split and, as Eladria glanced behind her, she saw a fountain of liquid fire exploding from the volcano's peak, as well as continuing to vent from the fissures on the ground. The air was filled with ash and the heat burned their exposed skin as they ran for their lives.

The animals of the forest were reacting in similar alarm. Flurries of birds filled the smoke-filled air, squawking in alarm, while the four-legged creatures of the forest floor raced across the land in search of safety.

Eladria's mind was surprisingly calm and clear as she focused all of her energy on reaching their commandeered craft. At one point it appeared they had taken a wrong turn and were lost, but fortunately Van'garat's sense of direction was sharper than hers and he directed them back onto the correct path.

After what felt like an eternity, they reached the landed True Way fighter, finding a distressed Janak, who was ecstatic at their return. Above the treetops they could see a stream of golden-red liquid spurting out of the mighty volcano, as the tremors continued to rock the island.

Eladria had no time to catch her breath as she boarded the fighter, strapped herself into the pilot seat and initiated take off. With a minimum of fuss, she fired up the engines and maneuvered the craft upward. Within moments they were flying above the island, passing not far from the volcano, which continued venting an endless stream of lava, running down the surrounding land in scorching rivers of red.

As they departed Naaryu, Eladria said a silent prayer of gratitude. Against all the odds, and having been forced to defy the greatest and most destructive enemy of all—the fury of nature herself—they'd made it.

Now it was on to their final destination, the forbidden land of Drantak.

Chapter 22

The Battle For Nubrak

The commandeered fighter sped through the sky, slicing through thick layers of cloud, beneath which occasional glimpses of the ocean were visible. Eladria again glanced at the navigational console, which displayed the jagged outline of Drantak, a lone island in the farthest expanse of the black sea.

"What you know of this place, Drantak?" Janak's voice came from behind her.

"I know that few have ever travelled there," she answered. "It's one of the remotest places on the planet."

"What is it like?"

"It's supposedly just a barren wasteland, uninhabited, with little in the way of animal or plant life. According to legend, it's a place of dark magic and secret underground civilizations. But none of the expeditions ever found any evidence of that. In fact, they didn't find much of anything at all."

"Yet the legends persist," Van'garat noted.

"Yes. Which is probably why it's called the 'forbidden land'. Few have any wish to travel there."

"What you expect us to find there?" Janak asked.

"I wish I knew. But there must be *something* there and I suppose it won't be long before we find out what."

"Yes, it seems the forbidden land is now the most important place in all of Tahnadra," Van'garat noted darkly.

"Where is that down there?" Janak asked, leaning forward and peering out the cockpit.

"That's the island of Nubrak," Eladria answered, alternating her attention between the controls and the navigational console, sparing just a moment to look out the glass cockpit. Far beneath them were rolling blue-green hills and forestland, crystalline rivers and sprawling reddish canyons.

"Nubrak," Janak echoed. "Nubrak is neutral territory?"

"Last thing I knew, it was, yes."

As a neutral land controlled by neither the Ha'shon or the True Way, Nubrak had been the source of great conflict and struggle. Both sides had sought a foothold in this strategic region. The Tahnadran Royal Military had established a base upon the island at the request of its inhabitants, who saw it as the only way to deter a potential invasion by either warring side.

Eladria was enticed by the knowledge they were nearing a TRM installation and she briefly toyed with the idea of making contact. She still had no idea what had been happening in the aftermath the Ha'shon coup and desperately wanted to know how the conflict was progressing. But she had no way of knowing who was now in control of the Nubrak outpost. It was possible that, like the other TRM bases, it had been overthrown and commandeered by the Ha'shon. If this was the case and she made contact with them, then she would alert the Ha'shon to her presence and they'd stop at nothing until they'd apprehended or killed her. The risk was too great. She knew she had to avoid making contact with anyone.

Similarly, she would have to steer clear of their flight space. She would have bypassed Nubrak altogether but that would have entailed a significant detour and they didn't have enough fuel for that. Judging by the rate at which the fuel gauge was dropping, they'd be lucky to make it to Drantak at all.

"Van'garat, do you still have the ring I gave you?" she asked her passenger. The Ha'shon looked round and nodded. "Can I have it please? I may need it again once we reach Drantak."

Van'garat reached into his pocket and hesitantly handed her the red ring. "I do advise caution, Princess," he said.

"After all that's happened, I'm cautious about *everything*," she remarked ruefully as she slipped the ring on the middle finger of her left hand.

"All the same, something is not right here," Van'garat pressed.

"I no longer know who our allies and who our enemies are, but I'm certain that we're being manipulated in some way."

"Can you elaborate on that?"

"No, it's just feeling, and one that's growing stronger the closer we get to Drantak. I feel a growing unease about this entire mission."

"Are you now saying we shouldn't go to Drantak?"

"No. I believe you've been sent there for a reason and that, whatever happens, your destiny is calling you there. But something has changed. The waters have been muddied. Things are no longer as clear to me. We must bear in mind that Drantak is a dark and dangerous place and maintain the utmost vigilance."

Eladria considered his words carefully before responding. "You're right, Van'garat, it's important to remain vigilant. But I've made my decision. I'm not going to turn back now. Zanel came to me in my darkest hour and ever since she's guided me. I know you don't trust her, but for some reason I do. It's like I *know* her somehow, as though I'm connected to her..."

"You're a young woman of extraordinary strength and conviction," Van'garat said. "I respect that and honor your choices. As I said, all I urge is caution."

"I agree with Ha'shon," Janak chimed in. "These dangerous times and we must be careful."

Van'garat turned to the young thief. "This may be the first time you've agreed with me on anything," he observed wryly.

"In spite of Janak's better judgment, you sometimes do speak sense...for a Ha'shon."

"I believe there may be hope for us yet," Van'garat said with a slight smile.

"Good, because we need all the hope we can get," Eladria said. "I appreciate what you're both saying. If Zinn were here, she'd no doubt echo your sentiments. She was always worrying about my welfare. When I was growing up, I must have pushed her nerves to the limit. I didn't always make life easy for her, or for anyone I suppose, including myself."

"If she harbored any resentment I saw no sign of it," Van'garat said gently. "All I did see in her was a fierce devotion and a bond of love as deep as I have ever seen."

"I wish she was here with us," Eladria said, feeling her eyes moisten as she pined for her beloved friend.

"Maybe, in a sense, she still is," Van'garat said.

Before Eladria could respond, her attention was drawn to a light flashing upon her console.

It was a proximity alarm alerting her to nearby aircraft—and not just one or two, but dozens of them! In her distraction she'd not only veered into the Nubrak flightpath but had flown into the periphery of an aerial battle.

She grabbed the control stick and tried to pull back. Ahead of her were two lines of aircraft—the TRM and the Ha'shon. They were engaged in fierce combat, gliding in and out of formation, releasing wave after wave of fire. Beneath them was the Nubrak TRM base. This was clearly a battle for control of the military installation.

A steady stream of fighters were being launched from the base, which was taking a battering from overhead raiders. The Ha'shon were numerous and relentless in their offensive. It nevertheless heartened Eladria to see that there were still TRM bases that had not yet fallen to the Ha'shon. The battle for Tahnadra was not yet over. But it was a fierce struggle. She watched helplessly as a number of military craft were destroyed or disabled by the Ha'shon and sent spiraling into the canyons beneath, where they combusted into balls of flame.

"I wish I could help them," she exclaimed as she reluctantly veered away from the engagement.

"Your people fight with bravery and resolve," Van'garat said. "And unless I'm mistaken, you have no experience in battle. There's nothing you can do to help them, Princess. You have other priorities."

His words stung. She hated the thought of abandoning her people when they were engaged in a life and death struggle, but she knew he was right. With a heavy heart, she prepared to resume her course for Drantak.

Just as they were about to leave, they suddenly lurched in the sky. The breath was knocked from Eladria's chest and her ears almost deafened by the sound of an explosion coming from the aft compartment.

"What was that?" cried Janak.

"We're under fire," Eladria exclaimed as she double-checked her display. One of the Ha'shon raiders had broken from their lines and was pursuing them.

"But we not part of their battle!" Janak exclaimed. "Why they firing at us?"

"Why do you think?" Eladria cried. "This is True Way craft we're in. The True Way are the Ha'shon's blood enemies."

Van'garat concurred. "The sight of a lone True Way craft must have been too enticing to ignore."

The craft was pounded by another explosion and then another as their attacker released a steady stream of fire. Eladria wished she'd had time to acquaint herself with the weaponry, but it was too late for that now. She couldn't return fire, so all she could do was try and outrun it.

Unfortunately, red lights were blinking all across the console. Her eyes darted across the cockpit display and her heart sank as she realized that the last shot had torn off the left nacelle and ruptured the fuselage. The damage was irreparable.

"Is there anything I can do?" Van'garat asked as he looked down at his copilot console.

"Yes," Eladria shouted. "Pray!"

The Ha'shon raider was relentless in its pursuit. They had a taste for blood and clearly wouldn't be satisfied until they'd inflicted the death blow. They fired again and again, causing the

True Way craft to buckle. Eladria shielded her eyes as the cockpit console exploded and ignited in flames.

"There's nothing I can do," she cried. "They've destroyed the propulsion system, the controls—everything! We're going to crash."

Janak cried in panic, while Van'garat closed his eyes in a strangely serene fashion and held on to his seat. Eladria grabbed the control stick, trying to regain control of the fighter as it hurtled downward, the ground getting closer by the second. This was her second crash-landing in the past couple of weeks. She swore that if she survived this, she'd never set foot in another aircraft for the rest of her life.

She kept her fingers tightly gripped on the control stick, tugging it upward, trying to raise the front of the vehicle as much as she could.

Closer, closer, closer the land appeared: intricately sculpted canyons of red rock.

Within seconds, their fate would be sealed.

The craft plunged into the open mouth of a canyon, bouncing off the rock-face as it tumbled and span.

Eladria was braced for death.

Chapter 23

Lost Light Of The Old Way

Deeper the craft plunged, ensnared by gravity's relentless pull.

Eladria tugged at the control stick in an attempt to elevate the nose and break their fall, but the controls were unresponsive.

Please, she cried inwardly, to whom or what she didn't know. *It can't end like this. It can't!*

At that moment she felt herself surge with a glowing radiance, as though her body was suddenly illuminated from within. The mysterious light pulsated through her being and spread outward to encompass the entire craft.

She instinctively knew that she had the ability to mold this energy with her intent.

With barely seconds remaining, she directed the energy to cushion their fall...

Their momentum slowed dramatically as though an invisible hand had reached down and caught hold of them. They landed on the canyon floor with barely so much as a bump.

"Impossible! I can't believe it," she exclaimed, breaking into nervous laughter. The energy that had flooded her mind, body and senses quickly dissipated and she was left with only a slight tingling in her extremities.

Van'garat looked round in bewilderment. "What did you do? It was as though something pulled us back just as we were about to hit the ground. If not for that we would have—"

"We alive!" exclaimed Janak from the rear. "By twin rivers of Taslock, I was certain we going to die. I actually see my life flash before my eyes—and it leave a lot to be desired, I admit—but we alive!"

Eladria slipped off her belt and got up from her seat. She stepped over to the exit and tried to open the hatch. It was stiff, evidently damaged in the fall, but with a little help from Janak she managed to heave it open and a shaft of daylight streamed into the fighter.

"What's that?" Eladria asked, looking down at her feet.

Janak looked up sheepishly. "Oh, I sorry, my last meal kind of revisited me. I tell you I hate flying, and I refuse ever to do it again."

Eladria frowned as she wiped her feet and stepped over to the locker in the aft compartment. She opened it and surveyed its contents. The craft was equipped with an array of supplies that may prove useful. She reached in and took out an electro-pulse pistol and holster, which she strapped across her waist. In spite of the clear skies and sunshine, Nubrak had a colder climate, so she took out three fur-lined overcoats and handed them to her friends, while slipping on one herself.

She stepped over to the exit and carefully climbed out the hatch. Along with virtually everything else, the mechanism controlling the landing steps was broken, so she had to jump. As the craft was partially submerged in the sparkling blue-green river that cut through the base of the canyon, she landed with a splash, ankle deep in water. She stepped across to the stony riverbank as the others followed behind.

The canyon walls stretched high above them, exquisitely carved red rock leveled in layers, decorated with occasional trees and patches of greenery. The sound of weapons-fire echoed around them like distant thunder. Thankfully, there was no sign of the Ha'shon raider that had attacked them. Once it had shot them down it must have returned to rejoin the battle.

Eladria stood on the riverbank and surveyed the smoldering wreckage. "There's no way to repair the damage. It's finished," she said with a sigh.

"And it nearly take us through gates of netherworld with it," Janak added.

"At least we're alive," Eladria said. "Which is more than we had any reason to hope."

"What exactly happened as we were falling from the sky?" Van'garat asked her once again. "I was aware of a sudden light and some force took hold of us, slowing our descent. The light came from you. It was *you* that saved our lives."

Eladria shifted uncomfortably, unsure what to say.

"You must have been aware of it," Van'garat pressed.

Eladria nodded awkwardly, unable to explain what had happened.

"It can only be the Dragon Star," Van'garat reasoned. "From the moment you emerged from the volcano, I sensed a change in you."

"What kind of a change?"

"There's something within you now, a dormant power that infuses every fiber of your being and is changing you from the inside out."

"Changing me? In what way?"

"That remains to be seen."

"Dragon Star?" Janak interjected. "Then is Dragon Star that saved us?"

Eladria nodded. "It must have been. All I wanted was for us to land safely, for something to break our fall. That's what was foremost on my mind."

"And that's what happened," Van'garat said thoughtfully. "Now you have a taste of the immense power that lies within you."

Eladria was uncomfortable with the conversation, as she didn't feel ready to speak of this. She'd been deliberately vague about her encounter with the Daykeepers. Perhaps because she still wasn't entirely sure what had happened when she merged with the Dragon Star, or what implications it held. She turned her attention to the smoldering True Way craft, eager to change the subject. "I don't know how we'll get to Drantak now," she said with a somber shake of her head.

"Whether by land or sea, I not care," Janak said. "Just so long as it not by air."

"We're so close to a TRM base," Eladria said, gazing in the direction they had come. "I'm so tempted to go there. They'd be able to give us transport to Drantak and we'd have a contingent of armed soldiers to accompany us."

"But as we saw, they're in the middle of a battle for possession of the base," Van'garat cautioned. "There's no guarantee that by the time we get there we'll be greeted by your Royal Military. Besides, should any of my people catch sight of you, you'd be captured or killed. Of that I'm certain."

"We must stay away from Ha'shon, no matter what," Janak agreed.

"You're probably right. I just wish there was a way I could make contact with my people and let them know that I'm still alive," Eladria exclaimed in frustration. She folded her arms and stared into the turquoise water, observing the shimmering reflection that looked up at her.

"You must focus on the task at hand," Van'garat told her. "You have your own path to follow now and although we're currently without transport, it is not over yet."

At that moment the ground shook, dislodging a chunk of rock on the canyon wall and sending it tumbling down into the river. As Eladria steadied herself, she sensed a faint electrical charge in the air, a sensation that was by now familiar to her. "There's another storm coming," she said, turning to her comrades.

"Not *here* as well," Janak muttered.

"These breaches are clearly happening all across the planet," she said.

"And their increasing frequency suggests that we're now running out of time," Van'garat added.

"Where should we go?" Eladria wondered aloud. "If it's not safe to go to the military base, then how else are we going to get off this island?"

"There has to be a way," Van'garat said. "I sense that we're here for a reason, that there's someone here, someone who may be able to help us."

Eladria looked round. "Can you be more specific?" she asked.

Van'garat closed his eyes and was silent for a moment. As he reopened his eyes, his face lit up in a wide smile. "Yes, he's here! And he's close by. I didn't even realize he was in physical embodiment. We must go to him. He will help us."

"Who?" Janak raised an eyebrow.

"One of the Old Ones, a mystic of the Old Way," Van'garat explained. "I've sensed his presence before and I saw him clearly in my mind's eye. He's living in a cave not far from here. If we hurry, I'm sure we can make there it by nightfall."

"You're certain we can trust this person?" Eladria asked.

"I would trust him with my life. Come, let us go."

"Very well," Eladria said with a measure of reluctance. Although there was still a lingering trace of doubt as to how far she could trust Van'garat and his mystical visions, she realized that their options were otherwise limited. If there was someone nearby who could help them, then it would be foolish to pass up the opportunity.

They left behind the wrecked craft and, with Van'garat in the lead, travelled along the riverbank as it wound through the canyon. Daylight was receding into dusk and as the sun gradually disappeared from the sky, the last remnants of turquoise dissolved into a deep indigo. The air was cool and crisp, but their brisk pace kept Eladria warm.

The sound of distant gunfire and aircraft engines had now ceased. Perhaps the battle for the Nubrak base was over? Eladria wondered if the military had succeeded in repelling the Ha'shon invaders, but there was no way to know.

Van'garat led them from the riverbank along one of the rocky trails that zigzagged up the edge of the canyon. Every so often the ground was shaken by a tremor; sometimes minor, but other times of considerable destructive force, causing chunks of the canyon wall to fragment and tumble to the ground beneath.

By the time complete darkness had set in, the heavens had erupted into another full-blown storm. The now-familiar ribbon of light pulsated amid the heavens, only this time it was larger than ever before. It discharged forks of lightning that filled the sky, sometimes reaching all the way to the ground. The howling wind and drum-like thunder reverberated through the canyon in almost deafening intensity.

Fortunately they soon reached their destination. Van'garat came to a stop, looking up at an opening in the canyon wall. It was a large cave, the entrance of which was lined with teeth-like stalactites, illuminated by the lightning to sinister effect.

"This is it," the Ha'shon said as he turned to his comrades, raising his voice to be heard above the storm.

"Then let's go," Eladria said, gesturing for them to move.

Van'garat approached the cave and cautiously entered. Eladria was about to follow, when Janak stopped her. "How we know is safe?" he shouted, steadying himself as another tremor rumbled underfoot.

"Would you rather stay out here?" Eladria shouted back.

Janak quickly shook his head and joined Eladria as she followed Van'garat through the mouth of the cave...

The interior of the cave was unlike anything Eladria had ever seen or experienced. From the outside it had appeared dark and lifeless, but the interior was alive with a warm, glowing radiance, the walls a translucent sea of shifting colors and the air tingling with a gentle static buzz. A thin membrane of light covered the entrance of the cave and Eladria could no longer hear the storm outside. It seemed far away somehow, as though an entire universe separated them from the outside world.

The cave branched into several tunnels, each pulsating with light. Van'garat was some way ahead of them, walking down the largest of the passageways, making his way deeper into the heart of this mysterious den. Eladria and Janak followed, looking around in wonder as they walked down the passageway. As they moved, they left a trail of light behind them, which glistened like dewdrops in the morning sun.

They soon came to the heart of the cave, an open chamber that was evidently home to someone, for there were chairs, a table and decor. Geode formations and antique tapestries adorned the walls, which continued to glow in kaleidoscopic pastel hues. At the center of the chamber burned a small fire with purple flames rising up from a spherical furnace. A sweet fragrance perfumed the air, calming Eladria's mind and senses. Whereas mere moments ago she had been in the midst of the storm, desperate and fearful, she now felt curiously at peace. The question was, who lived here?

As if in answer to her unspoken question, a figure emerged from one of the side tunnels, a trail of light sparkling behind him. At first Eladria thought it was an old man, but the closer he got, the younger he appeared. His face was changing before her eyes; one moment he was an elderly man with a lined face and short white hair, and the next he appeared younger and taller, his skin smoother and his hair darker. Wearing a flowing indigo robe, his features were those of a Nubrakian, for he had a narrow face with a pointed chin, olive skin and striking turquoise eyes. He walked with slow, purposeful steps and, whether young or old, he had impeccable posture and exuded an aura of immense power and dignity.

Van'garat bowed before him. "Master, I am honored to be in your presence," he said in a tone of deep reverence.

"I am pleased that you heeded my call," the man answered, with a hint of nonchalance. "But then, I would expect no less of an adept of Ko Tra Pah."

"You make it sound like you've been expecting us," Eladria said.

"Of course," the man responded. His face and appearance

again changed, he seemed now like an old man of indiscernible age, his face wrinkled and his expression bearing a trace of irascibility. "There are no unexpected happenings," the man continued. "Unless, of course, one fails to pay attention and is therefore heedless to the signs. In which case, it is one's own fault for being caught unaware. These times of unrest require our full participation, our full attention, or else we invite catastrophe."

"I'm Eladria," the princess introduced herself, stepping forward with a polite bow of her head. "These are my friends, Van'garat and Janak."

"Yes, I know of you all," the old man said. "My name, should you need it, is Nirataan."

"What is this place?" Eladria asked.

"It is my home and has been for more years than I care to number."

"I've never seen anywhere like it. The light, the colors, the very air; everything's different, somehow...*alive*..."

The man nodded curtly. "Of course. It is not of your world. The moment you stepped into the cave you entered a portal that took you into this, an intermediate realm, a buffer zone between the corporeal and non-corporeal realms."

Nirataan's appearance again changed. He was now a much younger man, his wrinkles dissolving into a youthful complexion, his silver hair suddenly thicker and darker.

"Why is your appearance changing like that?" Eladria blurted, unnerved by the transformation.

Nirataan sat on one of the chairs and gazed up at her, a look of wry detachment upon his face. "This place is unpinned in time," he explained. "The laws of linear time, so immutable in your realm, have greater plasticity here. Just as well too, for the body you see before you is of great age, born to the mortal realm over a hundred and thirty rotations of the sun ago."

"You're telling me you're over a hundred and thirty years old?" Eladria asked incredulously.

Nirataan nodded.

Eladria slowly shook her head. "It's not possible to live that long."

"Possibility is but a state of mind. I am a master of the art of the impossible, or, at the very least, the improbable."

"You look like you're from Nubrak?"

"Yes, this body was born to two farmers living in the Nubrak agricultural province almost a century and a half ago."

"How you end up here?" Janak asked as he continued looking around the cave.

"As a youth, I came across a wandering forest hermit who trained me in the discipline of Ko Tra Pah," Nirataan explained. "Like your friend Van'garat here, I left civilization behind and lived as a renunciant for many years. I was eventually led here, to this crack between realms, and here I have lived in solitude ever since. It was necessary in order that I fulfill my final purpose."

"You trained your initiates here?" Van'garat asked.

Nirataan looked up and nodded. "Yes, for many years I trained chelas in the ancient wisdom, but only those that were ready; those that were attuned enough to heed my call and find this place, which remains hidden from the ignorant and profane. But those days are long gone now. There are few today who remember the Old Way and fewer still who have any interest in our seemingly obsolete ways."

"Why is that?" Eladria asked.

"Times change. Rather like animals sense the onset of a storm and move to safer terrain, the masters of the Old Way could sense the impending darkness and they knew there was nothing to be done. Most of them chose to depart the mortal realm. They knew their time was over."

Van'garat stepped forward and again bowed his head in prostration before the old master, whose form had again shifted, ageing dramatically in the blink of an eye. Sat upon his chair, the man looked like an ancient statue, dignified and imposing.

"In the jungle, following my master's death, I often had visions of a great mystic living somewhere on the planet, yet somehow apart from it," Van'garat said. "I'm certain it was you, Master Nirataan, that I sensed during my darkest hours."

"I am glad you felt my presence," Nirataan said. "I was aware of you for many years, observing you from afar."

Van'garat's eyes widened and his voice became but a whisper. "Then you saw *everything* that happened?"

"Yes, I saw it all..."

Van'garat fell silent. Eladria noticed that the Ha'shon hermit was overcome by sudden and pronounced vulnerability.

Nirataan held him in his gaze, a look of compassion lighting his aged face. "It is a great wound that has eaten away at you all these years and you cannot be free until you have healed it, or at the very least acknowledged it. That is why you are here."

"What are you talking about?" Eladria asked.

Van'garat turned to her and took a deep breath. The ordinarily unflappable Ha'shon seemed shaken as he answered. "I suppose it is time you learned. You recall I told you that my Master Ustabak was murdered by True Way raiders?"

Eladria nodded.

"Well, that was not all that happened that day."

Eladria wasn't surprised, for she'd known all along that Van'garat had been holding something back. The whole time she'd been with him she'd felt there was something within him, a hidden burden that he constantly sought to restrain and repress.

"What I didn't tell you was that after they killed my master, I reacted in a fit of rage," he continued, his voice wavering. "I don't know what possessed me. Perhaps my grief triggered the violent impulses of my people, impulses that to this day I must exercise the utmost control over. But, in my state of grief and rage, I lashed out at the attackers, and with the power of my mind, I killed all five of them. Their bodies literally melted before my eyes as they were erased from existence."

Eladria stared at him, dumbfounded. Knowing what she did of him, it seemed inconceivable that he'd be capable of harming anyone, even in such extreme circumstances.

Van'garat was clearly uncomfortable sharing this horrific secret and was overcome by emotion. "I was horrified by my actions," he whispered hoarsely. "I couldn't believe what I'd done. I was an initiate of Ko Tra Pah. In spite of what had happened, I ought to have been in control of my faculties. But I gave in to my rage, and five people lost their lives. I violated every principle I believed in. I was a disgrace to the memory of my master."

Eladria stepped forward and tried to console him. "No. Like you said, you still have the blood of your people running through your veins, and there must be elements of their aggression within you. For one brief moment, that slipped to the surface and caused you to react out of pain. I understand that. I felt the same way when the Ha'shon killed my father. If I could have reached out and killed them all, I would have. But it passed. It was a momentary impulse and I can't spend the rest of my life judging myself for having felt that way. Neither can you."

"But I have," Van'garat shook his head. "I have spent the years since alone in penance, seeking forgiveness for my crime."

Nirataan spoke up. "You have punished yourself long enough," he said. "It is time you let go of this burden of guilt you have carried. You must forgive yourself for past misdeeds. You are still a mortal being, Van'garat and imperfection is the very nature of your realm. This you must accept. The past exists as but a shadow, a memory lingering in the mind. If you and your friends are to have any chance of succeeding in your mission, you must be free. You cannot let the shadows of the past bind you."

There was a long silence. Van'garat looked down at the ground, evidently deep in thought. "You speak great wisdom, Master Nirataan," he eventually said. "Perhaps I have carried this burden long enough. It is a pain I can bear no longer."

"Then let it go," Nirataan urged. "You have since atoned for your crime, through both your aspirations and actions. Forgive yourself and relinquish the past now."

Van'garat said nothing, but Eladria could tell he was deeply moved by Nirataan's words. She sensed that something had shifted within him now he had been absolved of his sin.

"Please tell me, Master Nirataan," Van'garat said after a pause. "You told us that the Masters of the Old Way have now left this world. Why do you still remain?"

"I remain because one final task stands before me," Nirataan said, his voice slow and measured.

"And what of myself?" Van'garat asked. "If the Old Ones have left Tahnadra in such great number and at a time of great crisis, then why was I led to this path? Why was I trained in the ancient wisdom when there is no longer a place for it in this world?"

Nirataan looked up. "The answers are already within you," he answered. "You are here neither by accident nor by chance and this applies equally to your young friends here. You were guided by the threads of fate and directed by the unseen hand of the Guardians. It was no coincidence that you landed so close to this portal and that you heard my call and heeded my summons. It was necessary for many reasons.

"For you, it was necessary for your atonement and to reaffirm that your journey these past years was essential to the great unfolding. In spite of your faith, there has remained within you a seed of doubt, a lingering fear that perhaps your life energy would have been better directed elsewhere. But that is not so. Your years of solitude, your training and your awakening, the triumphs and the tragedies, were all necessary, otherwise you would not be able to fulfill your destiny."

"Which is what?"

"You are the awakener and the guide. This you already know."

"I don't feel like I have been much of either."

"You still have your part to play. Do not seek to judge with the mind what the mind cannot begin to fathom. Know the truth in your heart. As you were taught by Ustabak, the highest level of Ko Tra Pah has nothing to do with exercise, combat or poise. It is to be attuned to the primordial essence, to be grounded in the root of existence and to work with it, flow with it and, if so drawn, to mold it with one's intent."

"What is the primordial essence?" Eladria asked, crossing her arms and starting to feel dizzy as the room continued to morph in a shifting screen of light and color.

Nirataan rose from his chair and stood before her, his body continuing to fluctuate between youthful vigor and elderly decline. "The primordial essence is central to the teachings of the Old Way," he explained. "It is the one substance out of which the ephemeral forms of this world arise and to which they return. To realize this and to become one with it is to see beyond all illusion: to see reality as it is and not merely as it appears to be."

"What do you see when you look at reality?" Eladria asked.

"I see endings and beginnings," Nirataan said. For a moment it seemed that he was going to say more but he hesitated, closed his mouth and remained silent.

"You've told Van'garat why he's here, but what about us?" Eladria asked. "You said we all had a reason for being here."

The ageless man was about to respond when he suddenly, with lightning-fast reflexes, reached out and grabbed Janak's arm. Janak gasped in surprise as Nirataan locked him in a martial arts grip, twisting his arm behind his back and holding him rigid. Nirataan reached into Janak's pockets and pulled out several artifacts he had evidently just stolen from Nirataan's cave, including two small gold trinkets and a geode formation. Nirataan released his grip, causing Janak to fall to the ground. He then returned the stolen objects to their proper places and folded his arms, looking down at the thief disapprovingly.

"Janak, I can't believe you," Eladria scolded him. He was certainly a gifted thief, for she hadn't been aware of him touching anything in the cave.

"I-I sorry," Janak pleaded as he got to his feet, his face white and limbs trembling. "Is just what I do. I had to steal to survive. It not matter where I am or what is going on, if I see something might help me later, I just take it. Is only way I manage to survive."

"It is time to change," Nirataan said in a raised voice, his eyes fixed upon the shaken thief. "This is no way to live your life, not any longer. You are worth more than this and capable of far greater things. You must rise above your past and relinquish those habits that no longer serve you."

"I...I try," Janak said in a fluster.

"You must do more than try. These are times of pivotal importance. You can no longer cling to the old ways. Rise above your limitations, if not for yourself, then for your family. They want better for you."

"My family?"

"They are with you," Nirataan said, his face softening. "They have been with you all this time. A bond of love, once forged, can never be broken."

"How...how you know this?"

"Masters of Ko Tra Pah can see beyond the veils that separate dimensions. That which was your family, their consciousness and essence, lives on. They are never far from you and they want more for you than the life you have given yourself. It is not too late for you to create a better life for yourself, an honorable life. That is their wish for you..."

"I will," Janak whispered, his eyes welling with tears. "I will...for them..."

"And for yourself. Your path will lead you to places you could never imagine. If, that is, you are successful in your mission to Drantak."

"What can you tell us of Drantak?" Eladria asked, stepping forward as Nirataan returned to his chair.

"I know that you are here because your journey to the dark land has come to a halt, but I can help you. That is why I have remained in this transitory realm just long enough that I might be here for you, to help and to warn you."

Eladria looked up in alarm. "Warn us? About what?"

"The moment you arrive in Drantak you will be walking into a trap."

"What...?"

"You have been deceived and manipulated," Nirataan said evenly, his eyes fixed upon her with piercing intensity. "The one calling herself Zanel, it is she that has deceived you. She is not one of the Guardians, or 'Others' as you call them. She is a treacherous mortal and it is she that has orchestrated everything that now endangers your world. She lies in wait for you at Drantak, desperate to acquire the power you now possess: the power of the Dragon Star. For only with the Dragon Star can she complete her plan."

Eladria took a step back and shook her head. "But the Dragon Star is gone," she said. "It disappeared into me. I have nothing to give her."

"It is part of you now. You must be aware of the change within you? It may be subtle as of yet, but you will learn to harness and direct its power. As an adept of Ko Tra Pah, your comrade Van'garat will be able to assist you in this."

Eladria looked at Van'garat, who nodded gently and then she turned her attention back to Nirataan. "So it's *me* that Zanel wants?" she asked, feeling a shiver run down her spine.

Nirataan nodded. "She needs the Dragon Star—she needs *you*—in order to complete her task."

"Which is what?"

Nirataan was silent for a moment before he continued. "As you know, there is a dark and deadly force seeking entry into your realm," he began. "It is now but a dim shadow, lurking in the periphery, but it is working intently, through any channels available to it, to open a passageway into your world. Zanel is a puppet, an instrument of the Shadow Lords, intent on releasing them from their dimensional prison."

"So they can invade our world..."

"Yes. If they succeed there will be no conflict, however, no war. It will simply be a mass annihilation. The Shadow Lords, assuming physical embodiment, will travel from world to world, across an entire universe, consuming and destroying all in their path. They feed off the life-force itself, in much the same way as other beings breathe air."

"You make them sound like parasites..."

"They are worse than parasites, for they kill their host immediately."

"And you really believe I can stop them?"

"You have the power, daughter of Chaldeen. Only you can seal the breach and undo that damage that has occurred. For even if the Shadow Lords are thwarted, there is still the danger this world will be pulled through the breach, into the void."

"What exactly is the void?" Eladria enquired.

"It is the buffer zone between dimensions," Nirataan explained. "Any physical matter that comes into contact with the void is instantaneously erased from existence. This is how containment between realms is assured, and it is this the Shadow Lords are attempting to subvert with the experiment."

"So what do I have to do?" Eladria asked in earnest. "You say I have the power of the Dragon Star within me? If that's so, then how do I use it?"

Nirataan exhaled, his lip curling in a terse smile. "You have already used it and you will continue to learn. It is a skill that will unfold, and when the time is right, you will *know* what to do. What I can tell you is that you will be made to look deeply into the face of your enemy, an enemy that has been lurking in the shadows your entire life. When your nemesis is revealed, you will be shaken to your core. But you must stand firm and muster all the courage you possess, for only then can you vanquish your demons and defeat your adversary. Falter even for a moment, and the result will be catastrophic for all."

"Master Nirataan," Van'garat interjected. "How are you able to sense all this? When I cast my mind to Drantak, I sense nothing. It is as though a screen has been placed over my vision."

"The dark ones have been watching you all along," Nirataan told him. "They have deliberately obscured your vision to keep the truth from you. As for myself, as long as I have existed in this pocket between universes, they have been unable to sense me. Until now, at least. Upon your arrival, they may have been able to trace me. That is why, as soon as you depart, I shall leave here. I will return to the dimension of the formless; an eager release, long anticipated."

"While in the meantime," Eladria began. "We have to somehow get to Drantak, knowing that we're walking into a trap and that the fate of the entire world is resting on our shoulders...and without a clue what we're supposed to do?"

"Is nothing you can do to help us?" Janak asked Nirataan.

"I did not say that," Nirataan rose from his seat and took hold of his cane. "You are tired and hungry, are you not?"

All three nodded.

"You will be given ample food and rest, and you may remain here as long as you wish."

Eladria shrugged. "I thought this was a situation of dire immediacy. We've been told we have to get to Drantak as soon as we possibly can..."

"So it is, and so you do," Nirataan answered. "But recall that you are in a pocket of the void here, existing outside of linear time. A century here may be only a heartbeat in the world outside, or it may be countless millennia. I will make sure that you arrive at Drantak in time. First, it is important that you rest and gather your strength. Because, believe me, you will need it for what lies ahead."

Chapter 24

Flight Of The Riders

When it came time to leave, Eladria found that she didn't want to go. Yet she knew their departure could be postponed no longer. Nirataan led her, Van'garat and Janak through the cave, toward the exit that would transport them back to their own world. Trails of light sparkled behind them as they moved through the ethereal passageway.

How long a time they'd enjoyed the safety of Nirataan's mysterious abode she couldn't say, for time here was indistinct and blurred. They had spent much time in quietude, resting and regaining their strength.

Ordinarily boredom and restlessness would have set in and Eladria would have found herself desperate to get moving. But her time here had changed her in some way. Perhaps it had something to do with the Ko Tra Pah exercises Nirataan had taught her and Janak. He had instructed them in the basics of meditation, breath control and taught them certain physical postures and movements designed to concentrate and balance what he called the 'life-force'.

Eladria had never found herself feeling quite as peaceful, and this was in spite of the looming encounter at Drantak. Her mind was more tranquil and her emotions had balanced, evening out the burden of grief she'd carried with her since the deaths of her father and Zinn.

The thought of leaving this sanctuary and stepping back into the tortured world she'd left behind filled her with dread, for she knew that in spite of all that had happened and all the pain she'd endured, the worst undoubtedly lay ahead of her. But she had no other option. She had to follow the path before her, wherever it might lead. She owed it to her mother, to her planet and to Zinn and her father and all the others that had been killed.

They came to the mouth of the cave. Outside, through a translucent screen of light, they could see the canyon illuminated by bursts of lightning as the storm continued to rage in the heavens.

"How long has storm lasted?" Janak wondered aloud.

"Barely moments have passed since you first entered the cave," Nirataan explained. "Barely moments of *your* time, that is. It was necessary that you return to the mortal realm before much time had elapsed. But, yes, the storm continues and I believe there will be no end to it now, not until the breach is sealed at its source. You must go now."

"Part of me doesn't want to," Eladria said.

"I not want to go either," Janak agreed. "Is far safer here!"

"You would not find safety even here for much longer," Nirataan warned. "If you do not act now, if you do not save your world, then even this pocket of space between realms will be destroyed."

"So when we leave here, what do we do?" Eladria asked. "Our means of transport was destroyed. How are we to get to Drantak?"

"You will fly there," Nirataan answered.

"Fly there?" Janak echoed, crestfallen.

Nirataan nodded, stepping forward and passing through the membrane of light that separated the cave from the storm-ravaged world outside. Eladria followed him, Van'garat and Janak close behind her.

Once again standing upon the canyon ledge, they were immediately exposed to the ferocity of the storm as it ravaged both sky and land. The howling wind made it difficult to stand, while the ground rumbled angrily underfoot. Fork lightning shot down from the sky, slamming into the canyon rock, creating small craters upon impact, sending up waves of fire and smoke.

Eladria looked at Nirataan expectantly. He raised his hands

high above his head. Now that he was out of the cave, his appearance had settled into that of an exceedingly frail-looking old man, which Eladria presumed was his true appearance, given his alleged age. He remained motionless with his hands raised and his eyes closed.

What was he doing?

She looked over at Van'garat, who had a knowing smile upon his face, while Janak simply shrugged.

After a moment, Nirataan opened his eyes and lowered his arms. "It is done," he said. "Your transportation is arranged."

Eladria was about to ask what he meant when she became aware of something in the sky. To begin with she thought it was part of the storm, perhaps a surge of lightning discharging from the rupture, but she quickly realized that it was something altogether different. It moved across the sky and shot toward the land like a bullet of light, accompanied by two other streaks of light.

As the sparks of light drew closer, Eladria realized they were actually *creatures* of some kind: great winged beasts, like the dragons of ancient myth. The three creatures approached the canyon plateau and alighted nearby, tucking their wings by their sides and lowering their tapered heads in what appeared to be a gesture of greeting.

"What are they?" Eladria gasped.

"In the ancient tongue, they were called the Uon'oi," Nirataan answered as he stepped toward the creatures.

"They're also known as the Riders," Van'garat added.

"These are the Riders?" Eladria asked in wonder.

Nirataan nodded. He stopped before the nearest creature and bowed his head in silent greeting. "They are from beyond the void," he explained as he placed his hand on the creature's side. "Only at certain times do they assume corporeal form. The rest of the time they exist as pure energy, riding the waves of light that encircle this globe. So fleeting is their presence, that few have seen the Uon'oi this close. But Masters of the Old Way, being one with the primordial essence, have the ability to commune with them."

Eladria was unable to take her eyes off the remarkable creatures, which remained still, heads lowered to the ground. They were larger than she'd imagined, being perhaps twice the size of an adult rhastopod. That they were from beyond the void—creatures that only occasionally assumed physical embodiment—explained their ethereal glimmer. They shone with a light from within, glowing through their translucent skin, a mixture of greens, yellows and blues, with a single streak of red running down their slightly ridged spines. They had large pointed ears and clear black eyes that conveyed a sense of peace that wasn't quite of this world.

"The Uon'oi will take us to Drantak?" Van'garat asked as he stepped forward, in clear awe of the magnificent beasts.

Nirataan lowered his head affirmatively. "I reached out to them and communicated our intent. They know where to go and how best to get there."

"Is it safe?" Janak ventured nervously.

"You can trust the Uon'oi," Nirataan said. "If anyone can get you to your destination, it is they."

"You not think we should wait till storm passes?" Janak suggested.

Nirataan shook his head in mild irritation. "As I said before, I do not believe it will. The longer you wait, the worse it will likely get. You must go now."

"Very well," Van'garat said.

Eladria stepped forward with a measure of reticence. "So we just climb onto their backs and they'll fly us to Drantak?"

"That is correct," Nirataan said.

"But surely moment we up there, we be struck by lightning, or maybe even sucked into whatever that is in sky," protested Janak.

"If you don't want to come with us, just say so," Eladria exclaimed, tiring of Janak's perpetual complaining. "I'd have no problem leaving you here."

"Well maybe I will stay," Janak huffed.

"No, you cannot remain here," Nirataan said, struggling to keep to his feet as another blast of wind swept through the canyon.

"If is because I took those things back in cave, I tell you, I very sorry," Janak said earnestly. "It never happen again. I learn my lesson, I never steal again."

"No, you cannot stay here because your destiny calls you elsewhere," Nirataan told him, having to raise his voice to be heard above the noise of the storm. "Muster what courage you have. I know it is there, otherwise you would not have survived on your own all these years. I assure you, the Uon'oi will get you to your destination."

Janak was silent for a moment as he stared at the old master. He then let out a sigh and shrugged his shoulders. "Very well," he said. "I go. I already come this far, after all."

Nirataan nodded and turned to Eladria. "Before you go, I have one final word for you, daughter of Chaldeen." He beckoned Eladria to come close and as she stepped toward him, he looked deeply into her eyes. As they stood, they were rocked by the wind and continued tremors. Nirataan almost had to shout now to be heard above the raging noise, his face filled with urgency, his eyes blazing with intensity. "By now, I am sure you must be aware of another world, another reality interlinked with this one. You have seen glimpses of it in your dreams. I know you can sense it, if only as a shadow in the corner of your mind. What you need to know is this: it is real, just as real as *this* world and it is calling to you, calling from across infinity."

Eladria was unprepared for this and wasn't quite sure what to say. "Why are you telling me this?" she asked.

"Because you need to know it is real. *He* is real: the one you dream of, the one whose face haunts you and calls to you..."

"What do you know of him?"

"Only that you are a part of him, and he of you. And he needs you!"

"I don't understand," Eladria said.

"You will understand, in time. For now you must concentrate on the task at hand, you must travel to Drantak and fulfill your destiny. Only then will it all become clear."

"Isn't there any other way?" Eladria asked, suddenly overcome with anxiety and doubt. "I don't feel ready for this, Nirataan. I've been told the fate of this world rests with me. But I know nothing of the world, I have no experience of anything! There must be someone better suited to do this."

"Do not underestimate yourself. Go now, knowing that you are not alone. You will be aided in your mission and guided along your path."

Eladria nodded and took a deep breath to steady herself. Again, the ground was rocked by a tremor, which sent rubble tumbling down the canyon walls. Lightning continued to bombard the land as the rupture swallowed the heavens.

The princess thanked Nirataan for all he had done. With a deep bow, Van'garat paid his respects to the mysterious master. Janak simply nodded nervously as they proceeded to mount the three winged creatures.

Eladria struggled to climb onto the creature and was mindful that she not alarm it. Once seated upon its back, she wrapped her hands around its neck.

The creatures immediately took to flight, raising their mighty wings and propelling themselves into the air, spiraling upwards into the center of the storm. Eladria's heart quickened as they soared upward. Every fiber of her being compelled her to remain as far away from the storm as possible, yet they were doing the opposite, they were flying right into the heart of it.

She looked down into the canyon below and saw Nirataan standing outside his cave, watching them as they departed. He raised his hand and waved, and then, much to her astonishment, he disappeared! It was as though his body had suddenly turned to dust and was dispersed by the wind.

He was gone.

Yet she knew in her heart that he was not to be mourned. For in a strange way, she could still feel his presence. It was vast and expansive, filling the canyon and reaching into the sky with them. She knew that somehow, in some sense, he would be with them on their journey.

Her attention was drawn skyward. They ascended at startling speed, the eye of the storm just above them. The rippling wave of distortion that filled the sky crackled with raw electrical power, spewing out lightning and showering fire upon the land beneath.

The Riders dodged the lightning with deftness and impunity, their reflexes as sharp as their speed was dizzying. It was no wonder these creatures just appeared as dancing light in the sky. Eladria held onto its neck, fearful that she might lose her grip and fall.

The light, heat and noise of the storm was almost unbearable. She closed her eyes tightly, and even then all she could see behind her eyelids was light. They were in the midst of the storm and she could feel her body tingling with electrostatic charge. She knew they were in immense danger. Nirataan had promised them the Riders would take them safely through the storm, but surely not even they could compete with this supernatural distortion?

Just as they were almost close enough to touch the crack in the sky, something happened. The Riders—diving in and out of the storm, dodging the twisting shafts of electricity and maneuvering themselves at incredible speed—merged into a current of energy. It was as if they'd entered a fast-flowing rapid and they settled into the flow, swiftly carried along by the current.

They were moving at startling speed. The Rider was no longer flapping its wings or actively propelling itself, instead it was being propelled by the subtle stream of energy.

They moved at such speed that the storm was no longer visible above them and neither was the ground below. All Eladria was aware of was a haze of light all around as the Rider, accompanied on either side by its two companions, travelled the energetic rapids. Her anxiety was replaced by exhilaration as she continued to hold on, now trusting that the Riders knew where they were going and would safely get them to their destination.

Several times she sensed the creature phasing in and out of reality, as though slipping from dense physicality into a place intangible and ethereal, taking her along with it. In such moments, the entire universe dissolved into light and she was aware of something beyond it: a place of vastness, invisible yet all pervasive, a force that stretched across infinity and throughout eternity. Was this the *primordial essence* that Van'garat and Nirataan spoke of?

It was an infinity of open space, an expanse of nothingness, yet filled with the pure potentiality of everything. Touching this realm, she sensed that everything which is, was and ever could be was but a play in form: a wave arising upon a vast ocean of oneness. Everything in the universe was composed solely of this invisible substance and everything would eventually return to it. With each glimpse of this, her mind froze and her old memories, beliefs and thoughts unraveled and dispersed into the winds of infinity.

She was uncertain how long a time they travelled in this manner. Her mind was absorbed in a state of mystic rapture and, for a brief time, she felt a surge of knowing rising up from the core of her being. For the first time in her life, it was as though she *knew*. She knew the secrets of existence itself.

That instantly faded, however, as they exited the energy stream and spiraled down to land. She was jolted back to reality with an unceremonious bump as the Rider landed on solid ground. As the creature lowered its wings and tucked them by its side, Eladria looked round and saw that the other two Riders, bearing Janak and Van'garat, had also come to a stop nearby.

She surveyed their surroundings. It was dark, bleak and barren. The only source of light came from the storm that continued to blaze in the skies above. The terrain was rocky and uneven, with craggy mountains rising to jagged peaks all around them. There was no sign of life of any kind.

Eladria dismounted the Rider and gently ran her hand along its back. She looked into its sparkling black eyes and reached out to kiss its cheek. "Thank you," she said, feeling an inexplicable bond with the creature in spite of the brief time she'd been with it.

As if in acknowledgement and farewell, the Rider lifted its head and arched its back, before stepping away from her. It joined its companions and together they took to flight once more, soaring high into the sky, circling overhead until they disappeared like shooting stars.

The storm was worse here. The blistering tear that ruptured the heavens throbbed in frenetic motion, discharging waves of electricity in every direction. Many blasts reached the land, causing explosions as they impacted the rocky wasteland. Fireballs shot down from the eye of the storm, slamming into the ground, waves of flame and smoke rising from the craters.

They had arrived in the depths of night, unless Drantak was always this dark, which wouldn't have surprised Eladria. The activity in the heavens lit up the land in bursts of light so bright that she was frequently forced to shield her eyes. The ground was being rocked by tremors of great intensity, making it a challenge simply to remain standing.

Waves of energy shot through the air like heat-waves spreading outward in rings. The ripples of energy were accompanied by a kinetic force that swept over them like bursts of wind, leaving a faint electrical charge as they passed.

In the far distance, Eladria saw a funnel of light stretching from the stormy heavens all the way to the ground, as if something was conducting and grounding the energy. It was similar to what she'd seen at Arnaast when the True Way had connected the energy of the storm with the temple's underground conduit. This appeared to be the apex of the breach and the source of the strange energy waves shooting across the valley. This was where they had to go.

She turned to her friends, whose expressions were understandably grim. "Welcome to Drantak," she called, shouting to be heard above the storm. "Apparently this is where it all began— and this is where it's going to end. Let's go!"

Fighting her way past the waves of energy that pulsated across the land, Eladria led the way as they began marching toward the source of the breach.

Chapter 25

Drantak

They hadn't been walking long when Van'garat suddenly fell to his knees and cried out in anguish.

"What's wrong?" Eladria stopped and knelt by his side.

"We can't go on," he cried, holding his head in his hands, his whole body shaking. "All I see is death!"

"What do you mean?" Eladria asked.

He looked up at her, his eyes wide with terror and his face drained of color. "In the blink of an eye I saw the death of every man, woman and child on this planet. I heard them screaming out in shock and terror..."

"It wasn't real, Van'garat," Eladria tried to calm him. "Perhaps this place is affecting you in some way. But it was just in your mind, a hallucination of some kind."

"No, it was real." He shook his head slowly as a teardrop rolled down his face. "It was real, and it was caused by us...by *you*."

"By me?"

"Yes. Something is going to happen here, something terrible, and it will be caused by you, Eladria. Perhaps the very thing you think you must do to save this world will destroy it. We cannot proceed."

"Listen to me," Eladria said, looking deeply into his haunted eyes. "We're here and we couldn't go back even if we wanted to. The Riders are gone and there's no way out of here. If we don't stop whatever's happening here, then it's the end for all of us. So we have to keep on going."

"But I saw it so clearly...the death of an entire world."

"You yourself admitted that your vision's been manipulated in some way," Eladria said. "So let it go, Van'garat and get ahold of yourself. Whatever lies ahead, we'll face it and deal with it."

"But what if he right?" Janak interjected as he stood over them nervously.

"There's only one thing I know for sure," Eladria snapped. "I've come this far and I'm going to see this through to the end. Now, come on! We're not safe out in the open like this. Get up and let's get moving."

Van'garat quickly regained his composure as he got to his feet. "Please, forgive me, Princess. I've never experienced a vision so strong. It overwhelmed me. But you're right, of course. We can't afford to second-guess ourselves at this stage. Whatever is to happen will happen."

"Can you sense what's up ahead of us?" Eladria asked, bracing herself as another ring of energy shot past them.

"No." Van'garat shook his head. "Aside for this momentary flash, my vision remains blocked. But whatever is ahead of us, it's most certainly dangerous."

"That much is guaranteed," Eladria said.

Following her lead, they resumed their journey toward the source of the energy ripples, which continued shooting across the valley in rings of kinetic force. The storm continued above them, howling and roaring, sparks of electricity exploding outward. Fireballs continued raining down upon the land, on occasion almost striking the travelers, forcing them to maneuver around the flaming craters created by the impact.

Another round of earthquakes shook the ground, causing a fissure that rapidly spread across the land. They had to walk around the fissure, and as they did so, a particularly violent burst of lightning caused a tear to form in mid-air, some way ahead of them. It was as though the fabric of reality had been sliced open and shadow-like figures soon began to pour through the rupture. Clad in black armor and brandishing swords and shields, the shadow-men spilled out of the breach and began marching across the rocky plateau.

Eladria reached for the True Way pistol attached to her belt, ready to defend herself. But the ghostly warriors didn't appear to notice them. They continued streaming through the tear and spreading across the valley. In the distance, another rupture formed and a second wave of armor-clad shadow-men emerged through the spectral doorway. It was only moments before the two armies met and, when they did, they engaged in fierce battle.

"Who are they?" Janak cried as they watched from a safe distance.

"Whoever they are, they're not of this world," Van'garat answered. "The barriers between realms are finally collapsing."

"I wonder why they're fighting," Eladria mused as she watched the ferocious battle.

"I don't know, but wherever they're from, they've obviously brought their conflict with them," Van'garat said.

The ground rumbled underfoot as another wave of tremors rocked the valley. Eladria fell to the ground and was helped up by Janak. The fissure etching its way across the valley had widened, creating a jagged chasm, splitting the land in two.

"It's getting worse all the time," the princess exclaimed as she struggled to catch her breath.

The sky was like a blazing inferno, filled with frenetic bursts of lightning, illuminating the sky and land beneath. Janak was first to notice that another tear had formed in mid-air, some way to their left, not far from the battleground. As the tear widened, something emerged through it: flying dragon-like reptilians, blood red in color, with outstretched wings and long forked tails. The creatures circled the valley like carrion birds in search of meat. Whatever they were, Eladria knew they were to be avoided. "Let's move," she called, hoping the dragon creatures would be too distracted by the battling warriors to notice them.

Her heart was drumming in her chest as they hastened their pace. This was like some kind of nightmare. Aside from the danger posed by the creatures spilling into this realm, she knew that at any moment they could be hit by lightning or struck by a fireball. There was nowhere to shelter. They had no option but to keep moving. Once they got to the center of the distortion, then perhaps everything would be clear and she would know what she had to do to end this.

Yet she couldn't shake Van'garat's vision of annihilation. What if he was right? What if she would inadvertently cause mass destruction? The thought horrified her, but she knew this was no time for deliberation. They had to continue onward.

Time was fragmenting and dissolving. A second seemed to expand into a veritable eternity, which then contracted into a single heartbeat. Eladria didn't know long they'd been here and had no idea of the amount of time it took them to cross the valley and reach the center-point of the distortion. But they arrived at the locus of the breach, where the pulsing funnel of light spiraled down from the sky and terminated in the ground among a cluster of ruins, possibly the remnants of an ancient town or city.

"What is this place?" Janak asked, raising his voice to be heard above the noise of the storm.

"I've no idea," Eladria called back. "But this seems to be at the source of the disturbance. This is where we need to be."

She led the way as they entered the ruins, bracing themselves against the energy waves that blasted out from ahead of them, apparently emanating from the funnel of energy that stretched between the sky and land. They found themselves among crumbling stone walls and pillars and the remnants of buildings undoubtedly thousands of years old. An archaeologist's heaven perhaps, but nothing of consequence and certainly nothing that would explain what was happening here. "There's nothing here but ruins!" Eladria exclaimed, turning to Van'garat. "Yet this *has* to be it! It all seems to be coming from here."

Another wave of energy shot outward, almost knocking them to the ground. "It is here," Van'garat confirmed, steadying himself upon a dislodged stone pillar. "I can feel it. But it's beneath ground. The source of the disturbance is below us."

"Below us?" Janak echoed.

"Yes, I'm certain of it. I've seen it before in my visions: subterranean tunnels and an underground base of some kind. It's right beneath us!"

"Then there must be a way underground," Eladria said.

She decided they had to get as close to the funnel of energy as they could. They climbed over debris, boulders and crumbling buildings, and the closer they got to it, the more intense the conditions around them became. The vertical shaft of light crackled with raw electrical force and was almost blindingly bright. Waves of kinetic force repeatedly surged outward, each blast knocking them backward. For every seven or eight steps they advanced, they were knocked back at least two.

More ruptures were forming around them. The walls between realms were collapsing in rapid succession. Objects and people from other dimensions were spilling into this one and, to Eladria's horror, she realized the same was also happening in reverse. A large tear formed to their right and a portion of the ruined city was sucked through it, disappearing before their eyes.

Another wave of distortion threw her to the ground and before she could get back to her feet, she suddenly had a flash of another place; another world entirely...

She was aware of forestlands, valleys and deserts—tribes of indigenous people, aggressive warriors with thick-plated grey skin and animalistic features—and a vast empire with armies of unstoppable robotic soldiers...

And she saw his face, the face of the boy with the dark hair and brown eyes—the face that seemed so inexplicably familiar to her—his eyes looking deep into her soul, enticing, inviting—calling to her—imploring her...

And then he was gone.

The images subsided as quickly as they had appeared.

She was back in the ruins at Drantak, so close to the eye of the storm as it stretched from sky to ground. Van'garat helped her up.

The place was being torn apart piece by piece. It was as though reality itself was collapsing. The storm was worsening, the ground shaking continuously and the light from the shaft of energy ahead of them was almost more than her eyes could bear.

Whatever was happening here was being caused by a force of unimaginable power. What could she possibly do to stop it? Why had she been led here? Was it to die? Was this all a cosmic punishment of some kind...?

"Come on," Van'garat called, sensing her hesitation and pulling her along by the hand as they climbed over the ruins. Closer and closer they got to the center of the ruins, to the apex of the distortion. The air was hot, smoky and buzzing with electrical charge.

Eladria was aware of other people here; people that had been scooped from their own dimension, pulled through the vortex and deposited here. Some of the figures were ghostly and intangible like the dueling shadow-warriors. Others were as solid and as real as she and her comrades. These lost souls wandered through the ruins, distressed and disorientated. Some reacted in panic and pain, screaming and howling, others responded aggressively, including more of the shadow-warriors, who immediately engaged each other battle. Others simply drifted like ghosts lost in space and time.

Eladria couldn't afford the distraction. She was here for a reason. She knew she had to keep on going.

Again she was thrown to the ground and this time Van'garat fell on top of her.

Once more, the moment her eyes closed she saw visions...

Visions of that far distant land and that familiar face staring at her, the young man calling to her from a place far beyond her wildest imaginings. He opened his mouth to speak, but she couldn't hear the words...

She opened her eyes and rose to her feet, along with Van'garat and Janak.

They continued moving through the ruins, ignoring all distractions and avoiding the displaced beings around them, until they reached the heart of the ancient ruins. It was here the shaft of light from the rupture in the sky touched the ground.

Initially Eladria had assumed that something underground was drawing the energy down from the sky, as had happened in Arnaast. But as she approached, she realized it was quite the opposite. The bluish-white funnel of energy was coming *up* from the ground, shooting upward to form the breach now covering the sky, while discharging the rings of kinetic force that swept over the valley. The source of the breach was evidently underground.

A fireball suddenly slammed into one of the dilapidated buildings. Debris went flying and flames leapt up from the site of impact, creating a thick screen of smoke. The impact caused a chain reaction, creating further instability as nearby structures began to collapse. Sharp reflexes were all that prevented Eladria and her comrades from being caught beneath the collapsing ruins.

The ancient city was disintegrating around them. They were surrounded by flames and smoke, which quickly filled their lungs. They ran, retreating from the billowing veil of smoke, coughing uncontrollably. Once clear of the smoke, they came to a stop and tried to catch their breaths.

As Eladria scanned the vicinity, her heart froze in terror.

They had company. Through the smoke ahead of them appeared six men with insect-like faces—scaly brown skin, compound eyes, short antennae and snapping mandibles. Each of them was clad in spiked armor and armed with electro-pulse rifles. They had caught sight of Eladria and her comrades and were closing in on them, snarling aggressively as they advanced through the smoking wreckage...

Chapter 26

Beneath The Surface

"Stay back!" Eladria cried.

Alas, she knew she was in no position to make demands. Their ambushers had a clear shot and she knew it would be suicidal to fight back. The creatures lumbered toward them and rounded them up, brusquely searching and disarming them.

"What do you want with us?" Eladria demanded as she was grabbed by one of the soldiers, feeling his nails digging into her arm, instantly drawing blood. Ignoring her, they began dragging her and her comrades through the rubble. They appeared to know where they were going and were unperturbed by the tremors and distortions that continued to ravage the ancient site.

Their captors led them to a roofless building, the stone masonry of which had gradually been devoured by time. Once inside, they came to a large metal hatch on the ground, gleaming in the reflected light of the storm above. One of the men cranked open the hatch to reveal a narrow staircase leading underground. The warriors marched them down the winding steps. The stone walls, smooth and dark, were lit by a series of lamps, causing their shadows to dance up and down as they descended the stairway.

Eladria had never seen creatures like these insectoid men before. She initially wondered if, like the shadow-warriors, they had been deposited through the breach from another realm. But that didn't appear to be the case, for they were clearly familiar with their surroundings. Was it possible they were native to Drantak?

When they reached the bottom of the stairway they were led into an elevator that took them even farther underground. Eladria and her comrades exchanged helpless glances as the elevator rattled and hummed, descending ever deeper into this subterranean world. The soldiers never once uttered a word. Some of them stared ahead blankly while the others kept their attention upon their captives, rifles poised, their faces as rigid as their bodies and their large black eyes cold and expressionless.

When the elevator eventually shuddered to a halt, they were pushed out and marched down a long straight corridor. Constructed of polished black stone with metal fittings, the corridor was faintly lit by a series of electric ceiling lamps. They walked in silence, the only sounds coming from the echo of their footsteps, and a distant low-level rumbling noise that Eladria couldn't identify.

The ground beneath them was shaking slightly, but aside for an occasional tremor, this underground facility was evidently shielded from the disruption that ravaged the planet surface. Perhaps it was because they were so far underground, or maybe this place was shielded in some way from the effects of the breach?

They came to a door and were ushered through it into a large room with gleaming black walls, metallic paneling and an arched ceiling with a single light dimly illuminating the room. At the heart of the room was a rectangular table, metallic, upon its surface a number of advanced-looking computer consoles. There was a large window on the wall directly ahead of them, covered by a metal shutter. Eladria looked around the room, taking in every last detail. She tried to identify the style of architecture and engineering, but it was completely alien to her.

The prisoners were ushered to the table and made to stand before it. Three of the insect-like men stood watch at the door, while the remainder hovered behind their captives, weapons in hand.

"What is this place?" Eladria asked.

Not to her surprise, none of the soldiers answered. But it was safe to assume that this underground complex was the very place she'd been looking for. It had to be here that the 'experiment' was being conducted.

They stood in silence for some time, before the door slid open and a figure in a hooded robe entered the room.

It was a woman, her countenance imperious and forbidding as she strode passed the guards, who nodded in respect, and approached the prisoners. Eladria sensed a heavy, dense and darkened aura around the woman, and there was an almost palpable chill to the air she approached. Although her face was concealed beneath the hood of her dark navy robe, Eladria immediately recognized her, not least by the quartz amulet around her neck. It was Zanel, the mysterious woman she'd first encountered at the temple in Arnaast.

"Welcome," Zanel said, her voice low and gravelly as she came to a stop before Eladria and her friends. "You have no idea how long I have awaited this moment."

"*You*...you're responsible for what's happening here?" Eladria asked.

"I am," the hooded figure responded with an air of nonchalance.

"Then you lied to me," Eladria growled. "You said you were one of the Others. You told me I had to come here to *stop* what was happening."

"I told you exactly what you needed to hear," Zanel retorted. "It was imperative that you come here and that you bring the Dragon Star with you."

"But why? What is happening here?"

Zanel paused before stepping forward and pressing one of the controls on the tabletop. The shutter covering the window ahead of them began to rise. Eladria stared out the window in amazement. It looked out on a circular, rocky chamber, dominated by an enormous cone-shaped crystal. Metal plating and wiring encircled the crystalline formation, which glowed brilliantly as it crackled with life, sending a steady stream of white light blasting upward.

"Behold the *psionic crystal*," Zanel said. "Buried deep in the heart of Drantak, it sits upon an electromagnetic conduit, one of several such conduits across the planet. The crystal amplifies the energy of this conduit, making it the most powerful conductor in all of Tahnadra."

"It's all about the crystal, isn't it?" Eladria asked in sudden realization. "You've been trying to use this crystal, haven't you? Trying to harness its power?"

Zanel nodded. "I was led here many years ago, through a series of ancient tunnels cutting deep into the heart of the land. Here, I found the psionic crystal. My masters instructed me to set up a base of operations and told me that, in time, I would be able to access the crystal's power and *use* it..."

"You can't have done all this alone," Eladria interjected.

"No. For a start, I enlisted the help of the Ornakai here," Zanel motioned to the insect-like soldiers. "The Ornakai were the only native inhabitants of Drantak, living underground, rarely venturing to the surface. They were a simple, unintelligent species—malleable and easily controlled."

"Controlled?" Van'garat echoed.

Zanel lifted her hand and raised the amulet around her neck. "This is a fragment of the psionic crystal. It grants its wearer certain powers, not least the ability to mold and manipulate the minds of others. I took the Ornakai, a weak-willed, backward species, and I made them strong, powerful and purposeful."

"You mean you enslaved them," Van'garat challenged her, a trace of anger in his voice.

"Call it what you will, Ha'shon. Under my supervision, they constructed this facility, which is built around the great crystal. I then set to work, doing what was necessary to harness its power. For, you see, whoever controls this crystal controls the fate of this entire world and beyond."

"What have you been using the crystal for?" Eladria asked, staring intently at the robed figure, wishing she could see the face beneath the hood.

"To reach into other dimensions," Zanel answered.

"Why you do that?" Janak asked, his face creased in bewilderment.

"Everything I've done, I've done because my masters, the Shadow Lords of Abidalos, have decreed it."

"So they can escape from their realm?" Eladria asked.

"Exactly!" Zanel answered, her voice lighting up. "They were falsely imprisoned there aeons ago by their enemies, the Guardians, or the 'Others' as you so quaintly call them. It's now time for them to break free of their astral prison. They've made contact with beings in several different dimensions and have endeavored to orchestrate their escape by whatever means they can, into whichever realm is ripe for their passage."

"Then the Others were right," Eladria said. "You've been using the crystal to open a doorway from their universe to ours."

"Yes," Zanel said, a trace of pride evident in her voice. "The moment I'm able to lock onto their dimension, they'll be able to enter this realm as easily as we might step from one room of a house to another."

"But is not Abidalos an incorporeal realm?" Van'garat asked. "How will they pass from there into our physical universe?"

"They have the ability to assume physical form, enabling them to function in this dimension," Zanel answered. "As discarnate entities they are known as the Shadow Lords, while in physical embodiment they are feared throughout the cosmos as the *Gr'noth*, or the *Narssians*."

"And what do you suppose will happen when these creatures come storming into this universe?" Eladria exclaimed.

"After countless millennia of captivity, they will have dominion over every world," Zanel said impassively, clasping her hands together and bringing them to her chest. "They will vanquish their enemies and destroy all resistance. All universes, all dimensions, all of life in its multiplicity will be cleansed and reborn."

"Why would you let that happen?" Eladria gasped, in equal measure horrified and astonished by Zanel's words.

"Because it's the nature of life to periodically cleanse and renew itself," Zanel answered blankly, her voice devoid of emotion. "Just look around at this world of depravity and chaos. My masters tell me this degeneration is prevalent throughout the cosmos, in every corner of our universe and beyond. They will cleanse this universe, bringing about a regeneration of this entire life-wave. What they promise is a universe of perfect order, perfect *unity*."

"What they promise is annihilation," Van'garat stated evenly. "Nowhere will be left untouched. And in spite of whatever they might have promised you, I can assure you that you'll be one of the first casualties when they break into this realm. The moment you've fulfilled your usefulness, you will be dispensed with."

Zanel turned to him. "What would you know of anything, Ha'shon?" she spat.

"I know more than you might think," Van'garat responded flatly. "The moment your friends here took us underground, the spell you'd placed over me dissipated. I can see it all so clearly now. I can see how you've been manipulated and deceived, how your strings have been pulled like those of a puppet. For that's all that you are: a puppet, no less so than these soldiers here that serve your every whim."

"You know *nothing*."

"I know that in spite of all that you've done here, you've yet to master the psionic crystal. The experiment has been a failure, hasn't it? For you've yet to find a way to control it. The breaches that are devastating this world were created quite by accident, am I not correct?"

"The breaches are byproducts of the experiment, yes. And it is true that until now I've been unable to use the crystal's power with any precision. But that is about to change now that *you* have arrived."

"What do you mean?" Eladria asked uneasily, getting the clear sense that Zanel was referring to her.

"You have the final key that I need," Zanel said, stepping toward Eladria. "You possess the Dragon Star. I can sense its power within you. It's the one thing I need in order to master the psionic crystal. Until now I've only been able to access other dimensions randomly. But now, with the Dragon Star, I can unlock the specific frequencies of Abidalos."

"But you don't *have* the Dragon Star," Eladria narrowed her eyes. "I do, and I'll never help you in any way."

"Your determination is admirable," Zanel said. "I'll regret having to break you of it. But I will, and then you'll find that you will help me, most readily."

"If you needed the Dragon Star so badly, why didn't you get it yourself?" Eladria growled. "Why did you need to involve me in your plan?"

"The Daykeepers would release it only to one of royal blood and pure motive. I could have tried to retrieve the Dragon Star, for I am of royal blood. But they would have sensed my motivation and prevented me from taking it. Only you, little girl, being ignorant of the true nature of your quest, could take possession of it and that is why I needed you."

"Wait," Eladria began, shifting on the spot anxiously. "You're of royal blood?"

Zanel nodded.

"How can that be? If you're of royal blood, then you must be related to me...?"

"Oh, I am more than *related* to you."

Zanel reached up and pulled down her hood, finally revealing her face.

Nothing could have prepared Eladria for the sight that greeted her eyes.

Chapter 27

The Face Of The Enemy

It was *her*. It was as though she was looking into a mirror—her own reflection staring back at her, only it was a warped and distorted reflection. Zanel's face and features were those of Eladria, although she was a great deal older, with extensive scarring disfiguring both sides of her face. Her hair was short and thin, her skin sickly pale and she had a haggard, deadened look about her. Her eyes were cold and dark like burnt-out stars, empty and lifeless yet filled with a lingering bitterness and stifled rage.

Eladria's mouth fell open as she continued to stare at Zanel's face. It was so like her own and yet so very different, as though she was looking at an older version of herself, one that had been broken and defeated by life. All that was left was a hollowed-out husk, twisted and barren, cold and desolate. She couldn't stop staring into her eyes. They pulled her in, almost drowning her in an all-consuming void of pain and emptiness.

"Yes, take a good look my face," Zanel whispered darkly, leaning toward Eladria.

"How is this possible," Eladria exclaimed, struggling to force the words out. "You look just like me..."

"Because I am you. We are the same person. We are one."

"No." Eladria shook her head, pulling back from her. "That's impossible..."

"It's true," Zanel said, narrowing her eyes. "I am you. Or at least, I *was* you..."

"But how?"

"You *created* me, and the irony is you have no idea how you did it or when." Zanel took a step back and began pacing, every so often stopping and staring at Eladria, her eyes drilling through her. "Cast your mind back to when you first arrived upon the planet after escaping the royal moon. You surely remember the first storm you encountered? You and Zinn ran for shelter and stumbled across the ancient temple of the Ara'buno."

"Yes...I remember..." Eladria could see herself back in the underground temple as if it had only been moments ago.

"As you wandered through the temple you came to a chamber, in which you found the Mirror of Souls."

"That's right." Eladria recalled the mirror vividly: octagonal shaped, set in an ornate emerald flame, sitting atop a stone platform beneath a hatch in the ceiling. Compelled to investigate, she had stepped up to it and wiped it clean with her dress, straining to see her reflection in the darkened glass.

"You then accidentally activated the Mirror," Zanel continued.

Eladria nodded slowly. She'd forgotten about it until now, but it all came back to her with vivid clarity. A tremor had rumbled underfoot and she was thrown forward, where she collided with the mirror. As she reached out to steady herself, she inadvertently pressed a lever on the side of the frame. An ancient, long-dormant mechanism had been set in motion. The ceiling hatch slid open and a vertical shaft of light descended, ensnaring the princess as it seeped through her skin, saturating every cell of her body.

Zanel stepped forward, her eyes blazing. "Do you have any idea what happened then?"

Eladria shook her head, continuing to stare at Zanel, overcome by a growing nausea.

"A history lesson then. The ancient Ara'buno used the Mirror to duplicate themselves, creating an etheric counterpart that could then travel to the formless dimensions, before returning and being reabsorbed back into the mortal frame."

"Is that what happened?"

"Yes," Zanel responded. "I was the etheric double. You created me, from yourself. You inadvertently initiated the process—and then you disrupted it. Or do you not remember taking your pistol and firing at the Mirror?"

Eladria nodded, overwhelmed and helpless. "I was trapped. I

couldn't get free. I panicked and I fired..."

"The electro-pulse fire reacted with the dimensional opening, creating what I'm told was a temporal disruption. The etheric double you created coalesced into physical form and was catapulted through the rupture, back in time."

"Back in time?"

"Yes. Due to the temporal destabilization, I was sent back in time almost twenty years."

Eladria took another step back from Zanel. "You're saying that you're a duplicate of me, created by the Mirror," she began. "That you were sent back through time...so you've been living on Tahnadra since before I was even born?"

Zanel nodded, her eyes still fixed upon Eladria with searing intensity.

"I didn't know," Eladria exclaimed. "I didn't realize. I did feel something strange happening to me as I stood before the Mirror. I felt myself being torn apart somehow, and some part of me being absorbed or swallowed by the Mirror. I saw your reflection and noticed it was different to me. But I didn't *know*. I couldn't have known!"

"In your ignorance you probably forgot about the entire experience," Zanel remarked coldly.

"So much has happened since then," Eladria admitted. "How was I supposed to know? What was I supposed to do?"

"Exactly as you have done...and I, exactly as I have done."

Eladria looked around the room helplessly, briefly making eye contact with Van'garat and Janak, who stood nearby, the Ornakai guards still hovering behind them. Janak had an expression of bewilderment upon his face, while Van'garat looked on bleakly, seemingly unsurprised by this turn of events. She turned back to Zanel, her mind racing as she grappled with the implications of this revelation. "What happened once you were sent back in time?" she ventured.

"You can't begin to imagine what I went through," Zanel

rasped, her voice betraying a mixture of anger and pain. "My very creation was one of violence and pain. I was literally ripped out of your body, displaced from time and thrown back into a world that was alien to me. When I awoke, it was to unimaginable agony."

Zanel stood before Eladria and pointed to the scars that ran down the length of her face. "As I was swept through time, my flesh burned. I was left in a smoldering heap, delirious and wracked by such pain you can never begin to imagine. I drifted in and out of consciousness, and with what little strength I had, I cried out for help. But none came. I don't know how I survived other than by the unseen hand of the Shadow Lords. From across the void, they became aware of me as I was catapulted through the temporal distortion. They reached out to me and a connection was formed. From across the veil, they nurtured me, guided me and gave me the strength I needed to survive."

Zanel again walked back and forth in an agitated manner, her hands clasped behind her back, her body tense and rigid as she moved. Everyone was silent as she continued to recount her tale. "As I recovered, my connection with my new masters grew and strengthened. I remained at the Ara'buno temple for many years. Using the Mirror of Souls, I was able to contact and commune with them directly. In a world devoid of human contact, they were my only company, my only family.

"I had been cast back in time, into an isolated and inhospitable jungle, with no one and nothing. *I was nothing.* Until, that is, they offered me the chance of life, of an identity and purpose. They even gave me a new name to reflect my resurrection and re-birth. They called me Zanel, which in their language means 'deliverance'. I became their primary connection with the mortal realm. I was made aware of their predicament, of their false imprisonment by the Guardians, and of their need to reclaim their freedom and to do as they were destined: to re-birth a universe collapsing into entropy and chaos. They promised that I would be spared the coming destruction that would cleanse this world, for I was now one of them."

Eladria said nothing, feeling a growing unease as Zanel continued her story.

"They gave me life and purpose," Zanel continued. She stopped and smiled a slight smile that failed to melt her icy dark eyes. "They trained me, enabling me to become a true instrument for them, giving me everything I have and everything I now am. They led me here to Drantak, where I built this complex with the help of some of the finest scientific minds on the planet."

"You had help?"

"Indeed. I 'borrowed' some of Tahnadra's most esteemed scientists and engineers. I'm sure you must have heard of the unexplained disappearances over the years?"

Eladria nodded.

"They were brought here, where under my direction they constructed this facility, as well as developing the means by which I could harness the power of the crystal."

"I can't believe you managed to do all this without anyone knowing about it..."

"The war between the Ha'shon and the True Way was the perfect distraction. All your focus was upon them. If I'm not mistaken, they were even blamed for the disappearance of the scientists. All of your attention, that of your father and the Royal Military, was directed in the wrong place."

The aggression of the Ha'shon and True Way had been overt and blatant. But Eladria could now see that the deadliest enemies were those like Zanel, whose evil was silent and secretive, subtle and hidden.

"In the meantime, I quietly bided my time, waiting for *you*," Zanel continued. "I watched from afar as you were chased from the royal moon by the Ha'shon, as you found your way to the Ara'buno temple where again, as was your destiny—and as was mine—you stood before the Mirror of Souls and I was created and sent back through time. Perhaps it was always meant to be, right from the start."

"Then you appeared to me at Arnaast," Eladria recalled.

"Yes. I knew I could manipulate you into bringing the Dragon Star here with you. Now, because of you, I can finally complete my task and free the Shadow Lords."

Eladria shook her head slowly. "I can't believe it. All of this: the experiment, the breaches...you're at the root of it all. You caused all of it. And you're a part of me..."

"Together we are two parts of a whole. It was only a matter of time before our destinies brought us together, for just as we were split, so will we again become whole."

"But you thought you were bringing me here to *help* you. Only that's not why I'm here. I'm here to *stop* you."

Zanel laughed coldly. "You have neither the strength nor the ability to stop me. If you could but see yourself: a spoilt brat, headstrong, foolish and utterly ignorant of what you truly are. The very notion that you could stop what I've done here is laughable."

"But you said it yourself, I have the power of the Dragon Star! That's the key, isn't it? You need it, and you can't have it."

"It will be mine," Zanel snapped back. "Just as you will be mine."

There was a long pause. Eladria wanted nothing more than to run; to run as far from here as she could. But there was no way of escaping and nowhere to go. "Tell me," Eladria began, trying to regain her composure as she locked eyes with her nightmarish alter ego. "You said my mother was here, that she's been held here ever since she disappeared?"

"It is true," Zanel replied. "Our mother is indeed here. She's been my guest for many years and has played an integral part in my experiment."

"What do you mean?"

Zanel stepped over to the window and gestured for Eladria to join her. Eladria refused to move, until the Ornakai soldier behind her nudged her forward, the tip of his rifle pushing into the small of her back. Zanel pointed out the window to the great crystal in the cavern beneath. "Observe," she said.

Up close, Eladria got a clearer view of the enormous crystal nestled underground. A metal walkway encircled the base of the crystal and around its perimeter a series of glass booths were connected to it by a network of cables and wiring. Each booth contained a human being, strapped in and standing upright, seemingly immobile. A larger booth dominated the center of the platform, also containing a stationary figure.

"Forty Starlanians," Zanel said with a wave of her hand. She looked round at Eladria. "Do you even know what a Starlanian is?"

"I heard the legends like everyone else," Eladria answered. "They're supposedly a race of powerful telepaths. Like the Lasan, they were meant to have seeded our world thousands of years ago. But I assumed that was just myth..."

"Then you were mistaken," Zanel said. "The Starlanians are real and they interbred with the people of this world. Their direct descendants opted to keep their bloodlines as pure as possible, for the ignorant masses of this world were unprepared for the gifts they possessed. They lived secretively, some of them eventually integrating into society, yet concealing their true identities, knowing that if others were to learn of their gifts, they would be endangered and exploited."

Eladria looked down again at the crystal. "What does this have to do with the crystal?" she asked.

"Only the Starlanians, with their advanced cognitive powers, are capable of focusing and directing the power of the psionic crystal," Zanel replied. "It took many years, but I sought out as many Starlanians as I could find—from the icelands of Rocasa and the caves of the Hanak desert, to the towns of Arkat and Kaesibar. With the help of the Ornakai, I brought them here. I found a way to connect them to the crystal and used their collective powers to activate it."

Eladria returned her gaze to Zanel. "My mother—what does this have to do with her?" she asked pointedly.

"Your mother, *our* mother...is a Starlanian."

Eladria stared at her, speechless.

"There are so many things you don't know," Zanel smiled. "Not even our father knew this. The Starlanians became so adept at concealing their true nature that they usually carried their secret with them to their deathbed. They renounced their powers, and their offspring, ignorant of their true nature, rarely had a clue as to who or what they truly were."

"How do you know this?" Eladria exclaimed.

"The Shadow Lords revealed all to me. The moment they made contact with me, they were aware of the dormant powers I possessed as a child born of both royal and Starlanian blood: the same powers that you also possess, albeit unrealized and untapped."

Eladria stared down at the booths surrounding the base of the crystal and then looked up at Zanel, overcome by a sudden horrific realization. "Mother...you hooked her up to the crystal, didn't you?"

Zanel nodded. "She occupies the central booth, for her powers are by far the strongest and most refined of all the Starlanians I brought here."

"How could you do that?" Eladria screamed, leaping at Zanel and grabbing her by the throat. The Ornakai guards intervened, pulling her back and restraining her.

"Our own mother!" Eladria cried. "How could you?"

"In many ways she's no longer my mother," Zanel said, her eyes darkening and her voice filling with a numbed grief and rage. "The moment I was pulled into the Mirror and catapulted through time, everything I was and everything I had been was lost. I died and was only reborn when the Shadow Lords found and restored me to health. They were my only family and I gave my full allegiance to them."

"I can't believe it," Eladria said, her entire body trembling and her eyes welling with tears. "It was you that abducted her all those years ago? It was you that took her from me! *You...*"

"Indeed," Zanel responded. "She was brought here to Drantak and held captive while I developed the necessary technology to utilize the crystal. Then, when the time was right, she was connected to the crystal along with the other Starlanians. Using their power, I then began my attempts to open a stable gateway to Abidalos."

"All this time," Eladria cried, struggling to break free of the guards. "All this time she's been here, used as some kind of slave..."

"It was necessary."

"Is she still alive?"

"In a sense. Her body lives, but like the others, prior to connecting her, it was necessary to wipe her higher cognitive functioning. The Starlanians' minds had to be focused solely upon accessing and directing the power of the crystal. I control them from a central station, with which I can direct their minds to unlock the dimensional frequencies."

Eladria let out a cry of rage, struggling against the guards, wanting nothing less than to kill Zanel for what she'd done. But the guards' grasp was unyielding and she was rooted to the spot, where she shook uncontrollably. Van'garat and Janak looked on helplessly.

"I demand that you release her!" Eladria cried.

"I intend to," Zanel folded her arms impassively. "She has now exceeded her usefulness. But once I disconnect her, she will need to be replaced and that is where you come in."

"Me?"

"Who better to replace her than her own daughter? Running through your veins is royal Lasan blood from your father's side and Starlanian blood from your mother's. And now you possess a third component, the ultimate means by which I can master the crystal: the power of the Dragon Star."

"I'll never help you," Eladria shouted, her voice burning with a hatred that ignited her entire being.

"You make it sound like you have a choice in the matter," Zanel said with a cold smile. "I assure you, you do not. No one can come to your aid now, not that old fool Nirataan and not your precious Others. The Ornakai will now take you to your cell. There you can reflect upon the irony of your fate and prepare yourself for what lies ahead. In the meantime, I'll make the necessary preparations for you to take your mother's place."

Zanel turned to leave.

"I'll stop you," Eladria shouted after her. "I promise! I'll make you pay for what you've done!"

Zanel looked round, her face etched with an icy sneer, her eyes narrow and deadened. "You've spent all these years underestimating yourself, little girl," she scoffed. "Don't start to overestimate yourself now."

Eladria wanted to protest further but she was unable to find the words. She watched impotently as Zanel left, her long grey robe swishing behind her as she disappeared through the exit.

The Ornakai soldiers rounded up the prisoners and led them out of the room. They were marched along the sleek black underground corridors, through a doorway and down a large flight of stairs.

At the bottom of the stairway they came to a landing with a dozen small cells carved into the gleaming black walls. Each cell was dimly lit by a ceiling lamp and furnished with a single metal bench. They were bundled into the first cell and behind them the Ornakai activated an energy barrier, a screen of faintly buzzing electricity that covered the front of the cell.

Zanel's revelations had left Eladria reeling in shock. She slumped down on the bench, her mind frozen and her body trembling. Now that she knew the terrible truth of what had happened—of how it was she herself that was responsible for this entire situation and for what had happened to her mother—she was devastated. Her universe had shattered into a million pieces.

She was her own nemesis, her own nightmare. And it was over. Everything she'd done and everything she'd been through had been for nothing...

Chapter 28

Light Amid The Darkness

"Eladria, listen to me," Van'garat began as he sat down by her side and looked deeply into her eyes. "You are not responsible for this. You can't hold yourself accountable. What happened was an accident and could not have been foreseen."

"He right," Janak agreed. "I not understand much of this, but one thing I know. In spite of what she say, and in spite of what she look like, she *not* you."

Eladria shook her head slowly. "But she is! Up until that moment in the Ara'buno temple when I stepped in front of that Mirror, she *was* me. She shared every experience I ever had. She'd lived her life in the royal palace, fled when the Ha'shon invaded, been forced to witness her father's murder, and before that she'd grieved for years when her mother was taken from her. And now I know the terrible irony: that she that was responsible for it, for the disappearance of our mother. It was she that inflicted that pain on us. I just don't understand how could she have done what she did..."

"She insane," Janak remarked with a shrug.

"I believe Janak's right," Van'garat continued. "It's more than just her face that's scarred. Whatever happened to her when she was duplicated and thrown back in time, it's certain that all that's good about you was stripped from her: your compassion, integrity, your sense of right and wrong. All that remains in her is bitterness and hatred."

"But I can recognize those qualities in myself," Eladria admitted, taking a deep and awkward breath. "Because that's what I felt toward the Ha'shon after they killed my father and toward the True Way for their part in Zinn's death. It wasn't until I saw it in her face that I realized...it all stems from me. It's as though she embodies all the pain I've ever felt, only whereas I've tried to hold it back, she's let it consume her."

"We all have our shadow side," the Ha'shon said. "Although mercifully few of us have to encounter it in the flesh as you have."

"Looking at her was like looking into a mirror," she confessed. "And what I saw was worse than any monster or demon I could ever have dreamt of. That's what scares me, because it clearly means I have the capacity to be just like her."

Eladria lowered her gaze and, as she moved her hand to her waist, she felt something in her trouser pocket. She put her hand into the pocket and pulled out the red ring Zanel had given her at the temple of Arnaast. Having been so distracted by all that had happened, she had forgotten all about it. Wanting to get it as far away from her as possible, she threw it across the cell.

"No, you never be like her," Janak said, watching as the ring landed on the ground not far from where he stood.

"You can't know that," Eladria said. "If it had been me that was pulled through the mirror and sent back through time and been in the same circumstances as she was in, then how can you say I wouldn't have ended up just like her?"

"Within each of us lies the capacity for both good and evil," Van'garat noted.

"So what determines which of the two triumphs?"

"Our choices in each moment," he replied. "How we choose to view our circumstances and interpret the world. Everything is but a choice."

"And if we choose wrongly?"

"Then we can make a different, better choice. It's never too late to choose differently. Most people are unaware they have the ability to choose how they see their reality and how they respond to it. They negate their power and lead lives of reactivity based largely upon habit and conditioned response. They sleepwalk through life. But not you, Princess, not any longer. This has been your awakening, a brutal but necessary one."

Eladria got up from the bench and began to pace the cell, deep in thought. Janak and Van'garat watched her quietly. Eventually she came to a stop and wrapped her arms around her chest as she leaned against the black stone wall.

"You speak of choices," she said thoughtfully. "I have a choice now, don't I? I can give up or I can carry out my original mission to stop Zanel. If I give up, then it's all over. Yet if I choose to fight, how can I possibly hope to defeat her? She's *me*. She knows me better than anyone, perhaps even better than I know myself. How do I destroy an enemy with such an advantage?"

"Maybe you don't need to," Van'garat suggested. "Like it or not, she is a part of you. If you tried to destroy her you'd be like a murracat chasing its own tail."

"Then what do I do?"

"She's a missing part of you. You're both fragmented souls, both hurting, both wounded and incomplete. I believe what you must do is reunite with her, merge with her."

"No," Eladria objected. "She's stronger than I am. She'd destroy me."

Van'garat got up from the bench and stood before the princess. "Don't underestimate your power. You have what she lacks." He placed his hand over his heart and continued. "You possess compassion, integrity and love, which are of a force infinitely stronger than the most potent hatred. Darkness is but absence of light and has no power over it. The mere presence of light illuminates and dispels the dark."

"But what if I'm not strong enough?" Eladria countered.

"Trust that you are," he said, his dark eyes gleaming. "You must now see why it was your fate to come here, why only you have the power to end this. You must face your shadow. You cannot fight it. You must heal and integrate it."

Eladria looked at the ground, listening intently but unsure how to respond.

Van'garat continued. "Now that the spell she placed on me has lifted, I can see that Zanel was right about a number of things.

The blood running through your veins is indeed a mixture of both Lasan and Starlanian lineages. The Dragon Star is the third aspect of the trinity; the key that will unlock your power and enable you to use it. You're more powerful than you could ever imagine, Princess Eladria. Pain obscures your clarity but now is the time to move beyond it and embrace your destiny. You must claim your power and be willing to use it."

"But I don't know how," Eladria exclaimed, fighting back tears of desperation.

"I can show you," the Ha'shon assured her. "That's my purpose here. That's why I was led to live as a hermit in the jungle, to awaken and be trained in the art of Ko Tra Pah. It's all clear to me now. It was all for you, Eladria, my entire life's journey. All so I could help you in your hour of greatest need, at a time when it's imperative that you claim your sovereignty and fulfill your destiny."

"Do you really believe that?" Eladria asked, a teardrop rolling down her face. "Because I don't see a grand design or purpose behind all that's happened. Life just happened, fitfully, painfully, one disaster and tragedy after the next. Whatever the truth is about my bloodline and whatever the Dragon Star has done to me, I don't feel there's anything special about me."

Janak stepped forward and shook his head. "You wrong," he said, looking up at her, his eyes wide and gleaming. "Moment I meet you, Princess, I know there something special about you, even though you not aware of it yourself. You have a light in you. Why else you think Janak join you and stay with you, even after we attacked and chased and captured and shot at? I had to be around you, because light in you shines like beacon of hope in a world of darkness. I not want to lose that light. I not want to be alone and lost in dark any longer."

"It is time, Princess Eladria," Van'garat said, his face lighting up with an enigmatic smile. "Time that you recognized that light within you and learned to use it."

"You're right," Eladria said, touched by the words of her comrades. She wiped away the last of her tears as she continued. "I can't just sit here and wallow in self-pity. I have to do whatever I can to stop Zanel."

"The situation is critical," Van'garat said. "We're somehow insulated in this underground complex but I sense the situation above ground is worsening. If we don't act soon, it'll be too late. Assuming this world isn't first consumed by the breach as Master Nirataan warned, Zanel will wipe your mind, connect you to the crystal and use you to free the Shadow Lords."

"No," Eladria said with resolution, feeling a spark of indignation igniting within. "I won't let that happen. I'll stop her and save my mother and all the others she's enslaved. If it really was me that did this—albeit some twisted, separate part of me—then I swear I'll undo it."

Eladria felt that for the first time in her life, she had a clear purpose and a true reason for being, one that was single-pointed and unmistakable. It was an electrifying realization. She turned to Van'garat. "This power you say I have within me," she began. "The Dragon Star and the lifeblood of the Lasan and Starlanians; this trinity you spoke of...you said you could teach me to use it?"

"Yes," Van'garat answered. "But there are dangers. I must lead you on a journey inward, into the very core of your being. It's the same initiation I undertook as the culmination of my training in Ko Tra Pah. I was fortunate to have had years of physical and mental preparation to ready me for the experience. You, however, have had little to none."

"You're saying it might not work?"

"There's no guarantee of anything. Once we undertake the process, there is no going back. Regardless of what happens, there will be consequences."

"I understand the risk. But I'm ready to do this. Tell me what I need to do."

Chapter 29

Emergence

The moment Eladria decided to relinquish her fears and embrace her destiny, it was as though everything came into sharp focus and she felt more alive than ever before. She had no idea what would come of this inner journey, but was determined to go through with it.

She spent a moment searching for signs of the Ornakai guards. After depositing their prisoners in the cell, the insect-like creatures had marched back up the stairway. But although they weren't visible, Eladria knew they were somewhere close by, undoubtedly watching their captives' every move. It was possible the cell was rigged with hidden surveillance devices. Eladria wouldn't have been surprised if Zanel had been watching and listening the whole time they'd been here. She tried to dismiss such a thought as she sat down upon the metal bench and tried to steady her nerves with a deep breath.

"What must I do?" she asked Van'garat as he sat down beside her.

"Listen and do as I say," he said, a look of utmost seriousness upon his face.

"What about Janak?" Janak asked nervously from the other end of the cell. "Is anything I do to help?"

"You can best help us by staying back and remaining quiet," Van'garat said.

"I still feel it within me, Van'garat, the pain and anger," Eladria admitted, repressing a shudder. "Will it prevent me from doing this?"

"No," Van'garat answered. "In fact, it's the very doorway that will lead you where you must go. Now, sit comfortably and close your eyes."

Eladria did as he directed.

"Allow yourself to feel the pain within you," he continued. "Move your attention into it. You've repressed and denied it, but you can avoid it no longer. Focus on the emotions, sensations and discomfort. Truly feel it. Be aware of it without *becoming* it."

Eladria felt a constriction stretching all the way from her gut to her chest and throat like a coiled serpent squeezing the life out of her. A sharp, searing pain came in waves of grief, despair and desolation. She had lost everything and everyone, including herself. "I can't do this," she blurted, with a shake of her head.

"Feel the pain," Van'garat implored. "Allow it to be there and truly *feel* it. That's the only way beyond it. You must bring your full attention into it."

Mustering all her fortitude, she did as he told her. She brought the light of her awareness into the emotional pain. So many years of grief—so many hurts, disappointments, fears and doubts—had accumulated within her, eating away at her from within. She'd done everything in her power to avoid and distract herself from it, but she could do that no longer. She had to face it head on and pray that it wouldn't destroy her.

As she continued to focus on the sensations within, a flood of images and memories spilled into her awareness. She saw herself as a child, with her parents and Zinn. She witnessed her life in the palace, the loss of her mother, her endless tuition and again felt her frustration and isolation as an only child and the over-protected daughter of the king. She saw Narat, the man who'd taken away her loneliness and stolen her heart, before betraying her in the worst imaginable way. She witnessed the invasion of her home and the death of her father, her escape to the planet surface and her arduous quest...the death of Zinn...her fateful journey to Drantak and her traumatic encounter with Zanel...

"It's time to let go of the past...and everything you have been and have believed yourself to be," Van'garat's voice echoed in her mind. *"You must willingly give it up and hold on to nothing..."*

A lifetime of regurgitated emotion had unraveled before her.

Eladria became aware of her deepest insecurities and her nagging sense of inadequacy as a princess in the royal lineage of Chaldeen. Although she'd always been headstrong and determined, deep down she'd felt unprepared for the duties that lay before her. She also felt she somehow didn't belong here, that it wasn't her home, that she belonged somewhere else entirely. Maybe that was why she had always yearned to escape? Was it actually herself she'd been trying to flee?

"You must willingly give it up..."

It was as though a tornado was tearing through her being, stirring up long-forgotten memories, lifelong fears and hurts that had festered beneath the surface. She had to confront all of it. There was no escaping it. Her entire psyche was unraveling...

"...and hold on to nothing..."

She refused to let herself be swept away by the deluge of memories, images and emotions. She observed them and watched as they passed by and faded into oblivion.

As they dissipated, she immediately felt lighter, freer and more spacious within and without. It was as though all that was unresolved in her heart, mind and psyche had been reconciled and was gone.

"Now, go deeper," Van'garat's voice echoed. *"Find that place within, beyond all thoughts, beyond all feelings. If a thought rises, resist the urge to lose yourself in it. Instead, trace it back to its source. Find the root of all perception...and allow yourself to rest there..."*

Eladria was aware of thoughts and perceptions drifting through her mind like clouds in the sky. They came and went, rising and falling, amorphous and ever-shifting. She realized that she'd spent most of her life completely consumed by these cloud-like formations, feeding into them, giving them a reality, solidity and importance they didn't inherently possess. For beyond the clouds was an entire sky.

The clouds no longer seemed as all-consumingly important, because she now saw that the vast expanse of sky—that which was beyond her thoughts; empty yet all-encompassing—was closer to who and what she was. Believing herself to be but an assortment of thoughts, beliefs and feelings, she had felt restricted, limited and small. But now, glimpsing a reality deeper than the content of her mind, she felt unbounded. Tracing each thought back to its source, she saw that they arose like droplets of vapor from a vast ocean of consciousness.

"Touch the core of your being," Van'garat's voice echoed across eternity. *"Feel and know this to be your true essence, the primordial essence out of which all arises and to which all returns. You had forgotten what you are, losing yourself in a realm of objects, thoughts and beliefs, a hazy world of dreams and illusion. It is time to awaken by coming back to your true nature and seeing all as it truly is. Go deeper...deeper into this ocean of being."*

Eladria was initially hesitant to do this, for she didn't want to lose herself in this ocean of spaciousness. But knowing that she could trust Van'garat, she quickly surmounted her fear.

She allowed herself to merge into the oceanic expanse of pure, unconditioned consciousness. As she moved into it, all notion of separation diminished. There was nothing but peace. She somehow knew that this ocean of light infused all of life, sustaining and nourishing everything in the universe and beyond. She was but a wave in this magnificent ocean; apparently separate, yet intrinsically part of it.

Following her difficult childhood and the nightmarish events following the Ha'shon coup, a part of her had given up on life. She had presumed that the universe operated on an axis of suffering and that all was in vain. But she'd been wrong. For she now could see that buried far beneath the surface events and the turbulent ripples that swept across the surface of the lake was a hidden perfection. Everything—every single atom in the universe—was bound together by a gravity of love, a love deeper than anything she could ever have imagined, an infinite light that could never be extinguished.

Everything and everyone that ever lived, at the core of their being, was rooted in this primordial substance. It was the wellspring from which all forms in the universe arose. Yet these forms—and all the 'people' that were but waves upon the ocean—were so ignorant of their true nature and so disconnected from their essence. They were lost in illusion and totally unaware of their true nature, of the interconnected vastness of the universe. It would almost be comical were the behavior of those apparently disconnected fragments of consciousness not so destructive.

"Find the light within," Van'garat's voice echoed across the void. *"Allow yourself to be drawn to it. It is calling to you."*

At first Eladria wasn't sure what he meant. There was light everywhere; everything was composed of light. But she moved her awareness deeper and found herself drawn to a pocket of blinding white light, shining at the core of her being like a thousand blazing suns. It had a certain feel to it that she immediately recognized, for she had experienced it before. It was the Dragon Star.

It had transferred itself into her consciousness where it lay shining at the core of her being, just waiting to be claimed. She had inadvertently tapped into its power before now, but now it was time to consciously integrate and utilize this spark of starlight, a gift from an ancient race that had been placed on her world so long ago, apparently just for her.

Van'garat was still with her on this inner journey and his voice carried across an immeasurable infinity: *"The power of the Dragon Star is the bridge that will enable you to access your true power and greatest potential. You must move into it. Merge with it and claim your sovereignty."*

The power was so great that Eladria feared it would destroy her. Yet she allowed the fear to pass through her awareness. By not engaging it, it quickly dissipated and she was ready to do as Van'garat advised, regardless of the risks.

She moved her awareness into the Dragon Star, opening

herself to it, allowing it to flood through her being. Waves of light consumed her, seeping through her being, overwhelming her. There was nothing she could do but allow herself to...

Melt into it...

Until she was no more...

How much time had passed she was uncertain. It had felt like an eternity, but it could only have been moments.

Her eyes opened and sight returned, although it was hazy at first. Her lungs filled with air and again she became aware of her physicality: head, neck, chest, arms, hands, torso, legs and feet. For a moment, it felt as though this body, this receptacle in which she found herself, was nothing remotely to do with her. It felt numb and leaden with drowsiness.

She looked around and found herself still sitting upon the bench in the underground cell. Van'garat sat beside her, while Janak sat on the floor at the other end of the cell, watching in curiosity.

"You okay, Princess?" Janak asked in concern.

Eladria nodded slowly.

"How do you feel?" Van'garat asked.

It took a moment for Eladria to answer. Initially it was a struggle to piece together the words and, even then, she found it difficult to elucidate her experience. "My head feels light but my body feels heavy, as though I've been asleep for years."

"In a manner of speaking you have been," Van'garat said. "But now you are awake. You have realized who and what you truly are. You moved into a level of consciousness far transcendent of the flickering dream-forms of the outer world. You have reclaimed your power."

"You seemed to know exactly what I would find and what I needed to do. How did you know?"

"I mentally connected with you so I could sense what you were experiencing and so guide and direct you," he explained. "I undertook the same journey with my master, Ustabak. After touching the primordial essence and realizing the truth of one's being, nothing can ever be the same. I took you even further than that. I saw the Dragon Star at the core of your being, waiting for you to fully merge with it and activate its power. You have now done that."

She looked up at him, feeling quite bewildered. "What does that mean?"

The Ha'shon mystic smiled. "It means that you can use your power to do anything," he said. "It is malleable and can be molded by your intent. You must now learn to channel and direct it. Adepts of Ko Tra Pah spend many years learning such skills and the power you possess greatly exceeds even the most revered of masters. You have the ability to create and destroy on an unimaginable scale. You now possess the power to birth entire worlds! You have been granted the power of the gods themselves."

"Then tell me, how do I use it?"

"I wish I could share all that I've learned. If we had the time I would systematically train you in the art of channeling and directing life energy. But instead you'll have to learn to use your power intuitively."

Eladria shook her head. "I can't do this alone. I can feel it within me, filling every cell of my body, but I haven't a clue what I'm supposed to do with it. I need your help."

"Very well," Van'garat said as he stood up and gestured for Eladria to join him. He took her arm and guided her a few steps back until they both stood facing the metal bench.

"What if the guards or Zanel are watching us?" Eladria asked in sudden concern.

"You needn't worry for now," the Ha'shon replied. "I've placed a temporary cloaking incantation around the cell. Even if they are watching, they won't be aware of this."

"How long will this incantation work?"

"As long as needed, or until we step out of the cell," he answered. "Now, concentrate. Close your eyes and feel the power within you."

Eladria did so and, sure enough, she could immediately feel her entire being tingling with energy. There was a vast reservoir of power buzzing within her; she could feel it all the way from her head down to her toes. When she moved her attention into it, it intensified until she could feel every cell of her body charged with light, a light that irradiated her mind and senses and electrified the air around her.

"Now focus on the bench," Van'garat said.

"The bench?"

"Reach out to it with your mind...and *move* it."

Eladria initially hesitated, doubtful that she could do such a thing. To move an inanimate object was a clear violation of the laws of physicality. But she recalled she had inadvertently done just that when she was trapped in the volcano cave-in and again when they were about to crash into the canyon in Nubrak. The power was within her. Back then she'd used it by accident, but now she would see if she could consciously direct it.

She set aside her doubts and did as Van'garat directed. With a combination of imagination and willpower, she pictured the bench moving to the left. As she consciously directed her intent, she instinctively reached out with her hand and could feel the power travelling from her fingertips as waves of invisible force. As she moved her hand, the bench mirrored her movement, slowly scraping across the smooth black floor.

"Is incredible!" exclaimed Janak.

"Do not disturb her," Van'garat hushed him, turning his attention back to Eladria. "Now, lift it in the air."

As before, she kept her attention fixed upon the bench and, with her focused intent, willed it to lift up from the ground. Almost the moment she set the intention and raised both hands upward, the bench lifted from the ground, as if being elevated by invisible hands.

"Put it down again," Van'garat said.

Eladria did so, and the bench landed on the ground with a clatter.

"Now, destroy it."

"Destroy it?"

"That's right..."

Eyes still fixed upon the object, Eladria sent out the intention to destroy it. Again the power surged through her and she watched as the bench began to disintegrate. The legs collapsed and the frame tumbled to the ground with a clatter. Remaining focused on the object, she reached out with her hands and closed her fists, watching as the pile of metal melted into a pool of molten liquid.

"I can't believe it," she cried.

"You did that?" Janak cried, gaping in astonishment.

"You saw it with your own eyes," Van'garat answered with a proud smile.

"I just imagined it happening and it did," Eladria said.

"That is but a taste of your ability," Van'garat said. "All you need do is connect with your innate power and direct it, molding it with your intent."

"Can...can you get us out of here?" Janak asked hesitantly.

"I don't know. I suppose I can," Eladria looked to Van'garat, still uncertain.

"The only limits to your power are those you impose upon it," Van'garat said. "Feel the power and direct it with your mind."

"This will take some time to get used to."

"Time is one thing we don't have. Everything you've ever been taught about reality has suddenly been overturned. The old laws of the universe no longer apply, for you have transcended them. Set aside your hesitation and embrace your power. There is nothing you cannot now do."

This was all so much to take in, but Van'garat was right. She could spend days trying to understand her newfound abilities, but there was no time for that. Eladria turned to the cell door, which buzzed with a screen of faintly visible electricity. With the power of her mind, she deactivated the barrier. The mechanism short-circuited with a bang and the electrical barrier immediately disappeared.

"Let's go," she said as she stepped through the open door.

"What about guards?" Janak asked.

"We'll get past them," Eladria answered, feeling a newfound surge of confidence.

Van'garat put his hand on Eladria's arm, stopping her in her tracks. "In spite of what I told you, you must not be overconfident, Princess. You dissolved a metal object and disabled a security field, but you've still much to learn when it comes to using your powers. Conceit can be ill-afforded."

"You're right," she replied. "But I know I can do this!"

Van'garat lowered his head. "I simply advise caution," he said. "Your greatest trial is yet ahead of you. You must not falter now."

Chapter 30

Crossing The Threshold

The Ornakai guards were aware of their escape the moment it happened. The insect-like men came racing down the stairway, rifles in hand.

Eladria acted immediately. Summoning her power, she mentally reached out and snatched the weapons from them. The Ornakai stopped in their tracks and watched in astonishment as the guns were plucked from their hands by an invisible force and cast down the staircase. Despite their initial confusion, the insect-like warriors were undeterred by the loss of their weapons and continued down the stairway, intent on apprehending the escaping prisoners.

Janak reached down and picked up the fallen rifles. There was one for each of them, but Van'garat refused the offer. Eladria admired his pacifism and checked to ensure that her own weapon was set to a nonlethal setting.

She and Janak took aim at the approaching guards and fired. Her aim was sloppy and she had to fire repeatedly before she succeeded in hitting her target. Within moments, they'd shot all four of the guards, who tumbled down the stairs, landing in an unconscious heap outside the cell.

"We have to get out of here now," Eladria said.

"Which way?" Janak asked.

Their cell was on a landing between two stairways, one leading up and the other down.

"If we go up, we'll end up where we came from," Eladria said.

"We have to go down," Van'garat stated.

"Are you certain?"

The Ha'shon nodded. "We need to go deep into the heart of this complex, for that's where the crystal is. Only there can we stop Zanel. I believe this stairway will take us where we need to go."

"Then let's move."

They ran down the smooth black stairway as fast as they could. Eladria knew it wouldn't be long before the rest of the Ornakai realized what had happened. She didn't know what to expect when they reached the bottom and was braced for the possibility that the enemy might already be lying in wait for them. Yet when they reached the bottom of the stairs she was relieved to see that her fears were unfounded.

The stairway led into a long empty corridor, illuminated by circular electrical lights fastened to the sleek obsidian walls, the air thin and musty. There was only one way to go and that was straight ahead. They made their way down the corridor, cautiously but hastily.

It wasn't long before the Ornakai caught up with them. Eladria was horrified at the sight of half a dozen armed warriors racing down the corridor behind them. The escapees ran as fast their legs would carry them, but the Ornakai—being larger, stronger and faster—were rapidly closing in on them.

The Ornakai opened fire, the electrical blasts ricocheting off the walls with the sound of thunder. It seemed they weren't yet close enough to score a direct hit, but they were getting nearer by the second. Realizing that they had no chance of outrunning their pursuers, Eladria stopped running and the others came to a halt beside her.

"Stop them," Van'garat said, putting his hand on Eladria's shoulder, his words almost drowned out by the relentless booming of gunfire. "You have the power to stop them. You did it before."

Eladria realized she needed to create a barrier between them and the Ornakai, something that would shield them from the weapons fire and prevent them from getting any closer. She closed her eyes and drew her attention inward, summoning the raw power at the core of her being and sending it outward. A wall of light appeared between them and the Ornakai. The barrier deflected the Ornakai weapons fire, reflecting it back, injuring several of them. The insect-men promptly ceased fire.

Eladria let out a triumphant laugh and turned to her comrades, who looked up in relief as they struggled to catch their breaths. "We have to keep on going," she declared. "That's probably just the first wave of guards. They'll be determined to recapture us. You can only imagine how angry Zanel will be when she learns we've escaped."

"Unless she wanted us to escape," Van'garat cautioned. "It's possible she's waiting for us at our destination."

"You mean it's a trap?"

"I don't know, but I believe she was expecting something like this to happen and has no doubt prepared for it."

"Well, if that's the case, I'm not going to keep her waiting," Eladria said, trying not to let her fortitude slip. "The sooner we get this over with, the better. Van'garat, are you certain we're headed in the right direction?"

Van'garat momentarily closed his eyes, then looked up at Eladria and nodded. "Yes, these tunnels lead into the heart of the complex. We're getting closer to the crystal. I can feel it..."

"Yes, I can feel it too," Eladria said. "And that's not all. I can feel the tremors again."

"They not as bad as on surface," Janak noted.

"No, but they're getting worse the farther we go. That must mean we're getting to the heart of whatever's happening here."

Before leaving, she took one last look at the trapped Ornakai, who were still struggling to find a way through the barrier and were getting angrier by the second.

They hurried down the corridor. Eladria could feel something leading her forward, as if an unknown instinct was pulling her toward her destination.

The corridor soon terminated at a series of steps leading up to a large arched doorway. The door was sealed and the surrounding wall carved with indecipherable inscriptions. As the ground was rocked by another tremor, Eladria climbed the steps and stood before the black stone door. With neither handle nor lock, there no obvious way of opening it. She tried pushing it open but it wouldn't budge.

As she sighed in exasperation, a red ball of light appeared across the doorway. She staggered back in alarm. The red light expanded to cover the entire doorway, increasing in brightness and intensity, pulsating and flickering like fire.

"Wh-what is that?" Janak stuttered.

"Unless I'm mistaken it's an astral guardian," Van'garat answered.

"A what?"

"An energetic entity created to guard whatever's behind that door. I've heard of them but never encountered one before. They were usually conjured to guard sacred sites in the ancient world."

"How do we get past it?" Eladria asked.

"You can only pass an astral guardian by providing it with the specific sound frequency with which it was programmed; the correct password, if you will."

"I hate to state the obvious, but we don't have a password."

"In which case our only option is to destroy it."

"How do we do that?"

Van'garat looked round at her. "You can use your power. I will guide you and use my own energy to aid you. You must concentrate and do exactly as I say. It won't be easy and there is extreme danger—"

"Extreme danger?" Janak echoed nervously.

"Either we'll succeed in destroying the entity or it'll destroy us," Van'garat said plainly. "The moment we try to interfere with it, it will retaliate and we must be prepared."

"Janak prepared all right," Janak said as he retreated several paces, keeping a tight hold of his rifle.

"We've no other choice," Eladria said, putting down her

weapon. "We can't go back that way and we can't stay here. The only way is forward."

"Then we're in agreement."

As Janak continued edging backward, Eladria and Van'garat stood side by side, facing the astral guardian, which flickered and oscillated as it covered the doorway, a force not quite of this world, but evidently posing tremendous danger.

"Focus on it," Van'garat directed her. "Together we can disperse it."

"I can feel it," she exclaimed. "It's alive!"

"It has no innate existence of its own. It's nothing more than a thought-form. It was created by the mind and can be destroyed by the mind. Project your awareness into it."

The astral guardian, sensing their interference, grew in size and strength, sending tendrils of red flame lashing out at them. As Eladria gazed into the red flames, she was certain she could see a face in the flickering energy field, and it bore an expression of unbounded rage.

"Is getting bigger!" Janak exclaimed from behind them.

"Keep your attention fixed upon it," Van'garat directed the princess.

Eladria wanted to run, to get as far away from it as she could, but she stood firm and continued to hold her attention on it.

"Now, disperse it!" Van'garat cried.

With all her might, Eladria willed the creature to dissolve. It was a struggle, for it put up great resistance, and she was aware that it had the power to overwhelm and destroy her mind from the inside out. The moment she had reached into it with her mind, she had invited it into her being. It was now within her and was determined to kill her.

But she reminded herself that it was just a phantom, an illusion conjured by someone's mind. She, on the other hand, was real, and she had the power of the Dragon Star. Her cause was noble and her intentions just. She would not let this entity stop her. She was strong and she was ready to use that strength.

The instant she banished all doubt from her mind, the astral guardian lost its struggle. With one last helpless splutter, the entity shimmered out of existence as quickly as it had appeared.

"You did it!" Janak cried in jubilation. "Is there anything you *not* do?"

"That remains to be seen," Eladria said, exhaling deeply. Although they'd managed to destroy the entity in a battle of wills, it had taken a lot out of her. She looked round at Van'garat, who appeared similarly strained. Alas, there was no time to rest. Another quake rumbled underfoot. Eladria knew that time was running out.

She climbed up to the door and pushed on it with all her might. It was stiff but it gradually creaked open. Beyond it was darkness.

They stepped through the door and it closed behind them with a resounding thud.

It took a moment for their eyes to adjust to the lack of light as they looked around, anxiously trying to determine where they were. They had stepped into an immense subterranean cavern, the limestone walls and ceiling lined with stalactites, some of which almost reached the ground. They were on the edge of a lake that stretched into the distance, the water surface choppy and undulating, agitated by each round of tremors. The air was thick and stale and the only source of light came from the fluttering of fire-bats and a diffuse white luminescence emanating from across the water. A low humming sound reverberated throughout the cavern, intermixed with the sound of the water lapping against the rocky shore and the steady tapping of water droplets falling from the ceiling.

"This must be part of the network of caverns out of which the complex was built," Van'garat noted.

"Why they go to such effort to keep people out?" Janak wondered.

"The crystal," Eladria said. "It has to be to keep people away from the crystal. I can feel it. It's just beyond the other end of this cavern."

"So how we cross water?" Janak shrugged. "Is a long way to swim."

"We don't have to swim," Eladria said, catching sight of a small boat perched upon the water's edge. By the look of it, it had been here for quite some time, perhaps even predating Zanel's arrival. The boat, which had two oars resting by its side, was made of wood and looked rickety and worn. But, as she approached it, she realized that it ought to be enough to get her across the water.

"It's just what we need," she said as she ran her hand along the hull.

"But is not big enough," Janak said.

"You're right. There's only enough room for two people at most."

"So what we do?" Janak asked as he folded his arms.

"Obviously I have to go," Eladria answered. "And I need Van'garat with me. I can't do this without him."

"On the contrary, this is a journey you will have to undertake yourself," Van'garat said. "Your final steps you must walk alone. But I will accompany you as far as I can, if that is your wish."

"But what about Janak?" Janak asked.

"You'll have to stay here for now," Eladria said. "But it should be safe here, certainly far safer than where we're going."

"But I be stuck here!" Janak looked around helplessly. "Is no way out of here."

"We'll be back for you," Eladria assured him.

"You promise?"

"You have my word."

Before he could answer, another tremor shook the cavern, knocking them to the ground and dislodging stalactites and rocks from the ceiling, some of which smashed to the ground, others landing in the water with a splash.

Eladria and Van'garat hastened their departure and, with Janak's help, pushed the boat into the water and climbed aboard. There was barely enough room for the two of them and conditions were cramped, but it would hopefully get them to the other shore.

They said farewell to Janak, who stood at the water's edge, looking on helplessly as Eladria and Van'garat picked up the oars and began rowing.

"Hurry back!" Janak called after them.

"Don't worry, we will," Eladria called back.

"Janak wish you luck!" Janak added as he nervously paced the shore.

Ordinarily the underground lake was probably motionless and still, but the increasing tremors were causing it to get choppier by the moment. Between tremors they made some headway as the water calmed, but the rest of the time they struggled as the boat was helplessly buffeted by the waves. It took them some time to get into a stable rhythm, to row the boat away from the shore and toward the eerie light on the horizon.

Another seismic blast shook the cavern, causing a deluge of water to shower over them, almost capsizing the boat. Eladria clung to the sides and spat out a mouthful of water. Both of them were unharmed but drenched, water dripping down their faces, their water-soaked clothes clinging to their bodies.

As the lake settled, they began rowing again with all their might, until the next tremor stirred up another round of churning waves. After each onslaught it took a few moments for them to regain their momentum. But they did so, and gradually they found themselves getting deeper into the heart of the cavern and closer to the light, which grew brighter as they neared. Translucent waves of energy now rippled across the cavern. They were clearly nearing the heart of Drantak.

All of a sudden, Eladria got the feeling they were in danger.

Before she could say anything to Van'garat, the boat was attacked. Something rose up from beneath the water. The first thing Eladria saw were six large, thrashing tentacles, followed by a head. It was a grey octopus-like creature with six black eyes, its scaly head dominated by an oversized mouth with gaping jaws and razor-sharp teeth. It grabbed hold of the boat and snarled ferociously.

As the creature reeled the boat in with its suckered tentacles, waves of water splashed over its frantic occupants. Breathless and terrified, Eladria knew she had to act immediately. Moving beyond her fear, she reached within and connected with the reservoir of power within her. She channeled it outward, intending to disable the creature, just enough for them to escape. A pulse of lightning surged from her body into the creature. The beast reacted with a shudder, momentarily loosening its hold on the boat.

But it quickly recovered its grip. What she'd done hadn't been enough.

Again she reached inward and called upon the power of the Dragon Star. She didn't want to injure the creature, but she knew it was imperative that they escape. A wave of energy leapt from her body and electrified the creature, causing it to convulse and release its hold on the boat. Eladria and Van'garat took hold of the oars and began rowing away from the creature as it thrashed about helplessly. Eladria watched as the creature eventually stopped moving and submerged beneath the water. There was a sudden stillness.

"I didn't want to harm it," she said breathlessly.

"You had no choice," Van'garat consoled her. "You did what you had to do."

"But there should have been another way..."

"There wasn't. If you hadn't acted, it would have killed us and all of this would have been for nothing. You had a hard choice to make and you made it."

"What's become of me, Van'garat? Death and destruction seem to follow me wherever I go. This isn't the first time I've had to take a life and I fear it won't be the last."

"You must let go of recrimination and remain focused. You're here for a reason and you know that."

"I know it's up to me to end this," Eladria began. "But I still don't know *how*. I don't know how I'm going to defeat Zanel..."

"When the time's right, you will know," Van'garat assured her. "But let me tell you this. It won't be by force. You cannot defeat fire with fire. It can be extinguished only by a different element, such as water or earth. In the same way, you cannot fight hate with hate. You can only dissolve it with love. No matter what Zanel throws at you, no matter what she tries to do, you must *transcend* it. You can never defeat her by being like her. You must be better than her, you must rise beyond her."

"I'm not sure I understand..."

"I trust that when the time comes, you will."

Without another word, they continued rowing toward the source of light, which was getting brighter by the moment. The closer they got, the uneasier Eladria felt.

They made it to the other shore just as the cavern was rocked by another series of tremors. Rocks fell from the ceiling and crashed to the ground, while a deluge of water swept over the shore, knocking Eladria down as she stepped out of the boat. As she tumbled, she gashed her arm on a sharp rock. She gritted her teeth and tried to ignore the pain as she forced herself back up and looked around.

The source of the light permeating the cavern came from a towering glass door ahead of them, atop a flight of steps. It was impossible to see what lay beyond the gold-framed door, or what was causing the light. Waves of semi-visible energy continued pulsating outward like heat-waves, emanating from whatever was beyond the glass.

"We made it," she exclaimed, wasting no time in climbing the steps to the door.

She was about to try to open it, when the door slid open of its own volition. Initially startled, she nevertheless walked through it and turned to await Van'garat, who by this time was climbing the steps behind her.

But before he could get any closer, the door slid shut. Eladria tried to pull it back open. There were no handles or latches and nothing to grab hold of. She pressed against the glass, determined to reopen it. Van'garat stood at the other side of the door, a look of resignation upon his face.

"There must be a way to open it," she called. She tried to force the door open with all her might, but was unsuccessful. She stepped back and looked behind her. There was another door just ahead of her. She didn't want to go near it until she'd found a way to get Van'garat through. Remembering her powers, she focused inwardly and tried to use them to open the door, but still it would not budge.

"You have to go on without me," Van'garat called to her. "This is the way it was meant to be."

"I won't leave you here," Eladria cried.

"You have to. You must face your final challenge alone."

Realizing that she had little option but to concede, she reluctantly nodded.

"Go now, Princess," Van'garat said, placing his hand on the glass separating them. "It has been my great honor to have assisted you on your journey. Remember all I've that told you. Be strong. Find and embody that which is best within you and you will not falter."

"I couldn't have done this without you," she said, feeling her eyes moisten with tears. "I still don't feel like I'm ready to do this."

"If you weren't ready you wouldn't be here. Go now. Go and do what you came here to do."

Eladria placed her hand against the glass and tried to muster a smile as a teardrop rolled down her cheek. Van'garat smiled warmly, a look of sad serenity in his wise old eyes.

She turned and walked up to the second glass door, which slid open the moment she approached it. She peered through it, but was unable to see anything for the light. Bracing herself for whatever might be lying in wait, she took a deep breath and stepped forward.

Chapter 31

Final Reckoning

As she adjusted to the light, Eladria found herself in a circular chamber that reached up as far as the eyes could see and plunged below into what looked like a bottomless precipice. At the center of the chamber was the source of the light: a colossal triangular-peaked crystal of magnificent opaque quartz. The crystal pulsated brightly, blasting a vertical shaft of light upward, all the way up to the surface and into the sky. This was the source of the breach that was ravaging the planet.

Waves of iridescent energy shot out like rings of smoke, charging the air with static, making Eladria's skin tingle. The tremors continued, apparently caused by the crystal itself, which vibrated and hummed as it discharged the shaft of light. The air was hot and laced with sulfur. Although still wet from her voyage across the water, she felt the heat from the crystal rapidly drying her hair, clothes and skin.

It struck her as strange that the crystal chamber had been left unguarded. Where were the Ornakai—and where was Zanel? Eladria had been certain that she'd be lying in wait for her. Wherever she was, it was safe to assume that she wouldn't be far off.

Eladria moved forward cautiously, looking all around. There were circular walkways beneath the crystal, with railings along the outer rim and steps linking them. Holding onto the rails and very conscious of the chasm below, Eladria stepped onto one of the aisles and gazed up at the crystal.

Although clearly a natural formation, the crystal had been harnessed in decidedly unnatural ways. It was strewn with wiring and electrodes, intersecting at a central point where a series of glass booths encircled the base of the crystal. Here the Starlanian captives were imprisoned: one in each booth, standing upright, held in place with wiring and cables. The booth at the forefront was more prominent, with extra cabling connecting it to the crystal.

Could it be...?

It was.

It was her mother.

Eladria raced along the walkway, occasionally falling as tremors convulsed underfoot. She ran up the steps leading to the circular plateau at the base of the crystal. Her heart was pounding as she approached the central booth and looked inside. It had been so many years since she'd last seen her mother and she was barely recognizable as the woman Eladria had once known, but it was definitely her. Her skin was pale and her face gaunt, her eyes open and staring blankly ahead. Her face and body were covered in electrodes and wires.

"Mother, it's me. It's Eladria. Can you hear me?"

There was no response. Her mother continued staring ahead, her expression vacant and unregistering.

"I'm sorry," Eladria gasped. "If we'd known...if we'd known you were here, we'd have come for you long before now..."

She reached out and touched her mother's face, but she was still unresponsive. Eladria was devastated. In some ways this was worse than finding her dead, for she was in what appeared to be a state of living death.

"What has she done to you?" Eladria exclaimed, feeling a surge of rage bubbling inside her.

Suddenly becoming aware of a presence nearby, she looked round and saw a robed figure strolling across the walkway toward the crystal.

"Zanel," Eladria growled, the full force of her hatred spilling into her voice. She felt an urge to attack and hurt her, to inflict just some of the pain that Zanel had inflicted on her. But she restrained herself and remained rooted to the spot as Zanel climbed the steps and strode toward her.

"I'm glad you made it here," Zanel purred, smiling coldly.

"You knew I'd come here?" Eladria asked, narrowing her eyes.

"Every step of your journey was precisely as I planned it," Zanel said. "I manipulated you so perfectly and you blindly complied."

"I should have seen through you from the start."

"But you were so blinded by your grief. Your Ha'shon friend was suspicious in spite of my attempts to block his vision, but you didn't listen to him. Not that it would have changed anything even if you had. Everything has transpired as it was meant to. All of it was necessary to bring you here to me."

Eladria motioned to her mother. "What have you done to her?"

"What I had to do," Zanel answered. "It was necessary to utilize her power, to use her as a conductor and bridge, giving me control of the crystal."

"So you just used her like some kind of inanimate object..."

"I did as I was directed by the Shadow Lords. And do not fool yourself, for it is exactly what you would have done had you been in my place."

"Never!"

Zanel laughed, her lip curling and her eyes remaining untouched. "Don't fool yourself, if it had been you sent back in time instead of me, you'd have done exactly as I've done. We are the same: the same being, the same essence, separated only by time and experience."

"We're nothing alike," Eladria declared. "I look at you and I see nothing of myself. You're just a lifeless husk without a shred of humanity left in you."

"I am what I am," Zanel countered, a trace of anger flashing across her mutilated face. "I've done what I've had to do to survive and to rebuild the future."

"But there won't be any future!" Eladria retorted. "If you let the Shadow Lords into this world, nothing will survive. Don't you realize that you'll be among the first to die? What can they have possibly offered you that's made you willing to do this?"

"They offered me *life*."

"But at what price?"

"A price I'm willing to pay. In many ways I died the day I was torn from your body and cast into the fires of time. But I was given the chance of life anew and I had to take it. It wasn't too late for me, and it's not too late for you either, little girl. I now offer you what was offered to me. You can join me."

Eladria shook her head, taking a step back. "Why would I ever do that?" Another tremor hit, forcing Eladria to take hold of the nearest railing.

As the tremor subsided, Zanel took a step toward her. "Because there's nothing for you in this world. They took it all from you and crushed it before your very eyes. They invaded your home, killed your father and your friends and loved ones. They destroyed your life and then hunted you like an animal. This world will burn and it deserves to. But you can join me. We can leave this world and go where we're meant to be."

"What are you talking about?"

A smile flashed across Zanel's face. "I have travelled through the breach. There's another world just beyond the barrier, a world that's twinned with this one and is accessible through the power of the crystal. I have walked upon its soil and encountered its peoples. And I've met *him*..."

"Who?"

"The one whose face haunts your dreams, whose presence you can feel in every waking moment, as though he is only a heartbeat away. You didn't think he was real, but he is—and I've made a connection with him, a link that can never be severed. If you come with me, we'll find him together. It's where we belong, where the tides of fate have long been carrying us all along. You can travel with me while the Shadow Lords cleanse this degenerate world. Take my hand...join me."

"No." Eladria shook her head slowly. "You just can't see it, can you? You've no idea what's going on here, what's happened to you. You've been used and manipulated and promised something you'll never be given. I look at you and all I feel is shame: shame that some aspect of myself could have fallen so low—willing to sacrifice an entire world, an entire universe—and for what? Some empty promise of salvation?"

Zanel stared at her, remaining silent.

"I'm sorry you had to suffer as you did," Eladria continued. "I've no idea what it must have been like or what you had to endure. But you lost more than just your face that day. You lost your soul."

"You're right," Zanel responded. "My soul was taken from me. Everything I've done since then was to get back what was stolen from me. You're the same as me, little girl. The only difference between us is that you don't realize it. They took your soul from you as well, and I'm offering the chance to reclaim it...the choice of life, the chance to survive what's coming. You don't have to remain here. You can come with we, for we belong together. I offer you the chance, one last time, to join me."

"If you think I'd ever join you, then you're even more insane than I thought."

"I'm disappointed. You really can't see why I've done this, how I'm acting for the greater good."

"You don't care about the greater good," Eladria declared, as she stared into the deadened eyes of her wraith-like doppelganger. "All you care about is yourself. You were so wounded, so hurt and desperate, that you gave your allegiance to the first thing that came along and promised an end to the pain. Maybe in time you even came to *believe* the Shadow Lords and what they told you, but you've lost sight of what you're doing. What of all the countless innocents that will die? This may be a troubled world, but we have to let the people of this planet work out their problems and learn and grow. Who are you or the Shadow Lords to act as judge and executioner?"

"We seek order!" Zanel cried. "There must be order, for the sake of all life. In that, we are no different from the Guardians. But they're too weak to intervene, and so we must! We must restore the natural balance. And, for that, this world, and everyone on it, must die."

"I won't let you destroy this world."

"Do you really think you can stop me?"

"Yes," Eladria took a step toward Zanel, her eyes blazing with indignation. "Because I'm stronger than you, and you know it. I have the power of the Dragon Star. That's the one thing you don't have, the one thing you wanted above all else."

"And that's the only reason you're still alive now. I need your power and I will have it. I'd hoped you'd give it to me willingly, but I can see I will have to take it from you forcibly."

"If you kill me, the Dragon Star will die along with me."

"I don't intend to kill you. But I will destroy your mind as I did your mother's and then you will take her place. I will use you to unlock the crystal and allow the Shadow Lords to enter this realm. You will be the instrument of their deliverance."

Zanel lifted the crystalline pendant from around her neck and it glowed brightly, the same white luminescence that shone from the crystal towering above them. A light discharged from the pendant, engulfing Eladria in a net of electrical energy that wrapped itself around her body. Zanel moved closer and, with a wave of her hand, knocked Eladria to the ground, where she lay immobile, paralyzed by the energy net.

"This is even easier than I'd thought," Zanel looked down at her, an expression of sadistic smugness upon her pale, scarred face.

"Then I'll make it harder for you," Eladria glared up at her, as she attempted to muster the power of the Dragon Star. She tapped into the energy within her and, allowing it to accumulate until she felt her whole body tingle, she used it to break free of Zanel's net. Using the power of the Dragon Star, Eladria lifted her arm and sent a wave of kinetic force that shot from her hand and impacted Zanel, making her fall to the ground with a cry.

Eladria rose to her feet and discharged another round of kinetic fire with the intent of disabling her adversary. But Zanel was strong. Through gritted teeth, she forced herself up and launched a counterattack, firing shot after shot at Eladria. The electrical blasts slammed into Eladria's chest and abdomen. She collapsed and screamed as the electricity surged through her body.

Zanel continued the bombardment, leaving Eladria unable to fight back. The attack was so brutal that Eladria felt herself teetering on the brink of unconsciousness, but she fought to remain awake at all costs.

"I don't want to have to do this," Zanel said breathlessly as she stood over Eladria. "Because it's literally myself that I'm hurting. But you've left me no choice."

In spite of her words, Eladria knew that Zanel derived some perverse pleasure from inflicting pain on her. Eladria tried to focus the power of the Dragon Star, but her body was in so much pain and her mind was so weak that she couldn't reach it. It was there, but elusive. If only she'd had more experience, more training in its use, she might have been able to stop Zanel. But now she was helpless as she writhed on the ground in agony.

Zanel encased Eladria in another energetic net that pinned her down and prevented her from moving. Zanel stood over her, a sadistic smile playing upon her lips. Now that she was closer, Eladria could see the full extent of the damage to her face. One side of her head was mutilated and scarred beyond recognition, her eye and ear distorted and misshapen. Her dark hair was pulled back, accentuating her disfigurement. In spite of all that she'd done, Eladria felt a strange pity for this woman.

"I wish it hadn't come to this," Zanel whispered, kneeling down by her side and placing the palm of her hand on Eladria's forehead. "In some ways it would be merciful just to kill you right now, to release you from this suffering. But I can't do that, for I need you alive. Yet I must break down your resistance and for that, I must reach into your mind and erase it from the inside out."

Eladria struggled to break free, but every muscle of her body was paralyzed. She tried to shout and scream, but found that she couldn't even move the muscles of her jaw. She remained pinned to the ground, aware of the pulsating crystal looming above them, sending waves of energy rippling in every direction and a steady beam of light shooting upward. Zanel continued to kneel by her side, hand pressed against her forehead as a pulse of energy passed from her into Eladria.

Eladria closed her eyes and found herself drawn inward.

Her outer senses shut down and she was aware of being pulled into the deepest recesses of her mind.

She was alone in a forest at twilight. It was a strangely ethereal place, ephemeral and dreamlike. A ghostly light shone through the trees, seemingly emanating from all around. It was unnervingly quiet, with not a sound to be heard aside from her own footsteps rustling through the dead leaves underfoot.

As she wandered the forest, Eladria noticed that some invisible force was uprooting the trees one by one. She began to panic, for she realized these trees represented aspects of herself— her memories, her loves, her hopes, dreams and fears—and with each tree that crashed to the ground, a part of her was lost.

She knew that Zanel was inside her mind and was pulling it apart, piece by piece.

She didn't know what to do. Did she run? Did she try to prevent the forest from being destroyed? And, if so, how?

She stopped in a clearing, around which the trees continued toppling down in rapid succession. "Please," she cried out, unsure who or what she was beseeching. "Please, help me! Tell me what to do!"

"There's no use struggling," came Zanel's voice, echoing around her. "It's too late. You can't fight me. I'm too strong for you."

"Where are you?" Eladria cried. "This is my mind and I demand that you show yourself!"

The robed figure of Zanel appeared before her. "Make it easier on yourself," she whispered darkly. "Surrender now. Give up the fight. Give in to me and let it happen."

"No..."

"There's no hope for you. Why make this more painful than it has to be? Give up now..."

"No! You're not as strong as you claim to be."

"I have all the power I need to erase your mind, to wipe away every last thought, memory and dream...as I did to your mother."

"To *our* mother," Eladria corrected her. "You've become so hardened, callous and unfeeling, but deep within you there's still a shred of humanity there, and that part of you abhors everything that you've done and everything you've become!"

"You *are* determined," Zanel remarked, her face tightening. "But it makes no difference. It won't get you anywhere."

Zanel reached out and grabbed her. Eladria fought back, shaking her off and together they scuffled, each trying to overpower the other. Eladria knew that this battle would determine ultimate victory. The trees were continuing to fall around them. Zanel was succeeding: she was systematically destroying Eladria's mind.

The two adversaries were faced each other, hands locked in desperate struggle. Zanel was pushing against her with incredible might and Eladria resisted with all her strength. Zanel not only had the power of the crystal, but she was fuelled by the full force of her bitterness and rage, as well as the lust within her. Lust for what? Lust for power, belonging, redemption...or simply peace? Maybe that was all Zanel really wanted? She'd been hurt so badly and all she wanted was some kind of peace?

Eladria suddenly realized that there was no way she would defeat Zanel by fighting her with force. She recalled Van'garat's assertion that she wouldn't be able to defeat her by fighting aggression with aggression or force with force.

As she stared into her opponent's eyes, Eladria could see the depths of Zanel's hatred. She clearly blamed Eladria for all that had happened to her, holding Eladria responsible for her creation and her suffering. Zanel's eyes blazed with fury and a consuming desperation to succeed. But Eladria could see something deeper. She realized that, at heart, Zanel was like a wounded animal and the only way to stop her was to heal her.

Eladria now knew what she had to do.

She had to give up and relinquish the struggle.

She suddenly let go of all resistance, dropping her arms and allowing Zanel to push her to the ground. But there was no fear within her. No resistance. No struggle.

Eladria let go of everything: all thoughts pertaining to her mission, her agenda, her past and all the judgments she'd made about Zanel. Her fear, anger and grief melted away and in an instant she felt her heart open—to *everything*.

At that moment, everything shifted. In the absence of her resistance, what had been an overriding force of repulsion instantaneously reversed and became a force of attraction.

Eladria felt her heart open and expand. Like the birth of a star in the heavens, a vast implosion of light was accompanied by a gravitational force that pulled all into itself. Like a black hole at the core of her being, she felt a force of attraction drawing all toward her, a force all-embracing and all-consuming.

It was not a force driven by fear or resistance; all that had lifted in an instant. Instead it was a force of sheer love, a love of uncontainable enormity and power, a force transcendent of personality and experience. This sublime love had but one intent: to reconnect with all the seemingly separate aspects of itself, fragments that had been projected outward to create a universe of so-perceived externals.

Zanel immediately sensed the shift and she reacted in fear, scampering to her feet and trying to flee. She could feel the gravity pulling her toward it, a singularity of unfathomable power, a force that threatened to swallow her up, leaving no trace.

Zanel had entered Eladria's mind to dismantle it and it ought to have been as easy as pulling the wings off a fly. She'd expected Eladria to resist, to fret and struggle and fight against her. She hadn't expected this. She tried to get out of Eladria's mind, to escape this consuming light. But she couldn't escape. She was ensnared by its pull, and dragged toward it like a piece of flotsam helplessly carried by an unyielding current.

Zanel cried in fear.

Eladria watched impassively as Zanel was pulled into the blazing star of light that had opened within her own heart.

"You were right," Eladria said softly. "We belong together. Just not in the way you'd intended. You came from me. It's time that you returned to me. It's the only way we'll ever be whole."

"No!" Zanel screamed, able to taste her own impending oblivion. "I don't want to go back—I can't go back!"

But she couldn't struggle against the force of gravity that wrapped itself around her; a magnetism of love that burned like a universal fire, inextinguishable and unconquerable.

Zanel was pulled into the heart of the vortex. She disappeared into the blazing light at the core of Eladria's being. Not a trace of her remained.

The moment Eladria had relinquished all struggle and resistance, the duality was ended. Only in her heart could either of them find unity.

Eladria could feel the remnants of Zanel inside of her. Eladria didn't fight her, instead she embraced her like a mother cradling her child. In doing so, Eladria absolved Zanel of all her bitterness and separation, all her fear, hatred and her desperate yearning for wholeness. It all merged into the vast ocean of love. The shadow vanished and the pain and suffering Zanel had both experienced and perpetrated dissolved...until nothing remained in Eladria but light.

A tremendous, unfathomable power now pervaded Eladria's being. The forest around her began to spontaneously regrow, only this time it was brighter and more beautiful than before and it glistened with newness, infused with a crystalline perfection and vibrant, dancing color.

Eladria knew it was time to leave this place and return to the outer world.

Her enemy was vanquished, revealed to be nothing but a shadow. But her ordeal was not yet over. Her world was on the brink of destruction. She had to save it—assuming she wasn't already too late.

Chapter 32

The Death Of Tahnadra

Eladria opened her eyes.

As she returned to waking consciousness, the first thing she realized was that she could move again. She was freed from Zanel's restraint, for Zanel herself was gone. Aside for her robe and boots, which lay crumpled on the ground by Eladria's side, there was no trace of her adversary.

Eladria rose to her feet and noticed Zanel's crystal pendant lying upon the ground. This had been the source of her power, the means by which she'd used the psionic crystal to manipulate and control others. She raised her heel and stamped on the pendant, smashing it to pieces.

Another tremor hit and the ground shook beneath her, forcing her to grab hold of the nearest railing. The tremors were becoming more frequent and intense. The crystal was pulsating uncontrollably, its emissions ever more frenetic.

It was time to end this experiment. That was why she'd come here. She looked over at her mother, who stood unmoving and expressionless in the central booth, her eyes open but vacant, staring straight ahead, seemingly unable to register what was happening around her.

"I'll get you out of this," Eladria promised her. "All of you," she added, remembering that it wasn't just her mother that was connected to the crystal, but dozens of others, each in the same cataleptic state. There were men and women of all ages strapped into the glass booths encircling the crystal, from a woman who looked to be in her seventies to a blonde-haired boy barely out of his teens.

Careful to keep her footing as the cavern continued to shake, Eladria stepped over to a control console at the foot of the crystal. It was clearly from here that Zanel had controlled both the crystal and her captives. Eladria was unfamiliar with the computer interface and struggled to decipher the controls. It took much trial and error before she found the mechanism that released the imprisoned Starlanians. As she pulled a small black lever, the clamps holding them in place retracted.

Eladria raced over to her mother and pulled the electrodes and cabling from her face, head and arms, fully disconnecting her from the apparatus. With an arm around her back, she guided her out of the booth. After a few steps they came to a halt, Eladria allowing her mother to slump down to the ground, her back resting against one of the metal railings. Eladria was appalled at how gaunt and malnourished her mother looked. Yet it was a wonder she was alive at all after all this time. There was no way of knowing how long she'd been connected to the crystal. She wondered if the crystal itself had somehow kept her alive, only marginally sustaining her body.

"Can you hear me?" Eladria whispered as she knelt by her side, looking deeply into her eyes.

Her mother was unresponsive, but Eladria persisted. "It's me, Mother...it's Eladria."

"Eladria?" her mother croaked in hoarse response. She slowly moved her head and looked into Eladria's face. Her eyes were unfocused and hazy, as though she'd been in a deep trance and was fighting to regain lucidity.

"Yes, it's me," Eladria laughed in joyful relief. "I came here to rescue you."

Her mother was drifting in and out of consciousness. One moment she seemed aware of Eladria's presence, then her mind slipped away again. Eladria gently shook her, trying to keep her awake.

"Eladria...but you...you're grown up," her mother eventually said, her voice soft and distant.

"It's been a long time since you last saw me," Eladria said, her eyes welling with tears.

"How long?"

"Over ten years have passed," Eladria said. "I thought you were gone. I didn't realize you were here. No one did. If we'd known what had happened, if we'd known that you were here..."

Again, her mother appeared to momentarily drift out of consciousness. This was hardly surprising. Zanel had apparently been unable to erase her mind as she'd claimed, but she'd apparently been kept largely unconscious for the duration of her captivity.

"Mother, do you remember what happened?" Eladria pressed, determined to keep her awake and lucid.

"Just like I've been in...a deep sleep, for so long," she whispered. "Dreaming...dark, disturbing dreams. The crystal...all I was aware of was the crystal..."

"Yes, the crystal. You were being used to control the crystal," Eladria explained.

"The woman that brought us here, she was using us to direct its power...to lock into a specific place...a dark place, a place of great evil. I touched it with my mind...the connection was made, but not stabilized..."

"It's over now," Eladria said, holding her tightly. "Zanel's gone and there's no way the Shadow Lords can get into our realm now. I've disconnected you from the crystal. You're free! And I'm going to get you and everyone else out of here. We'll get to safety and you'll be all right..."

"Eladria," her mother smiled weakly and again looked into her daughter's eyes, slowly raising her hand and stroking her face. "I can hardly believe it's you. You're no longer a little girl...you're a beautiful young woman. You came all this way...for me?"

Eladria tried to muster a smile. "Yes. For you."

The crystal chamber was being ravaged by the increasingly intense tremors, causing rocks to dislodge and fall from the surrounding walls, crashing into the walkways and tumbling into the chasm beneath. As the seismic disturbances worsened, the crystal was becoming ever more unstable, its emissions brighter, more intense and frenetic.

"I also came here to stop what was happening here," Eladria explained, looking up at the violently pulsating crystal. "Our world is still in danger. I thought that by disconnecting you the crystal would automatically power down, but I seem to have made things worse..."

"You...you shouldn't have disconnected us so suddenly," her mother rasped, shaking her head weakly, her eyes filled with alarm. "The crystal has been under our control for so long and so much power was being fed into it. Now there's nothing to keep in it balance. I can feel it...it's overloading...so much power and nothing to direct it. It's feeding back into itself..."

"What'll happen if we can't stop it?"

"It'll explode, destroying this planet along with it."

"That's if the breach doesn't pull us into the void first," Eladria said, overcome by a feeling of helplessness. She also felt a pang of guilt. Once again her headstrong impulsiveness had been her undoing. She'd disconnected her mother and the other Starlanians without considering the consequences. Instead of sealing the breach she had exacerbated it and, if she didn't act now, she would be responsible for the destruction of her world.

"Someone must link with the crystal," her mother said, struggling to get the words out, clearly in a great deal of pain. "I don't have the strength...I can feel myself...slipping away..."

"Don't say that," Eladria cut in. "You're going to be fine. I'm going to do whatever's necessary. I'll get you out of this, I swear it."

"I'm but one person. The planet will be destroyed...unless you seal the breach and stabilize the crystal. You must connect with it, connect with the crystal."

"But I don't know how..."

"You will. Just step into the booth and allow the connection to form...you'll feel its power infusing you."

"Then what?"

"You can use your mind to direct it. We were *used*...commands were programmed into our minds without our volition...but you must do so consciously. It's the only way."

Eladria looked around helplessly as the cavern continued to shake, the crystal pulsating ever more fitfully. She felt the weight of the world resting upon her shoulders and it was a crushing burden. Still, she couldn't ignore her responsibility. This was her world and she was the only one with the power to save it.

Her own reckless attempt to rescue her mother had worsened the situation immeasurably. The underground complex was crumbling around them. If the crystal didn't explode first then it would be crushed to pieces as the cavern collapsed. Either way, whatever remained of the planet would surely then be pulled into the void and erased from existence.

Eladria embraced her mother tightly. So many years apart, so many years of grief and finally they were together again. Eladria wished that she could take her mother from this place, that they could find somewhere to live in peace, free from the Ha'shon and True Way and far from the nightmare of Drantak. But that was a dream that was never to be, for her mother was dying.

Eladria could see her slipping away as she struggled for each breath. She didn't know if it was due to her abrupt severance from the crystal, but her mother's body and mind were unable to function and appeared to be shutting down with devastating rapidity.

"My sweet girl," her mother whispered weakly, before her eyes closed and her body went limp in Eladria's arms.

Eladria was racked by a sudden and overwhelming grief. Tears spilled from her eyes as she reached down, kissed her mother's forehead and laid down her lifeless body. Eladria lifted the gold necklace from around her head and placed it in her mother's palm, closing her hand tightly.

There was no time to mourn. The crystal chamber was

crumbling to dust. Huge boulders fell from the walls, pulverizing the walkways and aisles, fragments of rock battering the crystal and the surrounding consoles. The crystal was oscillating furiously, blinding bursts of light exploding outward.

Eladria got up and wiped away her tears. She was now Queen of Tahnadra and she was responsible for this nightmare in more ways than one. It was up to her to end it. She took a last look at her mother's body slumped upon the walkway and then turned to the central booth at the base of the crystal. The tremors were unrelenting, and she had to struggle to get to the booth, but once she did she wasted no time stepping into it and taking her position. She took the electrodes that had connected her mother to the crystal and placed them upon her forehead. She prayed that this would be enough to connect her with the crystal.

Tears continued streaming down her face as she looked straight ahead. She had a full view of the collapsing cavern as the falling rocks pounded it to pieces. There was very little time left.

Yet nothing was happening—she wasn't connected to the crystal. Perhaps someone was needed to operate the console, or maybe the mechanism had been damaged.

A wave of determination rose within her. She was resolute that she *would* do this, that her mother's death would not be in vain.

She closed her eyes and summoned the power of the Dragon Star. She directed this power to connect her to the crystal...and it worked!

In her haste, she'd been wholly unprepared for what she'd initiated. Her body and senses were electrified by the crystal, as a surge of raw energy ignited and irradiated every cell of her being, causing her to scream in agony. Her mind exploded, the boundaries of her consciousness bursting open like a dam.

She became the crystal and the crystal became her...

The crystal, she discovered, was an ancient source of unfathomable power. Reaching deep into the core of the planet, it was forged from the stars themselves. In that respect, it was the same as the Dragon Star, for they were two aspects of the same source. When combined, their energy was exponentially magnified.

Eladria was now one with the crystal, as her mother and the other Starlanian captives had been before her. But whereas they'd been kept in a semiconscious state by Zanel, Eladria was fully aware.

She learned with some astonishment that the crystal was not only connected to the core of the planet, but was also alive. She found herself drawn into its deep, primal consciousness, a repository for aeons of memories. Everything that had ever happened in the history of her world was somehow recorded and stored in this base intelligence.

Eladria approached it cautiously, touching it with her mind, becoming aware of a deep trauma and sorrow. She could sense how grossly it had been misused and violated, until the natural balance had been completely lost. Eladria apologized from the bottom of her heart. She felt partially responsible for what had been done, for it had been Zanel that had seized the crystal and attempted to subvert its power. How deeply the planet had suffered as a result. She could see that to exploit and abuse this power was to invite complete annihilation.

Eladria's vision expanded to encompass the entire planet. She could now see what was unfolding, and what she saw filled her with crushing despair.

The breach had spiraled out of control. This tear in the fabric of the universe was expanding by the second. Just beyond it was the void, the buffer zone between realities, an expanse of nothingness, the absence of matter and of life. She could sense myriad dimensions and universes interpenetrating each other, each safely sealed by the void to ensure containment. Tahnadra was now being pulled through the breach into the void—where all life would be instantly erased.

This can't have been Zanel's intent. She'd merely wanted to free the Shadow Lords and bring them through the breach into this realm. Eladria could see that, if properly focused and stabilized as Zanel had intended, the crystal would indeed have allowed travel between the two dimensions. But everything was now out of control.

Eladria could see it all.

As the planet was pulled into the breach, massive geological disruptions tore entire continents apart: raging tsunamis, devastating floods, earthquakes and tornadoes. Mountains crumbled as the planet's tectonic plates uprooted and collided. Cities were destroyed in moments and whole continents were submerged beneath the tormented ocean. Countless lives had been lost and the situation worsened by the second.

Eladria's soul was wracked with grief at having to witness the torturous annihilation of her world. Tahnadra was ensnared in the gravity of the breach, gradually disappearing into the tear between realms; all matter dissolving into nothingness the moment it touched the void.

She was aware of the myriad other worlds existing just beyond the void, so close they could almost be touched. The first she noticed was a dimension of darkness, of bleak and nightmarish terror, which she intuitively recognized as Abidalos, the realm of the Shadow Lords. She could sense the malevolent entities seeking escape from their realm, desperately wanting to claw their way into other dimensions. The consequences of this would be unimaginable. All they wanted was to conquer and consume. They fed off death and destruction the way most beings lived off oxygen and they craved to satiate their hunger, no matter the cost to the rest of the universe. They were hideous wraith-like beings, existing as pure energy, yet able to slip into physicality in order to devour the mortal realm.

They'd been so close to breaking free, but the connection

hadn't been sufficiently established to allow them safe passage across the void. They'd been thwarted. At the very least, Eladria was grateful she'd prevented these creatures from invading her world. She now knew how devastating that would have been. For they wouldn't have been content to stay on Tahnadra, they would have spread across the universe like a plague, the harbingers of death wherever they went.

There were other realms close by, beyond the depraved darkness of Abidalos. An infinite number of other worlds and other universes, tied together like pearls on a thread, inextricably bound, yet each distinct.

One world in particular seemed to pull her toward it, as though a distant, familiar melody called to her, mesmerizing and enticing her. She could sense his presence, the boy whose face had filled her dreams ever since childhood. He was there, somewhere beyond the void, so far apart and yet so tantalizingly close.

Her attention was drawn back to her own realm, as her dying world was devoured by the breach. Almost a quarter of the planet had now been sucked into the void, and the remainder was so destabilized that, by the time it was swallowed by the breach, all that would remain would be rubble. The planet's three moons were torn out of orbit, spinning uncontrollably and slamming into the planet, causing the planet to split into pieces.

Being at one with the crystal, she could sense the immense stress it was under: any moment now it would shatter and explode.

Eladria cried as she witnessed the agonizing destruction of her world. Countless lives had been lost and entire lands and continents wiped from existence. Deeper into the breach it went, into the gaping jaws of oblivion.

Desperation filled her. There had to be something she could do. She couldn't just watch as Tahnadra was wiped from existence. She'd joined with the crystal to save her world, not to stand by and witness its destruction.

She reconnected with the Dragon Star and, mustering the full might of her will and focused intent, she directed it to saving Tahnadra: to pulling it away from the breach. With all her heart and soul, she attempted to seal the rip in space that was dragging the planet into the void.

But it was too late. The void had already consumed too much of the planet. The gravity of the breach was too strong to nullify, even with the might of the Dragon Star.

There was simply no way to stop this and even if she could, all that would remain of the planet would be rock and debris.

It was simply too late for her world.

She had failed.

Tahnadra was dead.

Chapter 33

Beyond

Eladria was prepared to die along with her world.

The caverns around her collapsed and the great psionic crystal finally exploded like a star going nova.

In the aftermath of the explosion, all that remained of the planet were shards of fiery rock, which were then pulled through the breach, devoured by the void and wiped from existence.

Tahnadra was completely obliterated; every last trace of it erased by the void.

There were no survivors.

Yet Eladria herself was somehow still alive.

She was still conscious and aware, but her soul was crushed. Her world was gone and she'd been forced to witness its demise in agonizing clarity. So many millions had been killed in the most violent and horrific ways, or simply wiped from existence as the remnants of the planet passed into the void.

How she wished she'd been able to share their fate, for the guilt and desolation that wracked her soul was more than she could bear. Everything she'd ever known was gone. All the races and tribes of Tahnadra, and all of their histories and culture, had been erased from the universe.

Her legacy as Queen of Tahnadra had been to destroy it.

Eladria didn't know where she was, or what had happened to her. She was disconnected from the psionic crystal the moment it exploded, a forcible separation that was as painful as it was disorientating. She was now enveloped in a pocket of energy, yet she wasn't safe, for she knew that she too was being pulled into the void. In spite of having momentarily outlived her world, she was about to share its fate.

As she felt herself being pulled into the breach, she suddenly recalled the words of Van'garat:

"Everything you've ever been taught about reality has been overturned in the blink of an eye. The old laws of the universe no longer apply. You have transcended them."

She could almost feel his presence, reminding her of just how powerful she truly was.

"The power you possess greatly exceeds even the most revered of Masters. It is a power far stronger than anything you could ever possibly imagine. You have the ability to create and destroy on an unimaginable scale. You now possess the power to birth entire worlds! You have been granted the power of the gods themselves."

Could it be true? Could she be conceding defeat simply because she was still thinking in terms of old limitations, unable to grasp the profundity of the power within her?

"The only limits to your power are those you impose upon yourself. Feel the power and direct it with your mind and focused intent."

A spark of hope ignited within her. If she truly had the ability to create and destroy entire worlds—if she did have the power of the gods—then she had to use it. She'd failed to halt the destruction of her world, but could she somehow resurrect it and bring it back to life?

If Van'garat had been correct, then there was no limit to what she could do and the only thing that stopped her was her own lingering self-doubt.

Eladria turned within and was immediately aware of the blazing star of light at the center of her being. She allowed herself to move into it, to merge with it, until the power irradiated her entire being. This was the power that had enabled her to defeat Zanel, not with violence or resistance, but with acceptance and compassion. This energy, transcendent of space and time, was of the same primordial essence that infused and animated the entire universe.

Eladria merged with this power and she brought her mind and

consciousness into sharp focus. She had only one intent: to turn back time to the instant before Tahnadra was pulled into the void.

And that was what happened. Time reversed and sped backward, and she witnessed the planet reemerging from the breach and re-forming. It again occupied its rightful position in space and, as she held it with her razor-sharp intent, she consciously willed it back into a state of stability. The moons again came into orbit, the smashed continents were reformed, and the landmasses that had been submerged beneath the ocean were restored. The psionic crystal was pieced together and made whole again.

Eladria turned her attention to the breach, the tear in space that lingered above the planet like a gateway to oblivion. With her focused intent, she sealed it as though suturing a wound. The breach was closed and the tear between realms sealed. Dimensional balance had been restored.

She looked down at her world and felt like a mother gazing at her newborn child, with an immensity of love pouring from her heart. She had re-created and re-birthed it. Tahnadra was reborn!

But her work was not yet done.

She could not allow things to be as they had been. Her people had lost their way. Generations of war and hatred had taken its toll on the people of Tahnadra. Eladria had been just one of countless to experience the suffering perpetrated by the ignorance and brutality of the Ha'shon and the True Way. As Queen of Tahnadra, she could not allow that to continue.

Perhaps, incredibly, Zanel had been right in her own way. She could now see that her world had to be healed and renewed. A bloody history of war and oppression had led her people to an impasse that couldn't be surmounted without a fundamental shift in consciousness. With this in mind, she sent forth a wave of light that passed over the surface of the planet, cleansing and renewing.

Eladria decided to intervene further. The tyranny of the Ha'shon and True Way and their generations-long conflict had to end. She reached out and placed all members of the Ha'shon and True Way hierarchy and their followers onto El'shantal, an uninhabited island in the northern hemisphere. Around this island she placed a protective barrier. Until they learned to live and work together, they would be unable to leave the island.

Of course, it was possible the old conflicts would simply continue in this new location. Perhaps they would wipe themselves out before they agreed to live together on the island. Yet it was her hope that the shared adversity of living on an untamed island would allow them to set aside their ideological differences and find common ground. It seemed a necessary injunction. Her world had to be allowed to heal.

The remaining inhabitants, a mixture of nonaligned citizens and those that had lived under occupation by the Ha'shon and True Way, would have to rebuild their world. It was possible the human tendency to create divisive ideologies would cause new problems. But she had a sense that, following Tahnadra's death and rebirth, a newfound unity would allow the people of her world to come together and thrive. Hearts could no longer remain closed and minds no longer locked in false division. People could only survive by forging a renewed sense of kinship and mutual respect as they rebuilt their world and embraced the future.

She looked down upon her world, feeling almost godlike, with the ability to create changes as easily as an artist working with canvas and paint. One of the last changes she made was to locate and isolate Drantak, to keep it from being found again and prevent anyone from ever being able to misuse the psionic crystal as Zanel had done. She placed a protective sheath around the island and sealed off the underground caverns.

Eladria observed her world and was satisfied. From the ashes of its painful demise, Tahnadra had been reborn and renewed.

The devastation had been immense and though it would take time for civilization to be rebuilt, a stillness and peace washed over her world.

She was ready to return to it. She was the last of the royal lineage and it was now up to her to take charge of her world and oversee the coming changes. No longer willing to live on an isolated moon, she would make her palace upon the planet, where she could better connect with her people. They would work together in harmony, for the common good. With the power of her mind, she created a palace in the midst of a lush forest in the central regions of Lastaraad.

She knew who she wanted by her side as she took her position as ruler of Tahnadra. Van'garat and Janak were still trapped in the underground cavern at Drantak. She reached out and rescued them, pulling them from that dark land and transporting them to her newly-created palace. There they would remain by her side, her friends and comrades. Van'garat would guide and advise her and Janak would be her head chef as they'd agreed.

It was time for her to return to Tahnadra and take up residence in her new palace. She was filled with inspiration and renewed vision. It would be a long and challenging road as they rebuilt their world, but together they could create a world of prosperity and hope.

Perhaps, in a sense, the prophecies of the ancient scriptures had been fulfilled. The end times had come and Tahnadra had been destroyed and reborn. According to the ancient texts, an era of peace would follow this time of turbulence and transformation, a time in which all races would come together to ensure a better future.

But something was wrong. As hard as she tried, Eladria was unable to leave the cocoon that had encapsulated her and spared her from Tahnadra's destruction.

She tried again and again, but was held firm. She was trapped, unable to penetrate the invisible barrier that held her in place. She was so close to her world and yet a universe apart.

There was no going back. She realized with a growing sense of horror that she would never again return to her world...

Chapter 34

A Different Destiny

Disorientated, she cried out in alarm.

She didn't know what was happening. Still enveloped in the energy pocket, she found herself surrounded by a sea of golden light, swirling and diffuse, enfolding her and obscuring her vision. The planet she had resurrected from oblivion disappeared from sight and she had the sense of being pulled through space and time, into a whole other dimension of reality.

When the light subsided, she found herself in a place unlike anything she'd ever dreamt of. She was inside an expansive, multi-tiered golden temple. A series of pillars lined the ground level and high above the balconies arched an exquisite domed glass ceiling. Eladria stood upon a marble platform at the center of the temple, surrounded by an assemblage of people dressed in white ceremonial robes, with radiant faces and striking features, each exuding an ethereal radiance. Eladria got the impression that this wasn't their true appearance, but that they had simply assumed these forms for her benefit.

A sweet fragrance perfumed the air and she could hear a low, reverberating hum that seemed to emanate from all around. A sense of peace pervaded this place and a radiant gold light infused everything and everyone around her, a light that sparkled and danced with life. Everything was brighter here: the colors were more vivid and the air itself shimmered. The closest she'd ever experienced to it had been inside Nirataan's cave.

"Where am I?" she asked, her voice shaking. "What is this place?"

One of the robed beings stepped forward and joined her on the platform. "You are in Shanadon, and this is the High Council of the Guardians," he said. He wore a trailing white robe and was ageless in appearance, with long blonde hair, his eyes sparkling like gemstones and his manner both affable and serene.

"The Guardians?" Eladria echoed. "You mean you're the Others?"

The man nodded.

"But what am I doing here?" Eladria looked around in wonder.

"Your path led you here. It was always going to lead you here," the man answered.

"I didn't mean to come here," Eladria told him. "I wanted to return to my world. For the first time I felt ready to take my place, to assume my duties and lead my people."

"That will not be possible. You can never return to your world."

"Why not?" Eladria gasped.

"You have overturned the laws of the universe," the man answered, his every word carefully measured, his voice gentle yet resolute. "You turned back time and re-birthed a dead world. From the ashes of Tahnadra, New Tahnadra has been born. But you can never be part of it."

"But it's my world. I saved it! I belong there..."

"You crossed a line that no mortal before you has ever done, and there are consequences. You saved your world, but at a cost. It exists, but you no longer belong there."

"Then where do I belong?"

"Your destiny calls you elsewhere."

Eladria stared at the ethereal figure blankly as the impact of his words sank in. "What do you mean?" she asked.

"That, you are about to learn," the man smiled, his eyes twinkling like stars. "Shall we take a walk?"

Eladria nodded distractedly. The man took her hand and led her down the steps off the platform and through the crowd. As she passed them, the Others watched her in benevolent curiosity. Eladria's host led her out of the temple and into a seemingly endless garden, built in layers interconnected by crystalline walkways and surrounded by streams and waterfalls.

It was the most beautiful sight her eyes had ever beheld. The flowers, trees and shrubs pulsated with life; magnificent hues of pink, red, yellow, blue, violet and countless shades of green. As she and her host moved, their bodies left a trail of light behind them. High above, the sky was a shade of violet-pink and birds soared across the cloudless heavens. Eladria's senses were so captivated by the glorious sights that she almost forgot the dozens of questions that filled her mind.

"What exactly *are* you?" Eladria asked as they followed a path winding through the garden, passing by a large pond.

"We are known in many cultures as the Guardians," the man responded. "We are, in a sense, caretakers. We oversee the multiplicity of universes that coexist simultaneously, each separate yet interpenetrating. We prevent cross-contamination between realms. Each realm affects every other, for each is but a single cell in a vaster organism. A delicate universal balance exists and this balance can easily be disrupted."

He stopped and picked up a stone. "When one realm loses balance, this affects every other dimension of reality," he said, throwing the stone into the pond, where it landed with a splash, shattering the stillness of the water. "Like ripples spreading across the surface of a pond."

"And that was what happened on my world," she surmised.

"Yes. A tear was created between dimensions and the Shadow Lords were almost freed from their astral prison. If they had spilled into your realm, they would have been able to consume and destroy an entire universe. That could not be allowed to happen."

"What was my part in all this? Why did you have to involve me?"

"You were involved from the start. For it was you that inadvertently created Zanel and sent her back in time. As you know, it was amid the temporal vortex that the Shadow Lords latched onto her and used her as a means to secure their escape. Everything that happened was a result of your actions. You had to be the one to make things right."

"Tell me more about the Shadow Lords."

"Believe it or not, there were once Guardians, like us. Only they adopted a different perspective. No longer content with overseeing from afar, they wanted to directly intervene, to take a more *active* participation in universal affairs."

"Why?"

"They wanted to systematically cleanse impurity."

Eladria felt uneasy, knowing that this is what she herself did when she resurrected her world. She'd done the very thing the Shadow Lords wanted—she'd cleansed and renewed her world—albeit in a different, far less destructive way. Was this perhaps the reason she wasn't allowed to return to Tahnadra?

The Guardian continued. "This created in them a lust for power and control, which became their driving force and eventually destroyed them. They became twisted, wraith-like creatures that feed off life itself, stripping entire universes of all life. That is why they seek to break out and conquer other realms. Their justification is that they are cleansing those realms, but their sole motivation is now to satiate their hunger for life."

"Yet they're trapped in a separate dimension?"

"To our shame, we were slow to intervene. But when the Shadow Lords decimated an entire universe, we knew we had to act. They could not be allowed to continue. A bitter conflict ensued, but we were victorious, and we sealed them in their conquered universe. This astral prison is known as Abidalos, the Dark Dimension. In spite of the seal we placed around it, they have been unrelenting in their attempts to escape and on some occasions they have even succeeded. In such instances, we act swiftly and decisively. They cannot be allowed to be victorious. Were they to escape and consume another universe, the entire chain of existence would begin to collapse."

Eladria began pacing as she struggled to accept all she was being told. Her mind was racing. There were so many questions she wanted answered. "Did you know that Tahnadra would be destroyed?" she asked.

"All eventualities were foreseen," the Guardian replied.

"Was it really my fault that Tahnadra was pulled into the breach?"

"Your actions were hasty," the man admitted. "Had you not disconnected the Starlanians so suddenly from the crystal, it would not have destabilized as it did. It would have been possible for you to seal the breach before your world was destroyed."

"Then it *was* my fault," Eladria whispered. "All of it..."

"Your impulsiveness has often been your undoing, but you made things right in the end," he assured her. "You transcended your limitations and embraced the power within you. It is a power that all beings have to a lesser extent, but you were gifted an exponentially greater power. As you resurrected your world, you crossed the line between mortal and god...and there is a price to be paid. You were granted the power to re-birth your world, but you cannot now go back to it. New Tahnadra was created by you, but it is no longer your world."

"But why not?" she asked, coming to a stop beside a large tree, its pink blossom-heavy branches swaying gently in the warm breeze.

The Guardian stopped alongside her. "When you took possession of the Dragon Star, you accepted all that came with it. With a power so strong comes great responsibility. When you re-created your world, you violated the laws of the universe and there can be no going back. You can never return to Tahnadra."

"Because I interfered with its fate?"

The man nodded. "Such intervention carries a price."

"But you yourself intervened," Eladria countered. "You created the crystal waterfall and communicated with Lakandrian's people over generations. You directed me to Drantak. You left Nirataan where he could guide and help us. You condemn the Shadow Lords for their desire to interfere with the mortal realm, but this was all planned on your part, all orchestrated."

"Our involvement in shaping the mortal realm has been subtle, but necessary. Millennia ago, in your time, a number of us assumed physical embodiment and we visited your world, among others. We were known as the Lasan."

"The Lasan?" Eladria gasped. "*You* were the Lasan?"

"We brought civilization, culture and wisdom to the worlds we encountered. We also left behind gifts that we foresaw would be needed in future times. One of the gifts we left behind on your world was the Dragon Star."

"Of course..."

"Even back then we foresaw the rise of the Shadow Lords and their quest to destroy all. We knew they would attempt to invade your world and that they had to be stopped. That is why we seeded the Dragon Star on your world and paved the path for you to eventually find it. Everything was laid in place for when the time was right."

"If you knew beforehand they'd become a threat, why didn't you stop them?"

"Certain events are fixed in the fabric of time and space—keystone events—unalterable by any means. We prepared for it as best we could, but we were unable to halt their inception and development."

"I see. Then Lakandrian was right all along. You knew what my involvement would be millennia before I was born?"

"Past, present and future are one to us."

"Then tell me my future. You say I can never return to Tahnadra. So what am I to do?"

The man smiled, his entire body glistening with an ethereal splendor. "You have a vital part to play. Your power is now needed on another world."

"Another world?"

"Yes, and it is a world you already know of. There the conflict between light and dark has reached its zenith, for the Shadow Lords have broken free of their containment and contaminated that universe. Although they are but few in number, they seek to blast open the doors between dimensions. This cannot be allowed to happen."

"I don't understand what this has to do with me."

"The Dragon Star was given as a gift, a gift that you needed in order to save your world. But it was a gift that came at a price. You wield a power greater than any mortal has ever possessed, a power that is needed. That is why you are being called to this other realm. You must save it from annihilation by the dark ones. The universe of which I speak is a keystone. If it falls then every other dimension will begin to collapse. The void will consume all. All life, everywhere, in every realm, will eventually cease."

"And I can stop this from happening?"

"You must."

"You said I already know of this world...?"

"Throughout your life you have had visions of it, and visions of *him*. The threads of destiny have bound you across the vast distances between you. Your fates are linked and they always have been."

"I know who you mean," Eladria said, recalling the stranger whose face she'd dreamt of for so many years. "I never quite knew if he was real or just a figment of my imagination."

"He is real and he needs you."

"Tell me who he is."

"His name is David and his world is called Alanar. Your fates are inseparably intertwined. That is all you need know for now. The rest you will learn in time. Perhaps you can now see that everything that has happened was necessary in the grand scheme."

"Even the terrible things, the tragedies and accidents—Zanel, the breach, the death of Tahnadra...?"

The Guardian nodded. "They brought you here and they made you what you now are," he said. "There is an underlying perfection to all events. It is a perfection that is ordinarily obscured from the mind, for it is subtle and hidden. But there are no random events. How could there possibly be? Everything that has ever happened in the entire history of the universe, every cause and effect and chain of events, has led you here—now."

"What about the darkness and the pain?"

"The universe, as we see it, is but a play of duality, cradled in an infinite heart of unity. It is infused with a single life essence, a fount from which all forms arise. Darkness has its part to play. Without darkness, there could be no appreciation of light. Always the balance must be maintained: night must follow day, winter must follow summer and death must follow birth, all in succession, a never-ending circle with no beginning and no end. The Shadow Lords lost this sense of natural balance. They seek perpetual night, perpetual winter and perpetual death. That is why they must be stopped, for once the balance of the cosmos is lost, all is thrown into catastrophic collapse."

"I think I understand what you're telling me," Eladria said. "And when I took possession of the Dragon Star I was somehow *drafted* by you?"

"Yes, in a sense, you are now one of us," he answered. "You are a Guardian of the universal balance, and you are needed on the world of Alanar. That is where your destiny now pulls you. It is there you will find David. He is in danger and only you can save him. Together, you have the ability to safeguard the future of not only his world, but of every other world in every other universe."

Eladria stepped back and shook her head. "I've always wanted to make my own fate and my own choices in life. That's why I felt so stifled in my life as princess, because so many choices were made for me. I don't like being controlled and I don't like being manipulated."

The Guardian smiled again, his eyes filled with a mixture of patience, understanding and empathy, tinged with a touch of irony. "So it is with most mortal beings," he said, walking over to the tree nearest them, resting his hand on the sturdy trunk. "You have lived your life under the illusion that you exist independently of the universe, that you can steer your fate and manipulate life to satiate your desires and stave off your fears; and maybe you can in some circumstances. Yet the person you have long believed yourself to be is but a shadow of the mind. What you are is an expression of the primordial essence, an expression of the universe. You *are* the universe; you are life itself."

"I felt that myself," Eladria said. "When Van'garat guided me on the journey inward. I felt myself merge into the primordial essence until there was no separation, only unity. But the moment I opened my eyes, the experience began to fade again."

"The tendencies of mind re-create that false sense of division," the man explained. "The gravity of the mind, of thoughts, beliefs and conditioning is strong and exerts a tremendous pull. But once you have touched the core of what you are and have tasted truth, you can never again be the same. The prison of mind will eventually, inevitably, dissolve. Now, I ask you: setting aside this illusory sense of being a person separate from the unity of life...what will you now do? Where do you feel your destiny calls you? Answer from the heart, from the root of your being."

Eladria closed her eyes.

The Guardian's words had a profound effect on her. Everything she'd ever been certain of about herself—who she was, her past and intended future—had suddenly been revealed as hollow.

There was an emptiness within her, a stark and primal aloneness that nevertheless contained within it a deep interconnectedness and aliveness. Once again, quite effortlessly, she felt herself merging into the ocean of the primordial essence, dissolving into an unbounded field of unity, merging with the cosmos itself.

In this state of expansion, she was at peace and she knew that she wasn't separate from anything. She was part of it all. Yet there was also a remaining vestige of self amid the selfless. That which was she—temporarily enclosed in a body of flesh and blood—was still a part of the mortal universe. Her journey was not yet over. She had a task to complete. The entire cosmos directed her to heed the words of the Guardian, for he was guiding her to where she most needed to be.

She could see David's face clearly now. She was only a child when she first became aware of him and he had been but a small boy. Together they had grown up, so far apart, separated by the vastness of space and time, yet joined in consciousness. Their point of contact had been in the land of the unconscious, the intangible terrain of dreams and visions. Now he seemed so close, as though she could reach out and touch him.

She sensed that he too possessed a deep and innate power and that his life was one of noble sacrifice. He shone like a star amid the darkness of a twisted world and she could feel the pain etched in his soul. He had suffered and wrestled with the inner demons of hatred and grief, just as she had. Her heart filled with compassion and empathy. He had come so far and suffered so much, but he could no longer travel his path alone. He was in danger and so too was his entire world. He needed her. There was no hope without her.

Eladria withdrew from the universal unity and her mind and senses contracted, as though the ocean was drawn into a single drop of water. She was again aware of her body, a receptacle bound by the laws of physicality. She was still standing in the beautiful garden alongside the leader of the Guardians.

"Have you made your choice?" he asked softly.

"Yes," she answered. "I will go to Alanar. I have to go there, I can feel it. Whoever David is, I somehow *know* him and he needs me. Whatever happens, I have to help him."

"Then the decision is made," the Guardian smiled warmly. "We have the ability to transport you to Alanar from here. Though you must be warned, you will be stepping into a whole other realm and it may take you time to adjust. There will be immense danger. There are those on Alanar who would seek to possess the power within you and use it to their own ends."

"I understand that," she said. "But how will I know what I'm meant to do once I'm there?"

"Life will guide you, as it always does. Deal with whatever arises and follow your heart. Do not let confusion, doubt and fear blind you. These are obstructions to be overcome. Stay true to that which is within you, to that which you are, and you will not falter. Are you now ready to embrace your new path?"

Eladria bowed her head slowly. "I'm ready."

Eladria was led back into the great golden temple, where again she was surrounded by the assembled council members.

"It is time to go forth and embrace your destiny," the Guardian leader said to her. As his words echoed around her, the golden temple began to shimmer in a white luminescence. The Guardian council members disappeared from sight and Eladria was alone.

A doorway appeared before her, a rippling gateway of blue light that somehow beckoned her toward it. She knew that just beyond this portal was her intended destination, the mysterious world of Alanar, and that there was little time to waste.

Yet still there was an element of hesitancy within her. She didn't know what she would encounter in this new world or if she had the ability to do what was expected of her. The deeper part of her, however, knew that this was the next step in her journey and that she'd been led here for a reason.

She now had to take a leap of faith. She vowed to deal with whatever lay ahead of her while endeavoring to retain the knowledge and understanding she now possessed. All of the dramas were but expressions in an infinite play of the primordial essence. *She* was what lay behind, beneath and beyond the outer manifestations. On this level, she was invincible, invulnerable and could transcend whatever came her way. She was beyond the happenings and events of life, for she *was* life.

Before she stepped through the portal, she cast her mind back to her own world once more. It saddened her that she would never see Tahnadra again, but she had one last gift she wanted to bestow upon it.

Using the power within her, she reached out to her world and into the underground caverns of Drantak just prior to the planet's initial destruction. There she saw her mother lying upon the ground, just after she'd been disconnected from the crystal, but prior to her death.

Eladria used the power of her mind to take her mother and the other Starlanian captives from this place and to heal and revive them, restoring them to health and vitality, undoing the damage inflicted after the years they'd spent connected to the crystal. Once recovered, the Starlanians were returned to their homes and families, where they would live out the rest of their lives in peace and freedom.

Eladria placed her mother in the new royal palace, where she was, along with the planet itself, reborn. Eladria wanted to do the same for her father and Zinn, but knew that too much time had elapsed since their deaths. The universal laws would not stretch that far. But she was nonetheless delighted that her final task as Queen of Tahnadra had been to restore her mother as reigning monarch of New Tahnadra.

Eladria watched the succeeding months and years passing in the blink of an eye, unfolding as if like a play in her mind.

Her mother ruled with wisdom and compassion, overseeing the rebuilding of the decimated planet. She became very fond of Janak, who assumed his duties in the palace and eventually fell in love with one of the Queen's aides, whom he married and fathered four children with. She was delighted that Janak had been granted a new family, supplanting the loneliness and sorrow in his heart with love and happiness.

Van'garat remained in the palace as one of her mother's most trusted advisors. He spent his remaining years training initiates in the art of Ko Tra Pah, educating them in the wisdom of the Old Way and teaching them to connect with and embody the primordial essence. The wisdom of the Old Way had thus been preserved for future generations.

Eladria wished she could reach out to them and be with them, especially her mother. She yearned to rekindle their relationship and make up for all the years they'd lost. But she knew their destinies had diverged.

So she silently and tearfully said farewell to her mother, to Van'garat, Janak and to her entire world.

Assured that New Tahnadra was in good hands, she was now ready to let go of it.

Eladria stood before the portal.

Alanar was calling to her. Every fiber of her being was now pulling her toward this new world. She knew that, like the one she'd come from, it was a world of darkness and uncertainty. But she had a purpose to fulfill and she was now willing to embrace the power within her and use it as it was intended; as a force for good.

Taking a deep breath, she stepped forward and disappeared into the light.

Acknowledgements & Afterword

There are some people I'd like to thank, because without them I simply wouldn't have able to bring this novel to completion. First and foremost, I am exceptionally grateful to my amazing parents, who helped me through some difficult times and provided an enormous amount of support and encouragement; and also my sister, Holly, who is more than just a little sis to me, but one of my best friends as well. I couldn't have done this without their endless encouragement and unwavering belief in me.

Huge thanks to all my wonderful friends, of whom there are too many to mention here. My long-term Twitter posse and Mysterious Wisdom comrades in particular have been a great support. Special thanks go to Andy Weir who has been one of my biggest fans and supporters from the very start, and who was the first person to read the completed manuscript (so relieved he liked it!). I'm grateful to fellow author Harrison Davies, whose support and editing assistance has been greatly appreciated. Thanks also to healer and author Patricia Iris Kerins who kindly took the time to review my work and provide an endorsement.

Last and by no means least, I'd like to thank you. Yes, you! I appreciate the fact you bought my book and have read this far. I hope you enjoyed it. *Eladria* was written as the prelude to a series of books entitled *The Alanar Ascendant*. For reasons that would take too long to explain here, the first book in this series, *The Key of Alanar* was actually written prior to this one. If anything, it's an even more epic and ambitious tale and I can't wait to share it with you. Updates (and some free short stories) can be found on my website www.dreamlight-fugitive.co.uk. In the meantime, if you enjoyed this book, please tell your friends about it and if you feel so inclined I'd be really grateful if you left a review on Amazon or elsewhere. Your help and support is immensely appreciated.

Thanks for being part of the journey.